JOHN LAWRENCE REYNOLDS

SOLITARY DANCER

HarperCollins*Publishers*Ltd

First published in hardcover by HarperCollins Publishers Ltd: 1994
First paperback edition: 1995

Canadian Cataloguing in Publication Data

Reynolds, John Lawrence
    Solitary dancer

"A Joe McGuire mystery"
ISBN 0-00-647959-6

I. Title.

PS8585.E94S6 1995   C813'.54   C95-931385-0
PR9199.3.R48S6 1995

---

95 96 97 98 99 ❖ OPM 10 9 8 7 6 5 4 3 2 1

Printed and bound in the United States

For Suzanne McPetrie & Bruce Litteljohn

Friends, mentors, beacons

Work out your own salvation with fear and trembling.

— The Epistle of Paul the Apostle to the Phillippians

ONE

In the false New England winter, gray and damp, that envelops Boston in November, morning commuters emerge from subway stations beneath Boylston Street with expressions both purposeful and bewildered, as though waking from a sleep in which their destiny appeared in their dreams.

Among those who exited the subway one November morning was a woman with heavy Slavic features and a rotund body, her face pie-shaped and pink-cheeked and her pale eyes narrow and slanted, almost Oriental. Her legs, thick and sturdy as dock pilings, ended in scuffed vinyl boots salt stained from the previous winter's snows.

The woman's name was Stana Tomasevich. She crossed Boylston Street at Exeter and walked west toward Newbury Street a block away. At Newbury she turned left and glanced idly at a restaurant where wealthy housewives from Beacon Hill and the upscale suburbs to the west met to dally over smoked salmon, radicchio salads and California chardonnay.

Stana Tomasevich had never tasted smoked salmon or chardonnay. She had never enjoyed the luxury of a lunchtime spent exchanging gossip and muffin recipes over salad and chilled wine. Six days each week she cleaned the homes of people who indulged in such luxuries. She scrubbed other people's toilets, buffed other people's antiques and swept other people's floors before riding the subway back to her three-room flat in Dorchester at the end of the day.

Halfway along Newbury Street, she stopped in front of a four-storied nineteenth-century sandstone building, shifted the plastic bag to her other hand, gripped a cast-iron railing and pulled herself up a set of steps toward the twin front doors. Gilt lettering on the right-hand door identified "The Weiner Gallery," whose large brass-trimmed window on the ground floor displayed an impressionist painting of a Victorian terrace of houses seen across a park dappled with autumn leaves.

The door on her left bore only the numerals 206A, and it was here that Stana Tomasevich paused to retrieve a heavy ring of keys from the depths of her coat pocket. Each key bore a short length of adhesive tape with a name painfully printed on it in blue ink. She sorted among them until she found one marked *Lorenzo*, which opened the door.

Locking the door behind her, she glanced ruefully at the steep stairs ahead before climbing them one by one up two floors, her body tilting first to one side and then the other with each step, her breathing labored and wheezing from the effort.

At the top of the stairs she turned to enter a large sitting area. Positioned over a large elaborate Oriental rug were several pieces of furniture in a mélange of styles: a Chippendale table serving as a desk, two Eames chairs, a cherrywood Edwardian pendulum clock, a stripped Nova Scotian pine armoire, a parson's table bearing a porcelain vase filled with wilting flowers and an oak corner cabinet displaying dozens of tiny ceramic animals from Paraguay. The wall behind the desk was crowded with framed photographs, some black and white, some in color. The subjects in the pictures ranged from small children playing with puppies and kittens to shiny foreign cars that appeared to float in an expanse of dark space. There were also many food product packages, tropical scenes of palm trees and sunsets, and several nudes, both men and women.

As she always did, Stana avoided looking at the photographs of the nudes, resolutely crossed the room and pushed through two swinging louvered doors into a small kitchen.

It was eight a.m. The woman upstairs, the tenant of the apartment, would not descend from her bedroom until well after nine. Stana Tomasevich had time for tea and a short rest before beginning work.

Ten minutes later she was seated at the small pine table in the kitchen, watching the tea bag in the cup stain the hot water through shades of amber to deep mahogany.

The sounds of traffic on Newbury Street entered

the apartment, muted like storms raging in a distant world. Stana heard only the steady ticking of the pendulum clock and the slow drip of . . . what? She rose and walked to the sink, tightened the faucet handle and returned to sit again at the table.

She raised the cup to her lips, frowned and looked back at the sink.

Drip.

Three breaths.

Drip.

A horn sounded from Newbury Street, two short beeps, a greeting from a driver to a passerby. The door to the art gallery downstairs opened and closed.

Drip.

The faucet was dry. The sound was further away.

Stana turned in her chair. From the far wall of the kitchen a set of steep stairs rose to the fourth-floor level and its three rooms: a large bedroom, a bathroom opening into the alcove at the top of the stairs and, to the right of the alcove, an inner office whose walls were lined with bookshelves and filing cabinets. The pine stairs leading to the top level were waxed and uncarpeted, dangerous to a woman of Stana's age and weight. At their summit, opening into the fourth-floor alcove, was a door with several secure locks. The door would remain closed until the tenant chose to descend the stairs and greet Stana with a cool smile and a slight nod of her head, wearing perhaps a pink peignoir or an oversized man's silk shirt or, as she had on one oppressively warm summer morning, a pair of lace panties and nothing more.

Now Stana rose from the chair and walked across

4

the room to the foot of the stairs and stared up at the closed door.

Drip.

The blood had reached the third step from the top, gathering in a shining crimson puddle fed by the puddle above it and the puddle above that, all of it streaming from a partially coagulated pool on the top stair that leaked out from beneath the closed door, liquid seeking its own level down, down toward Stana Tomasevich's heavy feet and thick ankles and dock-piling legs.

Drip.

Tim Fox tested the strength of the Chippendale table, decided against resting his weight on it and remained standing to stare at the wall of photographs, his arms folded across his chest, a frown on his face. Naked men, naked women, naked men with naked women, naked women with naked women and, in the middle of them all, pictures of cake mixes, and cars and kittens, and bathtubs and flower arrangements.

"An agent. She was an agent for a bunch of photographers. Went out and brought in work for 'em, like a pimp." Standing behind Fox, Phil Donovan sipped coffee noisily from a plastic cup. "Guess these pictures, they're all by the guys, the photographers she went out and hustled for, right?"

Fox nodded and turned to the window overlooking Newbury Street. This was Donovan's first homicide case as lieutenant. "He's only an acting lieutenant until he writes and passes his exam," Fat Eddie Vance had assured Fox half an hour earlier.

"You're still running the team. So show him the ropes, but treat him like any other louie," the captain of detectives had ordered.

Fox had muttered in reply, "The son of a bitch is barely five years out of a whistle's uniform and he's an acting louie? Why, because he's a red-haired blue-eyed pink-cheeked potato eater?" Fat Eddie had just blinked and ignored him.

Ten years older than Donovan and with twelve years more seniority, Tim Fox had been promoted to lieutenant barely a year earlier and was still the only black cop above sergeant in the entire police force. And Donovan, whose reputation was based primarily on chasing women and being two months behind on his paperwork, was now an acting louie.

Somebody tell me again that Boston's not a racist city, Tim Fox thought.

Out on Newbury Street, traffic was jammed, drivers slowing as they encountered the murder scene where an ambulance and several police cars sat at angles against the curb and uniformed cops stood in the street, their faces calm, their presence signifying disaster.

"Coop's finished," Donovan said, and Fox walked through the louvered doors to the kitchen. Norm Cooper was descending the stairs, stepping carefully in his crepe-soled shoes, avoiding the pools of darkened and congealed blood on the steps. The ID specialist carried his oversized valise in one hand and gripped the railing with the other.

"Stairs like these, it's a wonder she didn't break her neck years ago," Cooper said when he reached the bottom. He set the valise on the floor, pushed his glasses up the bridge of his nose and swept a hand through his thinning gray hair.

"What'd you find?" Tim Fox asked, leaning against a windowsill, arms folded.

"Zip." Cooper looked up at Tim. "One set of prints, hers, I'll bet. Nothing else. Place was wiped down. Guy who did it knew what he was doing."

Fox grunted.

"Doitch'll want the body now," Cooper said. Two minutes after arriving to make an official death declaration, the overweight medical examiner had retreated to a restaurant on Boylston where he was eating a second breakfast of French toast and bacon, waiting to escort the body back to the morgue for an autopsy. Cooper paused at the door leading to the stairs and outside to Newbury Street. "Want me to send Mel up?"

Fox nodded absently. "Tell him to take his time," he said. All the specialists had completed their work. Death officially acknowledged, photographs taken, fingerprints lifted, the cleaning woman interviewed. Fox crossed the kitchen and began to climb the stairs to view, for the second time in an hour, the body of the woman identified as Heather Lorenzo, keeping to one side of the stairs, avoiding the blood. Jesus, so much blood.

Behind him, Phil Donovan followed. Acting Lieutenant Donovan, Fox reminded himself.

Heather Lorenzo had been severely beaten at various locations in her fourth-floor apartment. Blood was spattered on the walls of her bedroom where the assault had begun. A trail of blood led from the bedroom to the top of the stairs, along the hall to the office, back to the alcove and toward the bathroom where she had collapsed. A red smear traced her path as she had crawled to the door and slid into unconsciousness, her heart pulsing blood from her body.

The filing cabinets in the office had been ransacked and the contents of one drawer removed. In the bedroom, on a high ledge running across the wall facing the bed, a small steel bracket dangled as though wrenched violently from the wall. Flanking the bracket was a collection of earthenware vases; two lay shattered on the floor where they had toppled from the ledge.

All of the telephones on the top floor had been ripped from their wiring.

"She crawled from the john to the door, top of the stairs," Donovan had said when they viewed the scene upon arrival. "See the marks, there? Looks like she passed out, maybe, over near the bathroom, see how the blood's already hard?"

Tim Fox saw it all again. He stood staring at the streak of crimson leading across the carpet to where the body lay.

"Preliminary, I'd say she's been dead less than two hours," Mel Doitch surmised soon after arriving. "Unconscious longer than that, probably. She lay here bleeding." Then he announced he was going out for something to eat and hefted his oversized bulk through the door and down the stairs.

Fox nodded to himself now, understanding. "He stalked her," Tim Fox said aloud.

"With what?" Donovan stood with his hands in

his pockets, looking around through the open door to the bedroom, across the hall to the business office. "Musta had a weapon with him. Don't lay that kind of hurt on somebody with a pair of fists. Even Tyson on a mad-ass tear can't do that with his fists."

Tim Fox knelt to inspect the body of the woman again.

She lay on her back, one arm extended, her eyes clouded with death. She had not died in this position. The door at the top of the stairs opened inward and the officers responding to the cleaning woman's telephone call had pushed the body aside as they entered.

She wore a black silk dressing gown over black lace panties and brassiere. Her jaw appeared to be broken and there were dark bruises the length of her body, along her rib cage, down the inside of her forearms and across the line of her shoulders. The gown had been partially pulled from her body as she dragged herself, dying, toward the doorway. The middle fingers of one hand were shattered and several bones, white and delicate like ivory, glistened against the torn skin.

She had been stabbed once in the stomach, a deep abdominal wound that had leaked her lifeblood over a period of . . . how long? It was important to know.

Fox guessed her age at between thirty-five and forty. Her hair was dark and short and her figure was trim, lithe, the breasts unnaturally firm and round above tell-tale hairline scars. He had seen an exercise bicycle and weights in her bedroom.

"Whoever it was, he wasn't trying to boink her," Donovan said as Tim Fox stood upright.

"Go down and tell the foreign woman, the cleaning

lady, she can go home now," Fox said to Donovan. "Ask her if she can remember anything else, then tell her we'll get in touch with her."

Donovan paused for a moment, frowning. He's pissed because he's an acting louie and I'm giving him orders like he's still a whistle, Tim Fox thought. To hell with him. I've got seniority and I'll use it.

"Sure," Donovan answered and began descending the stairs.

Tim Fox stepped across the smear of blood marking the woman's path from the bathroom to the closed door at the top of the stairs, walked down the short corridor and entered the ransacked office.

She had fled into this room in terror. He saw the trail of blood on the floor leading to the old oak desk against the wall. But she had turned abruptly to flee again. Maybe going for the telephone. Fox peered over the far edge of the desk to where the telephone had crashed to the floor. The instrument was marked with a blue sticker initialled by Norm Cooper to indicate it had been dusted for prints.

Fox turned away, then looked back at the oversized telephone a second time, staring at its base where four gray buttons flanked a small black window. He knelt and bent forward, his weight resting on his hands, studying the lettering below the buttons. Message Play, he read. And Reset/Erase. Answer On. Record Greeting.

Two wires led from the telephone. One was a standard phone jack. The other was a thin power line, ending in a black box the size of a cigarette package. Fox unplugged the transformer, inspected it and replaced it in the receptacle, prompting a

10

mechanical click from within the phone. Replacing the receiver, he noticed the black window was now lit with the numeral "3." He pressed Message Play.

The whir of a winding tape sounded inside the answering machine. From the floor below rose the sound of Donovan's voice followed by laughter from the uniformed officers posted at the entrance to the apartment.

The tape stopped and the machine began speaking to Fox in the first of three voices he would hear. This was a man's, delicate in delivery with a prominent German accent. "Yes, I have the props we will need and Chill is bringing me model pictures to look at." The voice became plaintive, begging for understanding. "But, Heather, I cannot do this by Tuesday. Even working all weekend I cannot. Please call me and we talk, yes? Bye-bye."

Another voice, disembodied, mechanical, female, the voice of the answering machine: "Five. Forty. Four. P. M. Thursday."

The machine beeped like an electronic hiccup and a second man's voice, this one gruff and gravelly, made the tiny speaker rattle.

"Hi, it's me. Listen, I think we should talk. About what you said last night. If you're there, pick up the phone, okay?" In the short interval of silence that followed, Tim Fox heard Donovan climbing the stairs, returning to the fourth-floor office. "Heather, I know you're there." Anger rose in the voice from the answering machine. "Pick up the goddamn phone, will you?" Another pause.

Donovan called Fox's name from the top of the stairs.

The man spat an obscenity through the machine and the disembodied voice that resided within its circuitry said cooly, as though intentionally mocking the caller's anger, "Seven. Twenty. Two. P. M. Thursday."

Another electronic hiccup.

Donovan entered the inner office. "The fat Russian broad's gone home. Told her to stay put, we'll stop by for some questions later . . ."

Tim Fox waved a hand, silencing the younger detective.

But Donovan kept talking, lowering his voice this time, giving it a professional edge. "Doitch's back, wants to take the body."

Donovan's last word was drowned by a raspy baritone from the machine, the third caller, another man. He sounded drunk, nearly incoherent. And infuriated. Violently, vengefully angry.

"You know who this is, you bitch," the voice said.

Tim Fox sat back on his haunches and his eyes grew wide.

"The hell you think you're doin'?" the voice from the machine said. "I said no. I told you no, goddamn it. So stop bugging me or . . . or I'm coming over there and I'll rip off your face if you don't . . . stop it. Just stop . . ." A long pause as though the caller were collecting his strength. "You watch your ass, Heather," the man said, close to the receiver. "You got it . . . whatever it is, you've got it coming to you."

"Hey, now there's . . ." Donovan began, and Tim Fox, his eyes on the machine, said "Shut the fuck up for a minute," waiting for the woman with the halting, prerecorded delivery to speak.

"Eleven. Fifty. Three. P. M. Thursday."

12

"Maybe we've got us a time now," Donovan said quietly.

Fox's eyes were still on the answering machine.

"We might have us more than that," he said.

He looked up and avoided Donovan's eyes to stare out the window, his expression one of excitement tinged with sorrow. "I know that voice," Fox said in a near-whisper.

Donovan watched, waiting for him to continue.

"He's a cop. Or used to be."

Tim Fox breathed deeply, exhaled slowly and covered his eyes with one hand.

"Jesus," he said sadly, and shook his head.

TWO

F at Eddie Vance had gas. Not uncomfortable transient indigestion but chronic gut-wrenching, intestine-twisting, bowel-roaring flatulence that rumbled through his digestive tract like the bottom octave of a church organ.

Nothing he tried, not low-fiber diets or chalky antacid liquid swallowed directly from the bottle, prevented it. The root cause of his ailment, had Fat Eddie been honest enough to admit the truth, was the tension generated by his position as Captain of Detectives, Homicide Division.

"The problem, Mr. Vance," his doctor had advised Fat Eddie a week earlier, "is that you're dealing with too much pressure on your job and you're compounding the problem by refusing to admit it." The doctor had lowered his head and peered at Fat Eddie over the top of his glasses.

Fat Eddie hated it when the doctor did that. He hated it when anyone did it. The gesture reminded him of his mother who would stare at him over her glasses and demand to know if Teddy had completed his chores, if Teddy had finished his homework and if Teddy had banished evil thoughts from his mind that could lead to self abuse.

"Just remember," the doctor said, his head still bent, his eyes still fastened on Fat Eddie's from over the glasses' frame. "You can fool yourself, but you can't fool your stomach."

On this morning, Fat Eddie didn't want to fool his stomach. He wanted to pierce it with an open pressure valve and deflate it like a balloon. Instead, he crossed his legs, settled himself deeper into his leather chair, placed the tips of his fingers together beneath his chin and spoke to Tim Fox who had just burst into Fat Eddie's office.

"What've you got, Fox?" Fat Eddie asked in his deep, hollow voice.

"A just cause to haul somebody in on suspicion, murder one," Tim Fox replied. The black detective was wearing his crisply pressed beige Burberry over a gray-brown suit with subtle maroon pinstriping, the deep red tone of the worsted fabric echoed in the color of his tassled loafers and the pattern of his silk tie.

Fat Eddie paused for a moment to admire the detective's lean, fashionable appearance. Where do black people get that sense of style? he wondered.

"So do it," Fat Eddie replied. He shifted his weight from one buttock cheek to the other and winced as a small dagger-like pain sliced through his bowels. He wanted Fox out of his office. He wanted everyone out of hearing range.

"Listen to something first," Fox said. The detective withdrew a portable tape cassette player from a pocket of his topcoat and set it on Fat Eddie's desk. "This is the tape from the answering machine at the scene of that woman's murder on Newbury this morning. You heard about it yet?"

"Of course I heard about it," Fat Eddie said. He placed his hands on the arms of his chair, lifted his weight, lowered it again. "Tell me anyway."

Tim Fox smiled dryly and tilted his head.

Fat Eddie hated that gesture almost as much as he hated people staring over the tops of their eyeglasses at him. It meant he had been caught in a lie. Or a half truth.

"Victim's name is . . ." Fox removed his notebook from an inner jacket pocket and flipped through the pages. "Heather Arlene Lorenzo, age thirty-eight, separated from second husband, residing at 206A Newbury Street, occupation photographer's agent . . ."

"So get to the point." Fat Eddie unfastened his belt buckle. A sound like a Kenworth truck downshifting on a distant freeway rumbled from his gut. God, what was going *on* inside him? "I'll read all that in the summary."

"She was beaten to death with a blunt instrument," Fox said, returning the book to his jacket pocket. "And stabbed once, deeply, in the gut, right here." Fox touched his navel.

Fat Eddie blinked. What would happen, he wondered, if someone punctured *his* navel right now?

"Doitch figures maybe a fractured skull, for sure a broken jaw. Have the autopsy done this afternoon. Looks like she was knocked out and left for dead, came to, crawled ten feet to a doorway, passed out again and bled to death."

"Why are you telling me now?" Fat Eddie asked. He waved a pink hand at the portable tape player on his desk. "And what's it got to do with this?"

Fox reached out and pressed Play. "Listen."

Fat Eddie folded his arms and leaned back in his chair. Something large and furry seemed to be crawling laterally through his abdomen.

From the machine, the effeminate male German voice made its appeal for more time. Fat Eddie blinked impassively.

"One of the photographers she represented," Tim Fox said while the machine's voice announced the day and time of the message. "We think."

The second man's voice, lurching between pleas and anger, rumbled from the machine. Fat Eddie raised his eyebrows at the brutal, abrupt sign-off.

"We don't know who that was. But listen to this," Tim Fox instructed over the machine's voice. "See if you recognize this one."

"You know who this is, you bitch."

Vance jerked his head up as though a bird had flown into the room. He listened to the man's voice shape angry words whose endings were rounded and slurred, the vowels shaking, the whole effect somehow gelatinous and unstable.

"Is that . . . ?" Fat Eddie asked in a near-whisper.

"Sure sounds like it, doesn't it?" Fox shut off the tape player.

17

"Any other calls?"

Fox shook his head. During the playing of the tape his excitement had vanished and now he bit his bottom lip in concentration and avoided Fat Eddie's eyes.

Fat Eddie said, "I hear he's a drunk, living down in the old Combat Zone."

"Got a room over the Flamingo Club," Fox said. He slid the tape player from Fat Eddie's desk and dropped it into his coat pocket. "Strip joint off Tremont. Full of hookers."

"Can't say I'm surprised. Guy was a good cop once, but . . ."

Fox was staring over Vance's shoulder, out the window onto Berkeley Street. "Well, *I'm* surprised. You might've had problems with him but he was the best, him and Ollie. Those two guys taught me more about this job than anyone else."

"Flaws," Fat Eddie said, studying his fingernails. "Man was full of flaws, full of anger. When he didn't have this job to channel it through, he fell apart."

"I want to find him, talk to him," Fox said. "But I want to do it alone. I don't want whistles and I sure as hell don't want Donovan with me."

"He's your partner."

"Joe was my buddy."

"Well, sounds like your buddy's now a suspect in a first-degree." Fat Eddie lifted a pencil from his desk and waved it in the air as he spoke. "So far he's your best one, I'd say."

"I can't believe he would do anything like this." Tim Fox turned and began walking toward the door.

"You can't?" Fat Eddie sneered. "You don't think

18

he could kill anybody? Maybe you just didn't know him very well, Fox. Not as well as some people."

Fox closed the door behind him.

"Not as well as some people," Vance repeated, dropping a hand to his side, trying to rub the pain that was burning through his bowels.

The slimeball from Cambridge, the one with the beard who said he was a professor at Harvard, kept trying to stroke Billie's thigh; the third time he touched her she leaned over, close to him, a gesture she thought might be a mistake when she saw his eyes grow wide in reaction to her breasts dangling so close to his face. Billie said, "Look over there."

"Over where?" said the beard, grinning at her chest.

"Over at that son of a bitch, looks like a portable shithouse, standing behind the bar," Billie hissed. "Name's Dewey. Look at him, asshole." She gripped an inch of flesh on the guy's cheek and twisted his head so he faced the bar where Dewey stood watching the front door, his shaved head gleaming in the lights over the bar, a Bud in his hand, you can barely see the bottle his hand's so big.

"What about him?" the beard asked.

"I give the word to Dewey that you keep touching me and he'll come over here, pick you up, carry you outside and drop you tits-up on a fucking fire hydrant," Billie said.

The beard nodded, folded his arms and sat back while Billie finished dancing naked on the stool in front of him but her heart wasn't in it. When she finished the beard gave her a two-dollar tip and asked what her real name was. "Nancy Reagan," she said, and shrugged into her robe, jammed the two bucks in the same pocket where she kept her cigarettes and lighter, and headed for the front door, needing a smoke and some fresh air, cold as it was.

Sugarman, the owner, liked it when the girls took their breaks outside, standing in the doorway pulling on a Marlboro where the perverts going by on Laveche Street could see them, maybe with one long leg extended, red polish on the toenails, the guys knowing they had nothing on under their robes.

"Take your breaks there, the front door," Sugarman would say. "Brings the suckers in. Flash 'em a little thigh, casual like. Get 'em in for a beer, let 'em look at some pussy."

Billie opened the door on a gray early afternoon. She lit a Marlboro and French-inhaled, releasing the smoke in thick clouds from her mouth, pulling it up through her nostrils and deep into her lungs. She stood staring down the street toward Tremont. From inside the club, Mick Jagger's voice thundered through the speakers over the dance floor where Terri was just beginning her act, reaching behind her, unfastening the gold lamé halter top.

An electrician's delivery van drove by, the young mustached driver lowering his window and making a sucking noise at her. When she gave him the finger, he smiled, honked his horn, accelerated away toward Tremont.

"How you doin'?"

Billie turned to see a cool black dude who'd come up behind her. He was wearing one of those expensive raincoats made in England, nice pin-striped suit,

20

tab-collar shirt, loafers with those little tassels on them.

"I'm doing okay," Billie said. She stepped aside. "You wanta go inside, see some good-looking girls?"

He smiled. Nice white even teeth. Lots of them. "Not today. Looking for an old friend of mine."

Billie took a last drag on her cigarette. "What's his name?"

"McGuire. Joe McGuire."

"Never hearda him." She dropped the butt on the sidewalk, stretched a long leg out to crush it with a rhinestone-strapped stiletto-heeled shoe. The black guy was looking. She felt him watching her leg, admiring it.

"Guy's about fifty, dark hair gettin' gray," he said when she straightened again, her arms folded across her chest. "Got a scar here," and he traced a line with his fingertip diagonally from the corner of his nose to his upper lip.

"Never saw him either." She looked up and down the street, avoiding his eyes. "Listen, I gotta go to work, okay?"

The black guy reached out, grabbed her wrist, squeezed tightly. "How many times've you been busted?" he said, still smiling. Showing his teeth mostly, not smiling with his eyes.

"For what?" Jesus, if Dewey came out now . . .

"For anything. Hooking, snorting, public indecency, picking your nose, I don't care."

"None of your fucking business." Hell, first the bearded asshole said he was a professor, now this.

"You want to add another one or you want to tell me where McGuire is? Your choice."

People going by were watching. Stuff like this could hurt business, guys don't want to come into a place where there's trouble. "He's gone. Goes out in the morning, sometimes you don't see him for days even."

"Where's his room?"

"Around the back. Up the fire escape."

"You see him go out this morning?" The cop relaxed his hold on her wrist.

"One of the girls did. I think she's got a thing for him."

"Where does he go?"

Billie shrugged. "How the hell should I know?"

"Milt Sugarman still own this place?" He released her wrist.

"Yeah, but he's not here. Gone to Mexico with one of the girls. Acapulco, some place like that."

"When's he back?"

She rubbed her wrist where he had held her, gave him a sly grin. Good looking stud, wasn't he? She wondered how seriously he took the gold wedding band on his finger. "Next Wednesday or when he's tired a fuckin' his eyes out, whichever happens first." She took a step back into the club, glanced at the stage. Terri was showing her ass to the thin early crowd, bending over, touching her toes. "You comin' in?"

The black guy didn't answer at first, just leaned back to look around the building to where the fire escape came down to the alley. "Some other time maybe," he said.

"My name's Billie, you want to ask for me," she said. She pulled the robe tighter across her chest. The cold had made her nipples hard and they poked against the fabric.

22

"Sure." He flashed her a smile, put his hands in the pockets of his topcoat. "Maybe I will."

"Son of a bitch is pullin' a number on me."

Phil Donovan hitched his trousers a little higher over his narrow hips and tightened his belt a notch.

Fat Eddie Vance watched silently, holding a pencil by its ends, twirling it slowly.

"He sends me for errands, he tells me nothin'. Thinks I'm still a whistle." Donovan waved his arms in angry gestures, looked around and collapsed into a chair in front of the captain's desk.

"He *is* the senior partner," Vance said.

"Okay, okay, but we're both lieutenants. I'm acting, I know that, but when it gets final and I'm full louie I'm definitely not takin' his shit anymore."

Fat Eddie sighed. He opened the top drawer of his desk where a dozen pencils identical to the one in his hand lay waiting, their points sharpened, all facing in the same direction, like bullets in an ammo belt. "I can't give you a transfer yet. You know that. It would disrupt all the other teams." He added the pencil he had been holding to his cache and closed the drawer.

"I know, I know," Donovan muttered. "Just tell Fox to keep his black ass out of my way, that's all. He leaves me to write up the report on my own and now I gotta go down, watch Doitch do the broad's autopsy while he's out suckin' back a beer or something."

Vance raised his eyebrows. "He didn't tell you where he was going?"

"Not a goddamn word."

Fat Eddie frowned. "He's gone to talk to McGuire. If he can find him."

23

Donovan snapped his head around, the anger about to overflow again. "His old buddy? On his own? What's he doin', talkin' to a number one suspect and not tellin' me?"

Fat Eddie leaned back in his chair. "Did you finish writing your investigation report?"

Donovan nodded, staring off in the distance.

"And did Doitch specifically ask you to be present for a review of the autopsy findings?"

"Naw, that was Fox's idea."

"Then you needn't go. There's no regulation that says the investigating detectives have to be present for the autopsy, unless there are special circumstances." Vance opened another desk drawer and removed an unopened bottle of Maalox, keeping it from Donovan's view.

"So what do I do? Sit around here tryin' to guess what model of Louisville Slugger the guy used on her?"

"You've got a solid suspect, haven't you?"

Donovan looked back at Vance, his blue Irish eyes narrowing.

"Put a bulletin out on McGuire if Fox hasn't done it yet," Vance said. "If Fox finds McGuire on his own, fine. If not, maybe when he gets back, he'll find him here. Either way, you're getting somewhere."

"That's comin' right from you, huh?"

"You just heard it."

Donovan stood up. "Tim'll be pissed," he said. His freckled face was creased with a grin.

"He'll get over it. Besides, Tim has problems being a team player. I've been meaning to mention it to him. Maybe this will make my point."

"Actually, I thought about doin' that, puttin' out a metro call," Donovan said, reaching the door in three strides. "Didn't want to, you know, upset things too much. But this way . . . hell, you agree it's a good idea, right?"

Vance nodded. Right. One hand twisted the cap on the bottle. The point of a dagger traced its way along his lower digestive track. When Donovan closed the door, Vance tilted his head back and drank deeply.

The fire escape was crusted with layers of bird droppings accumulated over the years. As he climbed, Tim Fox wrapped his beige Burberry tightly around his body to keep the fabric from becoming soiled. He leaned slightly forward so that if he lost his step he wouldn't fall backward.

At the first landing, he looked up to the door of McGuire's apartment on the top level. From inside the building came the distant *whump-whump-whump* of the strip club's sound system.

On the second landing he paused again to look around and was startled to see an ancient Oriental woman watching him through a grimy window in the adjacent building, her toothless jaw moving in some kind of chewing action, her expression vacant and uncaring.

He began climbing to the third-floor landing, the bird droppings thicker and fresher, layering the soles of his nearly new Florsheims, his heart beating from the effort and from his fear of heights. He hated heights. Sometimes he hated his work. He sure as hell hated his new partner, Acting Lieutenant Philip James Donovan.

But he liked McGuire. He had always liked the snarly bastard somehow. He sure as hell wouldn't be doing this for anybody else.

Fox reached the door, raised a hand to shield the light from his eyes and wiped away a layer of dust that clung, thick as a penny, to the window in the door.

Through the dusty glass he could see an unmade cot, a sink, a long pine table, a shelf crowded with books, a straight-backed wooden chair, a naked light bulb dangling from the ceiling, a battered plastic radio, a low counter with a hot plate and a kettle, and a cheap floor lamp standing at one end of the bed. Fox knocked on the door, looked over his shoulder to see the ancient Oriental woman still watching him and knocked again.

He tried the doorknob. It turned easily in his hand and with one step he was inside the room, inhaling its stale air.

Billie was ready to go on after MaryLou, standing behind the stage in her pink gown with the pink halter and panties underneath, her silver G-string cutting the skin on her hips, wishing she could get a drink about now, a hit of scotch maybe, when the door opened and in came Django.

The Dancer, Dewey and Grizzly called him, but then Dewey and Grizzly could call people anything they wanted to and usually did. Nobody picked an argument with Dewey or Grizzly except maybe a goddamn platoon of Marines and then they'd better be sober and well-armed.

"Here comes the Dancer," Dewey grinned when he saw Django sidling between the tables, moving in rhythm to the music from the overhead speakers, snapping the fingers of his good hand and holding the other one, the one that was scarred and claw-shaped, out to one side. His close-cropped head bobbed, his eyes shone and he flashed his wide grin at everybody in the room, even Dewey. Django was wearing his black leather trenchcoat and gray tweed stingy-brimmed porkpie hat, the coat open so he could move his legs and feet easier, showing his dance steps, strutting his stuff.

His mother named him Elias for reasons she never explained, and he grew up in Buffalo as Elias Tetherton, just another runty black kid destined for a life in the projects or a death in a gutter, take your pick. Then Elias met Elsie, cute little Elsie who liked his sense of humor and his crazy way of dancing, telling him he made old Michael Jackson look like a tree stump, you come right down to it. Only thing is, Michael Jackson had the drive, the urge, and Elias Tetherton just had the joy, and joy alone gets you nothing but a grin and a nod and maybe a couple of bucks from white people downtown who would smile at his dance steps and broad grin.

The joy didn't get Elias any money for Elsie and him or for the baby boy who came along ten months after they met. Pretty soon they were a family of kids. Elias was eighteen, Elsie was sixteen and the baby was two when Elsie got pregnant the second time and Elias knew he had to do something more for his family than sweep out the pressroom and bundle papers down at the Buffalo *Evening News*.

It had to be something with a bit of risk, something that took a few smarts. Heisting cars, hustling watches on the street wouldn't do it. Had to be something bigger, something you could put your smarts to work on. Elias had smarts he hadn't even used yet and when Elsie's older brother offered Elias a thousand dollars, just take a big brown package down to Boston, don't ask what's inside, ride a gray dog bus along the thruway, Elias saw his chance and he took it and did it and got paid big-time. He decided to stay in Boston, just for a few weeks, get enough money to send home to Elsie and the boys, enough maybe to go to school, *really* exercise his smarts.

But that was nearly two years ago.

When there had been an Elsie to return to.

It was McGuire who named him Django when he first saw the small black man dancing with his crippled left hand extended. Elias's face lit up at the name. Django had a nice lilt, sounded like nothing nobody else was using on the street. People on the street had names like Grizzly and the Gypsy and Heckle and Cracker Jack. McGuire wrote the name out for him with a shaky hand on a piece of paper, telling Django there was once a jazz musician with the same name, some European guy died forty years ago, a brilliant wild man who had a crippled hand just like Elias's and who learned to play guitar in spite of it, learned a style of guitar playing that no one has quite copied since, good left hand or not.

McGuire took to Django right away and not just because Django was the source of McGuire's sole pleasure, the meperidine pressed within the small white pills Django sold for Grizzly. It was Django's insouciance that McGuire admired, the smaller man's inescapable optimism in the face of all the facts that said he was doomed, that he should nourish no dreams whose lives extended beyond a single rotation of the earth. And Django was drawn to McGuire in the way many people with limited power are drawn to those with strength, even when the strength is hidden and unacknowledged and almost broken as it was in McGuire.

They were the oddest of couples to see on the brief occasions they met for business and restricted social encounters, the ex-cop sunken to addiction and the wiry street person moving in dance steps to conceal the deadening effects of his daily life.

"Hey, Django," McGuire would greet the small man in his guttural whispery voice.

The more McGuire used it, the more Django loved the name. He needed something new, something to make him forget who he was and what he had been before they messed up his hand. "It's Django dancin' time, darlin'," he'd say when he'd see McGuire coming, and he'd move his feet in that nice soft-shoe rhythm, shove *that* up your ass, Michael Jackson.

After all, he had many reasons to change his name, reasons more than just hating the name his mama had given him.

Elias. Shit, who ever heard of a man with smarts named Elias? But Django, yeah, a nice touch. Man named Django had to have smarts, you could tell.

"Got a 'D'," Django said when he saw the name written by McGuire and McGuire told him, "Yeah, but you don't pronounce it, it's silent."

"The D don't talk," Django nodded. "Spread that word, man. The D don't talk, it don't say *nothin'* it ain't supposed to."

And so he became Django to everyone but Dewey, who Django never trusted and rarely spoke to, and Grizzly, who Django talked to every day, nodding his head in agreement because nobody ever disagreed with Grizzly, nobody ever told Grizz what to call nobody else, and the name created a special bond between Django and McGuire.

MaryLou finished her number and was standing there buck naked with her legs wrapped around the pole in the middle of the stage, trying not to yawn. She smiled across the room and waved at Django who waved back with his good hand.

Billie walked across the room, cut Django off before he reached the bar. Seeing her coming, Django threw her one of his big grins, the gold in a front tooth gleaming.

"Lady Day, Lady Day," he said in that voice of his that was always ready to laugh.

Django had dubbed Billie "Lady Day," which Billie later discovered was the nickname for Billie Holiday, which fit because that's who Billie's mother named her for. Billie liked her name until she was a teenager and found out that the singer named Billie Holiday had been a black junkie who had once hooked for a living, and then it didn't seem to be such a goddamn compliment.

"You seen McGuire?" Billie hissed at Django. The guys at the tables were pushing their hands together, giving MaryLou some half-assed applause while she stumbled around the stage picking up her clothes and blanket, looking forward to a hit of coke in the back room to get her through the day.

"Jolt?" Django said. His eyebrows, thick as steel wool, slid up and made his high forehead look like a black shiny washboard. "No, Lady. Ain't seen the man but I 'spec to see him soon. Man be needin' a few beats a Django's tune." As he spoke, Django moved from side to side, shifting his weight from foot to foot.

"A cop was lookin' for him, few minutes ago," Billie said. "He could be in deep shit. You might want to let him know, okay?"

"True, true I will, darlin'." Django threw a smile into the far corner, furthest from the stage, where a guy in a canvas hat and gray walrus mustache, kind of antsy looking, had been trying to catch Django's eye, nodding his head, his lips sort of puckered. Django had some business.

"You're on, bitch," MaryLou said to Billie, walking past, her clothes and blanket over one arm.

"And now, for your continuous pleasure, gentlemen . . ." Dewey drawled into the P.A. system from behind the bar.

Billie climbed the steps to the elevated stage, the lights flashing red and blue. Her music tape started playing, thump-thump.

". . . the Flamingo Club is proud to present the elegant and voluptuous *Shana*!" Django was side-stepping toward the customer in the corner. Mary-Lou stumbled once on her way to the dressing room, almost fell.

Break your fucking neck, Billie said silently, and she began to dance, moving her body for the men but keeping her mind in a different place, far away.

31

THREE

Tim Fox took barely a minute to skim McGuire's flat. No telephone, no TV, not even a refrigerator. The bathroom was barely bigger than a phone booth with just a toilet and a plastic shower enclosure. The books on the shelf above the bed were paperback biographies and histories, the food in the cupboard consisted of instant coffee and crackers, and even the clothing hanging on the back of the door was minimal: thick sweater, lightweight jacket, denim shirt, gray wool trousers, two blue button-down shirts.

Tim Fox dropped his card next to the hotplate on the chipped enamelled table and left, closing the door behind him.

What happened to the poor son of a bitch? he wondered, descending the fire escape while the old Oriental woman watched him from across the landing.

He wandered through what remained of the city's Combat Zone for almost an hour, peering through the windows of video shops, bookstores, Vietnamese restaurants and Chinese grocery stores where Peking ducks hung in the windows, their skin mahogany red and their smiling beaks encrusted with baked sugar.

When he returned to the Berkeley Street headquarters, Stu Cauley, on duty at the downstairs desk, called him over. "You're supposed to go downstairs," Cauley said. "Donovan's down there, him and a couple a uniforms. They brought him in, maybe half an hour ago, they're workin' through it down there."

"Through what?" Fox said.

"That case, broad got beat to death on Newbury Street. Yours, right? Everybody knows about it. Hell of a thing. Anyway they found him. Brought him in on it and he's down in the hole."

Fox swore and turned toward the stairs.

"Christ, does he look bad, Timmy," Cauley said sadly. "Looks like a barrel of yesterday's shit."

"Okay, maybe you're not drunk but you sure as hell look hung over."

Phil Donovan sat on a metal folding chair turned backwards, his tie askew, collar button undone. One of the uniformed cops, a young guy just two years out of the academy, watched from the far corner, his chair tilted back, a plastic cup of coffee in his hand.

Between them, a middle-aged man sat in a straight-backed wooden chair, bent from the waist, his elbows on his knees, his fingertips stroking his temples, looking like another street bum waiting on a bench in the Public Garden, hoping for a handout. Which was where two cops found him, staring blankly across Charles Street. The uniformed police officers didn't recognize him at first sight but one of them thought, What the hell, it could be him.

He admitted his name and right away one of the cops, the older one, started acting almost polite, practically invited him to get in the cruiser and come back with them to Berkeley Street. And he got in, not wondering why, just asking if he could have a couple of aspirin and a coffee when they got there.

"Still got your headache?" Donovan asked, grinning like he thought it was funny.

"I'm not a drunk," the man said.

"Naw, you're not a drunk. You just like to marinate your fuckin' liver," Donovan said. He glanced over at the young whistle in the corner who was smiling at the detective's humor. "Christ, look at yourself. You're a bum, you're worse than a bum. The bums in the Garden, most of them never had much of a break, never amounted to a hell of a lot in their lives. But *you* . . ."

The door behind Donovan burst open and Tim Fox stood there, his hand gripping the knob, breathing hard not from the effort of trotting downstairs but from anger. "I want to talk to you, Donovan," Fox said, the words escaping from his lips like steam from a pressure valve. "Out here. Now."

Donovan twisted in the chair and grinned over his shoulder at his partner. "Sure thing, Timmy," he said, standing up. "Don't go away now," he smiled at the middle-aged man, who lifted his head at the sight of Fox.

"Hello, Timmy," the man said to Fox.

"How you doing, McGuire?" Fox asked, and the other man smiled tightly and nodded.

Tim Fox strode past Donovan and down the basement corridor taking long quick steps like he was a whistle working Washington Avenue again, hustling to break up a street fight, ready to wade in with a billy club, cutting the air with it like Yastrzemski chasing a high and outside fast ball. Donovan tagged behind, his hands in his pockets, a smirk on his face.

"The fuck you think you're doin'?" Fox said, pulling up near the coffee machine and swinging around to face the younger detective, pointing his finger at him like it was a Smith & Wesson.

Donovan held his hands up, palms facing Fox. "Easy, buddy . . ." he said.

"Don't buddy me, asshole." Fox shook with anger and Donovan's grin grew wider at the sight of spittle forming at the corners of the black detective's lips. "You don't bring somebody like McGuire in and drop him in the I.R. like he's a piece of shit you picked up on the street."

"But, Timmy," Donovan said, "he *is* a piece of shit we picked up on the street. In the Public Garden, sitting on a bench, for Christ's sake, dressed like that."

"He's the best goddamn cop who ever walked into this dump," Fox replied. "Him and Ollie Schantz . . ."

"So what is he now?" Donovan spat back, the smile erased. He showed Fox a hand, the fingers folded down, and he popped them up one at a time as he spoke. "He's a has-been, he's a drunk, he's a bum and he's a suspect in a murder one. You seen the preliminary on that Lorenzo broad, Doitch's report?" He waved the question away before Fox could reply. "Deep penetrating wound through her gut. Plus severe concussion, cracked vertebrae, three broken ribs, broken jaw, two fingers snapped when she put her hand up to defend herself from that old favorite we've all come to know and love, a blunt fucking instrument." He arched his eyebrows. "She was one tough cookie to survive an ass-kicking like that as long as she did."

"Where's the weapon?" Fox demanded. "Where's the motive, the opportunity, the eyewitness, the forensics, to make McGuire an A-number-one?"

"I didn't say—"

"I was in his room, Donovan . . ."

Over Donovan's shoulder Fox saw two uniforms watching them from the far end of the hall, eaves-dropping on a face-to-face between a couple of hot-shot detectives, picking up some trash to spread through the cruiser network later in the day. "Should've seen Fox and Donovan going at it in Berkeley," they'd be saying. "Hammer and tongs, like street scum, two suits, two detectives." Rumor would feed rumor until, by the end of the day, the story would have Fox and Donovan rolling on the floor, squeezing each other's jugulars.

"You guys wanta find some traffic tickets to hand out or something?" Fox shouted down the hall to them, and the whistles muttered to each other and wandered around the corner toward the elevator.

"I was in his room," Fox began again, this time in a hoarse whisper, poking Donovan in the chest with a finger, "and there's nothing. No blood on the clothes, no sign of a weapon, not even a telephone."

"He was pissed enough to do it or to get somebody else to," Donovan said, his hands in his trouser pockets again. "Point is—"

"The fucking point is," Tim Fox said, raising his voice, "I'm the senior louie and if I say I'll deal with a suspect first, you keep your—"

"Fat Eddie gave me the go-ahead," Donovan said. The smirk was back.

Tim Fox froze his expression, except for his eyes which shifted sideways. "Who?"

"Vance." Donovan adjusted his tie, fastened his collar button. "Gave him a rundown, told him you were out lookin' for McGuire and Eddie said put some muscle on it, back you up. They bring him in, I take him downstairs, give the poor bastard some coffee, help him get over the shakes, read him his Miranda and be his buddy." He raised his hands again, palms open. "See? No rubber hose." Turning to leave, he said, "Now, you want to bitch to somebody, you go bitch to Fat Eddie. Otherwise, while we're runnin' up each other's tails here, we got a murder one gettin' cold."

"What do you need, Joe?"

Tim Fox sat on the same metal chair Donovan had occupied, facing McGuire. Donovan had retreated to the far corner of the interrogation room where the young whistle had been slouching until Fox entered and told him to get the hell out and stay out of the observation room too, he and Donovan would handle this on their own.

McGuire lifted his head to smile back at Fox. "I, uh . . ." he began in that low voice of his, the sound textured like a wet gravel road. "Nothing, Timmy," he said, shaking his head. "I'm okay."

He wore a faded cotton sweater, once white but now the color of dishwater, the frayed collar and cuffs of a blue oxford-cloth shirt visible beneath it. His denim jeans were oversized, the bottoms rolled above a tattered pair of Reeboks worn with no socks. A three-day growth of beard grew among the folds of a face as shrunken and bony as the rest of his body.

McGuire looked perhaps twenty pounds lighter and twenty years older than the last time Fox had seen him, less than a year and a half earlier.

"Donovan tell you about the woman on Newbury Street?" Fox asked.

McGuire nodded.

"We've got your voice on her answering machine tape, Joe," Timmy said. "Threatening the murder victim."

"So I hear."

"What got you so pissed at her?"

"Not sure."

"You on a drunk?"

McGuire thought about it for a moment. "No," he said finally. "Not yesterday."

"Where were you last night?"

"Beats the heck out of me."

"Where'd you wake up this morning?"

"My place."

"The room over the Flamingo."

"Home sweet home."

"I was there." Fox smiled. "You should lock your door."

"Nothing to steal. Besides," McGuire grinned, "it's never locked. Gets used when I'm not in."

"Girls from the club taking johns up there?"

McGuire ran a hand through his hair, longish, growing gray, the curls tighter than ever. "Pays the rent. Keeps the kids off the streets."

"Jesus Christ," Donovan muttered from the corner. McGuire looked at him without expression.

"You don't remember calling this Lorenzo woman?" Fox said.

McGuire turned back to Fox, shook his head.

"Can you remember why you were so angry with her?"

Another shake.

"How'd you know her?" Donovan called from the corner. "You bang her a few times maybe? Or were you just pimping for her?"

Tim Fox glared across at Donovan.

McGuire smiled and moved his lips.

"What's that?" Tim Fox asked, leaning forward and narrowing his eyes.

"Used to be related," McGuire said, loud enough this time for Fox to hear. He rubbed the back of his neck. "My ex-wife's sister."

Fox straightened up. Donovan pulled his notebook from his jacket pocket and began scribbling in it. "When was the last time you saw her?" Fox asked.

McGuire shrugged. "Not for years. Until . . ." He frowned, staring down at his feet. "Until a week,

39

maybe two weeks ago. I was, uh . . ." He pinched the bridge of his nose, stared up at the ceiling for a moment and nodded as though agreeing with himself. "I was over in the Esplanade one day. Just waiting, looking . . . looking for somebody. There were these women in fur coats and a photographer and a bunch of other people near the band shell and one of them kept looking at me, and then she came over and started talking to me. And I recognized her, I saw it was Heather. The photographer, he was one of her clients or whatever she called them, fashion photographers."

He sat back in the chair, raised his chin, spoke to the ceiling. "She, uh, she laughed at the way I looked, what I was doing. Said she knew who I was going to meet, what I wanted to see him for. Heard about me doing . . . doing what I was doing. Thought it was funny . . ."

"Who were you going to meet?" Fox asked.

McGuire pondered the answer. "A friend. Just a friend."

"He got a name?" Donovan asked.

"Django," McGuire said. "Just Django. And, uh, she asked where I lived and I told her over the Flamingo, and she thought that was even funnier, and I was, uh . . . if I'd felt better I might have hit her then and there . . ." McGuire grinned at Fox. "Jesus, Timmy, I just handed you an incriminating statement then, didn't I?"

"Sure as shit did," Donovan said from the corner. "Keep talkin' like that, we'll have your whole history nailed down."

McGuire shrugged. "My life is an open pamphlet."

40

"You didn't hit her?" Tim Fox asked.

"No. But I wanted to."

"What stopped you?"

"Guess I'm out of shape."

"So what'd you do?"

"Got up and walked away and she went back to the photographer and the models."

"Eddie Vance could use that statement to build a charge against you."

"Let him."

"You don't seem worried about it."

"I'm not. Nothing Eddie can do'll worry me."

Fox grinned. "Yeah, well, Fat Eddie's his own worst enemy."

McGuire arched his eyebrows and smiled. "Not while I'm around."

There was a knock at the door and a uniformed sergeant leaned into the room. "Got a message for you guys," he said, speaking to Fox and Donovan but unable to keep his eyes from the shrunken figure of McGuire.

Tim Fox looked at Donovan and angled his head. Donovan sighed and followed the sergeant out of the room and into the hall. When the door closed Fox stood up, took a step closer to McGuire, leaned from the waist and asked, "So what happened to you, Joe?"

McGuire sighed and allowed himself a smile. "I screwed up."

Fox shook his head sadly. "Last I heard you were down in the Bahamas mixing martinis, living the good life. When we got the word about you, bunch of us up here, we figured you scored a big one, you lucked out."

41

"For a while." McGuire leaned back in his chair and folded his arms, avoiding the other man's eyes. "For a while I did."

"And then?"

"Told you. I screwed up."

"Lot of guys screw up, but they manage to land on their feet."

The door swung open abruptly and Donovan was standing there, a sheet of paper in his hand.

"He's charged," Donovan said.

Fox scowled at him. "What the fuck you talking about?"

Donovan waved the paper back and forth as though taunting a bull. "Higgins got a briefing from Fat Eddie, says there's enough to book him. All in here."

"Higgins still P.A.?" McGuire asked calmly, and Fox nodded.

"It's a bullshit decision," Fox said, half to Donovan and half to McGuire.

"Need your shoelaces and your belt," Donovan said to McGuire as he entered the room, the sergeant and two whistles behind him.

McGuire bent over and began untying his shoes, Tim Fox watching sadly, McGuire fumbling with the laces.

McGuire was held on suspicion of the murder of Heather Arlene Lorenzo, age 38, resident of 206A Newbury Street, occupation: photographer's agent. He was ordered held in custody pending further investigation. He endured a strip search, a fitting for a pair of oversized blue coveralls and being locked into handcuffs and shackles. The young driver of the police van that transported him and two sullen black men in their twenties to holding cells in the jail on Nashua Street called him Pops, and McGuire smiled and ducked his head without responding.

Inside the brick walls of the jail reception area, McGuire emerged from the van and leaned unsteadily against the vehicle before retching violently while the black men watched blankly and the van driver made a joke about prison food.

He was photographed, fingerprinted and led down a narrow corridor to his cell, where he collapsed on the cot and listened to the slam of the cell door echo and decay.

In the cell facing him were two men, a large red-headed man whose oft-broken nose drifted at an angle across his face and who spoke with a strangely sibilant lisp, and a smaller older man who constantly moved a cigarette butt from one corner of his mouth to the other. Both stared at McGuire for several moments, the larger man blankly, the other with suspicion, until the red-haired man said simply, "Cop," and turned away to lie on his bunk.

"Watch your ass, buddy," the smaller one said to McGuire, who lay back with hands clasped behind his head. "'Cause it ain't worth shit in here. Me, I'd be proud as hell to do a few months in seg, just to say I offed a fuckin' cop. Wouldn't I, Red?"

The big man said, "Gimme a cigarette."

When McGuire's food was brought to his cell he could eat none of it.

"Good move, cop," the small man in the opposite

cell said. "They know you're a cop, the trusties piss on your food. You know that? Ain't that right, Red?"

When McGuire finally fell asleep he began to dream of drifting in boats through pastureland where grazing cows would lift their heads in surprise as he passed by, and of his father, dead twenty years, watching him from behind a wooden fence, the bleached unpainted boards covered in writing McGuire could not read. He woke and lay rising and falling through clouds of pain and perspiration before closing his eyes.

Almost immediately he began to dream again, visions of ice water flowing down his parched throat, tasting its freshness and cold salvation, and of walking woodenly along a city street toward a corner where flatbed trucks were passing slowly by in a convoy of sorts. The cargo shifted back and forth and side to side as the trucks passed, their movement propelled not by the motion of the vehicles but by some inner agony. At the intersection McGuire looked into the trucks and saw flayed bodies with amputated limbs, the skin and stubs of arms and legs cross-textured in blue and white, and as one truck passed another arrived to take its place and others stretched down the avenue of the city, their passage unending, their cargoes identical and agonizing and horrific.

Someone began choking him, thrusting a weapon into his mouth to block his breathing. McGuire cried out at the sight of the trucks and their cargo and at the attack on him by someone unseen. There were cries in his ears, the cries of the mutilated men in the trucks and the cries of others, and McGuire woke to find his own hand in his mouth and a guard poking him with a broom handle. In the opposite cell the small dark man called out, "You don't shut the fuck up, somebody'll shove your dick in your ear," while the big man with the red hair grinned across at McGuire and muttered something, and the small man laughed and lit a cigarette.

In the morning McGuire lay on his bunk with his forearm across his eyes. The two men in the opposite cell were escorted away, and as they passed McGuire's cell the small man hissed, "You're gonna get it, cop," and the other man said in his strange lisp, "Can't stop it happening, buddy. Can't stop what's gonna happen to you."

Half an hour later, McGuire was still motionless when he heard footsteps tread the corridor toward his cell and halt just beyond the bars. He raised his arm from his eyes and looked across the few feet separating him from an olive-skinned compact man in a brown suede windbreaker, faded jeans and white sneakers who stood watching him with concern. "Mother of God, I didn't believe it," the man said.

McGuire stared back at the man's dark eyes and curly black hair, the body slim and taut.

"Jesus, Joe, it's me, Scrignoli." The black-haired man shook his head and a nervous grin revealed white and shiny teeth in a handsome Italian face. "It's been a while, but hell . . ."

McGuire nodded and closed his eyes. "How you doin'?" he said. He remembered Scrignoli, an undercover cop, once Bernie Lipson's partner before Bernie joined forces with McGuire to replace Ollie Schantz. Bernie's retired and Ollie's paralyzed, McGuire reminded himself. A generation gone and

I'm in jail. McGuire pieced it together. Bernie retired. Kavander dead. Ollie crippled. Me in jail. On the whole, I'd rather be in Worcester . . . .

What the hell was Scrignoli's first name? The pain like a knife . . .

"Bunch of us back on Berkeley, Stu Cauley and the others, we heard about it and couldn't believe it." Scrignoli spoke in the broad accents of North Boston, a scrod-and-spaghetti accent Ollie Schantz used to call it. "This is horseshit, Joe. This is Fat Eddie at his worst."

McGuire nodded his head again. What's his name? Dave? Dominic? Something like that.

"So I got elected to come over and make sure you're okay, let you know we're with you, we're not gonna let nothin' happen to you. I mean, even some of the guys here, some of the guards, the older ones, they're wonderin' what you're doin' in here. So I came just to let you know you're gonna be all right, okay?"

"Sure." McGuire lay his forearm across his eyes again. Dell? Daryl? No, not Daryl. Maybe Darren . . .

"Anything you need? Anything we can get you?"

"Out," McGuire said.

"We're workin' on it. I mean, one of the guys's been talking to Higgins and you know what? Even Higgins, even he's not behind it a hundred percent, okay? He told the guy right up front, he said it's not gonna stick, the charge. You're outta here and you and me, the day you're out, the two of us'll go over to Hanover Street and suck up some clams, maybe pick up some broads." Scrignoli's voice dropped in volume and acquired a weight, a sense of everyone's daily sadness. "My wife and I, we split last year. Don't know if you heard."

Scrignoli's wife, McGuire recalled. Her name was Sue, plump, blond hair . . . the hell's *his* name . . . ?

A long pause, then, "Anyhow, you got problems, I can see that. But you got friends too, Joe, and we all know this is a chickenshit thing of Fat Eddie's, so hang in there, okay? Okay?"

Danny. Yes. "Thanks, Danny."

"You're all right," Danny Scrignoli said, and his voice almost choked with emotion. "You're gonna be all right," and he slapped the bars with his hand, in anger or frustration, and walked quickly, almost silently, away.

Listening to the details of McGuire's transfer to Nashua Street from one of the cops who accompanied the prisoner, Tim Fox absorbed it all with sadness. McGuire was more than an ex-cop not only to Fox but to an entire generation of police officers who had managed to rise from street duty to detective status.

Joe McGuire and Ollie Schantz had shown the way for a decade, working like guerrillas within an often incompetent system. Bending the rules to achieve success, they earned citations from the police commissioner in the morning and bought rounds of drinks for the duty cops that same afternoon, laughing at the pretentiousness of the award ceremony, knowing they had earned and deserved it but mocking it anyway, mocking everything except the reason they pinned on a badge each day: without daily encounters with the scum of life, without the silent trust handed to them to protect citizens who thanked them by sneering at their very existence, they would lack both identity and purpose.

For Joe McGuire, it all ended the day Ollie Schantz became eligible for his pension and decided that his identity and purpose now lay along the banks of a salmon pond. He retired leaving McGuire alone and bitter to manage without him.

Two weeks later, in one of those ironies of life that prompt some people to discover salvation in the Bible and others to seek it in a shotgun, the muzzle in their mouth, Ollie Schantz returned from his first fishing expedition almost totally paralyzed from the neck down. And soon after, McGuire escaped the complex politics and machinations of Fat Eddie Vance by retreating to the Bahamas for two years.

What brought him back? Fox wondered. What screwed him up so badly? What happened to the old McGuire, the tough son of a bitch who carried his anger like a junkyard dog with a toothache?

Fox didn't know. But he knew something had to be done about Fat Eddie.

He strode down the corridor to Vance's office and burst in on the captain who quickly closed the top drawer of his desk and looked back at Fox, startled.

"You're interfering, Eddie," Fox said, drawing deep breaths and glaring at the round pink face of the man who had once been his partner and was now his superior.

Vance blinked and raised his eyebrows.

"You don't like the way I'm handling a case, okay, tell me," Fox said. "But no more getting between me and Donovan, all right? Telling him to send out a P.Q. order while I'm still out there looking for the man. No more of that, okay?"

Fat Eddie smiled, closed his eyes and shook his head slowly from side to side.

"What's the deal?" Fox demanded. "I'm pissed and you think it's funny?"

"A little," Vance said when he opened his eyes. "You know who you just reminded me of? When you came in right now, so self-righteous and angry? McGuire, that's who. When he was still a cop, he'd be in here complaining all the time, to me, to Kavander, to everybody. McGuire acted like he carried all the rules and regulations around in his hip pocket and it was his duty to educate people about them. You sounded a lot like him just now."

"Thanks," Tim Fox said, turning for the door. "I'll take that as a compliment, Eddie."

"A compliment?" Vance called after him. "Are you nuts? Look where McGuire is now, Fox. You think being told you're acting like him is a *com*pliment?"

Ten minutes later Fox told himself Fat Eddie wasn't worth the spit it took to say his name and swung around in his chair to snatch Mel Doitch's autopsy report from Donovan's desk and scan the contents.

Heather Arlene Lorenzo had been in excellent physical condition with no visible scars except for the two crescent-shaped surgery marks beneath her breasts, marking silicon implants. Her injuries had been inflicted by a cylindrical wooden weapon, swung with substantial strength. Small samples of the wood had been removed from body tissues that had absorbed the blows and they were currently being subjected to laboratory analysis. . . .

The phone jangled at his elbow. He snatched the receiver from its cradle and barked his name into it.

The voice on the other end was deep and modulated. "Are you the gentleman who is investigating Ms. Lorenzo's death?"

"That's me," Fox said.

"My name is Gregory Weiner," the man said. "I own the building here. Heather was my tenant. I apologize for being absent this morning but I left early to do an appraisal of some watercolors in Cambridge—"

"We'll send somebody out to interview you," Fox interrupted.

The cultured voice faltered somewhat. "Uh, you *are* the detective heading the investigation, are you not?"

Fox assured the man he was.

"Then I would prefer to speak directly with you, if I may."

Fox frowned. "Look, we got maybe a dozen officers working on this—"

"Heather Lorenzo feared for her life," the voice interrupted. "She told me, just yesterday, when she asked me if I might be working late downstairs."

"We can take a statement . . ."

"That might be a good idea," Gregory Weiner said. "Heather told me a man might be trying to kill her. Somebody well-known and powerful. The gentleman apparently frightened her because he could get out of control. She had seen him that way."

"I'll be over," Tim Fox said.

When he hung up he thought about telling Donovan, then wondered what the younger detective could really offer. "Probably nothing," Fox muttered. "I'll tell him later."

* * *

It was there on his tray next to the powdered eggs, a small white envelope not much bigger than a postage stamp. The trustee slid his breakfast through the opening of the bars while McGuire watched from the corner of the cell where he lay on the floor, his stomach about to heave from the aroma of food, the pain in his head like a deep cleft through his skull.

He turned away and covered his face with his hand, a barrier against the smell of hot grease. His hand trembled like a captured bird and he remained motionless for several minutes before rising unsteadily and walking to the bars, planning to fling the tray out into the corridor until he saw the envelope.

He palmed it quickly and returned to the corner of the cell. Inside were four tiny white pills and he swallowed two before replacing the remainder in the envelope and settling back on the floor, his eyes closed, his brow less furrowed.

When the trustee returned for the tray, McGuire rose, walked to the bars, reached through to touch the man's arm. "Who gave you that?" he asked in a hoarse whisper.

"Gave me what?" The guy, skinny and gray-haired, his skin the color of old newspapers, avoided McGuire's eyes.

"The stuff on my tray, in the envelope," McGuire hissed.

"Don't know what the hell you're talking about," the trustee muttered.

A different trustee brought him lunch and he never saw the pasty-faced man again.

* * *

Stana Tomasevich sat nervously at her kitchen table, a cup of tea growing cold in front of her. There had not been a man of any kind in her apartment since her husband, Frank, departed with two plastic bags of clothing nearly ten years earlier, never to return.

And now there were three men here, the young red-haired one with blue eyes and a nose like a hawk's beak, smiling at her from across the kitchen table, and two policemen in uniform in the other room, searching through her belongings. She could hear the officers talking among themselves, quietly. She pictured them inspecting her room, touching, lifting, moving her possessions. She would have to clean everything when they finally left, wipe it all down.

The red-haired man was writing on the pad of paper he carried with him. "You ever meet anybody in her apartment?" he asked.

"Who?" Stana said. "Who would I meet there? Men? You think I meet men there?"

The red-haired man, Donovan, laughed aloud. "No, I meant friends of Miss Lorenzo. Anybody."

Stana shook her head. "Sometimes men are there, for business. I don't talk, I don't see. I scrub floors, I do dishes, I wash windows, then I go."

"So you wouldn't recognize anybody you met there if you saw them again."

Another shake of the head.

"Any men stay overnight with Miss Lorenzo?"

Stana blushed and lowered her head. "Sometimes."

"Recently?"

A nod. "Two, three weeks ago, Miss Lorenzo does not come downstairs when I finish kitchen, so I go upstairs, knock on door, say I am here. She comes, unlocks door. She is wearing blanket, no, sheet from bed around her body and she is laughing. She says, 'Don't do bedroom today,' and she runs back in room, closes door. And all time I am cleaning, I hear her in there with man."

"What were they doing?" Donovan sat back watching her, a wide smile on his face, tapping his teeth with a pencil.

She turned away again. "They laugh. And they make Ricky Chow."

The pencil stopped. "Ricky what?"

"Ricky Chow." Stana held her hands side by side in front of her, palms facing the floor, and moved them up and down. "You know, bedsprings go Ricky Chow, Ricky Chow, Ricky Chow . . ."

Donovan erupted in laughter, embarrassing Stana even more. His next few questions were interrupted by snickers and he mimicked her, muttering, "Ricky Chow, Ricky Chow," over and over. "What'd she keep up in her bedroom, among the pottery?"

Stana blinked. "Pottery?"

"The vases in her bedroom, up on the shelf near the ceiling. Something was screwed into the shelf on the corner and it looks like something else was fastened along the wall near it. Whatever it was, somebody pulled it out recently. Might've been the guy who killed her."

She shook her head. "I don't dust pottery, I don't dust ceiling. Too high."

Donovan rose from his chair. "Thanks for your help Mrs., uh . . ."

Stana pronounced her last name for him, rising

from her chair too. The police officers were waiting in the short hall near the apartment door.

"Anything else you want to tell us?" Donovan asked her, shrugging into his topcoat.

Stana held her hands together in front of her ample stomach and shook her head. Then, almost without thinking, she blurted, "She was not nice woman."

Donovan looked back at her, waiting for her to continue.

"Not nice," Stana repeated.

"That's no reason for somebody to kill her," Donovan said. "Just because she wasn't the nicest person in the world, right?"

"Bad," Stana tried to explain. She looked away, searching for the words a man once used to describe Heather Lorenzo as he stormed from Heather's apartment, his words shouted in anger. "Wicked and vicious," Stana blurted. Those were the words she had heard the man use. And they were true, Stana remembered. Heather had been wicked and vicious. When she had caught Stana on a ladder admiring the collection of pottery and the thing behind the pottery, black and shiny, she had shouted at Stana, telling her never to touch them again, the vases. "Wicked and vicious," Stana repeated, turning to enter her kitchen again, leaving the men to find their own way out. She would make a fresh cup of tea and drink it, and then she would clean her apartment, ridding it of evidence of those men, the cruel-mouthed red-haired one and the two police officers who touched everything with their hands.

Gregory Weiner was perhaps forty years old. He

wore his chestnut hair in a heavily sprayed, perfectly coiffed pompadour at the front and trimmed square across the back of the neck. His mustache looked as though it were shaped with a scalpel. His front teeth were oversized and his cheeks were round and full, giving him the appearance of a somewhat effeminate chipmunk, but his eyes were wary and conniving. He greeted Tim Fox by rising from the chair behind the oversized parson's table that served as a desk and extending a hand toward the black detective while his eyes scanned Fox's suit, shirt and tie in silent approval.

"This is terrible," Weiner said, turning his fingertips under and rubbing them against the palms of his hands. "Perhaps if I had listened to Heather . . ."

"Listened to her?" Tim Fox sat in the ladder-back chair facing Weiner's desk. Behind the desk loomed a bleached oak armoire with carved pediment, the doors open, the shelves crowded with small ceramic figures, silk scarves, embroidered pillows and antique photographs in pewter frames.

"She was *frightened*," Weiner said. "And yet she was laughing it off, as if it were a joke." He shook his head. "I realize now, of course, that it wasn't. She really was quite terrified of this man the other day."

"She didn't mention names?"

"Only that he was well-known."

"For what?"

Weiner looked confused. "I don't understand . . ."

"Was he an athlete? Ball player maybe? Somebody on television? A politician?"

"She never said. Just that he was well-known, well-connected." Weiner turned away. "She often bragged about her men friends that way but this time I could tell she was nervous and I asked what was wrong. She said she couldn't tell me but she asked if I might be working last evening or if Jonathan, that's the young man who comes in for restorations, if he might be here. I said no and asked why and she laughed in that nervous way she had and said she had been threatened, her life had been threatened. And I said, 'For goodness sakes, go to the police, Heather.'"

"And that's it?"

Weiner nodded.

"What did she say about your warning?"

"That she couldn't. She said the police couldn't help her."

"She have many men visitors?"

Weiner seemed amused by the question. "Oh, yes," he said. "Heather never seemed to lack for male company. Heather was . . ." Weiner shifted his weight in his chair. " . . . unconventional. And a free spirit, I should think."

Fox looked around the room at the paisley patterned wallpaper, the fancy cornices, the baroque brass ceiling fixture. "What's upstairs?" he asked.

"A small showroom, storage area. A restoration section. I have a refinisher who comes in when needed to perform simple repairs."

"There's no access to Heather's apartment from your quarters?"

Weiner shook his head.

"What was she like?"

"Heather?" Weiner smiled; his cheeks grew round and his eyes narrowed into slits. "Like no one

56

I have ever known. I don't expect to meet anyone quite like her again."

"Did you like her?"

"Like her?" Weiner was surprised by the question. "Oh, I don't believe I liked her. She was, uh, a difficult person to like. Attractive in a, um, I suppose, carnal fashion, but . . ." He shook his head as though the gesture was enough to finish the sentence.

"Did you ever criticize her about her lifestyle?"

"Her what?"

"All the men she brought up to her apartment. You said she brought lots of them home."

"Well, I never *saw* them you understand, not *all* of them . . ."

"She ever talk about your lifestyle?"

Weiner took a deep breath and smiled coldly. "How could my lifestyle have any bearing on your investigation, Lieutenant?"

"Just trying to get a handle on the victim, that's all."

"Well, as a matter of fact, Heather could be *very* caustic at times. A great many people found that difficult to take."

"Including you?"

"Sometimes." Weiner picked a gold-plated letter opener from his desk, holding it by the handle as though it were a knife.

"She call you names?"

Another cold smile. "Lieutenant, I've heard all the names. She didn't invent any new ones."

Fox placed his card on the desk. "Call me if you think of anything else."

He left Weiner toying with the letter opener and staring at Fox's card as though wondering if it were safe to touch.

FOUR

"Not enough," Don Higgins said, jutting out his bottom lip like a small boy pouting. "Not nearly enough. I thought you'd have more for me."

Fat Eddie Vance rolled a yellow pencil between his fingers and blinked at the prosecuting attorney across the pristine top of his desk. Tim Fox sat next to Higgins, his arms folded. He had not spoken a word since entering the captain's office ten minutes earlier. Phil Donovan leaned against the wall next to the window, staring out at a weak early morning sun obscured by high clouds, working hard at looking bored.

"It's borderline, I admit," Fat Eddie said as Higgins returned the various police reports to his briefcase. "But there's a link between them, McGuire and the victim. He can't account for his whereabouts—"

"Neither can we," Higgins said. "Everything I heard about threats against the victim, including one made within hours of the murder, sounded solid enough." He turned to Fox. "But there's nothing from the interrogation, nothing from forensics that moves the case forward." Higgins shrugged. "You haven't given me anything new."

"She said somebody might do her," Donovan said. "She told her landlord she was afraid of somebody heavy. What's that worth?"

"Nothing on its own," Higgins replied. "You'll have to give me more than that. Or we take another route, maybe a just cause restraining order, incarceration for his own protection, something to stick with for a few days until a lawyer files a habeas corpus." He jutted his bottom lip out again. "Faced with a habeas, I can't see any judge agreeing to extend a charge against McGuire based on what's here."

Vance swung his eyes to Tim Fox. "What do you think?"

"I got a fax an hour ago," Fox said. He reached for an inside pocket of his sports jacket and withdrew three sheets of paper. "Bahamas Police, Nassau."

Higgins shifted sideways in his chair, watching Fox intently. Fat Eddie Vance rested several of his chins on one hand, his elbow on the desk. Phil Donovan muttered something under his breath and turned back to the window.

"McGuire was deported from the Bahamas as an undesirable alien in July," Fox said, handing the report to Vance. "That was after he spent a week in the hospital recovering from a beating."

"What in God's name happened to the man?" Higgins asked with concern.

"He got himself involved with some rich guy's wife is what happened," Fox said, watching Vance as the captain read the Bahamian police report. "She was living on their yacht while her husband was back home making his next hundred million. One of the crew members called his boss in Chicago, told him about McGuire cutting the man's grass and the husband flew down with some muscle. They got McGuire on board and put the boots to him, apparently. Bruised all over, cracked ribs . . ." Fox shrugged and spread his hands. "They threw him overboard, the water revived him, some people in a boat saw him thrashing around and pulled him out."

"And what happened to the husband?" Higgins asked.

"What happened? The husband got McGuire deported, that's what happened. You've got money and influence, you can get that kind of thing done down there. And this guy has it. They never laid a hand on him. The next month the same guy, the Chicago millionaire, signs a deal with the government for some resort development in the outer islands. He's called a hero, a few palms get greased, it's all a tax write-off." Fox grinned coldly. "By the way, a couple of weeks after McGuire left the island the wife got drunk one night, fell overboard and drowned. Way of the world, right?"

"What else?" Fat Eddie asked, handing the report back to Fox. "Anything on this Lorenzo woman?"

Vance glanced at Donovan, who shook his head. "No appointment book, no telephone directory. Gone."

60

"Bank records?" Fat Eddie said. "You got her bank records?"

Fox nodded. "She was doing all right financially. Over thirty thousand in cash, another hundred and fifty or so in investments, blue-chip stocks. Lots of good jewelry, none of it touched. Drove a nice little BMW, all paid for."

"What was up on that shelf that interests you guys so much?" Vance asked.

"Still don't know," Fox said. "Or what was in the file cabinet either. But it wasn't forced. Unlocked, key still there, her prints on it."

"How about the other men on the answering machine tape?" Vance looked back and forth between Fox and Donovan. "You identified their voices?"

"We think one's a photographer, client of hers," Donovan said. "The other might be her ex-husband, runs some plumbing or hardware outfit. There's a boyfriend too. I'm talking to the husband today, check him out."

"What've you done about her landlord saying she feared for her life?" Fat Eddie asked. "She ever report it?"

Fox shrugged. "Nothing in the records about it. She told her landlord the police couldn't help her."

Fat Eddie raised his eyebrows and pulled at his mustache, lost in some private thought.

Higgins was on his feet. "McGuire's getting a court-appointed lawyer this morning," he said. "Whoever it is, they'll make a motion for release." He shook his head. "I can't oppose it."

Vance's telephone rang. He nodded at Higgins, picked up the receiver and barked his name into the mouthpiece. "Who?" he said, then turned to Fox. "It's McGuire's ex-wife, the victim's sister, came in from Florida last night. She wants to talk to you."

"I'll take it at my desk," Fox said, standing.

Vance nodded, a Buddha serene on the surface, his indigestion simmering like a stew within, but his mind fastened on something else for a change.

They took McGuire from his cell after breakfast. The guards clumped down the concrete corridor in heavy black boots with soles thick as watermelon rind. McGuire shuffled unsteadily between them, his feet flip-flopping in his sneakers with no laces.

They led him to a room with gray plaster walls that were cracked and peeling and gray metal furniture that was dented and bent. Harvey Hoffman, McGuire's appointed lawyer, lifted his head from the stack of legal documents he had been reading and nodded to McGuire, who sat facing him in the only other chair in the room. The guards retreated to the corridor, leaving the prisoner with his counselor.

"You okay?" Hoffman asked McGuire through his massive gray beard. The lawyer's bald head shone in the glare of the single overhead fluorescent light fixture. It was just after nine in the morning but already Hoffman looked as though he had run a marathon in his three-piece suit. Running any distance would have been a remarkable feat for this man, who carried his nearly three hundred pounds like an armful of inflated balloons, folds of it spilling out here and there. A pair of delicate gold-rimmed half-frame spectacles spanned his broad face. His salt-and-pepper beard sprouted untrimmed and untamed from the lower half of his face like shrubbery.

"I'm all right," McGuire said.

Over the years McGuire and Hoffman had encountered each other in various Suffolk County courtrooms, earning a grudging respect for each other, like sparring partners who know nothing of the other man's life except the sight of him crouching, jabbing and darting away.

"This is a crappy move, what they did," Hoffman said, suppressing a belch. He reached up and began unbuttoning his vest. "They couldn't even stick a charge of threatening on you. Can't threaten an answering machine." He chose a sheaf of papers from the stack and slapped it with the back of his hand. "Nothing in here, in your statement, constitutes a felony, not even sufficient grounds for suspicion." He removed his glasses. "Only reason you're here is that Eddie Vance doesn't like you very much, does he?"

McGuire smiled.

"Well, I've already talked to Higgins's office, told them I'd be filing a writ to get you in front of a judge and out of here. Word is, they won't fight it." He twisted his body and glanced around the room, the exertion causing him to wheeze. "Shouldn't even be here, short-term. Could've kept you downtown, in the courthouse holding cells. Didn't you raise hell about being sent here? Didn't you say this was a breach of your rights?"

"No," McGuire said.

"Why not?"

"Didn't give a damn."

Hoffman watched his client intently for several

seconds before leaning as far forward as his girth would permit and asking, "You sure you're all right?"

McGuire looked at the man as though he didn't understand the question. He was still staring at Hoffman when a knock at the door caused the lawyer to raise his head and motion one of the guards into the room. The guard handed Hoffman a note, studying McGuire's face as though imprinting it on his consciousness for a future test of his memory, before leaving and closing the door behind him.

"You're out of here," Hoffman said after glancing at the note. "But they're only going halfway. They've got some charges pending on other stuff and demanding you're not to leave the state without informing Berkeley Street." He tossed the note in front of McGuire who looked at it curiously. "I'll get that lifted this afternoon. It's another crappy move, got Eddie Vance's prints all over it." He stood up and gestured to the guard through the window. "I've got a couple other clients to see," the lawyer said. "Take about an hour which'll give you time to gather your belongings. You want a ride downtown?"

McGuire said yes and when the guard entered the room again he shuffled away, leaving Hoffman frowning and shaking his head, comparing the subdued man he had just met with the explosive homicide cop he once dreaded tangling with in a courtroom or jail corridor, a man with the same name and face but with something else in his eyes, something this man, this new McGuire, was lacking.

* * *

"I hope you don't mind meeting me here. But I just didn't like the idea of setting foot in Berkeley Street again."

The woman facing Tim Fox in the corner booth of the Gainsborough Pub was perhaps thirty-five years old, maybe younger. She wore a camel-colored cashmere sweater and brown tweed skirt. Her silken hair framed a startlingly expressive face, one that leaped between extremes of joy and sadness, rarely pausing between the two. Her eyes were large and dark and when her lips parted in a smile, deep dimples formed in her cheeks, soft-edged like craters in meringue. Her name was Michelle Lorenzo. It had once been Micki McGuire.

"Don't blame you," Fox smiled. "When I walk out of Berkeley for the last time, I don't ever plan to go in again." A waiter brought him coffee. Micki's sat cold and untouched in front of her. "How long were you and Joe married?" Fox asked.

There it was, the quick smile, the dimples. "Nearly five years. Plus a year and a half we lived together before that." Her hands, small and delicate, toyed with a coffee spoon as she spoke, and the smile faded. "He was so intense. It took me a long time to get used to it, how intense he was about things that mattered to him. I'd almost forgotten about it. Then I saw him earlier this year. I'd written to him, care of Berkeley Street. Just to see how he was doing, what he was up to. They sent the letter to Ollie Schantz and his wife who passed it on to Joe, over in the Bahamas."

She sat back in the booth, toying with the coffee spoon.

"I'd been involved in . . ." She halted again, looked across the almost deserted restaurant and started over. "I was working for an air conditioning company, they did repairs, installations." Then she added, like an afterthought, "Before that, I'd met some rough people, hung out with them for a while. It's not something I'm proud of. And when I found myself all alone I kept thinking about Joe so I wrote him . . ."

She reached to pat the back of her hair. "Anyway, I came out of work one day and there he was waiting for me, sitting in some car he'd rented." A smile that stayed this time, glowing with the memory of him. "He looked good. He looked really good. He'd lost some weight, had a great tan, smiled and laughed a lot. We had dinner and, um . . ." A shrug. "Went down to the Keys that weekend, stayed in a motel on the gulf side. It was nice. It was really nice." Still smiling. But crying now too. "And then, just like that, when Sunday came he took me back to Coconut Grove and caught a plane to Nassau. I haven't seen him since."

"He's changed," Tim Fox said. He told her about the Bahamian police report, McGuire's near-fatal beating on the yacht, the hospital stay, the deportation and the tiny room over the strip club whose patrons came to do more than just look at the young women.

She listened with her mouth partially open and her eyes darting back and forth. "That doesn't sound like Joe," she said. "God, that's not Joe, that's somebody else."

"Like I said, he's changed."

Micki stared down at her coffee before lifting the

cup to her lips. "You don't really think he killed Heather," she said in a low voice.

Fox shook his head. "But some people would like to."

She set the cup down without drinking from it and said, her head lowered, her eyes avoiding Fox's, "Some people will be happy to know my sister is dead too. Happy and worried at the same time."

Fox sat back, folded his arms and raised his eyebrows, urging her silently to continue.

She flashed her smile at him in embarrassment. "I know what my sister's been up to for the past couple of years," she said. "She didn't make all of her money from being a photographer's agent. Not by a long shot."

FIVE

Grizzly tossed a handful of old shingles on the fire blazing inside the rusting forty-gallon drum. When the black smoke and flames roared out Grizzly laughed and held his hands, large and brown like catcher's mitts, in front of him to feel the heat.

"Cops don't like it," the Gypsy muttered, wrapping her arms around her for warmth, huddled inside Grizzly's stained gray parka with the raccoon fur trim on the hood. Strands of her greasy black hair spilled out from around the fur trim, hair as dark and shining as her eyes. "Makes too much smoke. Might come by, just to raise hell."

Grizzly laughed again and rubbed his hands together. He was wearing a blue kerchief tied tightly around his head, a denim shirt open nearly to his navel, and brown army surplus pants. "We'll tell 'em we jus' sendin' smoke signals to your brothers 'cross the way. Maybe that's First Amendment rights." He looked across the flames at Django. "You figure that's maybe what it is?"

Django nodded and smiled, shifting his weight to one side and then the other, doing a shuffle around the blazing fire in the steel drum, sliding his feet in his white Reebok high-cuts. Django's black leather trench coat hung open and moved with his motion. A tweed pork-pie hat managed to remain propped at a sharp angle well back atop his small head. His eyes closed, he did a sideways step around the drum, staying near its warmth that softened the damp chill of the gray air.

Out on Washington Street at the end of the alley, a black Mercedes slowed to a stop. Its driver, an overweight balding man with an unruly salt-and-pepper beard, stared open-mouthed down the lane at the sight of Grizzly and the Gypsy, and Django prancing and stepping lightly around the fire that blazed in the steel drum, his head back, his eyes closed.

"Hey," Grizzly said softly.

The Mercedes' passenger door opened and a dark-eyed man wearing only a dirty and faded sweatshirt emerged. He was nodding in response to something the driver of the car was saying but he was watching Django intently.

Django's back was to the car. "Hear you, Grizz."

The man in the sweatshirt waited for the Mercedes to pull away. Then, with his hands thrust deeply in his pockets and his shoulders hunched against the wind, he walked unsteadily down the alley. The Mercedes drove off with a sound like a sigh.

"You got a customer." Grizzly stood motionless, watching the man approach. The Gypsy scampered toward the unpainted wooden shed set against the rear wall of the building housing Tremont Adult Novelties and began fishing in her pockets for cigarettes.

Django swivelled his small head to look down the alley. "It's the Jolt, come back to life," he called, extending his arms to welcome McGuire. "Hey, how you doin'?"

McGuire halted a few paces away. He nodded at Grizzly and glanced at the Gypsy. "I got twenty," he said, giving Django the crisp bill Hoffman had just handed McGuire in the warmth of the Mercedes.

"An' I got some D's for you," Django moved away from McGuire, his left arm extended. "Django's got some D's for his man, ain't he, Grizz?"

Grizzly smiled through the flames and smoke belching from the rusting drum. He motioned to the Gypsy who was taking long drags on her Camel Light and watching McGuire from the corner of her eye. She moved crabwise from the safety of the building wall to stand behind Grizzly, who reached into a pocket of the parka and withdrew a brown bottle the size of a coffee mug. In a quick, practised motion he removed the cap, shook ten small pills into his hand, replaced the cap and slid the bottle back into the parka. Then he was around the blazing metal drum, his hand extended to McGuire but his head and eyes in motion, looking everywhere.

McGuire counted the Demerol and said, "I used to get twice this much." Not waiting for a reply, he picked two of the tiny pills from his palm, placed them in his mouth and swallowed them dry.

"Supply and demand, Jolt," Django said. "Supply and demand."

McGuire approached the fire and its oily warmth. Soon, he told himself. Soon.

"Hey, you hear the word, Jolt? Lady Day, she thinkin' a you, missin' you all a time." Django nodded, smiling. "I tell her I see you, she gonna be glowin' again. She thinkin', worryin', wonderin' when you comin' back. Word is, you were kinda *mean* to a sweetie over on Newbury, one of your upward climbin' angora-style ladies."

"Tell Billie not to worry about me," McGuire said.

"Oh, Billie not worried," Django laughed. "She not worried, no darlin'." A long cackle, rising in pitch. "She egg-*sight*-ed, Jolt. She hear you get rough, she near to fallin' in *love* with you!" and he laughed again.

McGuire turned from the fire and walked away, down the lane, back to Tremont.

"Shouldn't," said the Gypsy from the other side of the burning steel drum. "Shouldn't do business with no cops."

"Ex," Grizzly corrected her. "He be an ex-cop."

"Cops are cops," the Gypsy said. "Dogs are dogs, shit is shit, cops are cops."

"He something special though, Gyps." Django twisted his shoulders from side to side and watched McGuire cross Washington on his way to the Flamingo. "Jolt special. And soon Jolt be special and happy. Happier'n he be now, for sure. Soon he be *real* again. The man be *real*," and Django turned to face the fire, closing his eyes, warming his body and moving it in rhythm, always in rhythm.

***

It was five blocks from Grizzly's back alley place of business to the Flamingo and the knife through McGuire's head, the one that blurred his vision and tilted the world around him like a slowing down spinning top, carved its way deeper into his skull with every step he took.

Reaching the base of the fire escape, he ignored the heavy crust of bird droppings that had repelled Tim Fox two mornings ago and gripped the railing to pull himself up step by step to his room, shouldering the door open and walking unsteadily past the bed.

In the ancient wicker wastebasket next to the toilet he counted five condom wrappers. He dumped them into a plastic garbage bag beneath the sink and washed the guano from his hands. Then, soaking a small towel in cold water and wringing it almost dry, he walked back to the single bed, pulled from the shelf the only hardcover book he owned, a battered copy of *Wild Animals I Have Known*, removed the five ten-dollar bills left between its pages and stuffed them into his pocket. Then he sat on the hardbacked chair, holding the cloth against his forehead, its cool dampness almost erotic in the pleasure it gave him.

When he opened his eyes a few moments later, there was a horse in the room. Small and dapple-gray, standing patiently in the corner. McGuire didn't look at the animal directly, knowing to do so would make it disappear.

"Hello, horse," he smiled. He rose, steadied himself against the wall, took two steps to the bed and lay upon it, placing the wet cloth across his face and feeling the room turn slowly beneath him.

It was on the horizon of his mind and approaching slowly, the warm cloud of numbness he craved.

When you do not wish to feel, you go numb. On your own, if capable. On the wings of a drug, if necessary.

Waiting for the full effect of the painkiller, he numbered the missing pieces of his life, beginning with the music he loved, the quiet jazz that had once served as the foundation of his sanity and the inspiration of his youth. Gentle rhythms and melodic improvisation, masking passion and intensity. That was the power of it, the way the passion and intensity remained concealed beneath the surface. Without passion and intensity and control, the music was nothing. Miles, Desmond, Zoot, Coltrane, all their intense melodies and phrases had once flown like lovers to McGuire's soul and made his head nod, his eyes burn, his smile arise like a dawn sun. They were gone, the music and the musicians, and he missed them.

And Gloria. He missed Gloria, his first wife, dead four years. You'll be commissioner some day, she told McGuire soon after they were married and he said, No, don't be silly, I don't want that, and she said, Then please figure out what you want because until you do you'll never be truly happy and you'll make everyone who is a part of your life miserable.

He lay there, feeling his eyes grow damp, for perhaps thirty minutes until he heard two sets of footsteps climbing the fire escape, one heavy, one light.

A girl from the club he figured, freelancing between shifts, leading a nervous morning customer on his way toward thirty minutes of fulfilled fantasy.

McGuire opened his eyes and the simple action drained weight from his body. Something had happened to his face and he realized he was smiling. The knot at the back of his neck had unravelled and the taut wire rope that had been his spine had fallen away. He watched as he extended his arms above his head, seeing the fingers spread, feeling the damp cloth slide from his face when he sat upright.

In the tunnels, moving through the tunnels of his mind, the warmth of the medication advanced like a gently rising tide.

He looked around the room. The horse was gone. Once he had seen a small black pig snuffling in the bathroom. And there had been snakes and toads the size of footstools. His hallucinations were often animals; animals were easy to accept, animals were fine. It was the others, the flayed corpses and staring naked women, that upset him the most when they appeared, daring him to look at them and vanishing from his sight but somehow never his presence when he did.

He was hungry, ready for a bowl of noodles and shrimp from a Vietnamese restaurant on Lincoln.

Voices were approaching his door, speaking softly, and he visualized them, the girl leading the way, the john nervous, maybe expecting a mugging and a knife in the ribs, then his wallet extracted and his body tossed from the landing to the alley below.

Shadows on the dusty window. McGuire rose to his feet, staggered slightly, walked to the door and swung it open before they could knock.

"How you doing?" Tim Fox, in his Burberry coat and small hound's-tooth check suit, smiled back at McGuire, then stood aside. "Brought somebody you know."

She said nothing at first. She simply pursed her lips and raised her eyebrows at him, her hands clasped in front of her.

"Hello, Micki." McGuire nodded as though confirming a fact.

"No surprise?" she said. Her eyes were shining.

"Maybe a bit."

"Lady wants to talk to you," Tim Fox said.

"And you want to listen," McGuire said.

"Joe, it's really cold out here," Micki said.

McGuire moved aside and gestured for them to enter.

Micki took a cautious step into the room. "It smells like . . ." Micki began.

"Like what?"

"Never mind."

She sat lightly on the edge of the hardbacked chair while Tim Fox leaned against the closed door, his arms folded, his face a solemn mask.

McGuire crossed in front of them and sat unsteadily on the bed until his body swayed to one side and he said the hell with it and lay back, his hands behind his head, and watched the ceiling turn in slow circles above him.

"No problem at Nashua Street?" Fox asked McGuire.

McGuire shrugged. "Three hots and a cot."

"Fat Eddie's holding the warrant open. Talked Don Higgins into doing it."

McGuire closed his eyes. Three hours, maybe four the pills were good for, and he would need one every hour after that. What did Django call it? His tune. Django's tune. The good feeling, the only good feeling available, and it comes in such small packages . . . .

"Joe?" Micki's voice, from a great distance. McGuire always liked her voice. High-pitched and feminine. Micki, she always wanted a deeper voice. And other things she couldn't have. Bigger breasts. Longer legs. Higher cheekbones. More of him . . . He began humming an old Duke Ellington song.

"Joe?" Again her voice.

"Yeah."

"What are you taking?"

"The 'A' Train."

"Drugs, Joe. You're taking drugs, aren't you?"

"Medication."

"The same thing."

Tim Fox leaned forward. "I gotta warn you, Joe. Guys in Narcotics know your source. I talked to them, Barker and Cummins, remember those guys? They got a file on Griswold and his weird Indian girlfriend that's as thick as your wrist. Soon as they work up a level or two they'll nail him and everybody connected with him."

McGuire remained silent but he felt his pulse increase, felt panic weigh him down like bricks on his chest.

"Joe?" Micki again. "Are you going to sleep?"

"Thinking about it."

"We have to talk."

"That's what you said a few years ago. I come home, you're sitting on your bags, you got all the money out of our bank account and you're pissed at me for doing behind your back what you'd been doing behind mine—"

"Joe . . ."

"—and you said we have to talk. So you talked. Not us, just you. Then you walked out the door soon's the cab arrived. Talk like that I don't need."

"I'm sorry, Joe."

"Sorry? Hey, we went through all that last summer, down in . . ." He opened his eyes, rubbed them with one hand, closed them again. "Florida. Down in Florida."

"Joe, you have to do something."

"Well, I could always puke on you."

Micki frowned and tilted her head, like a mother about to scold a child. "I'm serious, Joe."

McGuire grunted.

"Was Heather blackmailing you?" she asked.

McGuire opened his eyes and swung his head to meet Micki's steady gaze. "Was she what?" Still prettier than she knows, he thought. Not as attractive as she wants to be, not as young as she used to be. But prettier than she ever knew.

"Blackmailing you."

McGuire laughed. "Your sister? The woman who gave ball-breaking witches a bad name? Blackmailing me? With what? For what?"

Micki leaned forward in the chair. "Why were you so angry with her the night before she died? Tim played me the tape from her answering machine. You sounded ready to *kill* her, Joe."

"Prob'ly was," he slurred. He turned away to stare at the ceiling.

"Why?"

He shook his head. "Can't remember." He lay his forearm across his eyes. "She wanted me to do her a favor, hold some money, something like that."

"But she wasn't blackmailing you?"

"Said she could." He remembered now, something drifting through the fog.

"About what?"

"Don't know. Didn't need blackmail to make me hate her. Jus' came naturally."

"She was blackmailing other people," Tim Fox said. "Had been for three or four years."

"Who?"

"Different people," Micki said. "Wealthy men with wives and families who wanted to save their marriages and careers."

"What'd she have on them?"

"Pictures."

"Of what?"

"Heather and the men. In bed together."

McGuire lifted his arm from his eyes to stare at Micki. "Heather? Your sister Heather was running that old scam?" Micki nodded. McGuire smiled. "How'd you know?"

"She told me," Micki said. "In Florida. She came to see me, gloating like she used to . . . ." She shrugged.

McGuire stared at her in silence.

"She came down to visit me and flashed all this jewelry, said she was going over to Tampa for a dirty weekend with some guy, and then she laughed and whispered how she was going to show him some pictures when they got back. The pictures had been taken the previous weekend in her apartment. She would sell him the negatives. 'Never take less than five thousand,' she said. 'They want to play, they gotta pay.' She said she'd rather take less from more men than go for the big kill, a hundred thousand. She said she usually got ten because after a hundred thousand, ten sounded like a bargain and they could hardly wait to put money in her hand for the negatives. She always gave them back the negatives. Always."

"An honest businesswoman," Tim Fox said dryly.

"S'what makes America great," McGuire added.

"Figure somebody she was blackmailing decided it was cheaper to cash her in than a check," Fox said. "We think she had a camera in her room mounted on a wall, peeking out from between some vases on a shelf in her bedroom. And an infrared flash. We found receipts for infrared film. Camera was probably set on a timer, she'd know how to do that. Crank the stereo up high to cover the sound of the camera, going click-click every couple of minutes. Probably kept the negatives and prints in a file cabinet that was ransacked."

"Sounds like somebody made an astute business decision," McGuire muttered. He turned back to Micki. "How many of these stunts did she work?"

She shrugged. "I think maybe six or seven a year. I don't think she did it just for the money. She always used to say, 'Living well is the best revenge.' But I think Heather did it for the excitement too. And she said she always chose good-looking men. They had to be good-looking, married and rich. She'd give herself a month with them. She said sometimes she was juggling two or three at a time and that was good, she said, because the others would get jealous or possessive and that's when she knew she had them."

"This woman," McGuire said. He swung his feet to the floor, steadied himself and sat upright, looking at Fox. "This woman, Heather, she was kind of like Miss Congeniality with hobnailed boots and a hard kick to the crotch."

Micki smiled, a little embarrassed. "She was always a little wild, Joe. You know that."

"Told me her only regret in life was not sleeping with her high school football team," McGuire said. "S'true," he added when he saw the expression on Fox's face. "Heather's the woman everybody had in mind when the sexual revolution started."

"Sounds like we have ourselves a motive," Fox said. "And it's not you. Thought we should let you know. When I report it, Eddie and Don Higgins'll have to burn the warrant."

"You got a diary, appointment book?" McGuire asked Micki.

She shook her head. "They're gone."

"Good luck, guys." McGuire stood up and closed his eyes until the dizziness passed. He was thinking of noodles and shrimp, some of that Vietnamese molten metal hot sauce on it, a cold Molson's . . .

"If she was trying to blackmail you, it's a motive," Tim Fox said.

McGuire leaned against the wall, his head down. "Never slept with her. Never would've. Be like sleeping with a porcupine."

"Heather called me a week ago," Micki said.

"Looking for a partner?" McGuire said.

"She was afraid," Tim Fox said. He nodded at Micki.

"She thought she might have picked the wrong man to do business with this time," Micki said. "She wouldn't tell me anything more. She just said she might be down in Florida soon to stay with me. 'I might be over my head on this one,' she told me, and then she laughed like she did when she was nervous."

"Names?" McGuire asked.

Micki shook her head.

"You want to get involved?" Tim Fox asked, stepping aside as McGuire approached the door.

"Get what?"

"Help out. I can use you. Donovan's a jerk. I could use somebody to bounce things off."

"Bounce things off?" McGuire stepped through the door. Christ, it was cold. He reached out to steady himself as he began descending the stairs. "Bounce things off?" he repeated over his shoulder. "The hell you think Fat Eddie's head's for?"

SIX

"Three names," Tim Fox said, avoiding Fat Eddie's eyes. "We nailed the names of the guys whose voices are on her answering machine. Plus we picked up some good leads and a couple more possibles."

Fat Eddie's gas was back. He blinked and shifted his bulk in his chair.

"First caller is definitely the photographer," Fox said. "One of her clients."

"He's the kraut, sounds a little loose in his loafers," Phil Donovan said. He was sitting in the chair facing Vance's desk, one leg over the other and a grin on his face, like he was having a beer at a buddy's house, waiting for the football game to start on TV.

"Name's Posner, the photographer." Tim Fox flipped through the pages of his notebook. "Siegfried

Posner, Ziggy for short. Runs a studio off Summer Street. He was her biggest client. Does a lot of work for ad agencies, here and out of New York."

"Siegfried," Donovan sneered. "Shit."

"The other voice, besides McGuire's, belongs to her husband, guy named . . ." Tim Fox turned a page. "Steve Peterson. Her sister recognized it. He runs some kind of plumbing supply outfit on Lansdowne. They separated four, five years ago, never got divorced."

"But she used her maiden name," Fat Eddie said.

"Always did, even when she was married to this schmuck," Donovan said. "An original feminist. You know, one of them broads hates men so much they wanta be one?"

"And McGuire's the third voice," Vance said.

"Best lead of the bunch." Donovan curled a lip and poked a thumbnail at something between his teeth.

"What other names do you have?" Fat Eddie asked.

"Some boyfriend," Donovan said, inspecting the tip of his thumb. "Weiner, the landlord, says he met him a couple a times. Thinks they split up last month. He remembered this guy was smooth, a lot of talk. He's some big advertising dude. Gave his card to Weiner, said maybe they could do something together to promote his gallery. His name, the ad guy, is Hotchnik, Marty Hotchnik."

"You talked to them yet?" Vance asked.

"I covered off the ex-husband," Donovan said, taking over now, not letting Fox jump in. The black detective turned away, his arms across his chest, to stare out the window. "He admits he called her 'cause he was pissed at her. Apparently she promised to loan him some money or something and then welshed on it. He blew off some steam and went home to boink his common-law over in Cambridge. Soon's we leave here we're talkin' to the kraut and the ad guy."

"What else do you know?" Fat Eddie said.

Donovan uncrossed his legs and stood up, his hands in his pockets. "McGuire's ex-wife says her sister was pumping some rich guy, got his own company. Sounds like this heavy-duty dude made her think she might be over her head on this one."

"No name?" Fat Eddie raised his eyebrows.

"No," Tim Fox said, turning from the window. He was annoyed at Donovan. Micki Lorenzo had given the information about the businessman to Fox in confidence and Donovan was spreading it around like he had unearthed it himself.

"When's the funeral?" Fat Eddie asked. "The victim's?"

"Tomorrow." Donovan was up and pacing the floor. "We'll have an ID car, get everybody on tape. All laid on."

"What about the guy she was afraid of?" Vance said. "The one the art gallery owner told you about?"

"Can't find a thing," Tim Fox said. "Looks like she was the kind of woman who could piss off men pretty easily. But there's nobody special we know about. Except her ex-husband."

"And McGuire." Fat Eddie pointed a finger at Fox.

"McGuire's a non-issue," Fox said.

Donovan exhaled noisily in disgust at his partner's comment and Tim Fox glared at him.

"How can you say that when he and the victim knew each other and he made a threat on her life the evening she was murdered?" Fat Eddie demanded.

"She wasn't blackmailing McGuire," Fox said. "For one thing, the guy's broke. For another, there's nothing to put him at the scene. Nothing at all. Whoever did her, he'd be splattered with blood, there'd be something to tie him back to the victim."

"Maybe he didn't do her himself," Donovan suggested. "Maybe he got somebody to off her for him."

"That's a fucking crock," Fox said. He took two quick paces toward the door and stopped to stare angrily away from Donovan and Vance toward an empty corner.

"Hey, you gotta admit, McGuire's not exactly hangin' out with Eagle Scouts," Donovan said. "He's mainlinin' something and he's dealing with pushers, hookers, pimps, known felons . . . . You don't think he's got the connections?"

"It's crap," Fox said. "Total crap."

"McGuire's warrant's suspended," Fat Eddie said to Fox. "Only suspended. If I were you, I wouldn't dismiss McGuire quite so fast."

"Crap," Fox repeated, walking to the door, seizing the knob, slamming it shut behind him.

Donovan spread his arms, palms up, and shrugged his shoulders at Fat Eddie. Then he shook his head and followed his partner out of the captain's office and down the corridor to the cubicle he shared with Fox.

McGuire was clumsy with chopsticks and he had splashed too much fiery Vietnamese pepper sauce on his shrimp and noodles. Chewing his food, he looked around the storefront restaurant. The lighting was harsh and glaring, the tabletops were worn Formica and, except for two women dental students from Tufts University, he was the only Caucasian in the restaurant.

He had become a regular patron because he enjoyed the taste of the food and because it was both healthy and inexpensive. The restaurant, whose name McGuire had never bothered to learn and never would have been able to pronounce anyway, sold no beer. But Chet's, a working-class bar on Tremont near Essex certainly did, and after paying the small Vietnamese waitress whose face shone when she smiled, McGuire set off unsteadily through the door and into the gray afternoon chill.

He paused in the doorway of an empty pornographic movie theater, scooped two small tablets from his jacket pocket into his hand and swallowed them. The warm damp fog bank in his head, he knew, would linger for a few hours yet.

It had been twenty years since Martin Griswold crouched in the corner of the kitchen in the Dorchester apartment and watched his father shoot his mother. Martin Luther Griswold had squeezed his nine-year-old body against the wall at the first explosion of his father's rage and when his father withdrew a large and very ugly black pistol from his heavy topcoat and aimed it carefully at the woman who lay on the floor holding her head in both hands and crying, Martin swallowed once and forced himself to keep his eyes open, told himself that what was about to happen was natural and expected. His father fired two shots into Martin's mother. Then he returned the gun to his pocket and bellowed through the door at neighbors who wanted to know what in hell was going on in there, telling them to shut up and mind their own business, and walked to the refrigerator for a beer.

Martin remained in the corner, wedged against the side of the battered cupboard, and watched his father drink two Miller High Lifes while the blood from his mother's body ran toward Martin Luther Griswold in small crimson rivers.

"That's what you gotta do when they fuck wid you," his father said to Martin when he had finished his first beer, for his father had known of Martin's presence all along. "They fuck wid you, they give you no respec', you teach 'em. One way or 'nother, you teach 'em."

When he finished his second Miller High Life, Martin's father rose to his feet and tossed a five-dollar bill in the boy's direction. "Go buy yourself a pizza, somethin'," he said and left the room. "'Member what I tol' you."

Martin never saw him again.

After waiting for the sound of his father's footsteps to fade beyond the din of the television set in the next room, Martin walked carefully around his mother's body and followed the same path his father had taken down the stairs and out into the summer air. He walked to a nearby park where he sat for an hour while dusk gathered and he wondered what to do.

Then he ordered two slices of double cheese and pepperoni and a large Pepsi from the take-out on the corner and went back to the park to eat it.

When he returned home the blood on the floor had hardened and dried. A neighbor stuck her head out the door of her apartment. "The hell goin' on there?" she asked Martin. "You all right?"

Martin said he was all right.

"Your mother all right?"

Martin said she was dead.

When the cops left, some social worker took Martin to a children's shelter and later to a foster family in another neighborhood. Martin remained there until he was twelve years old, stood five and a half feet tall, and weighed a hundred and sixty-five pounds.

Martin Luther Griswold became simply Grizzly. And Grizzly, when he was fourteen years old, chased a teacher from the classroom, swinging a brass fire extinguisher in his hand and threatening to bury it in the teacher's skull.

Grizzly became a street person, scamming whatever was available, sometimes wondering what happened to the man his mother called her husband, who told Grizzly he should think of him as his father.

Didn't make a helluva lot of sense to Grizzly. Man sleeps with a woman, doesn't make him her husband. Woman's got a kid, doesn't make her man the kid's father.

They arrested Grizzly for the first time when he was sixteen after he organized a pay-off three-day gang rape of a fifteen-year-old girl who had told Grizzly she loved him, keeping her tied up in a back alley shed and charging local kids five bucks a go. Some adults came around too, fathers of some of the boys who were Grizzly's customers, grown men who heard about it while he kept the girl there. They slipped Grizzly the money, went inside the shed, came out maybe five minutes later, the young boys laughing and talking, their fathers and their fathers' friends skulking away in shame. For three days Grizzly fed the girl, slapped her when he had to, and made a pile of money.

Until somebody squealed.

Grizzly spent two years in a reformatory where he acquired enough formal education to expand his street smarts.

Nobody had more street smarts than Grizzly. When Grizzly learned about marketing in prison, when he grasped the concept of keeping both demand and prices high, he rose head and shoulders above everybody else when it came to dealing narcotics.

"Make it scarce an' you makes it valuable," he told Django once. "So you wanta sell, you sell the scarce stuff, hear me?"

Django nodded but he didn't understand completely. The more you sell the more you make, he believed. If something's scarce, there ain't much of it so how can you sell more? Didn't make sense. But disagreeing with Grizzly made even less sense.

"You always gotta be either the first on the street or the last on the street sellin' your stuff," Grizzly added. "Guy in the middle don't make shit."

Django nodded again. It's safer in the middle, Django wanted to say. But he didn't.

The first man Grizzly killed was a street tough named Bones, a bully who claimed to have downtown connections and who made the mistake in a bar one night of reaching across Grizzly to stroke the breast of a girl Grizzly was with. It was a year after Grizzly came out of reformatory.

When Grizzly raised an eyebrow at Bones, the older man slapped Grizzly's face with one open hand and showed him a knife in the other. "Don' say a word, pussy," Bones sneered, and Grizzly nodded and slid off the stool, leaving Bones laughing and groping and the girl crying in fear.

Ten minutes later Grizzly returned with a .357 Magnum revolver inside his jacket. Bones had his arm around the girl and when Grizzly walked up to him, Grizzly said, "Show me yo' knife."

Bones said, "You got one?"

Grizzly said, "No."

Bones said, "Knew it. Pussies don' carry steel."

Grizzly took the gun out and shot Bones through his left eye. Then he turned the gun on the girl and shot her too. Twice.

"She shoulda left," Grizzly said when he told a friend about it the next day. "She shouldn'ta been there so long."

No one in the bar could identify Grizzly. None of the investigating police officers felt the incident was worth more than a day's investigation.

Only fools challenged Grizzly again. And they only challenged him once.

Grizzly finished his whispered conversation behind the bar with Dewey and returned to the table where Django and the Gypsy waited.

Dewey was more than the Flamingo's bouncer. He was also assistant manager, talent scout and Grizzly's bouquet man. Bouquet men profited from drug sales but never carried, never used, never sold the product themselves. They functioned as conduits of information and directors of traffic. When sweeps occurred and arrests were made, Dewey and the handful of other bouquet men would be questioned and released for lack of sufficient evidence. "Come out smelling like a bouquet of roses," one of them had boasted, and he and others were dubbed bouquet men from that day forward.

Now Grizzly settled his massive black bulk in the chair between Django and the Gypsy. "Heat's on," he said, watching the tiny stage set against the far wall of the room. He extended an arm to the Gypsy, his index and middle fingers spread in a V sign. His lidded eyes remained on the small brown girl who was prancing back and forth across the stage, strutting her stuff in a long green satin skirt open on one side all the way up to her tiny waist. The Gypsy quickly pulled a pack of Camel Lights from a pocket of her red and black plaid woollen shirt.

"Heat?" Even when sitting, Django moved with the music, his shoulders swinging, his head bobbing, like a featherweight boxer watching for a jab, waiting for an opening. "Hell, ain't no heat," Django laughed. "World's colder'n a witch's tit. No heat at all. Put your pecker out the door, Grizz, it be a chocolate popsicle faster'n Sienna up there can aim her money-maker at you."

The Gypsy placed a Camel Light between Grizzly's waiting fingers and he transferred the cigarette to his mouth. "That her name?" he asked, still watching the stage. "Sienna?" He leaned toward the Gypsy who had the match already lit and was applying it to the end of the cigarette. "Nice name for a little gal like that."

Sienna whirled once and dropped the satin skirt to the floor of the stage revealing a gold G-string and slim legs.

Grizzly drew in a deep breath of cigarette smoke and nodded.

Beside him the Gypsy studied her glass of beer, her face a mask.

"Who feelin' heat?" Django asked. His eyes darted from Grizzly to the stage and back again.

"People I know."

"Same people I know."

"Not the same. Special people. People you don't know 'bout, you don't *wanna* know 'bout, hear me?" His voice softened. "You know this little girl, this, what'd you call her?"

"Sienna. From the islands. One a them itty-bitty places named after them saints down there. Thomas or John or Ralph."

"Ralph? There a St. Ralph?" Grizzly looked at Django with interest.

"Sure. Church gotta name saints just like you and me get named. What, Grizz, you think the Pope, he gonna pick a new saint and he say, 'We callin' this next sucker number two-five-eight'? They name 'em, the saints."

"After who?"

Django shrugged.

"Tell you one thing," Grizzly said, shifting the cigarette to a corner of his wide mouth. "They ain't never gonna be no St. Django."

Django erupted in laughter. "Whoa, darlin'!" He slapped his thighs and bent from the waist. "I'm doin' my part to make it a fact, I surely am." The small brown girl was prancing in long strides around the perimeter of the stage. Her hands were busy at one hip, unfastening her G-string. "I surely am."

Grizzly held his breath until the stripper removed the last piece of fabric covering her body. Then he exhaled slowly and spoke softly, watching the girl promenade in her nakedness. "Wait out the heat. Gotta wait out the heat, monkey."

"Hear you, Grizz," Django nodded.

"We be like that little gal up there, you know. What her name again?"

"Sienna, darlin'. She Lady Sienna."

Grizzly grunted and took his eyes from the woman to inspect the tip of his cigarette. "Not as pretty, understand. Not as pretty as that little thing. But we be as naked, you hear me talkin'?"

Django nodded, his face clouded.

"We don't carry nothin' for nobody 'til it cool again, understand?" Grizzly swung his massive body to Django and leaned to look directly into the small man's eyes. "Special not for that cop friend of yours, hear me?" His breath smelled like a musty room and Django sat back in his chair. "Tell me you hear me talkin' to you."

"The Jolt, he all right," Django said. He avoided Grizzly's eyes. "Don't be askin' me to leave the Jolt dry . . . ."

"I be talkin' to you all this time and you ain't started listenin' yet," Grizzly said. "I ain't axin' you to dry the man up. I *tell*in' you, you hear me?"

Django watched Sienna doing knee-bends at the edge of the stage where men gripped long-necked bottles of beer and stared back at her with open smiles. "I hear you, Grizz," he said. "Hear you." He bit his lip, looked around, tried to stay cool, then he said, "Other guys, Garce 'n' Drew, them guys, they dry too?"

"What you wanta know for?" Grizzly shot back. "None a your damn business. I say you dry, you dry."

Django sat back in his chair. Garce and Drew, he only met them a couple, maybe three times, they were dealers for Grizzly, Grizz liked to keep everybody separate, nobody get together on a conspiracy against Grizzly, no sir.

"You do like I tell you?" Grizzly said.

"No question, Grizz," Django said. "Never any question 'bout it."

Grizzly grunted and sat back in the chair, his eyes on Sienna again. "Little brown girl nice," he said to no one in particular. "But Billie, she still the best 'cause she *like* it up there, you know? Don't she like it up there?"

"Oh, she do," Django agreed. "She like to show her jewels all right." He was no longer moving in his chair and his face was glum. "Can see she like it."

The Gypsy played with her fingers, her eyes downcast.

The sports channel was running a replay of last night's hockey game and the Bruins were again getting their asses kicked, this time by the hated Rangers, a reprise of organized chaos traced on the screen of the television set above the noisy, smoky bar. The inept play and repeated miscues of the hometown team generated shouts of derision, cries of anguish and peels of sardonic laughter from the patrons, nearly all men, virtually all of them out of work and low on hope.

McGuire slouched at a table in a rear corner next to the washroom door, a half-finished glass of beer in front of him. The rim of the glass was chipped and the beer was flat. Men in soiled caps passed McGuire on their way to the urinals and many offered him a curt nod, acknowledging him not as a friend but as a regular patron of Chet's, almost the same thing. Two weeks earlier one of the regulars recognized McGuire and had spread the word that he was an ex-cop, and for a few days the patrons withheld their greetings. But it soon became evident that ex-cops have every bit as much to lose as ex-truck drivers, ex-welders and ex-mechanics, and eventually they accepted the common bond although they still moved past McGuire warily. None chose to sit with him and offer to buy him a beer, or cadge enough money from him for a draft and a hamburger.

McGuire swallowed another Demerol. He waited for the fresh wave of relaxation and numbness to creep through him. It would displace the tension in his body, dissolve the furrows between his eyes.

Soon, he lied to himself. Soon he would turn things around, get himself organized, go back to the Bahamas . . .

He lowered his head to his hand, rested it there.

They almost killed him.

They would have left his body rotting among the mangroves or being flayed apart in the surf. He heard them discussing it between the blows of the heavy boots striking his back, his groin, his head, talking about it in the casual tones of shade-tree mechanics pondering a reluctant car engine.

"Take the son of a bitch out past the reef, throw him in." That was Charlie, Patty's husband, the industrial mineral king from Chicago.

"We can work him over a little more, you give us the word." The taller of Henshaw's two employees who had flown down with their boss on a chartered jet that afternoon drew his foot back and drove it into McGuire's side, and pain like a rapier shot through McGuire's abdomen.

"You start her up, Mr. Henshaw, take us out to deep water and we'll drop-kick the prick over the side." The smaller man, the more vicious of the two, seized McGuire's hair and yanked his head up. "See what happens when you fuck around where you shouldn't, asshole?" he spat in McGuire's face.

The yacht was anchored in the middle of the harbor. Music drifted across the water from the bar of the Horizon Club where McGuire had promised to meet Patty Henshaw and where, half an hour earlier, the taller of Charlie Henshaw's men had found him sitting on a bench at the water's edge. "You McGuire?" the man asked and when McGuire nodded he said, "The missus wants you to join her on board." He jerked a thumb behind him. "I got a whaler over near the dive shop to take you across."

"Who are you?" McGuire asked.

"New crew member in from Man O' War Cay for the week," the tall man replied. He thrust a calloused hand at McGuire. "Name's Unsworth. Came down from Chicago last month and lucked out. Got a crew job'll take me through the summer."

McGuire followed Unsworth, stepping aboard the motorized flat-bottomed skiff to join Patty Henshaw, the shattered wife of a domineering and abusive husband. For the past two weeks she and McGuire had been a diversion for each other, McGuire living alone in a cabin overlooking the harbor, Patty spending the winter aboard *Savarin*, her husband's eighty-five-foot yacht.

"This boat and me are the same thing to Charlie," she once smiled at McGuire. "We both wait down here for him to climb on and enjoy himself."

As soon as McGuire stepped aboard, Charlie Henshaw and the other man emerged from a cabin, Henshaw with a brass chain wrapped around one fist, the smaller man beside him and one step behind, his teeth gleaming in a broad smile, and the beating began.

"Get up!" Henshaw screamed at McGuire when the small man offered to throw McGuire overboard in deep water. "On your feet, you scum-sucking bastard!"

McGuire pulled himself to his hands and knees, retched once and rolled onto his back.

"Pull him up," Henshaw muttered and Unsworth, his back to the low railing, rolled McGuire facedown on the deck and gripped his collar, yanking him to his feet. McGuire held back, waiting for Unsworth to apply more strength and when he did McGuire flew at him. Surprised, Unsworth stepped aside, prepared to deflect a punch, but McGuire continued his forward motion and dove over the railing and down, through the darkness and the soft Bahamian air, into the water.

A couple from Maryland, sailing with their children for a year through the Caribbean, pulled him aboard their boat and called the police. But beyond transporting McGuire to hospital in Nassau, the police offered him no assistance and asked him no questions. Two officers arrived at his hospital bedside three days later to give McGuire the alternative of being charged with robbery and attempted rape aboard the *Savarin* or accepting immediate deportation to the U.S. upon his release from hospital.

"We have witnesses sworn to testify against you," one of the Bahamian police officers told him. "You will receive a fair trial, of course, but I would caution you against such a choice. Should you be found guilty, as I believe you would be, you would face several years in jail."

In hospital while his ribs mended and his bruised kidneys healed, the doctors prescribed meperidine for McGuire's constant pain; within weeks the drug became his deliverance from agony and his entry into a world of peace and solace where he could escape not only the pain but himself. Upon his release he was deported to Miami where he sold his possessions and sat for two days at sidewalk cafés in Coconut Grove, squinting against the sunlight and the pain.

In downtown bars he made enquiries, then a cabbie drove him as far toward Liberty City as the driver dared to go, and a block further along he met two men who offered him 'ludes and codeine and heroin and crack, and he chose the codeine, buying a hundred capsules from them, and returned to Coconut Grove.

The release from the pain was a freedom he had never experienced, and the agony fell from him like discarded clothing that he stepped out of on an empty beach. For the next few days he smiled and drifted and when he was mugged by three teenagers who took his watch and gold ring he smiled again because they had not found his capsules hidden in a small plastic bag in the crotch of his underwear.

A week later the pills were gone and he returned to Liberty City. But the men were not to be found. He asked a street vendor where they were and the vendor said, "Dead," and shrugged and pushed out his bottom lip.

McGuire called Ollie and Ronnie Schantz who wired him enough money to return to Boston. The pain was back and when the doctors at the Mass General walk-in clinic refused to renew his drug prescription, he sought and found sources as he had in Miami, settling on Django, the compact black man with the withered left hand who dispensed codeine and meperedine and who heard the rhythm of the saints in every phrase spoken to him, responding with smiles and laughter.

McGuire leaned back in the chair, his hand gripping the glass, his eyes closed. On the television screen the Bruins intercepted a pass and the men in the bar abandoned their sense of loss and defeat and cheered the hometown player who broke through the Ranger defense to glide across the ice and flick the puck into the far corner of the net with a deft wrist shot, the perfect play making those in the bar feel like winners for a precious few moments, lifting them above their own lost lives.

* * *

Boston's Summer Street boasts no major tourist attractions nor is there evidence that Paul Revere's horse ever carried the patriot over its cobblestones or that British regulars performed unspeakable acts of violence against innocent colonists. But it remains one of the oldest thoroughfares in the city and the short distance from its beginnings near Filene's in the heart of the shopping district to the ancient docks on Fort Point Channel is a journey that extends backwards, from the city's present adversities to its past glories.

Fort Point Channel, a finger of fetid water extending south from Boston Harbor proper, is lined with rotting docks and rusting railway lines, virtually all that remains of the city's former role as a major east coast seaport. The docks are ugly and dangerous, long past any hope of repair and restoration.

But not the massive hundred-year-old buildings that line Summer Street in the docks area. Built a century earlier as manufacturing plants and warehouses set conveniently close to the rail and shipping terminals, most have had their red brick exteriors sandblasted and their interiors converted into offices and studios for architects, lawyers, wholesalers, advertising agencies and other professionals whose working environments are assessed as keenly as their talents.

"What's a guy who takes pictures want to be down here for?" asked Phil Donovan, emerging from the gray Plymouth parked at the curb. He looked up at 270 Summer Street, six stories high and constructed of yellow brick.

Without replying, Tim Fox led the way into the building, staring at the directory for a moment before pressing the elevator button. "You read Doitch's report?" he asked his partner.

"Big deal," Donovan said. "Takes a doctor to say she died because she got the shit beat out of her."

"Important thing is the time," Fox said. "It throws everything off. If she'd died right away we'd have a fixed point, we'd know when the guy was there. Now all we have is a window. Doitch said she could have lived three, four hours, maybe more, maybe less. Makes it tough to call it down."

The elevator arrived and the door slid open silently. Fox stepped in first. "We put this one away, either we're geniuses or we have horseshoes up our asses," Fox said. "Fourth floor."

Donovan pushed the button. "You know the best way we can get lucky on this one?" he sneered.

Fox looked at him blankly.

"Put the squeeze on your buddy McGuire."

Tim Fox stared at Donovan until the younger man, still grinning, muttered something under his breath and turned away.

The cool gray walls of the building's upper corridors were broken by a series of evenly spaced white doors. Suite 403 featured double doors with the words Posner Studios traced in black strips of photographic film. Fox and Donovan entered, Fox leading the way.

They emerged in a small cluttered alcove with a reception desk, two chrome and leather sofas and a display wall lit by chrome track lighting and hung with framed advertisements for food products, clothing, appliances, restaurants and luggage. Directly ahead stood another set of white doors. One of them was ajar and through the opening they could hear a woman shouting in a vaguely European accent, her words echoing within a large and empty space.

"*I tell you and I tell you but you are never listening to me, Ziggy!*" the woman was screaming. Something shattered like glass on a concrete floor.

Donovan looked at Fox, his eyebrows arched.

"Chill, Chill." The voice from within the studio was male and German, passive and patronizing in contrast with the woman's.

"*Well, I've had it! This time I've really had it!*" The woman was approaching the reception area, the sound of her high heels marking her advance with a staccato beat. "I spend all morning looking for just what you want and it's not good enough. It's never good enough! You are so stubborn . . . ."

The door flew open and the woman, whose face was screwed into an angry frown, glanced from Fox to Donovan in surprise. In less time than it took her to blink, a wide smile had replaced her frown. "Hello," she said brightly. "Were we expecting you?"

She was somewhere south of fifty and her heavy body was wrapped in a dark brown shapeless dress that might have been a monk's robe. The plainness of the woman and her dress was offset by an excess of gold: heavy gold chains around her neck, gold rings on most of her fingers, dangling gold earrings, gold-framed harlequin glasses perched in front of narrow brown eyes and a gold-edged cap on one incisor that gleamed brightly when she smiled. The gold theme was continued in the short bobbed hair, more brass than gold, that framed her face. She was a woman intent on extending what little natural beauty she might have possessed in her youth through her middle age.

"We're here to see Mr. Posner," Tim Fox smiled in return. He held his detective badge in front of him and she leaned forward to study it.

"It's about Heather, isn't it?" the woman said flatly.

Fox nodded. Donovan was peering through the open doorway into the massive studio beyond.

"Ziggy didn't do it, you know," the woman said. "He's the gentlest man. He wouldn't hurt a fly."

"And your name is?" Fox asked.

She extended an undersized hand to him. "Jill Beauchamps," she said. "I am Ziggy's partner and assistant."

"You gotta see this," Donovan said from the open door. "They got enough equipment in here to light the Garden for a Celtics' game and a camera the size of a Honda, all to take a picture of a plate of bagels." He looked back at Tim Fox and Jill Beauchamps, the woman smiling indulgently at him. "A plate of bagels, for Christ's sake!"

"I was a client of Heather's, yes."

Ziggy Posner sat cross-legged in powder-blue coveralls on a low stool in a corner of the cavernous studio, a long-stemmed crystal glass of red wine resting on the palm of one hand, steadied by the other. He was perhaps forty-five years old and his body was slim and athletic. His long hair was silvery-straw in color; a neatly trimmed Vandyke beard set off an angular face ready to break into a shy smile without notice.

103

Softening his harsh German accent was a docile voice that seemed incapable of rising in anger.

"You talked to her answering machine the night she was murdered," Phil Donovan said. He was fingering a strip of exposed film retrieved from the floor, and he rolled it back and forth between thumb and forefinger as he spoke. Tim Fox sat facing the back of a folding metal chair, his arms crossed, letting Donovan lead the way, watching the photographer's reactions.

"Yes, yes, I did." The photographer bent his head and smiled. "Heather, she could be demanding at times. You ask Chill and she tells you, yes?"

"Explain demanding," Donovan said.

"She would make promises and expect me to keep them." The photographer raised the glass to his lips but continued speaking. "She would tell an advertiser, a magazine, somebody who wanted something, she would say, 'Ziggy will have it for you tomorrow if it takes him all night,' yes? Then she would tell me, she would say, 'I work hard for you, now you work hard for me,' but she would forget that I am an artist, I take my time." He sipped the wine.

"You ever go to her place on Newbury?"

Posner sampled the wine again and nodded. "Sometimes, when I must, yes."

"You ever hear Heather talk about a man named McGuire?"

A telephone rang somewhere in the far corner of the studio.

"Who?" Posner asked.

"McGuire. Guy named Joe McGuire," Donovan said.

"No, I hear of him, I think, but I don't know where."

Jill Beauchamps was speaking loudly into the telephone, her harsh voice echoing back from the other side of the studio.

"You ever process any infrared photos for her?" Fox asked.

Posner looked down and smiled sadly into his glass. "Yes, I make those pictures for Heather. I know what it is she is doing. I develop the film, I make the contact sheets for her. But I don't look at them, not close. I look at them the first time and I know what she is doing and I say never again will I look. And I give her back everything, film and prints, yes? Because she sends me lots of work, I am her favorite she tells me, and without her I don't get so much work, yes?"

"What's the big deal about infrared?" Donovan asked.

"It is so that no one knows," Posner said. "She has an infrared flash near the camera. In the dark no one knows when it is on. You cannot see it, the light. Only the film sees. The men, they are surprised."

"Did you take any pictures in Charlesbank Park a few weeks ago?" Tim Fox asked.

Posner turned to face Fox. "Yes, I take photographs there. For a fashion advertisement. I remember, it was very cold that day and Heather was there for some reason, I do not remember why." He frowned into his glass. "I remember now, yes," he said, nodding his head. "The photography was for an advertising agency and the man from the agency, I hear he was a very good friend, a boyfriend maybe, of Heather's. That is why she is there. Otherwise Heather would leave me alone to work."

Tim Fox flipped through his notebook. "His name Hotchnik?"

The photographer nodded again. "Yes, Hotchnik."

"What's he like?" Donovan asked.

Posner arched his eyebrows and tilted his head to one side. "He is not so bad, yes? Not so bad."

"Do you remember Heather mentioning anybody else—" Donovan began, but before he could finish Posner snapped his fingers.

The click-click-clicking of Jill Beauchamps's heels was approaching.

"That is where she mentions his name," Posner said. "This McGuire man. He is sitting on a bench watching us and she talks to him and she comes back laughing . . ."

"Ziggy!" Jill Beauchamps called in a pleasant sing-song voice.

". . . and calls him names, some names. She is glad to see him and says he deserves to be there on a park bench. And then she says—"

"Ziggy, it's Saatchi and Saatchi on the phone," the woman interrupted, ignoring the glares from Fox and Donovan. "I have to talk to you, it will take just a minute."

Posner looked at Fox who nodded.

"What does she say?" Donovan asked.

Posner rose and set his wine glass carefully on top of the stool. "She tells me she must be careful with this man. She must be careful with him because she tells me and everyone else there, she tells us he is very mean and very violent, they never like each

106

other, he would kill her if he got the chance. That is what she says. 'He would like to kill me if he had the chance.'"

Posner excused himself and followed Jill Beauchamps across the studio floor, the woman leaning her body toward his to whisper in his ear.

"Bingo."

Tim Fox looked over to see Donovan holding one hand thumb up and grinning back at his older partner.

Hunched over their glasses and long-necked bottles of beer, the men gave only passing notice to the white-haired woman who entered Chet's and stood in the doorway wearing a plain dark woollen coat, a red kerchief on her head, her dark eyes snapping from side to side, working their owner's gaze deep into the recesses of the smoky room. Then the eyes ceased their movement, the woman's chin rose and she began walking purposefully toward the table in the far corner.

"Gotta be a pissed-off wife," one of the men at the bar muttered. "Somebody's gonna catch hell."

Men both younger and older than the woman stepped aside in deference as she swept past them like a ship of state, neither pausing nor looking to either side until she reached the table in the corner where she pulled a chair out, sat herself on it and stared silently at the man across from her whose eyes were closed, his face relaxed, his lips toying with a smile.

When he opened his eyes and saw her he showed no surprise and only a hint of pleasure. "Hello, Ronnie," McGuire said.

The woman softened her severe expression for the first time since entering the bar. "Hi, Joe," Ronnie Schantz replied.

"Want a beer?" McGuire asked.

"You know I don't."

"Right. You're here for the ambience."

"No. I'm here for you."

McGuire turned his head away. "Oh, shit," he said, because he knew this woman well enough to understand that she would never leave without him.

SEVEN

"When you finally do something late in life like I did to get my driver's license, you should do it as well as you can, don't you think?"

Ronnie Schantz swerved the station wagon around a line of cars waiting to make a left turn and bounced down the curb lane, narrowly missing a parked panel truck.

"I mean, you'd better be damn near perfect at it."

McGuire stared out the passenger window as the car sped past dusty storefronts where sullen young men huddled in the doorways and beaten old men stood near lampposts. "You're perfect, Ronnie," he said. "You're a perfect driver." He closed his eyes. The car sailed over the crest of an intersection and McGuire was nearly weightless for a moment with the rising motion of the vehicle and the effects of the meperidine.

"Ollie never thought I'd get my license," Ronnie said. She sounded the horn at a driver who had begun to pull into her lane and steered around him sharply enough to toss McGuire against the side of the passenger door. "Neither did I. Neither did you, I'll bet." The right front tire thumped against the side of the curb and Ronnie overcorrected to the left, causing the driver of an oncoming brewery delivery truck to honk his horn and glare at her as she passed.

"You're right. I didn't." McGuire's eyes were still closed.

"Somebody told Ollie, somebody from Berkeley Street, you're taking drugs or something. Oh, shit."

The car shuddered and screeched to a halt. McGuire threw his hands against the dashboard and opened his eyes long enough to stare back at several faces looking down at him from the windows of a tour bus sitting perpendicular to Ronnie's car, perhaps two feet from the front bumper.

"Now where in heaven's name did he come from?" Ronnie asked.

McGuire closed his eyes again.

Hodgson Slater Advertising occupied three floors of a chrome and glass building two blocks off the Common. The reception room was dimly lit and furnished in antique patio chairs covered with flower-print cushions. Fox and Donovan sat waiting for Marty Hotchnik. Fox read a newsmagazine while Donovan smiled and nodded at the receptionist whenever their eyes met until the receptionist rose from her chair. She walked to a coffeemaker where she bent from the waist to open a cupboard door, the fabric of her skirt tight across her buttocks.

Donovan leaned toward his partner. "You see the ass on that?" he asked Fox. "Jesus, how'd you like to come home to that every night?" Donovan grinned.

A door to their right swung open and Fox and Donovan turned to see a tall, stooped man approaching. He was in his mid-fifties, pink scalp shining through thinning gray hair. His eyes were downcast at the corners, giving the man's face a perpetually saddened look as though he habitually received and delivered tragic news, like an undertaker. He wore a gray sweatshirt, faded blue jeans and white canvas boat shoes.

Donovan glanced at the man and turned away, wondering where the hell this bum had come from, hanging around a big expensive advertising agency, until the gray-haired man stopped near them, thrust his hands in his pockets and asked if they were waiting for Marty Hotchnik.

"You him?" Donovan asked, and the man nodded and blinked and his lips tightened and spread into either a grimace or a smile, Donovan couldn't tell.

"You're here to talk to me about Heather, I expect," Hotchnik said.

Tim Fox was already on his feet, his badge and ID out, but Hotchnik just glanced at it and turned to lead the way back through the same door, Fox behind him, Donovan at the rear looking at the receptionist still making coffee, her back to him, hoping she would turn around so he could wink at her.

"He's getting better," Ronnie said, leading McGuire up the walk. "Better than the doctors thought he would be six months ago. One of them said he'd be dead by now, remember?"

"I remember," McGuire said.

Ronnie Schantz paused at the front door of the small white clapboard house in Revere Beach and fumbled for her keys. The chill breeze off the bay, a block to the east, was like a burn on McGuire's cheek and he shifted his weight, uncomfortable about what he was about to encounter inside the house.

The door swung open and for a moment McGuire waited there, absorbing the aromas of home baking, spices and coffee wafting down the hall from the kitchen, and then he followed her inside.

"You got him?"

Ollie's voice, sharp and edgy, sounded from his room at the back of the house.

"I've got him," Ronnie said, still shrugging out of her coat in the hallway.

"Send the horse's foot in," Ollie barked.

Ronnie smiled at McGuire. "I'll bring some coffee," she said, and McGuire edged past her down the hall and into the room with its window overlooking Massachusetts Bay and its paralyzed occupant, McGuire's former partner, Ollie Schantz.

She's right, McGuire thought as he entered Ollie's room. He does look better. More weight, more color to his skin.

Before McGuire could speak, Ollie's face became a fist. "What've you been doin' down there, the city?" Ollie demanded, and his one good hand waved in McGuire's direction as though making a feeble attempt to strike the other man. "And what's eatin' at you? You look mean enough to start a fight in an empty house."

"I'm okay." McGuire sat in a wooden chair next to Ollie's bed.

"Yeah, right, and I'm Carl Lewis. You still playin' landlord for a herd of hookers?"

"It's a living."

"Don't be a smartass with me."

"I said it tongue in cheek—"

"And no brain in head. The fuck's gotten into you?"

"It's a bad time, Ollie."

"Yeah, tell me about bad times."

Ollie Schantz had not left this same small room for three years. Surgery and physiotherapy had restored his nerves and muscles enough to permit him to swing his head in a small arc from left to right and his right hand to move, like a seal's flipper, across his bed to grip a remote control for his wall-mounted television set or slap a button to summon his wife for food, for drink, for the warmth of her company and devotion.

McGuire could tell Ollie nothing about bad times that Ollie Schantz failed to experience day by day, so he shrugged and avoided the other man's eyes.

"Heather and I began dating last summer, but it was usually, uh, a sometime thing, you know?"

Marty Hotchnik leaned on the large, badly scarred pine table that served as his desk. Across from him Tim Fox sat hunched forward, watching the advertising man carefully while Donovan slouched in a restored Windsor chair with his legs crossed, pencil and notebook in his hands. One wall of Hotchnik's office displayed reproductions of advertisements for beer, packaged snacks, fur coats and imported cars. Another wall, the one behind Hotchnik's desk, bore framed certificates, advertising awards and several photographs of Hotchnik with groups of people, the women young and artificially attractive, the men older and intense, all of them with their arms about each other.

"How'd you meet her?" Fox asked.

"We'd known each other for years, through business." Hotchnik stretched his arms above his head. "Then I was on a shoot up in the Berkshires and she dropped by and um . . ." He shrugged his shoulders.

"You married?" Fox asked.

"Three times. Divorced three times."

Donovan held Hotchnik's business card up and looked from it to the advertising executive. "You really a senior vice-president in this outfit?" Donovan asked.

Hotchnik nodded.

"Sure don't dress like one. How big is this company anyway?"

"We billed a hundred million last year," Hotchnik said. "Might do a hundred twenty this year."

"And you can't afford to wear a fucking *suit*?" Donovan said. He laughed and looked across at Fox.

"Why should I if I don't have to?" Hotchnik said. He seemed amused.

"Why should you if you don't have to," Donovan echoed, and wrote something in his notebook.

"Where were you, night before last?" Fox asked.

"I was working here on a presentation until about ten o'clock. There were three other people with me, a writer and two art directors. We all went out for something to eat and a couple of drinks in a bar on Stuart Street and I left there sometime after eleven o'clock, caught a cab back to Cambridge."

"What time'd you get to Cambridge?"

Hotchnik searched for the answer on the ceiling. "I'd say between eleven and midnight."

"Anybody see you come in?"

Hotchnik closed his eyes and shook his head slowly.

"How about the next morning?"

"I was in here at seven o'clock. The presentation was at nine."

"You got names of these people who were with you that night?" Donovan asked.

Hotchnik nodded. "I'll write them out if you'd like."

"I'd like," Donovan said.

Tim Fox released a long breath, noisily.

Hotchnik began writing on a sheet of lined paper.

"She ever talk about a guy named McGuire?" Donovan said. "Joe McGuire?"

"Not that I recall." Hotchnik flipped through a diary of names and addresses, copying them on the sheet of paper. "Although it sounds familiar."

Fox scanned the advertisements mounted behind Hotchnik's desk, and his eyes lighted on a photograph of three women modelling furs in a park setting. "Where was that picture taken?" he asked.

Hotchnik twisted his neck. "That one, with the trees? Down by the Esplanade."

"Ziggy Posner take it?"

"Yeah, as a matter of fact he did." Hotchnik grinned up at Fox, impressed. "How'd you know that?"

"Were you there that day?"

"For a while."

"With Heather?"

"I drove her over."

"Do you remember her talking to some man sitting on a bench near the band shell . . ."

"That's him," Hotchnik said. "McGuire. That's right. She came back laughing about it. Said he was a drunk or a doper, a big-time loser anyway. Said he was her . . . what? Ex-brother-in-law? Something like that. Anyway, I remember her saying she had something on him."

"What?"

"I don't know." Hotchnik resumed making notes. "It just seemed to please her that this guy, this McGuire fellow, was so down and out." He shook his head. "Heather had quite a mean streak in her, I'm telling you."

"How often did you see her?" Tim Fox asked.

"Couple of times a week," Hotchnik said. "For dinners, usually. She might drop in here on business, maybe we'd go for lunch."

"Were you in love with her?"

Hotchnik folded the paper once and handed it across the desk to Donovan. "Hardly." He lowered himself into his chair. "It was mostly physical or business, one or the other. Heather was attractive and lively and we enjoyed each other's company. But like I say, she could be tough and mean."

"You know anything about a scam she was pulling?" Donovan said.

"Scam?" Hotchnik looked from Donovan to Fox and back again.

"She may have been blackmailing people," Fox

said. "There's some evidence of that. Did you know anything about it?"

"No." Hotchnik turned away to the window for a moment and lowered his eyes. "No, I knew nothing about a blackmail scheme, but . . ."

"But what?" Donovan demanded.

A sample of a smile. "But I wouldn't be surprised. She wasn't blackmailing me, but I wouldn't be surprised by anything Heather was doing. Not a bit."

"You know how I found out about you, where you were, what kinda shit you'd gotten yourself into?" Ollie Schantz rasped.

"Never thought about it," McGuire said. Ronnie Schantz entered with coffee, fluffed Ollie's pillow and departed, touching McGuire's shoulder with affection as she passed.

"Don't think about much anymore, do you?" Ollie said after his wife closed the door. "Well, it was Danny Scrignoli came by to see me, tell me about you."

"He was at the jail too," McGuire said. "Nashua Street. The guys on Berkeley elected him."

"That right? Well, Danny's concerned. Says a bunch of people down there are. He wants to talk to you, soon's you're ready."

"Whenever that is," McGuire said.

"How about tonight?"

"Aw, hell, Ollie . . ." McGuire said.

"I told him, come by about six o'clock, pick you up."

McGuire stared back at the paralyzed older man, who returned his stare with a pale smile.

"'Course, you don't have to be here, you don't wanna be," Ollie Schantz said. "But Ronnie's sure as hell not gonna drive you back downtown and you don't look ready to haul your ass that far on your own."

"You mind staying out of my life?" McGuire said.

"Yeah, I mind." Ollie's good hand flapped twice in McGuire's direction. "I mind a hell of a lot. Ronnie and me, we've got an investment in you. You wanta stick your ass in a meat grinder, you can go ahead and do it, I guess. But you think Ronnie and me are gonna sit around and watch you act dumber'n a barrel of hair and not say anything, not try to keep you out of your own way, you're nuts."

McGuire's hands began to shake and the hollows of his head filled with angry ghosts and rusting nails. The last of Django's pills remained in his pocket and he feared they would be insufficient to hold back the flood of pain poised on the horizon.

"Danny'll be here in an hour, take you down to North Boston and feed you some of that good pasta and Valpolicella he likes, introduce you to a bunch of his Italian buddies. Get you half alive again. Shit, your eyes're so tight, they look like the assholes of two eagles in a power dive."

"Okay," McGuire said weakly, wondering how long he would be able to remain where he was without vomiting. "Okay."

"Do a check on Hotchnik," Tim Fox was saying. "Talk to those people who were with him that night and the next morning, see what they remember about him, how he acted."

Donovan grinned coldly, like a smartass teenager ready to throw a line back at a teacher, daring the teacher to deal with him, watching Tim Fox manoeuvre the Plymouth down Boylston Street. "Me? You want me to do backgrounding? What for? The guy's straighter'n a pimp's pecker on Saturday night. Get some whistles to do it. We got other people to talk to, right?"

"Look, you do that, I'll check some other stuff out."

"Who with, your dope-head buddy McGuire? You think that hotshot's ever gonna find anything heavier'n an old cigar butt in the bottom of a wine bottle?"

Fox looked away, out the passenger window, his hand gripping the top of the steering wheel. "Hotchnik's an opening," he said quietly. "Talk to him, run him down."

"Opening? What opening? So he was banging her, so what?" Donovan began picking at his teeth with a matchbook cover. "So does that make him a number one perp or just another guy gotta start lookin' around for some fresh pussy?"

Tim Fox's face was a mask. "You want to clean up your language?" he said.

Donovan's jaw dropped open. "What, you only work with choirboys? Huh? Is that what's buggin' your ass? Hey, I'm no choirboy, Timmy. I spent six years in South Boston wiping brains off car fenders before I was in Berkeley Street long enough to take a piss. So what do I owe that guy back there, makes probably two, three hundred grand a year and dresses like he's going out to do yard work? I owe him maybe some college English, some Harvard horseshit language?" Donovan leaned forward, his arm on the dashboard, his head almost meeting the windshield, trying to catch Fox's eye, stare at him as he talked. "Comes down to it, what the fuck do I owe *you*?"

* * *

Danny Scrignoli had come out of Boston's North
End twenty years ago ready to make his mark, get
enough money to buy a house in Brookline or Cambridge and go back to the old neighborhood, cruise
Hanover Street in a black Caddy, the radio blasting
some good doo-wop music and Danny waving to
the old dagos standing outside the espresso bars,
wearing their topcoats with the black velvet collars,
talking the old country language.

All Danny had was high school, which was more
than Danny's old man, the florist, had, but it wasn't
enough to get Danny anything better than a messenger job downtown at a branch of the Bank of
New England. Not a hell of a lot, and a long way
from a Cadillac, but sometimes that happened to
Italian kids in Boston, even street-smart ones like
Danny and his older brother Gino, proving that having some talent and working your ass off doesn't get
you the American dream all the time.

All it got Gino was dead.

Gino Scrignoli was the best shortstop the Boston
school system had ever produced, soft hands, speed
on the bases and able to turn the double play at second, jumping like a garlic-eating kangaroo to avoid
the slide coming in from first, the guy with his
spikes up, trying to break the throw. Boston College
picked Gino up like he was a diamond bracelet lying
in the grass and he made varsity baseball as a sopho-
more, playing every day, going three-for-four some
games, making maybe one, two errors all season. In
his junior year Gino Scrignoli the baseball hero took
courses in American History and Art Appreciation

and dated blonde co-eds with blue eyes and tight sweaters and names like Buffy and Rebecca, showing them the North End, walking them down Hanover Street while his kid brother Danny jumped around them, slipping his hand into the girl's or running behind to grip Gino's bicep and say to anybody listening, "This's my brother, Gino Scrignoli, the Indians are scouting him."

And it was true. Cleveland offered him a contract, big bonus and all, and Gino was ready to go, ready to sign, but the old man said no, not until you get your education. Gino's twenty years old, he can sign if he wants, but the old man's word was law, had been all of Gino's life. "Sign, for Christ's sakes!" Danny begged his brother, five years older, soft hands, great speed on the bases, but Gino just smiled and said, "Lotsa time, Dinny." That's what Gino called him, Dinny.

"You could be down in Florida, sleeping with broads there, getting some double-A experience," Danny begged him, but Gino shrugged and said, "Maybe the old man's right. Get the education, have something to fall back on, keep the grades up."

Then, middle of his senior year, Gino finally signs, just a couple of courses away from graduation. Cleveland management said he could finish his studies at spring training and through the first month of the season playing double-A ball in Davenport or Albany, some place like that. Then he could write his exams, graduate. They'd wait. Speed like that, hands like those, hit a curve ball the way Gino could, they'd wait.

And they gave him a signing bonus, twenty grand.

Gino passes half of it on to the old man and spends some of the rest on a restored fire-breathing Norton 900, the last of the British motorcycles made back in the days when Limey bikes could still kick anybody's ass, even a Harley's, down a winding road.

The next day, Gino gave Danny a ride on the Norton, tear-assing over the Longfellow Bridge into Cambridge, Danny smiling all the way, thinking he'd get bugs in his teeth unless he closed his mouth but smiling anyway.

That was Saturday afternoon, a cold dry February day. Gino had a plane to catch for Daytona Beach on Monday.

Early Sunday morning, Danny woke to hear the Norton being fired up outside, the sound of its steel muscle cutting the quiet of the North End neighborhood, Gino taking it out for one last ride along the river before storing the bike for the season. Danny smiled and rolled over, went back to sleep.

Danny had never heard his father scream before, never heard anybody scream like that again, and as soon as it woke him up, he knew.

"Cold weather like this, a bike's tires don't grip so well," one of the cops at the door said, as if trying to explain the mechanics, the physics of it, trying to make sense of the death of a kid with soft hands, good speed on the bases.

Gino lost it tearing down Memorial Drive along the river in the gray dawn light. Nobody saw it happen. The cops found the body on the road near a gap in the fence where the Norton had torn through, sailing riderless into the water.

"Leave the son of a bitch in there!" the old man cried when the police said they were searching the river for the motorcycle.

Maybe they did. Danny never knew.

Danny was a decent athlete but he didn't have Gino's hands or speed and he wasn't able to track a curve ball all the way in from the mound. Danny never had a lot of things his brother had except the craving to walk down Hanover Street and have the old dagos nod at him and recognize and respect him, as they had his brother, the Big League Kid.

So there he was a couple of years later, eighteen years old and a messenger boy for a bank, working on Congress Street for a lousy two hundred bucks a week, and he comes around a corner one night with his head down, scuffing his sneakers, pissed off because he had to stay late while the jerk accountant finished some stuff, and he looks up and right there on Franklin two guys are putting the boots to a cop. The cruiser door is wide open in the middle of the road and the cop's on the sidewalk, one guy holding his gun on him and both of them kicking him, so much blood in the cop's eyes he can't see, he's just trying to protect himself.

They spot Danny and Danny doesn't think, he jumps into the cruiser, afraid to turn his back and give the guy with the gun a good target. He slips the Ford in gear and peels that sucker out of there, half expecting the rear window to be blown away, blasting the horn like hell as he drives, not knowing how to work the police radio. He gets around the corner, still leaning on the horn, and he clicks something on the radio until he hears the dispatcher's voice and yells where he is, "Franklin south of Congress, there's a cop down, get your asses here!" into the microphone, hitting every goddamn button in sight.

Then he turns the cruiser around, points it back up Franklin, and the cop is still there on his back, rolling from side to side, but the two guys have taken off, and by the time he reaches the cop he hears the sirens.

The city gave him a commendation and a press conference, Jack the Bear Kavander shaking his hand and smiling at the cameras. Right there on TV Kavander asked Danny if he'd ever thought of being a Boston cop. Danny said, "Not until now," and Kavander told him to come by Berkeley Street some day, any day, Boston needed more brave young men like Danny Scrignoli.

Might just do it, Danny thought. Not too many cops drive BMWs. But they get respect. And Gino would've approved. Gino would've been impressed.

Danny showed up at Kavander's office the next day and he was fast-tracked into the academy two weeks behind everybody else, they had to bump some turkey to make room in the first-year class for Scrignoli the hero, Gino's kid brother. And Danny caught up with the others and graduated in the top ten in his class. Scrignoli the cop now.

The cop Danny saved, the one rolling around on Franklin Street who let two guys jump him and take his .38 Police Special, was Stu Cauley. A month later his gun was used in a fatal holdup on Columbus Avenue and Cauley never worked a beat again, never got anything more demanding than counter duty on Berkeley Street.

124

They said it was because of the damage to his eye but everybody knew about the holdup with Cauley's gun.

Everybody knew.

The doorbell rang and a moment later Ronnie Schantz ushered Dan Scrignoli into Ollie's room, the undercover cop wearing a chocolate brown suede windbreaker over a Penn State sweatshirt and blue trousers.

"Hey," Scrignoli said, grinning at McGuire like he was going to hug him. He reached his arms out to grab McGuire's biceps and squeeze.

"Get his ass out of here," Ollie Schantz growled. "Feed him some good pasta, clean the crap out of his system, maybe get him laid."

Scrignoli released his grip on McGuire's arms and walked to Ollie's bedside. "How you doin'?" he said to Ollie softly. "You still mean enough to go bear huntin' with a willow switch?"

"I'm okay," Ollie nodded. "I'm doin' okay." He lifted his good arm in McGuire's direction. "But he's not. If I could get up, I'd kick his ass, what he needs."

Scrignoli placed his arm across McGuire's shoulder. "Son of a gun's too tough for me to tackle," he said. "But I'll do my best."

"Just give me a ride downtown," McGuire said, and headed for the front door without a goodbye.

"I'm out of it." Tim Fox had his jacket off and the sleeves of his shirt rolled up, exposing a gold Omega watch with an alligator leather strap and thick forearms that made him look like a heavyweight sparring partner. "If Donovan's on it, I'm not. It's as simple as that."

Fat Eddie closed his eyes and shifted his weight from one buttock to the other. It was well past six o'clock, he had reports to finish and a visit to the gastroenterologist to endure the next morning, and here was his most professional lieutenant, his only black detective, sitting across from him in a snit because an acting louie didn't show him enough respect.

"You can't just walk off a case, Timmy," Vance said.

"Watch me." Tim Fox sat back in his chair, his heavy arms folded across his chest, the light catching the gold on the Omega. "Just watch me. I'll put up with a lot, Eddie. A hell of a lot. But I won't put up with a racist bastard telling me that my black ass doesn't belong behind a full louie's badge."

Vance frowned. "He tell you that?"

Fox nodded.

"He said he doesn't think a black person should be a lieutenant?"

Fox leaned forward and his eyes locked onto Fat Eddie's. "That's what I said, didn't I, Eddie? Didn't I just say that?"

Vance nodded. Well now, Fat Eddie thought. Sparks between teams you expect. Sometimes it's even beneficial, it shows intensity. But open racism was something else again. "I'll have to call a hearing," Fat Eddie said.

"I don't want a hearing." Tim Fox sat back in his chair. "I don't want any fingerpointing or name-calling. I just don't want to cross paths with Donovan on a case. Any case. I can't work with the man and that's it."

Fat Eddie stared down at his stomach, its inner workings about to betray him with an inevitable emission of gas in the presence of Tim Fox, the elegant Tim Fox. "I'll look after it," he said.

"How?"

"I'll remove his acting lieutenant status."

"And?"

Vance shrugged. "Reassign him."

"Who do I work with?"

Fat Eddie sighed. "Give me time," he said. "We're stretched, Tim. You know that."

"This Lorenzo case is tough," Fox said. He stood up and adjusted the crease in his trousers. "There'll be a lot of interviews to make and sift. I need help, Eddie."

"You'll get it," Vance promised. Just get out of here, he pleaded silently. "I'll leave a note on Donovan's voice mail that he's off the case, that he's to see me as soon as I'm back tomorrow."

"Back?" Tim Fox had turned to leave. "Back from where?"

"Doctor's appointment. Nothing serious." Fat Eddie smiled, creasing his mustache. "Checkup, that's all. Relax, Tim. You're the best on the team, I know it, the commissioner knows it. And we can't tolerate racial slurs. I'll do everything I can, you'll see."

"Thanks." Fox strode thoughtfully to Eddie's office door. "I appreciate it."

"No problem," Vance said. "No problem at all." Please get the hell out, he wanted to say.

EIGHT

"We built this goddamn town, people like you and me, our families," Danny Scrignoli said to McGuire. "The pasta-makers and the potato-eaters, the guineas and the shamrocks, right? Where'd this town be without us micks?"

They were in La Venezia on Salem Street, and the conversation from other tables in the crowded restaurant masked the traffic sounds of the elevated expressway a block away. The voices were loud and vibrant, charged with passion and life, a fusion of Italian, English and Portuguese.

"Not me," McGuire said.

"What? Whattaya mean, not you?" Scrignoli lifted a glass of Chianti to his lips and held it there. "You're Irish as hell, it's all over you."

"Worcester," McGuire said. "I'm from Worcester."

"Yeah?" Scrignoli took a long sip of wine. "I never knew that," he said. "I thought all the time you were a Boston kid."

McGuire had palmed his last pill and swallowed it dry, riding down from Revere Beach in Scrignoli's car, Danny not noticing because he was babbling on about some woman he was chasing. "Little redhead, no boobs but a great ass." The pill had begun its work. To McGuire's surprise he discovered himself smiling, enjoying himself, glad to be where he was. He sipped the wine and savored its astringency. "What'd you order for us?" he asked.

Scrignoli had taken charge from the moment they entered the restaurant, greeting the owner and patrons and waitresses with a broad smile and Italian phrases interrupted by quick embraces. "Leave it to me," Scrignoli had said when the menus arrived, and McGuire had not even listened as Scrignoli ordered the meal in Italian to a woman who looked like an overweight Liza Minnelli, all eyes and lips and hips.

Now Scrignoli answered. "We got some arancini coming, that's a baked rice ball stuffed with meat and cheese." He kissed the tips of his fingers. "Orgasmic, McGuire. Fuckin' orgasmic. Then I ordered baked cavatelli for me, that's with ricotta, egg, mozzarella and Parmesan in a marinara sauce and you got some veal paragina coming 'cause I thought you'd want something like that, all that Anglo-Saxon stuff rattling around in your genes."

McGuire said it sounded good and he drank more wine, wondering when the defenses of the Demerol would begin to crumble, how soon he would become headachy and nauseous again.

The arancini arrived with a salad and it was as good as Scrignoli promised. It had been years since McGuire had eaten at a North End restaurant, never with Danny Scrignoli.

"Did you hear, they make anybody yet on that case they were trying to hang you for, the one on Newbury Street, woman beat to death?" Scrignoli asked. He finished the remains of the arancini on his plate, pushing it onto a last scrap of Italian bread, raising it to his mouth and washing it down with more wine.

"Don't know," McGuire answered.

Scrignoli frowned. "Somebody said you were related to her."

"Only by divorce."

The other man laughed. "Christ, I went through mine two years ago." He set the plate aside, turned the stem of the wineglass in circles, watching the patterns. "Miss the kids. That's what I miss most of all. My kids."

"It happens."

"So this woman was, what? A sister-in-law?"

McGuire nodded. Heather is dead, he reminded himself. All those years I wished her to be and now she is. Somehow it wasn't sufficient, satisfying.

Scrignoli turned away, looked at the floor for a minute, then back at McGuire. "Look, I gotta ask you something. The victim, her name was Heather Lorenzo, right? Lived over an art gallery on Newbury?"

McGuire nodded. "Antique store. She lived over an antique store."

Scrignoli closed his eyes and nodded. "Son of a bitch," he whispered.

The waitress arrived to remove the dishes and Scrignoli waited for her to leave before resting his forearms on the table and leaning forward, holding McGuire in his gaze. "I knew her," he said softly. "I mean, I never *met* her but I knew about her." His fist came down on the table, rattling the eating utensils. "Jee-*sus*, this could be a real screw-up. I gotta tell you about it."

"Doesn't matter to me," McGuire said.

"You're still a suspect, I hear. It's gotta matter to you."

McGuire shook his head.

"Anyway, it matters to *me*."

McGuire was about to ask how when the waitress returned with the main course. "I'll tell you about it later," Scrignoli said, and began eating distractedly. McGuire wanted to tell Danny he didn't give a damn, he was out of it, out of police work, out of anything that smacked of responsibility, including relationships, but he said nothing. When Scrignoli asked how his food was, McGuire told him it was damn good and Scrignoli nodded but didn't appear pleased, just kept eating, mechanically, his mind in a distant place.

They refused the dessert menu and ordered espresso instead. Scrignoli made small talk about police department personnel they both knew until two women entered the restaurant and stood waiting to be shown to their table. Scrignoli commented on their figures but without the zeal he might have shown an hour earlier, then paid the bill and led the way through the chilly night to his car, saying nothing, as though weighing what he might tell McGuire who didn't care to listen anyway, who was wondering only where Django was and when he might see him next.

"You know I'm undercover, right?"

They were skirting Government Center in Scrignoli's Buick, the buildings gray and empty. McGuire grunted.

"Have been for, what? Three, maybe four years now." Scrignoli turned onto Tremont. "Probably not much longer, blown it too many times. Can't work the streets anymore. So I'm doin' white collar stuff." He looked across at McGuire who caught his glance with eyebrows raised. "Oh yeah, I can spin that shit out when I have to. Did a bunch of Cambridge yo-yos dealing hot computer equipment out of a place down near Central Wharf last year, and a whole family running insurance scams out of a big office on Copley Square, stuff like that. This spring, somebody tipped us to a bunch of stockbrokers in town running a game. Not S.E.C. stuff, you know, churning accounts, privileged information, none of that, that's out of our league. But little deals between them that's got nothing to do with taxes or anything, borderline stuff but big money, some really big money. Tough case. Turn here?"

They were approaching the Flamingo, the streets dark and crusty. McGuire had told Scrignoli to drop him off at the club, not knowing if the other man knew where he lived, how he lived.

"So we got a guy on the fringe, a heavy hitter. Not involved in things, not a perp himself but he knew what was going on, made some money on deals, we coulda nailed him as an accessory if we wanted to push it. Piece a cake. Dead to rights, but maybe if we nailed him he'd just get a fine, couple a hundred grand's all he'd pay."

Scrignoli glided the Buick to a stop in front of the strip club. Two of the girls, Billie and Dakota, were standing in the doorway, flashing their thighs from under their robes, having a smoke. Billie bent from the waist to look through the car's windshield. She saw McGuire, puckered her lips, raised a hand in greeting and touched one open palm with two fingers of the other hand.

"You know her?" Scrignoli grinned at McGuire.

McGuire nodded.

"What's with the signal?" Scrignoli raised his hand and imitated the woman's gesture. "The hell's that mean?"

"Somebody's using my room." McGuire stared out his window to the other side of the street where a Korean woman was leading her two children quickly along the sidewalk, gripping their hands. "One of the girls, with a john."

Scrignoli studied McGuire for a moment, his mouth open, surprise and amusement in his eyes. Then he looked away and shrugged. "So whattaya do? Wait 'til they're finished?"

"It's a living."

Scrignoli laughed. "Jesus, I never thought . . ." He shook away the rest of the sentence and leaned forward, resting his arms on the steering wheel. "Anyway, about this guy. He's a broker. Independent. I mean he's more than a trader, this guy's got a full operation, a whole floor of offices downtown, branch office in New York, another in Chicago.

Maybe thirty-five, forty people working for him here. A house on the Cape, condo over on Marlborough and a hell of a big place out near Natick, private lake, horses, the whole bit. Married to this woman who's related to the Cabots, kind of broad they made up the word 'classy' for."

"So what's the point?" There would be at least ten dollars waiting for McGuire in his room and maybe Django was inside the club, Django and his handfuls of tiny white relief. The agony was perched on McGuire's doorstep, waiting to burst through his skull and pounce on his well-being.

"Two points." Scrignoli twisted in the seat to face McGuire. "Two points I gotta make to you. First one. This guy, the broker, he turned for me. Took a hell of a lot of doing but I laid it out for him and his lawyer and his lawyer said, 'Tell 'em,' so he told us. It wasn't the fine that scared him, hell, he spills a hundred grand a year through the cracks in the floor, wouldn't bother him. But he'd lose his license, and that'd be a bitch. And if his wife figured out some other shit. . . . Well, he'd probably have to find honest work."

Scrignoli shifted in his seat, instinct directing his eyes to scan the street as he talked, watching for the unexpected face, the threatening motion, the movement where movement shouldn't be.

"He's gettin' ready to finger some buddies who've been filling their pockets with coin, big coin, for a long time," he began again. "In return, he doesn't testify, him and his company come out of this with roses in their teeth. We're almost there, goddamn it. Almost there. Soon as we get the word in from the forensic accountants, that's what they call themselves, bunch of pencil pushers tracing money transfers and stuff, we move. We get their evidence nailed down and I make this one, we call in the Bureau, hand over a bunch of interstate scores for 'em, and I'm up a couple of notches, maybe get my ass off the street 'cause I'm tired, Joe. I'm really getting tired, and I'm too well-known. Can't work the Zone any more, not around here. And I'm losin' it too, losin' the edge."

"Sounds like you've got a good source." McGuire lowered his head, pinched the bridge of his nose.

"This guy's a gold mine, Joe." Scrignoli became animated, like a man describing an expensive new car or a voluptuous woman. "He's a fuckin' mother lode. This guy can blow the whole scam in this town to the moon, trust me on that."

"So what's the second point?"

Scrignoli exhaled slowly and struck the top of the steering wheel with the palm of his hand. "We start digging into his records and there it is. He was banging her, the Lorenzo woman. The broad you used to be related to. He'd get it on with her, her place, business trip to Florida, it's all there. Then she started blackmailing him and he paid her off but she came back for more. So that makes him a suspect. But he couldn't've done it. No way could this guy have done it, Joe."

"Why not?"

Scrignoli poked McGuire's shoulder with a fore-finger. "Because when Lorenzo got hers the other night, I was with the son of a bitch at his place on the Cape, working out his evidence. He never left my sight, Joe. All night long, except maybe to go have a whizz. Never left my sight."

Dakota dropped her cigarette to the sidewalk, stubbed it out with her shoe and turned to enter the club with Billie, who headed for the john. Just inside the door two guys with long greasy hair and trucker's caps asked her to table dance for them. She said, "Not now, maybe later."

Dakota recognized the guy McGuire had been sitting with outside in the car, fingered him. Didn't know his name, only that he was a cop. A while back, couple of years maybe, he'd busted her and some friends who were dealing a little snow, not a hell of a lot, just enough to keep them on top of things. They dropped the charges against her but she remembered the arrogant little Italian guy, undercover turd, would never forget him.

Jesus, was McGuire one of them too? All this time, McGuire mumbling and hanging around here, watching and listening, was the son of a bitch working undercover?

She'd better tell Dewey. And maybe Grizzly, and Django. Tell them what she saw, tell them maybe to take a hike from McGuire, hang him out to dry.

"You gonna tell me any more about your buddy, the broker?" McGuire was leaning forward, his elbows on the dashboard of Scrignoli's car, his head in his hands. Wait, he told himself. Wait until Danny's gone. Find Django, make the connection.

"What's to tell?" Scrignoli shrugged. "He's worth maybe fifty, sixty million. Keeps himself in shape, hell of a tennis player I hear. He's got a workout room in his house with enough Nautilus machines to train an army regiment."

"And you're convinced he didn't do it."

"No fuckin' way." Scrignoli's voice grew stronger. "Told you, I was with this guy the night she was put through the wringer. All night long. Out on the Cape, going through his books, taking statements, putting everything in place. We started at nine and worked through till three. Almost finished off a bottle of Remy Martin between us, but who needs to know that, right? We crashed about three-thirty and were up before seven, having breakfast at a Denny's near Hyannis. Got back in town about ten and I was a mess the whole day but I had what I needed."

Scrignoli slapped the steering wheel again. "See, here's where I can get screwed. Somebody starts sniffing around, thinks my guy's involved in a first-degree and spills it to his wife that he was having little romper room parties with your former sister-in-law over on Newbury, and there goes six months of work down the toilet. Along with my plan to spend a big chunk of my life in a hammock with unlimited beer and lots of broads close by. 'Cause there's no way this guy'll cooperate if his wife picks up on the Lorenzo bitch. No way. She'll put him out of business if she goes for a divorce. She gets half the company, I can't protect him any more from the P.A., he loses his license and he'll tell me to take a hike. You see what I'm sayin' here?"

"Just because your guy's with you on the Cape doesn't mean he didn't have it done," McGuire said. "Somebody else does it for him, he's got an alibi with you."

Scrignoli looked out his window, staring absently down the alley leading to the back of the Flamingo. "Can't see it, Joe. First, the broad's only touching him for ten grand. That's pocket change to him. He'd paid her some already, then she came looking for ten grand more, said she'd wait a month, she wasn't greedy, just wanted to know it was coming. He'd a paid it, trust me. Second, I had a noose on his nuts when it came to money. Poor bugger couldn't buy a book of matches without me knowing about it. That's how I found out about her in the first place. So how's he gonna lay off whatever it takes to pay some street hood to do her without leaving a trail?"

McGuire shrugged. "Wasn't professional either," he said. "Whoever did her took his time, beating her up like that. Not like a professional hit. Somebody enjoyed doing Heather."

"Got a point there," Scrignoli said. "You got a point. So whattaya think I should do?"

McGuire had had enough. Whoever was in his room should be finished by now. "Don't know why you're asking me." He wrenched the door open.

Scrignoli seemed surprised by McGuire's sudden departure. "Just wanted your advice, Joe. That's all. What, I should go to Fat Eddie on this, ask him to be cool?"

McGuire stepped from the car. "Tim Fox," he said. He felt a steel rod where his neck used to be, a white-hot steel rod extending out of his skull. "Tell Timmy, he's handling the case. Timmy'll know what to do. Thanks for dinner."

He turned, stumbled once before pushing open the door of the club, and entered the darkness and the noise, not even glancing at the naked woman writhing in the glare of the lights.

His mother named him Byron because a lover had once given her a poem written by somebody with that name, a lord or count or something, and because the gift of the poem was the lone romantic memory in her life, she had preserved it, or tried to, in the name of her only child.

But a boy growing up in South Boston soon learns Byron is not a name to command respect on the street. By the time Byron was fifteen years of age he stood almost six feet tall and boasted a record of two convictions for theft and one for assault. He also carried a new name, Dewey. You don't fuck with a Dewey, especially Dewey Robinson who contradicted normal physiological development by, at age thirty-five, managing to accumulate equal quantities of fat and muscle on his six foot three inch body, ballooning out to more than three hundred pounds.

Dewey loved his job, managing the floor at the Flamingo. He loved the girls, especially those who were good to him in the back room, the ones who would perform any little act he wanted if he sweet-talked them and laid a little coke on them. He loved intimidating customers, assholes who couldn't keep their hands off the girls like they were supposed to until Dewey showed up, casting a shadow over them with his presence before leaning down to whisper in their ear, "How'd you like your nuts shoved up your nose, cowboy?" Which tended to slow them down a little, decide that copping a feel probably wasn't worth being taken outside and dropped like a sack of potatoes on a fire hydrant. Dewey had done that to a couple of them. When word got around, people knew he meant business, and it added to the whole intimidating package. Like shaving his head did, and wearing sleeveless vests so he could flash the tattoos on his biceps.

Dewey especially liked grabbing the microphone and announcing the girls' names over the p.a. system as they climbed the stairs to the stage, imitating those big-time radio jocks who screamed about drag races in between beer commercials and Rolling Stones records. Some day Dewey'd go to one of those radio stations, get a job as a nighttime DJ. Make some of that big bread, get his picture in those ads on billboards and on the side of the MBTA buses, maybe with a hip line like, "Dewey Does It For You Every Night," something like that. Christ, he'd have women crawling all over him, begging him for it.

Sienna was starting her third tune, down to nothing but skin now, rolling on her red velvet blanket, Risa waiting to go on, then Billie, then Dakota, then MaryLou when she got back. Risa was new, nice build, lots of thick dark hair . . .

"Dewey?"

He turned to see Dakota standing there, biting her bottom lip. What, she needs something to snort in the back, Dewey thought. It'll cost her. "What's up?" he asked.

"I gotta talk to you."

"So talk."

Dakota looked around. Snakes, the bartender, was pulling a couple of drafts and laughing with two bikers. The music was rolling behind Sienna and every guy in the place, maybe a couple dozen of them, was watching her. Some had their mouths open and a couple were nodding, liking what they saw. "You know McGuire?" Dakota asked.

"Haven't seen him."

"Yeah, well, I just did. Out front. Sittin' in a car with a cop, guy who does undercover work."

Dewey's head didn't move but his eyes swung over to look at Dakota, something happening to them when he did that, and Dakota's hands started playing with themselves, fingers soothing fingers.

"You sure?"

Dakota nodded. "Guy busted me and some friends a while back." She shrugged. "They didn't nail me for nothin', you know? The two guys, they got three to five, I didn't have to testify or anything."

Dewey's eyes swung back to the stage. He didn't speak, he just breathed in deeply, a long intake of air that made his chest expand like a balloon and made the lines of his neck stand out like rope.

"Everybody knows McGuire used to be a cop, long time ago," Dakota said. "He never tried to hide it, never talked about it or nothing. Maybe this guy's just an old buddy givin' him a ride. Hell, no way he'd meet an undercover right out front, out in the open like that, right? I mean, Billie says there's no way, she was with me, she says McGuire's not like that."

"Billie's got the hots for him, she'd say anything." Dewey was frowning at his thumbnail.

"She knows him better'n me, that's all I'm sayin'."

"Yeah." Dewey was watching Sienna again. "That's right."

Dakota stood there for maybe another minute, wondering if she had done the right thing and then she said the hell with it, picked up a stool and walked back to the two greaseballs with the 49ers caps, ready to show it all, do it all, five bucks for five minutes.

It happens, it happens, it happens, MaryLou kept telling herself over and over, silently, behind the tape that covered her mouth. It happened before, twice before, and she lived, she survived it, she could survive this, and when she did Dewey or somebody would hunt this fucker down and oh God!

She had never seen the guy before, didn't even notice him sitting in the far corner until she had finished table dancing for a couple of college kids and was heading back to the bar and he waved her over. Harmless looking but they all are at first. Glasses, short haircut, skinny guy wearing a heavy tweed jacket over a Hawaiian shirt.

"You wanna go out?" he asked her.

"Cost you a hundred," she said.

"Got it."

"Ten more for the room."

"Got it."

"I have to be back here on time, half an hour, that's it."

The guy nodded.

"Meet me out back, bottom of the fire escape," she said.

She'd told Billie and one of the other girls, let 'em know she had a john, then left by the rear door where the john was standing in the shadows and led him up the outside stairs to McGuire's room, knowing

McGuire was never there between six and midnight, that was the deal. The john with the glasses and the nerdy haircut was behind her, she could hear him breathing hard.

She pushed open the door and there was the cot and the small light at the back, and as she reached behind her to shrug out of her robe the john pushed her face down on the cot, and she felt a knife against her neck and the son of a bitch was breathing in her ear telling her he'd cut her right there and now, *Now!*, if she made a noise, made a move, did anything except what he told her to do, and she thought, "Oh, Jesus, not again!"

He must have done it before because he had the tape already cut to size and across her mouth and more tape around her wrists, her hands behind her back. Then he rolled her over and sliced through her robe and bra and G-string with the knife blade, watching them fall from her body with no expression, not even pleasure, not drooling, not laughing, none of that stuff, and his silence was more frightening to her than laughter or lust.

When she was naked he studied her body like a gardener surveying a plot of land, spade in his hand. But instead of a spade, he reached inside the waistband of his trousers to withdraw a length of garden hose, maybe two feet long. An inch or two of butcher's string formed a loop at one end and she realized he had concealed it within his trousers, hanging it inside so you never saw it, and in spite of herself, her fear, her panic, she thought, "Are you glad to see me or is that just a garden hose in your pants?" and then he brought the hose down hard on her stomach and she began the long vomit of silent screams.

Django was sitting in the far corner of the Flamingo, his teeth gleaming in a wide smile, his small head moving to the music, watching the stage where Risa was prancing and showing it off, playing to the audience.

McGuire ignored the woman on the stage and walked toward the small black man, steadying himself against tables as he moved. There would be money upstairs, enough for some pills to ease the pain, enough to play a few notes of Django's tune.

When Django saw McGuire approaching, the smile vanished and he turned back to Risa and her lovely long legs.

"I need some candy," McGuire said, sitting heavily on the chair next to Django. "There's some money waiting . . ."

"Candy?" Django's smile returned but his eyes remained on the stage. "Rot your teeth, Jolt. Do like your mama tell you, eat up those veggies. Get your *greens*, all them vitamins."

"You know what I mean," McGuire growled. "Gimme a couple now and when . . ."

Django's head shook from side to side. "Out," he said. He brought his thumbnail to his teeth and began probing the crevices.

"Hey, I've got it," McGuire said. His voice was hoarse and his hands began to quiver from the pain. "Codeine, whatever you've got, just roll me a couple for now."

As the first of Risa's three songs ended, she removed her halter top with a flourish, revealing heavy breasts, their skin the color of buttermilk, and the men began applauding vigorously and a few appreciative whistles cut the smoky air.

Django clapped too, bringing his hands together in a slow rhythmic pattern, until McGuire leaned across the small table and seized the black man's arm, yanking him close. "Come on, damn it," McGuire spat in Django's ear. "Give me a break here, just a couple until I get the money from the room."

"Can't, Jolt." Django pulled away and smoothed the leather sleeve of his coat. "Couldn't sell my mama a aspirin, way things are. Nothin' personal, understand. You a good customer, good guy, but . . ." Django glanced behind McGuire and sat back in his chair again, his arms folded across his chest. He returned his eyes to the stage where Risa's second tune had begun, whump-whump-whump, the tall black-haired woman striding back and forth across the stage, her hands supporting her breasts, thrusting the nipples forward so they bloomed like young roses.

McGuire reached for Django's arm again. "What do you mean, the way things are?" he said, and a large hand settled heavily on McGuire's back. He turned his head, winced at the stab of pain that raced across the base of his skull and locked eyes with Dewey.

"Don't want no problem here," Dewey said calmly. He kept his hand on McGuire's back but he was looking across the room at Risa. "Just want everybody to have a good time, sit down, enjoy a drink, look at the pretty women, okay?"

"Aw, Jesus, Dewey," McGuire said, then Dewey added, "'S'all we wanta happen here, so whyn't you

145

go outside, tell your buddies from Berkeley Street for me, okay?"

Django's eyes grew wide and his head swivelled back and forth, from McGuire, to Dewey, to the front door where Grizzly and the Gypsy would be walking through any minute and finally down at the floor as though there might be a message for him there, telling him the Gypsy'd been right, he should never trust a cop, even an ex-cop.

"Berkeley?" McGuire said. "What's with Berkeley Street?" but Dewey just stood there watching Risa on the stage and Django slid off his chair, looking to put room between himself and McGuire, who sat for a while with his head in his hands before rising and walking out the front door, wondering what the hell he was going to do now.

He rolled her on her stomach. His jacket was off, she didn't know when he removed it, didn't even know how long she had been there, but she remembered coming out of a faint maybe. Like she was somebody watching it all in a movie, she saw that his jacket was off and his ugly red Hawaiian shirt was stained under the arms from the effort of raising the rubber hose and bringing it down again and again across her body while she writhed to escape the blows.

Now her face was buried in the folds of the cot and when he began working on the backs of her thighs she knew she would either throw up or pass out or maybe both and if she did she would choke to death on her own vomit. My God, how long had it been going on? How much more could she stand?

Another blow from the hose on her thighs and then another, and she knew, she *knew* he wouldn't stop until he killed her and the knowledge settled like a force within her. There had been times when she was coming down from a drug high and she owned and controlled nothing but her body, whatever she could do with it, those were times when MaryLou wished she were dead. She had said it aloud when she felt too much pain and too much sadness, when she had taken too much shit from her boyfriend or her father, and now she told herself that her wish was coming true, this is what happens when you get your wish.

The blows ceased and she heard only the man's heavy, labored breathing. MaryLou imagined him reaching for a knife and she repeated do it quick do it quick do it quick in her mind, her eyes squeezed shut.

But she heard only his breathing and then not even that when he held his breath, and she realized he was listening to something.

She heard it too. First a step on the landing beyond the door, and now the sound of the door opening.

McGuire stood absorbing the sight of MaryLou bound and gagged face down on his cot, and the man in the sweat-soaked red Hawaiian shirt with one arm raised and his eyes on McGuire's. They were frozen for a moment, each stunned by the other's presence, until the john dropped the hose and whirled around in search of the tweed jacket he had tossed over McGuire's small table.

McGuire remained in the doorway, his thoughts moving slowly toward action, like someone swimming through syrup, and here was the john charging for the door now, holding his glasses against his face with one hand, the other gripping his jacket, aiming his body for the opening between McGuire and the door frame.

The scene was filtered through the pain and the residual effects of the Demerol but they failed to dull McGuire's instincts entirely. He reacted without thinking, extending his arm out to clutch the man even while his eyes remained fixed on the sight of MaryLou bound and naked on his bed, her body crisscrossed with cranberry-colored stripes.

The man twisted out of his grip, stumbled backwards past McGuire and out the door, then bounced off the railing and turned to flee down the stairs. Now everything was clear to McGuire, who turned and hurled himself against the man's back, throwing him onto his face and McGuire, gripping the other man's shoulders, rode him down the stairs like a boy on a sled. At the landing they settled in a heap and McGuire, still laying atop him like a lover, seized a handful of hair and hammered the man's head against the metal grates again and again until his face was layered with blood and bird droppings. Then he rose to his feet, lifted the man by the back of his shirt collar and walked slowly down the rest of the stairs to the ground pulling the bloodied mess behind him, the man's feet striking each step of the fire escape, thunk, thunk, thunk.

McGuire rolled the man on his back, then limped back down the alley to the front door of the club where Sienna was standing with her robe partially open. "Tell Dewey there's a piece of shit waiting for him out by the fire escape," McGuire said when he caught his breath. "And have him call an ambulance. For MaryLou."

Then he sat down right where he was on the sidewalk, his back against the crumbling brick wall, waiting for everything to unravel as he always knew it would some day.

"What'd you do to him?"

One of the cops handed McGuire a black coffee in a plastic cup and McGuire nodded his thanks. The others stood a few feet distant, chewing gum, making notes.

"Stopped him from killing the girl," McGuire said. He was in the same spot in which he had collapsed fifteen minutes ago, his back against the wall of the club. Small knots of people grouped themselves across the street, staring down the alley now crowded with police cars and two ambulances.

Billie, her robe peeking out from beneath the hem of a cheap fur coat, knelt beside McGuire and used a damp cloth to dab at a cut over his eyebrow.

"Sure as hell did that," the cop with the notebook said. "Berkeley Street lit up like a Christmas tree when we sent the guy's description and M.O. in. Guy did two girls in Cambridge last month and one down in Quincy, all of 'em hookers. Same routine. Beats 'em with a hose and when he gets tired or bored, I guess, slips a knife between the ribs."

"You see his face?" another cop asked McGuire.

"Too dark." McGuire took another sip of coffee. Billie's hands were soft and soothing on the back of his neck and for a moment, a brief passing moment that frightened McGuire, he felt his eyes begin to sting with tears.

"I mean just now, when they wheeled him into the ambulance?"

McGuire shook his head.

"Son of a bitch was at McDonald's, they'd put his face on a grill, fry it up into a Big Mac."

"Good." Billie's voice was full of venom. "Joe shoulda killed him's what he shoulda done."

"You wanna tell us how they got into your room, the two of 'em?" the cop with the notebook asked.

"Door's always unlocked," McGuire said. "Anybody can come and go as they please." He drained the coffee, handed the cup to Billie. "How's MaryLou?"

"Probably be back in there showing her ass to the world, couple a weeks," the other cop said. "You don't mind coming in, signing a statement when it's typed up?"

"Sure." McGuire struggled to his feet, steadying himself against Billie who rose with him. "Let me know when."

"Where do we reach you? Be a bunch of ID people in your room for a while."

"At my place," Billie said before McGuire could respond. "He'll be staying with me for a couple a days over on Chandler Street." She recited an address and a telephone number while McGuire watched her, a small smile on his face.

The cops told everybody to break it up, damn it, the show was over. Standing in the doorway, Dewey announced the Flamingo was closed for the night and everybody should do what the police officers—dragging every syllable out with contempt—do what the po-lice off-i-cers said to do.

Billie edged past Dewey to run inside for her purse and call a cab. The cop who had brought the coffee moved sideways toward McGuire. Keeping his eyes on the crowd as it parted to make way for the ambulance, he said, "You gave that pervert one hell of a ride." Instinctively he patted McGuire on the back and strolled down the alley toward the back of the club.

Across the street on the fringe of the crowd, Grizzly watched the gesture impassively, the tip of a freshly lit Camel glowing precariously close to his wild untrimmed mustache. Standing next to him, the Gypsy's face mirrored hate as her eyes flew back and forth between the police officers. "Cops are shit," she muttered. "All of 'em, can't trust a one of 'em."

But a few feet away Django stood smiling among the grim faces of the onlookers, happy for McGuire and his new hero status, repeating over and over, "Yes yes yes yes Jolt, you the one, you the *man*!"

NINE

P hil Donovan was pissed. All those years he tried to get along with people, no matter what color they were or how big an ass they could be, he'd always made an effort and where'd it get him?

He made an *eff*ort. Found a way to work with Fat Eddie, never made wisecracks about him like the other clowns did. Worked with Howie what's-his-name, that chink over in Forensics, got along great with him. Didn't bitch when they teamed him up with Fox, told him he had to take orders from a black man. And where'd it all get him? Flat on his ass is where. One day he's an acting louie, the next day he's back to sergeant. Who the fuck they think they're dealing with?

Donovan twisted a paper clip in his hand into a knot, swiveled in his chair, tossed it at the wastebasket and missed.

Which put him over the edge. Rising from the chair he took one step toward the wastebasket, drew his right foot back and launched the gray plastic receptacle in a short arc that ended against the radiator on the far wall.

"Gotta keep your head down, boy."

Donovan turned to see Danny Scrignoli watching him from the open doorway, grin on his face, stick of gum in one hand. The undercover cop was wearing a suede windbreaker with grease marks on the collar, red wool turtleneck, black chinos and a pair of beat-up Adidas.

"You can tell if you made it through the uprights from the crowd noise, see," Scrignoli said. "Didn't your coach tell you that? You wait to hear the crowd, then you lift your head."

"The fuck you want?" Donovan sat down in the chair again, leaned back, lifted his feet to the corner of the desk.

Scrignoli spread his hands and looked around the room. "Want?" he said in exaggerated surprise. "I don't want anything, man. What's to want?" He popped the gum into his mouth and talked around it. "Question is, what the hell do *you* want, man? Word's out Vance dropped you back to sergeant and now you're ready to slip his balls in a wringer. What, you wanta make captain overnight? You want Fat Eddie's job? You know what Ollie Schantz said about Fat Eddie's job, being a captain here?"

Donovan picked up another paper clip from the desk, started twisting it in and out of shape. "You think I give a shit?"

"No but I'm gonna tell you anyway. 'Cause that's the kind of guy I am." Scrignoli leaned against the open door, chewing with his mouth open, looking like the street-smart punk he pretended to be in undercover work, busting heads and asses on Mass Avenue. He leaned forward to catch Donovan's eye and frowned. "You remember Schantz? You ever meet Ollie?"

"Couple times. What about him?"

Scrignoli laughed. "Funniest son of a bitch you'd ever wanta meet. He had more lines . . . ." Scrignoli folded his arms and smiled down at his sneakers. "Talkin' about Fat Eddie one day, this was 'way before Vance made captain, he's still Sergeant Eddie Vance. Ollie's over there, end of the hall, watchin' Eddie whose belly's spillin' out over his pants and he's tryin' to be Paul Newman. Eddie's glasses are slidin' down his nose and he's pullin' at that mustache of his, always looks like a toothbrush, sweet-talkin' some new honey in the steno pool, just started the day before. She's lookin' around saying to herself, 'Where'd this loser come from and when's somebody gonna take him away and lock him up?' And Ollie and me and a couple other guys, probably McGuire and ol' Dave Sadowsky, we're watchin' from the doorway, and Ollie says to us, 'You know somethin'?' he says. 'Eddie Vance couldn't get laid in a woman's prison with a fistfulla pardons,' and that did it."

Scrignoli grinned and shook his head at the memory.

"Christ, we laughed so hard everything stopped in the steno pool and Fat Eddie stood there lookin' over at us until Kavander, he was captain then, he comes out of his office and yells across at us, 'You comedians want a laugh, I got a couple autopsies you can look at.' Then he points at Fat Eddie and says, 'Vance, stop trying to fuck the stenos. It slows down their work and annoys 'em all to hell.'"

"Terrific," Donovan said dryly, but he permitted a small smile to play at the corners of his mouth.

"Hey, speakin' a McGuire, you hear he just about offed a pervert over at the Flamingo last night?" Scrignoli's expression changed to one of admiration. His eyebrows shot up his forehead, his jaw ceased its ferocious chewing and his bottom lip shot out. "Christ, I'd just dropped him off there maybe ten, fifteen minutes before. I'm a couple blocks away and McGuire's preventing a homicide."

Donovan tossed the paper clip across his desk. "Big deal. Now everybody's sayin' he's a hero. Never heard such bullshit."

Scrignoli stepped into the small office and closed the door behind him. "What, you got something against Joe?"

"Nothin' except maybe he's weaselin' sideways out of a possible murder one, murder two maybe."

"You mean the woman over on Newbury Street?"

"Yeah. Used to be my case, Tim Fox and me. Now Fox thinks McGuire's a goddamn altar boy and me, I guess I'm just another nigger-baitin' freaked-out cop. So here I am, waitin' around for somethin' to happen and Fox, he's off runnin' the case on his own like he's General MacArthur."

"You don't think McGuire did that woman."

"I think he knows more than he's lettin' on."

"Like what?"

Phil Donovan rubbed his eyes with the tips of his fingers. "Like maybe what she had on him."

"You wanta tell me about that?"

"She was ballin' men and blackmailing them. I think she had something on McGuire and was usin' it on him."

Scrignoli gave a short, sharp laugh. "You gotta be kiddin' me. What's she gonna get from McGuire? Guy doesn't have a pot to piss in."

"I dunno. Drugs, maybe. Inside information. Hell, her own landlord said she was scared shitless of somebody she knew. McGuire's got a way, okay, he *had* a way of scaring people, intimidating them." He shook his head. "Somethin' fits there, damn it. He knows somethin' he's not tellin' and it's behind the whole thing. You know, we never did a search of his room. What's he got up there we should know about? Guy's a murder one suspect and nobody even gets a warrant to search his place?"

"Probably done it now, after last night." Scrignoli thrust his hands in his pockets.

"Bullshit. All they're lookin' for last night is felonious assault stuff, the broad bein' worked over on McGuire's bed. They got the victim, a witness, the perp." Donovan shook his head. "There's somethin' there, damn it."

Scrignoli rested his hand on Donovan's shoulder. "You better get over this one," he said. "McGuire's not the guy, you're not on the case, Tim Fox is as good as they come around here and Fat Eddie'll make you golden again in a couple of months. Just gotta keep the faith, boy."

Donovan looked up, mildly amused. "Faith? Who the hell are you, Billy Graham?" he said.

* * *

McGuire stared at each of them in turn for several minutes before deciding he liked the brown-haired one best of all. She had the kind of wide-eyed innocence that always appealed to him in young women. And she was dressed more conservatively than the others. Nice red gingham apron, little matching bow in her hair. The blond next to her looked like a tart in one of those fifties sheath dresses that clung to her ass, even under the cheeks. The redhead was a phony, anybody could spot it. Probably had a nose job too, real noses don't turn up at the tip so neat. But there was a real body on the black-haired honey at the end, look at that chest. Jesus. He reached an unsteady hand toward her. Footsteps and the aroma of coffee drifted down the hall. Billie would catch him in the act but McGuire didn't care. His fingertips brushed the oversized breasts.

"You're awake."

Billie was wearing a silky sky-blue robe trimmed with white lace. Her blonde hair was gathered on the crown of her head, a few strands permitted to fall across her face. She carried a tortoiseshell tray bearing two cups of coffee, two glasses of orange juice, a stack of raisin toast and the morning newspaper.

"You like my dolls?" She set the tray on the bed next to McGuire. "That's Carmella, the one you were reaching for. She's Spanish. I mean, I didn't *get* her in Spain, I've never even *been* to Spain, but I saw a picture of a Spanish woman once and I thought, 'She looks like my black-haired doll,' and Carmella, I don't know where that came from, I just like it."

McGuire pulled his hand away from the dolls lined up on the table next to Billie's bed.

"You probably think it's nuts, a woman my age collecting dolls, but . . ." Billie shrugged. "It's harmless, just a hobby. Actually, a lot of girls at the club collect dolls. Terri does, she gave me Cheryl, that's the blonde doll, one night. You take your coffee black, right?"

McGuire nodded and raised himself to a sitting position.

"How'd you sleep?"

"Okay." McGuire took the coffee from her. "I slept fine."

"Damn right, all the pills I gave you. How's your headache?"

"Gone." McGuire sipped the coffee. Something floating within his head collided gently against the inner walls of his skull. "Thanks."

Billie sat on the edge of the bed, watching him. "You want a shave later, I got a razor in the bathroom. Old boyfriend of mine left it here. Long time ago."

McGuire nodded.

"I don't do what MaryLou does, you know." Billie picked at her fingernails, her head down. "Never turned any tricks. You start that, where the hell're you gonna end up, right? I mean, all there is for you is gettin' beat up, maybe killed. I know some girls who just disappeared one night, never seen 'em again. I knew one, Molly or Dolly or something, little bitty thing, they found bits of her floating in the harbor, a leg here, an arm there. Never did find her head. Jesus, I don't want to wind up like that. What I'm saying is, I don't hook, Joe."

"I know." McGuire sampled the orange juice.

"I could, easy. Could use the money too. Mary-Lou, Terri, Josie, sometimes they make an extra thousand a week easy, right in their pockets. That's tempting, you know."

McGuire grunted, drained the glass of juice.

"I just wanted you to know I never did that, Joe."

"I hear you, Billie."

"I don't even have any boyfriends any more." She dropped her hands in her lap and stared out the window, the winter sun shining weakly through layers of grime. "Used to but he got . . . he got sent away."

"For what?"

"Assault with intent. Somebody promised him a couple a thousand dollars to rough up a guy, owed the other guy money. My boyfriend and a buddy, they got caught doing the guy with a crowbar. Guy recovered, he's walking the streets today. But Gene, that's my boyfriend, used to be my boyfriend, he gets five to ten upstate. His buddy, who turns evidence against him, he gets two years suspended."

"Five to ten?" McGuire sampled more coffee. "Not a first offence term."

"Gene's had a rough life."

"Bet the guy he worked over with the crowbar will too."

Billie shrugged. "Thing is, that was nearly six months ago and I've been on my own ever since. You know, at the beginning I told him, I told my*self*, I said I'd wait for Gene, go see him once, twice a month, but Gene's having a tough time in there. Been in a coupla scraps already, he's in solitary now for two months, can't have visitors. Way he's goin', I'll be an old broad by the time he gets out and I don't think it's fair for a woman like me to spend the best years of her life alone, do you?"

McGuire sighed and set the coffee cup aside. "Your call, Billie. Your life, your call."

"One thing Gene did, just on the side, you know, was use. A little snow, he tried horse once, made him sicker'n hell so he laid off it. He liked downers, codeine and 'ludes." She slid the tray, her food untouched, from the bed and stretched out beside McGuire. He could smell her cologne, lilacs and cinnamon. "Left some here at my place, never kept any where he lived."

"Why are you telling me this?"

"Because I know you need them. I know Django's your source. He really likes you, Django I mean. Says you're his man. He knows you're in pain. Hell, everybody can see you're in pain. Stuff I got, stuff Gene left here, you can use. Long as it's here, you can use it."

She moved closer to him, and one hand reached out to stroke his shoulder. "Jesus, you know what it's like to stand up there at the club, night after night, gettin' those guys turned on, gettin' your*self* turned on, then comin' back here alone?" Tears began to flood her eyes. "It's hell, man. Sometimes it's fuckin' hell and . . . and I almost wish I could do what MaryLou does, not now, not after what happened last night, but sometimes I wish I could do that just once, you know?"

"You've been good to me," McGuire said.

"Oh, Christ, you haven't seen anything yet." She pushed herself onto her hands and knees over him, lifted one hand, brushed the tears from her eyes, then sat up and back on her haunches. "You haven't seen a damn thing yet," and she shrugged out of the robe, letting it fall to her waist. Raising both hands she stroked her breasts, watching McGuire's eyes, and McGuire realized that everything Billie was about to do was an extension of her act at the club, the teasing, the posing, the surrender, the need to be used, and it swept a wave of overwhelming sadness through his soul.

He lay back and closed his eyes and Billie was bending over him again, brushing her breasts against his cheek, swinging them back and forth, their texture like crumpled silk within cool satin. He reached for her and Billie stretched herself prone over him, the rhythm of their breathing syncopated, their hands moving over each other's bodies in search of forgiveness, acceptance, defiance against what time was doing to them.

Tim Fox hoped Fat Eddie never assigned another partner to him, never found him anybody, just left him alone to do his job. He worked better that way, nobody to adjust to.

But somebody new would be sent to work with him, somebody junior probably, because you needed corroboration and you needed backup, you needed somebody to talk to, bitch at even, otherwise the job would kill you one way or another.

He wheeled the gray Plymouth into a loading zone on Lansdowne Street and remained behind the wheel for a moment. Fat Eddie would have a new partner for him this afternoon, some whistle looking to move up to a gold badge. Bunch of crap. Fox didn't care. Whoever Fat Eddie chose, he'd be better than Donovan.

Fox stepped out of the car, tightened the belt around his Burberry and started across the street toward the low yellow-brick building with the faded sign proclaiming Van Ness Plumbing Supplies—Wholesale Only.

Inside, in a tiny reception area furnished with two plastic and metal chairs, Fox told the woman behind the sliding glass window that he was from the Boston Police Department and he had come to see Steve Peterson. Within a minute the door to the office area swung open and a man with short-cropped gray hair growing out of a bullet-shaped head stood looking directly at Fox. His body was blunt, like a tree trunk, and he wore a creased white shirt with the sleeves rolled above the elbows, a striped tie pulled away from his collar and blue trousers with red fireman's suspenders. The man introduced himself as Steve Peterson, shook Fox's hand once and turned to lead the detective through a maze of filing cabinets, computer desks and shipping cartons to a glass-walled office in a far corner.

"You here about Heather?" Peterson said, fishing a pack of cigarettes from the pocket of a suit jacket draped over the back of his desk chair.

Fox nodded and sat in one of the uncomfortable metal chairs across from Peterson. From somewhere beyond the walls of the office came the sounds of forklift trucks and the shouts of young men.

"Already talked to some detective, coupla days ago. Irish guy, Donovan, something like that."

Peterson had a gruff voice and a directness that acted as a barrier against small talk.

Tim Fox had heard that voice before.

"This is kind of a follow-up visit," Fox said. "Just take a minute."

"Other guy didn't want much except to know where I was the night Heather was killed. So I told him. Same's I'm gonna tell you."

Tim Fox withdrew his notepad and sat with his pen poised. "Did you call your former wife the evening she was murdered?" he asked.

"Yeah, I did." Peterson placed a cigarette in his mouth and left it there while he talked. "It's on the answering machine, right? Knew you guys would hear it. I called her from here about, I dunno, quarter after seven, seven thirty, something like that."

"From the sound of the tape, you were pretty upset with her. You want to tell me about that?"

Peterson pulled a battered Zippo from his trouser pocket, lit the cigarette and inhaled deeply. "You know what she was doing?" he asked, avoiding the detective's eyes.

"Doing?"

"Her scam, the pictures and all that shit. Don't tell me you don't know about it. Other guy did, the Irish cop."

Fox nodded. "We know about it," he said. "We just want to know how you fit in."

Peterson studied the end of his cigarette. "Listen, maybe I should get a lawyer in here while I'm talking to you."

"Can if you want to."

"I mean, I didn't kill her, understand. Like I told the other guy, I'm living with a woman over in Charlestown, she's got a couple of kids. I was home there by eight o'clock, her and the kids and I went out for dinner, and I was in bed by eleven. I can prove it."

"So far you're not a prime suspect in her murder, if that's what you're worried about," Tim Fox said.

"Yeah, well, all this shit's upset my girlfriend all to hell but she knows, she told the other cop where I was, offered to sign an affidavit, whatever he needed." Peterson took a deep pull on his cigarette and released the smoke slowly. "Heather was a pain in the ass to me in more ways than you'll ever know but I didn't kill her. Felt a little bad when I heard about it, understand. Not too bad, mind you, just a passing twinge."

"How long were you married?"

"About two years. I refer to it as the Heather Incident. Second marriage for me and my last."

"When were you divorced?"

"Three years ago. We kind of kept running into each other. Or she'd phone me for a favor, some damn thing. Most of the time I'd tell her to go take a flying leap but every now and then . . ." Peterson took another long pull on his cigarette, leaned his head back and aimed smoke rings at the ceiling.

"How involved were you in the blackmailing?" Fox asked.

Peterson swung his chair sideways to the desk, tapped the cigarette against a glass ashtray and spoke without looking at Fox. "This is where I gotta be careful," he said. "See, I was never involved at all. It didn't surprise me what Heather was doing. She was screwing around on me when we were married, that's what broke it up, the marriage." He smiled coldly. "Heather got off on the power more than the pleasure. I'm telling you, I was married to one strange woman."

"But you knew she was blackmailing men."

"Oh, sure. She bragged to me about it. Pulled up here once in her shiny new car, BMW. Showing off. Talked about leaving for Europe on the Concorde, all of that shit. Rubbed my nose in it." He shook his head. "Jesus, she was a strange broad, I'm telling you."

"She try to involve you in it?"

"Yeah." Peterson butted the cigarette in a sudden violent motion, and Fox noted the man's deep chest, powerful biceps and aggressive manner. "Near the end. That's where I gotta be careful, like I said." He turned to face Fox, resting his forearms on the desk. "You don't give a damn about criminal intent, do you? You know, just talking about doing something with somebody, something that might be construed as illegal? Is that, what? Conspiracy?"

"Was the other person Heather?"

"Could be."

"There's no way we're going to pursue a conspiracy case where the second party is dead. Especially if she was a homicide victim. No way at all. You want to talk, go ahead, but I don't give a damn what you and your ex-wife might have speculated about. Unless it concerns her murder."

Peterson stared back at Fox in silence. "Yeah," he said finally. "Okay, I hear you." He leaned back in his chair. "Look, I've been working in this dump for over twenty years. I bought a big piece of it a few years ago, right around the time everybody in the state decided they didn't want any more bathrooms. That's me, the guy with great timing, okay?"

Fox watched him in silence, waiting for him to continue.

Peterson breathed deeply once, picked up his package of cigarettes, thought better of it and tossed them aside. "She calls me, couple of weeks ago, says she's on to something big. Too big for her, she could use some help."

"What kind of help?"

Peterson shrugged. "Kind of a partner. For protection. She never admitted what she was doing, the scam with the pictures. See, she never laid it out for me in detail but she let me know, bit by bit. You know, brag about her new boyfriend of the month. No names, but she'd tell me they gave her big chunks of money and I'd ask why and she'd laugh and say there were two things she knew best. 'Two things I know best are fucking and photography,' she'd say and laugh like hell. Plus she'd talk about all the money she had invested. I knew she wasn't making it all as a photographer's agent."

"How'd you feel about that?" Fox asked.

"About what? About my ex-wife screwing other guys? It was old news to me. Old news when our marriage split up, old news now. Didn't bother me none."

"So why did she suddenly need a partner?"

"She was going after some kind of score from a big name and she wanted some backup, somebody who knew what was going on in case she messed up."

"She offer you money?"

Peterson nodded. "Not a hell of a lot. Ten thousand up front and a couple of grand a month just to hold on to some stuff for her, I don't know what. Right now I could use it, the money. This place was bleeding, still is. The bank, wise asses over there, they'd just told me I couldn't draw more'n twenty-five grand a year in salary for Christ's sake until things get turned around and that'll take maybe a year. They saw me taking out more, they'd call their loan, that's the only deal they offered. So when Heather starting talking about how she'd pay for some help, I jumped for it. I said, 'Sure, long's I don't have to get rough with anybody, do anything too illegal myself.'"

"Why did you call her the night she was murdered?" Fox asked.

"She never came through." Peterson picked up the cigarette package again and toyed with it as he spoke. "She was supposed to meet me with the ten grand. Said she'd be home that night, I was to call and we'd meet somewhere. I mean, this was important to me, you know? One day the bank's saying they're ready to close me up, put me out of business after years of pouring my sweat into this place, the next day Heather offers me enough money to pull me through, just for backing her up, holding on to some stuff, let some guy know she wasn't strictly freelance. I *counted* on that. Then I call and she doesn't answer and I know she's home because . . ."

Fox waited a moment before asking. "Because what?"

This time Peterson removed a cigarette from the package. "Because I went over to her place and rang the bell. About six o'clock." He placed the cigarette in his mouth, flicked the Zippo lighter and brought the flame to the tip. "She answered on the intercom and told me there was a change in plans, somebody else might be doing the deal for her. Told me to call later, she couldn't talk just then."

"You figured she was backing out?"

Peterson filled his lungs with smoke and exhaled slowly. "That've been like her."

"And you'd already spent the money she promised you."

"Something like that."

"Where'd you call her from, when you left the message on her machine?"

"Here. I came back here really pissed."

"If you've got anything else for me, I need to know," Fox said.

Peterson took another long puff on his cigarette and stared past the detective, lost in thought. Finally, he said, "Yeah," set the cigarette on the ashtray, then stood and walked to the door where his suit jacket was suspended on a brass hook. Reaching inside he withdrew a black leather wallet and returned to the desk. He took a business card from the billfold, glanced at it absently and tossed it to the detective. "She gave me this when we first started talking."

Tim Fox picked up the card, printed on heavy linen stock, and turned it over. The lettering was in gold script: Bedford Investments Incorporated. An address on Winthrop Square appeared beneath it followed by a name: Harley DeMontford. "This the man she was blackmailing?" Fox asked.

Peterson nodded. "He owns the joint, the Bedford outfit."

"Why'd you take so long to give it to me?"

The other man smiled and tapped the end of the cigarette on the ashtray. "Can't you figure it out?"

"You were thinking about running your own scam on the guy?"

"You got it. But it never got past the thinking stage."

"Smart move."

"Yeah, I'm an upstanding Boston citizen." Peterson placed the cigarette in his mouth. "Truth is, I woulda done it except when I heard all the details about what happened to her. How bad she was beaten up. If this guy's involved and he did that to Heather, maybe I should stay away from him."

"You figured this DeMontford, he's the one who killed her?"

"She was scared shitless of *some*body," Peterson said, squinting through the cigarette smoke at Fox. "Something about the guy or the deal really spooked her. And believe me, Heather didn't scare easy."

"We might have to talk to the woman you're living with again, doublecheck your alibi."

"You do that."

"You going to the funeral this afternoon?"

"Hell, no."

Fox rose to his feet. "We'll need to talk to you again."

"Anytime."

Fox was at the door when Peterson said, "The bank's shuttin' me down, end of the month, looks like. Coulda held them off with the money Heather promised."

"Sorry to hear that," Fox said. "Things are tough all over."

Peterson swore under his breath and stabbed the ashtray with his cigarette.

"You want me to make some more coffee?"

Billie was speaking to McGuire but her eyes were fixed on the stained gray rug beneath her bed. She lay on her stomach, her head over the edge of the mattress, one arm dangling to the floor, a finger tracing patterns in the cheap carpeting. A bed sheet lay across her lower body, placed there by McGuire, who reached to stroke her shoulder before rolling onto his back.

McGuire said, "No, thanks." He was looking up at the ceiling, finished in cheap stucco-like white paint, creating patterns by joining with imaginary lines the small gravelly lumps scattered randomly above him. A triangle there, a parallelogram here, and over there a diamond . . .

"Lemme guess," Billie said. "You never had this problem before, right?" When McGuire didn't answer Billie rolled on her side, facing him. Her voice had lost its warmth, its caring tone, its seductiveness. "I mean, isn't that what you're supposed to say? 'Gee, I never had this problem before.'" Charging each word with sarcasm. "'I've always been able to get a diamond cutter up, first snap of a brassiere.' That's what you're supposed to say, right?"

"Billie, I'm sorry." McGuire rubbed his eyes with one hand. "I'm really sorry."

"You know how many guys I've had up here in the last five, six months? You know how many I've invited home with me?"

"No idea."

JOHN LAWRENCE REYNOLDS

"One, that's all. Well, one plus you. No, two. Okay, two guys and you, that's only three in, what'd I say, four, five months? What I'm sayin' is, I'm no slut, Joe. No cheap lay. I gotta care about the guy before I let him into my bedroom, you hear what I'm sayin'?"

"You want me out of here, Billie, I'm going."

Billie rolled onto her back and folded her arms across her chest. "I mean, hell, Joe, you gotta see my point. Six times a day I get up on that goddamn stage and show my crotch to a bunch of guys I ain't never seen before and hope to hell I never see again and I know I'm turnin' them on. I *know* it. They're all picturin' themselves with me in bed. I take *care* of this body, Joe, you see that? I'm not stuffin' myself with grease, I don't smoke too much, I do fifty sit-ups a day. Guys appreciate it, right?"

"I appreciate it, Billie." McGuire sounded weary, ready to roll over and sleep.

"Yeah, well, your cock doesn't."

As soon as she said it, Billie felt like a shit and she reached across to stroke his face with her hand.

"I'm sorry," she said. Then, "It's the drugs, isn't it? The drugs can do that, can't they?"

"Probably," McGuire said.

"So drop 'em."

"I get pain. Too much pain. Migraines, they feel like."

"And you start throwin' up, right?"

"The pain gets that bad, yeah, I do."

"And you get the shakes, you sweat like a pig, your ears start to ring."

McGuire turned his head slowly to look into Billie's eyes.

171

"You're wired, you dumb shit," Billie told him. "You're fuckin' fried."

"I'm not a junkie."

"Yeah, and these melons on my chest aren't tits either, I just got a couple a swollen glands. Who're you kiddin'? You got so many chemicals in your system, no wonder your dick's in a coma. Same thing happened to Gene, my boyfriend, when he was usin'. It's all connected, McGuire. You want drugs, you forget about screwin'. You wanta get it on, you better cut back on the chemistry. Hell, every basket case on the street knows that except you."

"I'm not taking that much," McGuire said lamely.

Billie erupted into a long rattling sarcastic laugh that descended into a racking coughing fit until she rose from the bed and walked to the bathroom, tears in her eyes, McGuire turning his head to avoid the sight of her nakedness.

Bedford Investments Incorporated said the sign on the twin walnut slab doors as Tim Fox pushed through them to enter a dimly lit reception area finished in deep reds and gray tweeds. The woman behind the reception desk looked up at him brightly until he showed her his detective badge, slid a card across to her and asked to see Mr. DeMontford.

"He's out of town," she replied. "I don't expect him back until tomorrow."

"Where is he?" Fox demanded.

"Florida."

"You know his hotel?"

"Yes, but he won't be there right now. He's in meetings all afternoon."

Fox pointed at his card. "You call him, you tell him I want to talk to him. Either he calls me or I'll send somebody to find him."

The woman bit her lip. "Will he know what this is about?"

"Damn right." Fox flashed her his warmest smile and left.

TEN

McGuire lay back with his eyes closed, listening to the pelting of water against the plastic curtain surrounding the tub as Billie took her shower.

Of all McGuire's qualities ascribed over the years by friends and enemies alike, weakness had never been among them. He had been praised and condemned for his stubbornness, lauded and criticized for his inability to compromise, admired and rejected for his refusal to play politics with colleagues. Depending on the source, McGuire was brave, foolish, tragic, heroic, perceptive, intuitive, bullheaded and any of a hundred other contrasting and contradictory qualities.

But never weak.

Which was how he felt now.

There were reasons, he told himself. There were always reasons. And he began to number them now, reclining on Billie's bed with his eyes closed.

He began with the realization that he had never stopped loving Gloria, his first wife; awareness of this fact had crept within his marrow during the long vigil by her deathbed in a lonely room at Mass General.

Janet Parsons' rejection of him a year later, after they both escaped to Green Turtle Cay in the Bahamas, had left him questioning his assumptions of independence and self-reliance. Ignoring McGuire's pleas to stay, she had returned to Boston alone. McGuire had loved Janet, something he never admitted to her. He justified his aloofness by telling himself that love, like happiness, resonated loudest in memory. Janet, the first woman to make detective sergeant and now married to Ralph Innes, loving and nursing him through the physical and psychological trauma of being wounded in a fusillade of shots on a soft evening in California three years ago.

McGuire was there that night in Palm Springs. He heard the shots fired, heard Ralph's screams of agony as the bullets carved through his abdomen. That was all McGuire had done. Listened. Absorbed. Survived. It's all I *could* have done, McGuire assured himself again and again, even now, years later. I was unarmed, handcuffed to a corpse.

And it was true. But there was no escape from the shame and sense of failure the memory generated in McGuire, and it gnawed at him like a rodent.

What had he felt for Micki, his second wife? Little, until recently. Years before, after leaving Gloria, McGuire had reached for Micki with perhaps the most common and forgivable of motives: a lonely confused man stumbling into middle age, seeking to boost his ego with the casual giddiness and slim beauty of a much younger woman. Micki had been a narcotic for McGuire, a prescribed cure for an incurable affliction caused by time and healed only by love or death, whichever arrived first.

But the healing process was incomplete, with nasty side effects, eruptions of rancor and fevers of jealousy until Micki left him and McGuire teetered for several days on the fulcrum between despair that she had abandoned him and satisfaction that he had finally driven her away.

And now when McGuire held back the rising tide of pain with Django's drugs, he acknowledged the deeper currents that drove his addiction, the sluggish flows of despair and solitude that ran through his soul, the dark side of him he had tried to deny throughout his life.

It was only when emerging from the depths of sedation that McGuire surrendered to this deeper blackness of his being, and encountering it was reason enough to sink again into oblivion. Because he knew the source of his despair was also the source of his abiding anger, and the knowledge that these twin forces powered his psyche, sweeping tenderness and compassion aside, had begun to frighten him in recent years. There was a time when they had been enjoined with an almost intrusive intuition, and the combination produced a superb police detective, a crossbreed of a man with narrow and incisive talents who, like a natural athlete, could demonstrate his abilities again and again but could never explain them, never teach them to another in step-by-step detail, not once, not ever.

Now McGuire's intuition, his most powerful and positive quality, was blunted by drugs whose effects were like mind music that enabled him to dance to Django's tune, permitted him to trace a weaving, stumbling walk through each day, a frolic performed with a crooked smile on his face and a thousand-yard stare in his eyes. Anger and despair were held at bay by the same chemical cocktail until they would explode unbidden and unbridled, as they had the previous night when he discovered the man beating MaryLou with a rubber hose and rode him like a sled down the stairs, gliding on the bird shit, releasing all that had been pent up within him in an eruption of fury and justice.

The shower noises ceased. McGuire closed his eyes again.

"How ya doin'?"

He opened them to see Billie standing naked in the open bathroom door, rubbing her wet hair with a neon-pink towel.

"I'm okay." McGuire lay his forearm across his eyes. "I'm okay."

"Listen, I gotta go downtown, pick up a few things, then I'm goin' to the club. I got a one o'clock start." Billie reached for a white terrycloth robe and slipped into it. "Dewey wants me to, I might work a double shift, I dunno. You gonna drop by later'n see me?"

"Maybe." He watched clusters of stars erupt behind his eyes and he listened to the panpipes ringing in his ears, sustained notes played unbidden in the blackness of his mind, the sound echoing as though reaching him from deep within a thick forest.

"Do whatcha want. Just make sure the door's locked before you go, okay?"

McGuire said okay and he remained motionless, not opening his eyes, not making any movement at all, even when Billie, fully dressed in tight white jeans, pink sweater and waist-length coyote fur coat bent to kiss him lightly on the cheek. He heard her walk to the door and leave and he counted to twenty before rising from the bed and walking purposefully to the medicine cabinet. He chose three vials of pills, stumbled once on his way to the kitchen where he poured himself a large glass of orange juice from the refrigerator and retreated to the bed again. Then he tuned Billie's clock radio to a jazz station in Cambridge, fluffed the pillows behind him, swallowed four capsules of meperidine and lay back with his eyes closed.

The world would make another revolution on its axis and McGuire would refuse to record or acknowledge it.

To avoid sensations of feeling—pain, concern, sorrow, affection—you first become numb.

Numbness was no longer an absence of sensation to McGuire. It was a chosen response, a comfort zone, a refuge.

Tim Fox glanced up the street at the gray van where an ID man was preparing to videotape mourners arriving for Heather Lorenzo's funeral. Then he entered the funeral chapel and slid along a pew next to two grim-faced men who nodded to him in silence.

One of the men was from Internal Affairs and the other from ID. The Internal Affairs man had a thick black mustache squared-off like a formal bow tie tucked beneath his nose and a Hungarian name Tim Fox could never pronounce correctly. The ID man was a bearded computer nerd named Brookmyer. Fox, Brookmyer and the Hungarian together represented one third of the mourners.

At the front of the small chapel sat Micki Lorenzo, staring straight ahead at a point somewhere above her sister's coffin. A row behind her were the photographer Posner and his assistant Jill, who was hissing something at Posner, her face contorted in anger. Gregory Weiner, Heather's landlord, sat against the far wall, studying his fingernails. In the corner of a pew furthest from the coffin, Stana Tomasevich sat watching the others.

The sound system was playing a creaky pretaped version of a Bach organ prelude. Brookmyer glanced sideways at the black detective, used his pinky finger to push his black-rimmed glasses up to the bridge of his nose and nodded again.

"Won't get much out of this," Fox said, looking from Brookmyer to the Hungarian, whose name Fox recalled was Zelinka. "Aren't enough people here to fill the hearse."

Brookmyer nodded again.

"All we'll wind up with is a bunch of snapshots," Fox said, glancing around. He was wasting his time.

Zelinka leaned across Brookmyer and spoke to Fox. "I happened to see Eddie Vance before coming over here. He wants to speak to you, something about your new partner. Asked me to tell you."

Fox sat back in the pew and scowled.

"You got anything?"

It was Brookmyer, looking straight ahead at the coffin as he spoke.

"What, on the victim?" Tim Fox asked, and Brookmyer nodded. Zelinka remained bent from the waist, staring across Brookmyer at Fox with sad brown eyes.

Fox reached for his wallet, withdrew the business card Steve Peterson had given him and passed it to Zelinka. "You recognize him?" he asked the I.A. man. Brookmyer looked at the card with interest before the Hungarian took it from Fox's hands.

"I know it, the man's name," Zelinka said. "Not the company, just the name."

"Where? You remember where? On a case, something active, what?"

The Hungarian shrugged.

"I can do a global search when I get back," Brookmyer said. He withdrew a pen and small notepad from an inside jacket pocket and wrote Harley DeMontford. "Let you know then."

Fox nodded and extended his hand to retrieve the card from Zelinka. "Do that for me, okay?" he said to Brookmyer. "Leave something in my electronic mail at Berkeley if I'm not back."

A minister whom Fox considered far too young to be wearing religious vestments stepped onto the platform from behind a purple curtain, a prayer book in his hand, and he stood in front of the microphone, smiling uncertainly. "We are gathered here today, friends of our departed sister Heather . . ." he began, and Tim Fox folded his arms and stared at the ceiling.

* * *

Micki Lorenzo approached Fox's car outside the funeral home just as he was about to start the engine. She wore a two-piece dark blue knit suit with a black shoulder bag and she bent from the waist to speak to him.

"Joe hasn't called me at all," she said. "I thought he would. He was with Ollie and Ronnie yesterday but he never went back last night, and I heard he was in some sort of fight at the place where he lives now."

"He saved a girl's life," Tim Fox said. "Caught a pervert beating a hooker to death with a rubber hose. Nearly killed the guy." He smiled. "Joe's feeling better. Better'n the guy whose voice box he nearly crushed anyway. Joe's probably hiding for a while, trying to stay out of the limelight."

"That's just like him, isn't it? Always wants to be the hero, then doesn't know how to handle it." Miki's mood changed, became sober. "I'd like to see him, talk to him."

"Where you staying?"

"I was in a tourist home over on Marlborough. But I might move into Heather's now that it's cleaned up . . ." She withdrew a thin black pen from her purse and scribbled a telephone number on the back of a pharmacy receipt. "If you see Joe or if you're talking to him, would you have him call me? I can't go to that place where he lives, not by myself anyway . . . ."

"I'll tell him," Tim Fox said.

"Are you coming to the cemetery?" she asked him.

Fox shook his head and smiled.

"You were only here because it's your case, weren't you?" she said. "And those two over there, the ones who sat with you. That's the only reason they came."

"That's right." Fox started the car.

"I'll bet . . ." Micki hesitated and began again. "I'll bet if all the men Heather loved over the past three, four years, I'll bet if they'd come to her funeral the place would've been so crowded, you couldn't get a seat."

"Loved?" Tim Fox asked, his eyebrows arched.

"You know what I mean," Micki said. "God, even her ex-husbands and her other clients didn't come. None of them."

"Was she that bad?" Tim Fox asked.

"I guess she was," Micki said, and walked back toward the hearse, her head down, her slim ankles teetering slightly on her high-heeled shoes.

The meperidine dose was temporary death, a drifting into blackness which promised no dreams and no awareness until McGuire felt himself rising upward again, with sudden and unbidden release, into the light. It was a return journey made with a sense of regret, and McGuire believed that if there were any benefit to be derived from addiction, it was a dilution of the fear of dying.

McGuire squinted his eyes against the glare penetrating Billie's bedroom window, then closed them again and listened to the sounds of a world intent on life and sensation. Traffic noises in the street, music from an apartment somewhere in the ancient tenement building, pigeons cooing to each other on a ledge beyond the curtains.

It was mid-afternoon but time was unimportant. McGuire remained motionless for several minutes before trying to rise and falling back to the bed. His second effort succeeded and he slid from the bed and walked unsteadily toward the bathroom. Fiorinal, he remembered. He had seen some Fiorinal in Billie's medicine cabinet. Lovely stuff.

Baby food. Fat Eddie was living on baby food now. Yogurt and bananas, custard and tofu. No fiber, no meat, no taste.

He opened a drawer in his desk and removed the half-finished cup of peach yogurt left from lunch. God, two days of this and he was already hating the stuff, he'd give anything right now for a cheeseburger or even a strip of beef jerky.

But the maelstroms that once swept through his intestines had begun to dissipate and that was a relief. A massive relief. He lifted a spoonful of yogurt to his mouth and was about to force himself to taste it when someone knocked on his office door. Before Fat Eddie could respond and put away the yogurt, Tim Fox entered.

"You wanted to see me," Fox said, striding toward Vance's desk.

Again Fat Eddie was impressed with the black detective's style. Fox was wearing a gray sharkskin suit over a maroon pin-striped shirt and paisley tie. Who the hell dresses him in the morning, Vance wondered, assuming that only a woman, and a cultured one at that, could choose a man's wardrobe with such flair and elegance.

"What's that you're eating?" Fox asked, slouching in one of the chairs facing Vance's desk.

Fat Eddie held the container up for the detective to see. "Yogurt," he said. "Great stuff. Good for you, full of vitamins. I'm eating healthy now, cutting back on cholesterol and animal fats." He sampled a spoonful. "This stuff is *really* good. I have more in the fridge. Want some?"

Tim Fox grinned. "Naw, I think I'll stick to ribs and collard greens, thanks."

Vance smiled, unsure of the black detective's humor, then shrugged and set the yogurt and spoon back in the drawer of his desk. "I'm having a problem adjusting the staff list," he said, stroking his mustache to remove droplets of yogurt. "There's Stanton, you know him? Young guy, just got his detective status last year?"

Fox nodded, his face blank.

"Trouble is, Stanton's got a trial next week so he'll be unavailable for a while. Then there's Orwin, used to work with Sergeant Parsons, but she'll be taking a leave of absence for a few months—"

"Janet?" Tim Fox asked. "What's up?"

Fat Eddie leaned across his desk and lowered his voice like a racetrack tout. "She's pregnant."

Fox smiled and tilted his head. "Hey Eddie," he said. "It's all right. Being pregnant is legal now, haven't you heard?"

Vance sat back in his chair. "It's Ralph Innes's—" he began.

"Hell, I *hope* it is," Fox laughed. "They've been together for a couple of years now."

Fat Eddie nodded quickly. "Anyway, how do you feel about working with Orwin?"

"Better'n Donovan."

184

"I have to deal with that, too. He's pretty upset, Phil is. He felt he was making progress on this Lorenzo woman."

"Bullshit." Fox spat the word at Fat Eddie, then sat back in the chair. "He talked to the victim's ex-husband two days ago and didn't get a damn thing except the same old alibi. I saw the husband today and picked up a lead on the guy who was spooking her, the best connection we've got so far. Donovan missed it completely."

"I asked Donovan to transfer all of his files to you."

"I haven't seen anything yet."

"If you don't have them by the end of the day, let me know. Meanwhile, fill Orwin in on what you've got on this Lorenzo thing and anything else that's on your plate, bring him up to speed, start teaming with him tomorrow." Fat Eddie removed the yogurt container from his desk drawer again. "Sure you won't try some of this?"

The Gypsy's voice was a drumbeat, a pinched, tight, rhythmic sound penetrating the wall behind Django's head. "Uhn, uhn, uhn, uhn," over and over, a tattoo of pain or pleasure, Django could never tell.

Nearly an hour ago Grizzly had tossed Django half a bottle of that good Canadian whiskey, comes in a glass container shaped like a crown, ritzy stuff. Then Grizz went back into his room, the one next to Django's in the Warrenton Hotel, where the Gypsy had been waiting with something shot up her arm and something else wrapped around her body, maybe black leather. Django had seen her in the black leather outfit once, sitting on the edge of the bed waiting for Grizzly, looking glum and crazy, pink flesh spilling out between a laced-up vest and trousers with no crotch, waiting for Grizz, a strange sight, strange, yes.

Word had it, Django'd heard Dewey or somebody say it, that the Gypsy was North American Indian, Mohawk or Iroquois, one of those northern tribes. Liked to sniff gasoline out of a glass jar, walked around the little Maine town carrying it with her like it was lunch. Got on a bus one day, higher'n two hawks flying kites, stuffed herself behind the rear seat and fell asleep. She woke up in the Greyhound maintenance yard and Grizzly spotted her on the street trying to figure out where the hell she was, how the hell she got there.

She was kind of pretty back then, nice dark eyes, skin the color of faded chestnuts, long black shiny hair. In a month Grizzly owned her, had her doing everything he wanted her to do, doing things she couldn't dream up herself, doing them with people she'd never met in her worst high-octane nightmares. Six months later she looked twice her age and if you stared into her eyes long enough, if the pupils were wide enough and their gaze steady, you could look over the rim of the hell that was her life and know somewhere beneath it, broken into cinders, were memories of a young girl from the north country who had once sat on logs over crystal ponds in the summer sun and watched tadpoles swim beneath her bare feet, who had cuddled in her mother's lap on cold winter nights, hearing wolves howl and moose crash through the brush.

Grizzly, as he had done for Django and Garce and others, had given the Gypsy salvation and sanctuary, but at what cost? Now he extracted pleasure from her in the same manner as he extracted money from Django and the others, leaving enough for them to cling to his network, his protection, his demands of unquestioning obedience.

"We be dry," Grizzly had told Django, and Django wondered again what Grizzly knew and how he knew it and where he learned it, but there was no asking Grizzly, never.

Django never asked because that was one of the rules, the ones that came with the deal, with everything that Django owed Grizzly from nearly two years ago. Day before Christmas it was, just a month after Django arrived in Boston, looking for a way to put some extra money together to send back to Buffalo, to Elsie and the two boys.

Careful, fool, Django told himself, remembering. Careful, careful. There be some doors you don't ever want to open, some alleys you don't ever want to walk down, not again, not ever.

Django's eyelids quivered and he lifted his left hand, the one they had broken under the wheel of the truck and held in the fire, and lay the crippled hand across his eyes and felt the scar tissue, like corrugated paper, against the skin of his face.

"Uhn, uhn, uhn." The Gypsy was singing on the bed with Grizzly, and Django's eyes began to sting and he remembered, ignoring his own warning.

"Dealin' on the street," Django told Elsie over the pay telephone, long distance back to Buffalo, and

Elsie said, "Hush, you don't know who listenin'."
Elsie was worried, but she was happy when Django
sent her the first thousand later that week and then
the next thousand a week later, sending it back for
Elsie to spend on clothes for the boys and to put
food in their bellies and save the rest in a bank
account, using the money to keep the boys healthy,
keep the dream alive.

He was working strange turf there on Dorchester,
other people's turf in a strange city, but you had to
take risks, that's what business is about. His brother-
in-law Percy sent the coke in from Buffalo, bus ship-
ments marked Books and Clothing and Personal
Affex, Percy never much of a speller, but that was
good, that was okay. Django was living in a room
on Mass Avenue, cooking the coke into crack and
dealing it along the river, selling to college kids and
white suburban guys in their Buicks and Jap mini-
vans so they could take some back to the wife or
girlfriend in Newton or Waltham, try some of this
here nigger sin. But most of it he sold to black
dudes who needed the stuff, they'd rip off whoever,
whatever was around to get a boost, a bit of that
good crack, smoke it out of an empty Pepsi can,
that's what they lived for, that's what life was all
about, that's *all* life was about.

Two different times the competition warned him,
couple of heavy black brothers in Raiders jackets,
pulling up to the curb in a beat-up Ford, calling him
over, telling him they knew all about his rat's-ass
tenement back in Buffalo, telling him he don't get
the cream if he ain't on the team, and Django'd nod
and smile and dance away for a day or two.

But he had to go back to the same place, no choice about it. Regular customers, they came by and if Django wasn't there they got spooked or went somewhere else and *stayed* there because you needed loyalty in the business and Django was loyal, yes indeed.

The third time the brothers came around they arrived in a dump truck, three of them this time, where'd a bunch of young black dudes get a truck like that? Django never knew. One put a gun to Django's head, big mother of a gun, the end of the barrel in his ear, another one of the brothers gripped his hair and yanked his head back, the third twisted Django's arm up between his shoulder blades until Django screamed and when they started dragging him he ran with them, anything to cut the pain, ran with them to the truck and through the open door. They flung him to the floor where he lay while two of them kicked him all the way to the bridge where Dorchester crossed the channel, taking the last exit and turning into a dead-end lane.

"Told ya, motherfucker," one kept saying. "Told ya."

They tossed him from the truck and jumped on him before he could crawl away and he was flat on his back, one of the brothers standing on his fore-arm, a second pulling a gray container, looked like a coffee thermos, out from behind the seat of the truck. The third dude stayed behind the wheel and started backing the truck up, swinging it closer to Django lying there, until the dual wheels crushed Django's hand against the pavement with a sound like popping corn, pop pop pop, like that, and the truck rumbled on and stopped ten feet away.

"Shoulda done the other," said the dude with the gray container that wasn't a thermos bottle but a propane torch, because now there was a quiet blue flame hissing from a brass tube on the end of the container. "Shoulda done his right one."

They played the flame across Django's shattered hand, back and forth, and they watched Django writhe and scream with no expression on their faces, none at all, until the propane was exhausted and the flame died. One of the dudes said, "Shit," and shook the container before throwing it away where it clattered against a brick wall and landed at the feet of Grizzly who'd been standing there watching it all from a doorway, the Gypsy behind him.

The guy in the truck recognized Grizzly who held his hand out to the side and the Gypsy drew an ass-kicking Colt from a pocket of her parka and placed it in Grizzly's hand. In one motion, his eyes never leaving the kid in the truck, Grizzly raised the Colt to shoulder level and it jerked in his hand and a copper-jacketed forty-five splashed the dude's brains all over the inside of the cab before anybody could react.

"You boys're too far from home," Grizzly said, and he fired again, this time into one of the other dude's knees, and his howls of pain echoed off the warehouse walls over and over. "Warned you to keep your asses clear a me. Warned you what I'd do, you pull this shit around me."

The third dude was already gone, snap, like that, running like hell out onto Dorchester because he knew Grizzly, knew the man's rep, knew he was right, the man was *right*, you didn't go into Grizzly's area unless he knew you were coming, gave you the okay word. But that's what they planned to do, that's what they'd been *told* to do, take this dumb little mother from Buffalo and dump him on Grizzly's turf, and if he lives, you let him walk around town, let everybody know what happens when you don't get on the team.

That's how you played the game, the game had *rules*, everybody knew that. Django broke the rules and he paid, and then the dudes in the truck, they broke Grizzly's rules and they paid. But a week later, a week after Grizzly and the Gypsy took Django to their place and wrapped his hand up and waited for it to heal, Elsie paid and Elsie didn't *break* any rules, Elsie had been four hundred miles *away*, but Elsie paid anyway. They made her pay and made her little boys watch and the guys who did it, friends of the dudes in the dump truck, they took pictures of it all and sent them to Grizzly who showed them to Django, the Gypsy taking them out of an inside pocket because these pictures were *bad* and Grizzly never carried anything bad on him, never. Another one of Grizzly's rules.

"Word come with the pictures," Grizzly said. "You okay here, it's over, account's been settled, hear me? This shit started 'fore you came along, between me an' them, you just got yourself sucked in. But you don't go back to Buffalo, understand? And you don't go back on the river, not your turf. You go back, either place, it starts again and this time they maybe get your little boys." Grizzly put a big paw on Django's shoulder. "Give you a chance," Grizzly said. "Me and the Gypsy could use a buddy, a partner. No crack, understand. You handle pills and such, lotta action happening there. Little bit a bread in it for you, little taste now and then, and protection. Specially protection."

Django had nodded, staring dry-eyed at the dirty bandages on his hand, the pus oozing through, the fingers twisted like a chicken's claw, and he avoided looking at the pictures of what was left of Elsie.

Alive, he told himself. You be alive, the boys be alive. That counts. That *counts*, damn it. You a little different, a little crazy maybe. He knew that, he knew he had to go a little crazy now to save himself, keep himself from living those few minutes with the brothers and the dump truck over and over in his mind, keep himself from thinking of Elsie being raped and cut open while the boys watched and screamed. He would celebrate the fact that he survived by dancing through life, one way or another he told himself. He would let whatever music that entered his mind carry him above all he had suffered, and he would dance to it.

Django closed his eyes and rolled onto his right side, his scarred and crippled left hand against his chest, and willed himself to sleep.

Gerry Orwin was an experienced cop who never played the political game or tried to raise his profile in the department, which was why he had not moved past sergeant after ten years as a full detective. That was how Tim Fox assessed it, and he was quietly satisfied to have Orwin as a partner.

They began their review at Orwin's desk in the new open-concept office arrangement that Fat Eddie had installed a year earlier and that every detective hated because there was never any privacy. When Fox suggested they retreat to the basement lounge for coffee he and Orwin gathered the file summaries and spent two hours in the small, harshly lit room, Fox pointing out key details on the Lorenzo murder, autopsy report and interviews along with three other investigations that were still open on his docket. Orwin nodded his balding head and filled several pages of yellow notepaper with neat and tidy handwriting.

When they finished, Fox noted it was almost six o'clock; he slapped Orwin on the back, arranged to meet him at eight the next morning and trotted three floors up the stairs to Homicide. A scattering of detectives were still bent over paperwork at their desks, leaning back in their chairs with telephone receivers at their ears or huddled in knots of two and three, plastic coffee cups in their hands and intense expressions on their faces.

At his desk Fox dialed his home telephone and while it rang he punched his electronic mail code into the keyboard of his computer terminal. The messages began scrolling past just as Adelaide Fox, Tim's wife of four years, answered the telephone. Tim began to explain that he would be home within an hour, then paused and leaned closer to the terminal.

"Hold on a minute," he said to Adelaide, and read the message on the screen again, the one from Brookmyer, the text preceded by the case number for the Lorenzo murder:

Re: 892-774/Lorenzo—Subject of inquiry, H. DeMontford, under restricted access code, reference 1415-94. Not to be contacted without notification of

> Felony Team Green. Cross-reference
> between two files reveals common subject
> you may wish to pursue, one Joseph P.
> McGuire, former BPD officer, last known
> official address, 217 Medford Street,
> Revere Beach, MA.

His wife was talking to him, something about Cecilia's teacher, but Fox wasn't listening, he was digesting the text in front of him, absorbing all that it meant and what it might lead to.

Team Green was code for undercover officers whose activities were isolated from other departments for a number of reasons—including the possibility that their work could reveal the involvement of police officers in the crimes being investigated. Fox could obtain access to the DeMontford file in Team Green by citing the Lorenzo murder investigation, but that could only be arranged through Fat Eddie, who had departed for home an hour earlier.

What's McGuire up to? Fox asked himself.

"Is that okay?" Adelaide was asking him, and Tim said, "What?"

"Is it okay if Cecilia stays with your mother?" she repeated. "Are you listening to me?"

"No, I wasn't," Fox confessed. "Look, I may not make it there before eight after all. Give Cissy a goodnight kiss for me and I'll pick up some of those pink jelly beans she likes, slip 'em to her for breakfast tomorrow."

"You're spoiling the heck out of her," his wife said, and Fox told her, "Yeah, but it worked for you, didn't it?"

194

When he hung up, he called Ollie Schantz in Revere Beach at McGuire's last known address. Ronnie Schantz told him she hadn't seen McGuire since the previous day but she'd heard about him saving the poor girl being beaten to death in his room and Ollie wanted to talk to him about it, hear all the details. Fox told her he would pass on the message. The file on MaryLou's beating provided him with Billie's address and telephone number, but after counting seven rings he hung up, snatched his Burberry from the armchair where he had tossed it and rode the elevator down to the basement garage, staring fixedly at the floor and frowning.

The Gypsy's moaning had long ago ceased and when Django awoke the light beyond the window had faded. He rose and stretched, his belly empty, his mind free of the spiders that had been whirling in his head, and slipped into his long leather coat.

He tapped lightly on the door of the adjacent room before opening it. The Gypsy was curled in the only chair in the room, wrapped in a blanket from the bed, a cigarette in her hand and her tired eyes fixed on the television screen.

"Where Grizz?" Django asked, and the Gypsy shrugged her shoulders. "I'm goin' to the Bird," Django said and she nodded her head.

Django turned to leave before looking back at her. "Hey, Gyps," he said. "You all right?"

He hadn't noticed the tears at first but there they were, making her cheeks shine.

She didn't answer, kept staring at some dumb game show on the TV, running her teeth across her bottom lip over and over, like she was skinning it, cleaning it.

Django reached out a hand to touch her but she pulled away like his hand was a shaft of hot metal, like she was an animal fearing a whipping, and Django told himself to stay back, fool, leave it alone.

"Keep cool, Gyps," Django said and gave her a smile, but now her head and eyes were in motion, swinging wildly from side to side, scanning the room like someone following the flight of a frenzied bat.

The detritus of the previous night's police investigation remained scattered on the ground behind the club, lengths of yellow plastic tape marked POLICE LINE DO NOT CROSS, an empty photographic film box, plastic coffee cups and gauze bandage wrappers.

Tim Fox glanced up at McGuire's room. No light shone from within but the door was ajar, and he began to climb the steps, one by one, avoiding the bird droppings and the puddle of congealed blood on the landing where the man who had beaten MaryLou had landed face down with McGuire on his back.

Django saw the lights of the Flamingo ahead, the scene different from last night, everybody gone, things back to normal. He remembered McGuire, the Jolt in a fog from those pills but still sharp enough, still mean enough to handle that creep who'd been doing MaryLou. Damn, Jolt's a bad cat, Django told himself. Get a man like him on your side 'n you can ride anything out. Hell, between Jolt and Grizzly, Django'd never have to fear anybody on the street again.

Gotta tell him that, Django thought. Gotta let him know he's still my man, he's the meanest, explain to him how it ain't me, how Grizzly said we be dry for a while and Jolt shouldn't take it serious like.

Don't wanta upset Jolt. No sir.

He turned down the alleyway, moving through the darkness lightly and without sound, like a bird.

From inside the club Fox heard the thump-thump of music urging another young woman to strut across the stage while men watched, the girl holding a hand on her waist and beaming her one smile, the only one she owned.

At the top of the stairs the heel of Fox's loafer caught in a strip of the metal strapping that formed the landing; Fox stumbled forward against the open door and into McGuire's darkened room, feeling clumsy and silly but keeping his balance, lifting his head just as a figure burst from McGuire's small bathroom and fired once, the sound of the shot like a cannon's roar and the muzzle flash like a fleeting dawn in Fox's eyes.

ELEVEN

They came for McGuire at ten o'clock, using Billie's key to get into the apartment and clumping down the hall to the bedroom, four uniformed cops, their police specials out and held in a two-handed grip, moving them from side to side. McGuire lifted his head lazily from the pillow when they entered the room, thinking maybe he was in the midst of some codeine nightmare, until two of them yanked the covers from him and two others prodded him naked from the bed and ordered him to lie face down on the floor while the others stood in their balanced stance, their revolvers aimed at his head.

"What's going on?" McGuire managed to say as they cuffed him, his hands behind his back. None of them spoke but one wrapped him in a blanket before they half-carried, half-dragged him outside where a crowd had gathered on the street, drawn by the sight of three cruisers with gumball lights on their roofs scattering red and blue flashes across the walls of the other buildings.

The codeine hangover was so heavy that even sitting with his hands cuffed painfully behind his back and being bounced from side to side in the rear of the cruiser, McGuire managed to sleep through most of the trip to Berkeley Street.

When they arrived he was conscious enough to stumble down the corridor from the basement parking garage, suspended between two of the uniformed cops, to the interrogation room where Fat Eddie, Orwin, Phil Donovan and Zelinka, the Internal Affairs investigator, were waiting. Zelinka was dressed in a dark suit, crisp shirt and patterned tie. Donovan was in sweatshirt and jeans while Fat Eddie, looking as uncomfortable as McGuire had ever seen him, shifted his weight nervously from side to side in a far corner. Vance was wearing a knit golf shirt whose fabric stretched across his stomach and casual slacks. Two uniformed police officers stood in the opposite corner from Vance, their hands behind their backs.

They set McGuire on the folding chair in the middle of the room, snapped the cuffs off and, at a curt nod from Fat Eddie, left the room, closing the door behind them.

"The hell is this?" McGuire said, looking from Vance to Donovan to Zelinka. The blanket had fallen from his shoulders and McGuire pulled at one corner to conceal his nakedness. "Feel like a goddamn Roman."

"Would you like some coffee?" Fat Eddie Vance said, clipping his words and speaking in the deep voice that always made McGuire think he was talking from the bottom of his balls.

"Yeah." McGuire nodded. "Yeah, coffee would be good."

At a nod from Vance one of the uniforms left the room. McGuire lowered his head and ran his fingers through his hair.

"Where's the weapon?"

It was Donovan, staring at McGuire with his hard Irish eyes, his arms folded across his chest.

McGuire looked up. "Me? You talking to me?"

"That woman's room, the one you're living with," Fat Eddie said. "It's being searched for evidence."

"I'm not living with her," McGuire said. "Somebody tell me what this is all about."

"He died an hour ago," Donovan said.

"Who?" Jesus, his head hurt.

"Tim Fox."

McGuire raised his eyes to meet Donovan's. "Timmy?" Vance, Donovan, Zelinka and the remaining uniformed officer were staring back at McGuire. "Timmy?" McGuire repeated. "Jesus. What happened?"

Donovan exhaled noisily, dropped his hands and turned his back on McGuire.

"Tell us where you've been for the last four hours," Vance said.

"Been?" McGuire lowered his head and studied the floor. Tim Fox dead? Timmy was one of the best, Timmy was the kind of stand-up guy McGuire admired, Timmy didn't have an enemy in the department . . .

The door opened but no one looked up as the uniformed officer entered the room carrying a plastic cup of black coffee and a paper sack stuffed with McGuire's clothing. He crossed to the center of the room, placed the coffee cup in McGuire's trembling hands, set the clothing at McGuire's feet and retreated to a far corner.

McGuire raised the cup to his lips with both hands. The heat of the liquid scalded his tongue but his head began to clear and as it did the first rays of rising agony burned on the rim of his skull. "What happened to him?" he said, staring at the floor where his bare toes peeked out from under the hem of the blanket.

"You tell us, asshole—" Donovan began.

McGuire threw the coffee in an overhand arc and dove out of the chair at Donovan, the blanket slipping from his body, a demented, naked man weary of the pain and the humiliation, driven by fury from his private crevice of darkness into the light again.

"Are you perhaps feeling better?"

McGuire nodded in response to Rudy Zelinka. He was back in the interrogation room, showered and dressed, and he raised a hand to touch the bandage above his right eyebrow that covered the gash suffered when Orwin and the two uniforms wrestled him away from Donovan an hour earlier. He had consumed two cups of coffee since then with the awareness that, to a meperidine addict, caffeine not only stimulated consciousness but encouraged the pain to burn more fiercely and sear his nerve endings.

"I didn't do it," McGuire said.

"You and Doitch are beginning to make a believer of me," Zelinka said. He threw McGuire a tight smile. "Do you have any idea how many pills you took today?"

McGuire shook his head.

"There was an empty container of codeine on the floor of the bathroom in that apartment. Your woman friend says there were at least a dozen in it this morning."

"That many, huh?" McGuire looked around the perimeter of the room where Donovan was stroking a fresh bandage set across the bridge of his nose, his sweatshirt stained with blood. Fat Eddie sat in a folding chair and stared at the opposite wall.

"You are a serious addict," Zelinka said.

"No, I'm not," McGuire replied.

"If you weren't, Doitch says you should be dead by now."

"Just keep that red-haired son of a bitch away from me," McGuire said, tilting his head toward Donovan.

"Would you like him to leave?"

"I would like him to take out his goddamn liver with a chain saw."

Zelinka looked up at Donovan. "Would you mind excusing us for a few minutes?" he asked pleasantly.

Donovan glanced at Fat Eddie, who nodded once, and Donovan was out the door in four long strides.

"Tell me what happened," McGuire said, stroking his temples with the tips of his fingers. "To Timmy. Tell me what happened."

"Someone shot him as he entered your room. The shooter was inside. One to the chest. It severed the aortic artery, exited through his back. The detective choked to death on his own blood. The killer stepped over him on the way out."

"Weapon?"

"We don't know. We haven't found the bullet yet. Doitch thinks it's a thirty-eight."

"Who found him?"

"An old Oriental woman called it in. Lives in a tenement next to the Flamingo. Says she didn't see it happen. She finished her dinner, sat down by her window, saw Fox's feet extending through the door to your room, and called her daughter, who called us."

"What was Timmy doing at my place?"

"We were hoping you could tell us that," Fat Eddie said.

"No idea." A cleaver in his skull. That's what the pain had begun to feel like.

"Your name came up on a Felony Team Green code. Would you like to say something about it?" Zelinka said.

"Undercover? I'm not doing anything undercover." McGuire's neck grew damp and the room began to turn.

"You're cross-indexed on a Team Green file with a man named DeMontford."

"Never heard of him." The pain was a living thing now, creeping through the breach between skin and skull.

Zelinka studied McGuire as though pondering a puzzle. Then he said, "Would you like to come out of this clean?"

"Clean?" McGuire lowered his head.

Zelinka knelt in front of McGuire trying to catch his eye. "I don't think you've been in any shape to hit a barn door with a snow shovel lately, let alone shoot a man through the heart from twenty feet. But you've become something of a shit magnet, McGuire. Your sister-in-law's found dead with a recording of you threatening her on her answering machine. Which makes you a suspect. Then you rescue a young prostitute from a serial killer and turn his face into hamburger, so for a while you're a hero. The next night one of the best cops in the city is shot dead on the doorstep of your room, and you're a murder suspect again. And through it all, you know what else you've been?"

McGuire was unable to sit still. Adrenaline flowed through him like a river in flood and his skin grew damp with sweat.

"You know what you've been?" Zelinka demanded, thinking McGuire hadn't heard.

"I know what I'm going to be," McGuire said weakly.

"What?" Zelinka said just as McGuire leaned from the waist and vomited all over Zelinka's brand new honey-colored suede oxfords.

"Cold turkey it," Mel Doitch advised McGuire. The others had left, leaving McGuire alone with the overweight medical examiner. "Your best way. Drink liquids and eat light because you'll throw up a lot. Stay in a dark room. Give yourself two, three days, maybe a week. You want it badly enough, you can do it."

Ronnie Schantz drove down to Berkeley Street, bringing with her some clothing that McGuire had left from last summer. She clucked her tongue at the sight of him but said nothing except to ask if he was okay when he lowered his head between his knees. McGuire said, "Sure." Then she drove him in silence back to the small white frame house on Medford Street in Revere Beach.

It was after midnight when McGuire stretched out naked between the crisp white sheets of the guest room bed, a plastic bucket on the floor beside him, a container of orange juice on the night table. He lay there like a moth in a web while the entire menagerie of his nightmares battered against the inner walls of his head.

In the beginning, McGuire told himself, it wasn't his doing, he never sought it out, it was all due to lack of energy, an inability to care about anything, anything at all, and that made it passive and easier to accept.

Once he had believed in the wisdom of seizing life and shaking it until it did his bidding. By taking charge he would avoid being a victim, a goal that reflected his view of people as either victims or perpetrators, winners or losers, spectators or participants.

But over the years McGuire committed the unforgivable yet very human error of telling lies, rarely to others but often to himself. During the disintegration of his two marriages, the abandonment of his career in police work and his slide into barbiturate addiction, he assigned his destiny to others while telling himself it was all his choice, his decision. One of his decisions was to coast through the latter half of his life.

Coasting. He turned the word over and over in his mind, feeling the gyros in his head spin and his stomach turn and jerk like a wild horse being broken on the perimeter of a wheel. He was weary of pedaling uphill, of rising against the gravity of his own environment, lifting himself from the sullen violence of his parents' house to prominence as one of the most decorated police officers in Boston's history.

Two years ago he had grown tired and wanted only to coast for a while.

He closed his eyes and began to construct peaceful images in his mind. He visualized Micki lying on her side with him, her back to him, both of them naked, his arm slung over her body and his hand cupping one breast, the two of them fitted together like spoons in their bed, and the line he could see stretching straight and unbending toward the horizon, that was their life together.

Hours later the image appeared as a dream, both of them sleeping in this same darkened room, their backs to the door, and while they slept the door opened and someone entered the room to lay on the bed next to him, someone unknown and threatening. McGuire felt the bed sag beneath him from the weight of the visitor and he woke to discover he was in fact lying on his side in this room with no light. But there was no Micki pressed against him and he was torn between a sense of immediate loss and a fear that in fact someone *was* on the bed behind him. He listened to his own heart beating and tried to grasp the pain radiating from his brain stem and failed, and cautiously he rolled onto his back to confirm he was alone and safe in the small guest room of Ollie and Ronnie's house.

He lay trembling with resonating fear and nausea and when he grew sick to his stomach, the sound of his retching echoed loud and obscene in the small quiet house. Ronnie tapped at the door and asked if he was all right and McGuire assured her he was before drifting blessedly back to sleep again, free for a time of the pain.

He dreamed of his parents' home, the home of his childhood, set against the embankment leading down to railroad tracks which hummed like twin sets of steel strands that began in the shunting yard a half mile away and ended somewhere west of the passenger terminal. The metallic clash of boxcars and grunting diesel locomotives dominated the neighborhood, soothing in their immutable logic, their sense of ordered assembly, of defining a place for every element of a journey. For years as a child McGuire envied railroad workers for the logic of all that they did, the defined destinations, the fixed schedule of arrivals and departures, the imposed imperatives of their lives.

At the edge of the shunting yards several blocks away, a steel bridge carried streetcars across the expanse of the embankment, the railroad tracks like a river sunk beneath the level of the city, and when the streetcars crossed the bridge on late summer nights the unyielding sound of metal upon metal, steel wheels on steel tracks set in steel foundations, spoke to McGuire of escape and deliverance all through his childhood.

Now in his dream he heard the streetcars, the sound drifting in through the windows of the house, open to catch the cooling summer night air, and he felt the presence of his parents again, his father distant and brooding, his mother silent and curiously inert. Both were long dead and little mourned by McGuire, but in his dream he tried to rise and go to them and bury himself between them, seeking and dispensing love. He drifted up and out of the dream, waking with his cheeks wet and a sob poised to erupt in his chest. He swallowed the emotion, unaware of its origin and its intent, then he closed his eyes and imagined himself with Micki once more, safe in the knowledge that sleep would arrive before he would take her, naked to him, even in his imagination.

He woke several hours later, his memory flooded with a clear recollection of the railroad tracks again and an incident from his childhood.

Word had swept the neighborhood one Sunday morning that some boys had lain a dead dog across a rail beneath the Pearl Street bridge ahead of a late-night train. McGuire, nine years old, had run to the bridge and stacked three pieces of two-by-four and stood on them to peer over the railing.

The beagle lay on the tracks, its head and front paws on the gravel bed and the rest of the body between the rails, severed like a frankfurter divided by a kitchen knife. McGuire remembered the dog's brown eyebrows and white tail, and saw that its eyes were closed, the entire scene, viewed from twenty feet overhead, strangely calm and surreal.

The image haunted him still. Not the gore or the stunning reality. But how immaculate it all appeared. How easily acceptable the horror was.

He lay there perspiring and shaking, probing for the reserve of anger that had once fueled his resolve, a reservoir of strength that had been there to meet his need but had dissipated some time in his past. The hell with it, he told himself, the hell with it, the hell with it, and he rose from the bed, fell to his knees and rose again at the sound of footsteps outside his door.

"Joe?" Ronnie called. "Are you all right?"

He fell against the door, turned the knob and opened it, the glare from the overhead light in the hall shining off his body.

"My God, Joe, put some clothes on," Ronnie said, her eyes darting from the sight of him.

"I need some," McGuire said. He stretched out a hand, touched Ronnie's chenille robe until she pulled away, her head still turned.

"Joe, go back to bed . . ."

"Just two or three, Ronnie. Just a couple to get me through the night . . ."

"No," she said, and spun away. "I don't have any, and even if I had—"

"There's an all-night drugstore down the street . . ."

"Joe, don't even ask me—"

"*Goddamn it, you don't know what it's like!*"

At the sound of his anguish she stopped, breathed deeply and turned to stare at him, her eyes locked on his. "You go back in there and you wait until it's over," she said. "And that's that. Or you leave here now and you never come back to bother Ollie and me again. Never. And for God's sake, put some clothes on. You're embarrassing both of us."

"All right," he said. "Fuck you both. I'm . . . I'll get out, get the hell out of here."

He closed the door, angry at her refusal. But the anger opened another door and he stumbled back to the bed, determined to wait it out, to overcome the tyranny of the narcotic.

From the corner of the room he thought he heard a snuffling sound. In the shadows, he was sure he could see them, waited two small pigs and perhaps a dog, a sad beagle. "Where's the horse?" he asked. He grinned to himself and began to laugh, except the tears kept flowing and the laughter hung in his throat like a bone.

McGuire woke to a gray dawn. Ronnie entered the room and steadied him with a hand at his back while he sat up and sipped from a glass of juice before curling on his side again.

"Sorry," he said.

"About what?" Ronnie asked, fluffing his pillow.

"About last night."

"A bad dream," she said. "We both had the same bad dream." She paused at the doorway and permitted herself a sly smile. "But a little bit of mine was actually kind of fun."

When he lay back, shivers racked his body and his skin acquired a sheen of perspiration. Within an hour he vomited the juice into the bucket, leaning over the edge of the bed and retching uncontrollably. He was enveloped in a rankness that seeped from within him, rising through layers of perspiration, an aroma as warm and cloying and greasy as chicken soup.

The bed was an airship and a vault, and when he closed his eyes he felt himself simultaneously rising weightless and sinking within the folds of the bedclothes, held down like a small animal in a snare. The nausea rose within him again and he opened his eyes to steady himself. The room ceased its spinning but small articles began to move: the cornice molding slithered along the wall, the heavy oak-framed picture glided slowly to the floor and his clothing, tossed casually across the back of a rocking chair, rolled itself into a ball.

The rest of the day passed in short spells of sleep and violent spasms of sickness. In the evening Ronnie persuaded him to swallow a few spoonfuls of broth which McGuire managed to keep down until some time in the middle of the night when he awoke from a dream of Timmy Fox and Janet Parsons and McGuire together in Green Turtle Cay. He remembered nothing of the dream except the location and the people who had been there with him. When he fell asleep again he imagined himself walking on a floor constructed of writhing gray snakes whose bodies moved within a glassy slime and he felt himself sliding among them, knowing that to fall was to never rise.

He woke in the fading dusk light. His skin was dry and he shivered uncontrollably, feeling his body quiver as though driven by some unknown, ungoverned engine within him.

"Don't need to know why." Grizzly leaned against the door frame and stared past Django down the alley beyond the fire blazing in the steel drum. "Just need to *do*. You axed to *do* it, you *do* it, hear?"

Django stood shifting his weight lightly from one foot to the other. His hands were in the pockets of his long leather coat and his tweed hat sat on the rear of his head, its brim up, the effect like a laughing cat with its head thrown back. "Don't know where to find the Jolt," Django said. "Ain't seen him since the black dude got it right there on Jolt's doorstep behind the Bird."

"You find him, he finds you, no difference," Grizzly said. He hunched his shoulders and tilted his head, the gray beard beneath his chin thick and pliable and impenetrable like a sponge, and he stared down his wide flat nose at Django. "You put him where I can get him, all that matters. He find you when he need you."

"Find me?" Django's small mouth broke into a grin. "Why the man find me? Ain't nothin' I can do for him. We dry, remember? Leastwise, I'm dry. Drier'n a nun's pussy on Good Friday, that's what you tell me I be."

"Gonna make you a little damp." Grizzly nodded. "Here she come now. She late but dependable, ain't she?"

Django turned to look down the alley where the Gypsy was trudging toward them in a moth-eaten gray sweater-coat that fit her like a dress, her tiny feet moving quickly in white ankle socks and tattered Nikes. She glared at Django as she always did and withdrew her hand from the pocket of the coat. Opening her hand, she offered a small plastic vial to Grizzly who took it from her, glanced at it and nodded approval. Then he tossed it in an underarm motion to Django and said, "You not dry anymore, monkey."

Django counted twenty small tablets in the vial before dropping it in the pocket of his topcoat.

"Your man comes lookin', tell him you back in business again, hear me?" Grizzly held the first two

212

fingers of his right hand up, making the V sign, and the Gypsy reached in another pocket of her sweater-coat, looking for her Camel Lights.

"Don't know where he's at," Django said.

"Man's got the whore Billie, ain't he?" Grizzly said. The Gypsy was lighting a cigarette for him, the flame of the match dancing in the breeze.

Django nodded, feeling glum.

"Lucky fool, got a woman like Billie givin' him what a man needs now and then. Woman's got time on her hands these days, what with the Bird closed. So you go see his whore, you start there." The Gypsy slid the cigarette into Grizzly's waiting fingers and he brought it to his lips, still watching Django through narrowed eyes. He took a deep pull on the Camel Light and when he spoke his breath was a blend of condensation in the cold November air and exhalation of tobacco smoke. "Ain't askin' you to *waste* the fool. Jus' tellin' you to *find* him. An' put him where *I* can find him. Ain't so ball-breakin' tough. Izzit?"

TWELVE

There were four doors on the second-floor landing and Donovan squinted in the dim light until he found number three, the brass numeral bent and corroded.

He rapped sharply on the door twice and stood there sniffing the air. Sauerkraut. Somebody's cooking goddamn sauerkraut for dinner. Jesus, you can smell it everywhere.

"Who is it?" The woman's voice was flat, as though she had just woken up.

"Police." Donovan removed his shield from inside his jacket. "Like to talk to you for a minute."

"What about?"

"Homicide investigation."

"I don't know nothin' about it."

Somebody was moving behind the door of apartment two. Donovan could hear the floor creak.

"You want me to come back with a warrant and three pissed-off uniformed cops I can do it, lady." Donovan turned to stare at the door of apartment two and slipped his hand inside his jacket to grip the Police Special nestled in the shoulder holster. Probably just a nosy neighbor but you never know. . . .

The door to number three opened and the blond was standing there in a pink chenille robe. Her eyes were puffy and her hair looked like she'd set it with an eggbeater but you could see she had a good chest and healthy hips. Donovan flashed his shield, and Billie nodded and said, "Come on in."

Donovan walked past her into a living room that surprised him with its cleanliness and order. Good solid furniture, clean and not too glitzy. Couple of paintings on the wall, nice crystal chandelier over the dining room table. No dust, no dirty dishes, none of the whorehouse atmosphere he'd seen in other apartments where women like this one lived, a stripper with a criminal record, probably a part-time hooker like the rest.

"Your name's Chandler?" Donovan said, standing there in the middle of the living room, looking around.

"That's me."

"First name Billie?"

"Only one I got."

Donovan bent to lift a ceramic figure from a walnut hutch cabinet. "Chandler your maiden name?" He turned the figure over, raised his eyebrows at the Royal Doulton signature on its base and returned it to the hutch.

Billie grunted.

Donovan turned to look at her.

She was sitting in an upholstered armchair, her legs crossed, shaking a cigarette from a pack that had been resting on a side table. He watched her light it with steady hands, take a deep breath and tilt her head back blowing smoke toward the ceiling. Donovan walked across the room to sit opposite her, watching her with a crooked smile on his face. "Know why I'm here?"

Billie tapped the cigarette against a glass ashtray. "Don't have a fucking clue." Pronouncing each syllable carefully, like she wasn't just another tough street broad.

"It's about Heather Lorenzo."

"Never heard of her."

"And Detective Fox."

"The guy who got shot at Joe's the other night."

"That's him. He talked to you at the Flamingo a week ago."

"Black guy." She took another drag, still not looking at Donovan. "Him I remember."

"Your buddy McGuire's involved in both of them."

"No, he's not."

"Well, I think he is. And I'm gonna prove it."

"So prove it. What're you talking to me for? He's not here."

"Maybe I don't want to talk to him. Maybe I want to talk to you."

"About what?"

Donovan shrugged and dropped his eyes down to where her gown had slid open exposing a leg. Nice calf, slim ankles. "Maybe something that slipped out, something he told you that he didn't tell us. Hell, you were fuckin' him, weren't you?"

Now she looked at him for the first time, burning her eyes into his, staring at him like he was a stack of fresh shit, the look she used to give guys at the Bird who came on to her, thinking she's an easy lay just because she makes money by taking her clothes off in front of people.

"Let me know if you ever get a red-hot poker up your ass," she said. "I'll come and applaud."

Donovan's grin widened. "Oh, you're one tough lady, aren't you, Wilhelmina?"

"I answered questions half the night when they took Joe out of here," Billie hissed. "Then you guys come in here, tear my apartment apart, rip open my mattress, threaten me with jail, upset my neighbors. . . ." Jesus, she was starting to cry. Damn it . . . "I'm out of a job, I got bills to pay, and you're still on my ass and there's nothing else I can tell you. . . ."

She bit her lip and tilted her head back again which made the tears well in her eyes.

"Hey, sweetheart," Donovan said. "We got a dead cop and a dead civilian, and both of them're linked to McGuire. We're gettin' heat, lady. If you think those gorillas who came in here last week are something, I'm telling you they're only the beginning. Only the beginning."

Billie took a deep breath, which made her chest do wondrous things for Donovan's imagination. "You wanta tell me what you want from me?" she said.

Change of tactics, Donovan told himself. "Hey, I'm sorry I upset you, okay? Okay?"

"Yeah, sure."

"Just need to ask a few questions, that's all. Cop gets killed, all hell breaks loose, you know that."

"Joe and me, we had nothin' to do with it."

"You were at the club the night Fox got it. Maybe you saw something."

"I didn't see anything. None of us, we didn't see anything, didn't hear anything until about fifty of you guys came through the door of the club and grilled us, all of us, most of the night, and the next day the city shuts us down."

Donovan watched her, waiting.

"So me and the rest, we're out of a job and you guys still won't leave us alone."

"Yeah, well, I said I'm sorry."

Billie looked at him like he'd just said he was born on Mars.

"I'm sorry about all that stuff, okay?" Donovan spread his arms, opened his hands. "I wasn't with the first team, the guys who put the pressure on the Flamingo, all you people down there. But now I am. Hell, everybody is. Cop gets shot in this town and it's like somebody bopped the president. So I heard about you and I thought maybe I could do something, ask a few questions from a different angle, you know?" He grinned, lopsided. "I mean, I'm workin' on my own time here, okay? I just put in ten hours on Berkeley Street. I got a right to go home, have a beer."

"What happened to you?" Billie asked, referring to the bandage across the bridge of Donovan's nose.

Donovan touched it hesitantly, remembering how McGuire had knocked him against a doorjamb in the interrogation room. Son of a bitch should've been charged with assaulting a police officer. "Had to get rough with somebody on the street," he said.

"Broken?"

"Naw, just cut a little. No big deal."

"So I still don't know what you're here for." She pulled a strand of hair away from her face, tucked it behind her ear.

Donovan shrugged, started to speak, stopped and thought, ah, why not? If it works, wouldn't it be something to hit McGuire with? Hey, asshole, I porked your old lady last night, how's that make you feel? Then, laying his warmest smile on her, "Thought you and me, we could go out for a drink, talk about things a little."

Billie looked up at him, a smile playing at the corners of her mouth. "Jesus Christ," she said, and Dono van shrugged again, watching her. "Jesus Christ," she said again, looking around her apartment as though she'd just woken up. Then she threw her head back and laughed, her body shaking a little, and said "Yeah, sure." She rose to her feet. "Sure." She covered her eyes with her hand and stared at the floor for a moment. "Give me ten minutes to get ready," and Donovan watched her walk away from him toward her bedroom, combing her hair with her fingers, her shoulders shaking with laughter. "I don't believe this," he heard her say. "I don't fucking believe this."

He told Billie he knew a bar down Mass Avenue near Huntingdon, asked if she'd like some dinner with the drinks, maybe a decent steak. She said sure.

Walking down Mass Avenue he sneaked sideways looks at her, the way she cinched her light raincoat tight around her waist so it made her chest look better. Good-lookin' broad, you gotta admit. Not the kind you take home to your family but, Jesus, you'd have to be a goddamn robot not to wonder what it'd be like riding her in bed, hands under that great ass of hers.

They were passing the Christian Science Center, heading down Mass Avenue, the streets wet with the light rain that had fallen all day. Donovan was enjoying himself, going out for a beer with a good-looking woman, a sleaze and maybe a witness to Fox's murder, but you couldn't argue with that chest. Besides, after more than ten hours in that pressure cooker on Berkeley Street, everybody trying to solve Fox's murder on his own, he needed a break. Spend a little time with a sexy broad, might tell him what he needs to know.

Fox is dead, he reminded himself. Any regrets you got won't do a damn thing to bring him back.

"You wanta take a picture?" she asked, looking straight ahead.

"Picture?" he asked. The bar was a block ahead, light spilling through the windows onto the street.

"You wanta see what's on my chest, you can buy a ticket, soon's I get another job in a club," said Billie glancing sideways at him, looking him up and down as she walked.

"Can't blame a guy for using his imagination."

"So how come you're not using it to find the guy who killed your buddy, Fox, whatever his name was?"

"Imagination never found anything. I'm looking for facts, stuff you can tell me, maybe you forgot to tell somebody else."

"Aw, shucks," Billie said in a corn-pone accent. "And I thought this was gonna be a real girl-boy date."

They entered the bar and Donovan noticed how the guys on the stools watched Billie as she passed, Donovan staying a pace or two behind, his gaze either on her ass moving so nicely under her raincoat or looking up at the expressions of the men nudging each other, and he would catch their eye, let them know who she was with, who they'd have to get past if they wanted to make a move.

She chose a booth in the corner near the back and he asked her if she'd mind moving to the other side.

"Lemme guess," she said, sliding out and sitting opposite the way she'd been facing. "You don't like your back to the door."

"Something like that," Donovan said. He sat across from her, elbows on the table, hands clasped in front of him. "Just like to know where the threat's coming from, that's all." He scanned the bar, the guys on the stools going back to their talk about broads they'd known and those dumb-ass Patriots.

"You guys are all alike." Billie glanced down to her waist, unfastened the buckle of her coat.

"Men?"

"Cops." She opened the coat and slid out of it, arching her chest forward. Donovan made no effort to help her.

"You run into a lot of them?"

"Some. Dated a couple back in Portland. My old man was a cop, can you believe it?" She was out of her coat and looking at him.

"Funny thing for a cop's daughter to do, isn't it?"

"What is?"

"Working at the Flamingo, walking around naked." He was staring down the bar, watching who came and went, trying to catch a waiter's eye. "Hanging out with dope pushers."

"Hey, listen to me," Billie said. She jabbed his hand with her finger until he looked at her. "Look, I don't know where you come from and I don't care. You're a big city cop, spend your time looking at dead bodies, well, I guess it's a living. But people like me and the other girls, and guys like Django, okay, he's black and I'm white, but you gotta understand. We do whatever the hell it takes to survive, okay? I show my tits and Django deals a little drugs on the side. So maybe we're not Ozzie and Harriet, okay? But that doesn't make us scum, him, me, any of us. Maybe the people we deal with, maybe they're scum. But Django's just tryin' to make it and so am I and if you gotta act tough around us or rough me up a little, so do it if you get to keep your job. Just remember that Django and me and Dakota, some of the rest, we'd rather not be doing this shit, okay? Okay?"

She leaned back and stared out the window, her face flushed with anger.

The waiter, whose expression said he'd rather be anywhere else except where he was, was walking toward them. He tossed two greasy menus on the table. Billie ordered a vodka gimlet and Donovan asked for a Michelob.

When the waiter had gone, Donovan placed his hands on the table and leaned forward. "Tell me about yourself," he said.

"What's to tell?"

"Where you were born. Where you grew up. You ever been married?"

"Portland, Portland and no."

"Why not?"

"Never wanted to make the same mistake once. You?"

"What?"

"Ever been married?"

"Once."

"What happened?"

"We stopped."

Billie took a cigarette from her purse. "You miss her?"

"No." Donovan found a pack of matches in an ashtray, lit one and held it while Billie leaned across the table toward him.

"Why'd you bring me here tonight?" Billie asked. She put her head back, aimed a stream of smoke at the ceiling.

"Told you. Have a drink, nice little steak. Get to know you. Your old man really a cop?"

"That's what I said."

"What's he think about you now, what you do for a living?"

"He's dead. Died when I was fourteen years old." She took a long drag on the cigarette and looked down at it as she spoke. "He used to paint, if you can believe it. Watercolors. He was really good at it too. Said it helped him relax. And he'd sing, he liked opera. My old lady was a jazz freak but Pop loved opera. I'd wake up in the morning and hear him singing right through the noise of the shower, this great big booming voice. Then he'd put his cop uniform on and go to work. He was a hell of a guy."

"You close to your parents?"

"Used to be. They were older." She took another long drag, turned her head to blow the smoke away from his face. "Pop was almost forty when I was born. Mom, it was her third marriage, she was in her mid-thirties. Pop was a real character. Nothing special as a cop, just a desk job was all he wanted. He liked the regular hours, liked being off the street, Mom not having to worry about him walking through warehouses at night."

"What happened to him?"

Her eyes were shining. "Like I said, he liked to paint. One year, middle of October, he took off upstate for a long weekend. Had a couple of days off coming to him for some overtime and he packed a sleeping bag, bunch of paints, box of sandwiches and stuff and headed north, other side of Squaw Mountain."

She leaned back in the booth, one hand holding the cigarette in front of her mouth, the other hand supporting her elbow.

"The next morning he wakes up, rolls out of his sleeping bag and some son of a bitch shoots him from the other side of a bunch of bushes, fifteen feet away. With a shotgun. Said he thought Pop was a moose."

Donovan watched her, saying nothing.

"I remember I came home from school and they told me, a bunch of Pop's friends from the station came to the house. I went nuts, I lost it. I still don't remember what I did for two weeks after that. It's all a blank to me."

For a moment Donovan saw her as a fourteen-year-old girl who worships her father and is told he's dead. He glanced away and when he turned back again she seemed to be younger, softer, almost innocent.

"You got a hate-on for hunters?"

"They're scum."

"So how come you don't like cops either? That's what your father was."

"It was a job to him. Wasn't his goddamn life."

"And that's what stripping is to you?"

She smiled at him coldly. "We prefer to call it exotic dancing."

"How'd you get into it anyway?"

"None of your business."

"Most of those girls, they have some guy sweet-talk them into it. Won't turn tricks for him but they'll strip. You have an old man like that?"

"I had a boyfriend with a habit."

"Let me guess. He was a friend of Dewey's."

"No flies on you, are there?"

"You ever want to get out of the racket?"

"I think I'm out of it now." One last pull on the cigarette and she stubbed it out in the ashtray. "There's no way the Flamingo's gonna open again. I hear they're gonna tear it down, turn it into a parking lot."

"So what'll you do?"

She shrugged. "Maybe get a job as a waitress in a place like this. Give me a chance to meet some new men anyway."

"Woman like you shouldn't have much trouble meeting men."

She smiled and tilted her head. "Yeah? And a guy like you wouldn't know what the hell I was talking about."

Donovan was trying to think of a reply when the waiter came back, asked if they were ready to order and Donovan told him to bring T-bones for both of them, medium rare, stack of fries, salad on the side.

"So," she said when the waiter left. "How come you don't miss your wife?"

McGuire woke in the dark, knowing the answer. Just a few, he told himself silently. "Just a few," he said aloud. His hand opened and closed and he imagined someone dropping the pills into his palm. "Thank you," he muttered, "Thank you, Django," and he raised his hand to his mouth and opened it, licking his empty palm eagerly and squeezing his eyes to keep the tears in.

She paused only a moment at her door, the key in the lock, but it was all Donovan needed, and when she asked, "You wanta come in for a coffee?" he kissed her, probing for her tongue with his, wondering when she parted her teeth if she might bite down on it, but she didn't and the rest was familiar and exciting.

On the sofa, Billie on her back and Donovan running one hand up the inside of her skirt, the flesh of her thigh feeling like a warm peeled fruit beneath his fingertips, she said, "This is crazy, this isn't like me." Donovan breathed into her ear, ran his tongue around its edge and bit the lobe.

"My boyfriend," she began, and held her breath as his hand moved higher, closer. "My boyfriend

moved out . . . six months ago and you . . . you
know how many guys I've had here since then, oh
God! Don't touch it, don't touch it, oh Jesus! . . ."

Stroking her wetness, the thin fabric of her
panties soaked already and her hips rising and falling
with each pass of his hand.

"Two, that's . . . that's all. Okay, three, counting
McGuire. Just three and you. I mean, I don't do
this all the time, see?"

THIRTEEN

The interior of McGuire's skull was a vacuum, a dark empty place where nothing moved and only pain resided. In the morning Ronnie brought fruit salad and tea, and at noon some soup. He was nauseated and dizzy the rest of the day but by evening he felt something settling within him like a precipitate, heavy drifts accumulating in static waves, flake by flake, and he recognized it as strength.

He remembered Green Turtle Cay, his helplessness during the beating he suffered.

He thought about the final night he'd spent with Patty, how she cried in fear of her husband and pleaded with McGuire to take her away, she would go anywhere with him, anywhere at all. McGuire refused, he never wanted to leave the Cay and, besides, Patty was just another in a long string of women, one who drank too much. He couldn't believe her husband was an animal who would try to kill McGuire the following evening and succeed in murdering his wife two weeks later.

For months he had thought of revenge.

When he was finished with the pills, he would tell himself. When I no longer need the pills I will find him and I will find those two men and I will correct what they did to me and to Patty.

Meaning what? he asked himself now. Meaning you will visit a city you don't know and move among people you don't know to break the bones of men who would prefer to see you dead?

He remembered an Arab proverb: Choose your enemies carefully for they are the people you will most resemble.

I'm sorry, Patty, he said silently. I'm very sorry, but I don't think I'm capable of it. Of what I promised I would do.

As if she gives a damn now, he added.

Through the rest of the day he slept more soundly than he had in months, and when he awakened the following morning he showered and dressed himself in the worn corduroy trousers, button-down oxford shirt and crewneck sweater Ronnie had laid out for him. He walked unsteadily downstairs, following the aromatic trail of brewed coffee to the kitchen table where Ronnie looked up from her newspaper, rose to embrace him, then held his head in two hands and looked into his eyes.

"Welcome back," she said, and McGuire nodded.

* * *

Fat Eddie had converted the third-floor squad room to a Task Force Center in which teams of detectives could assemble in their quest for the killer of Detective Tim Fox, centralizing everything. Centralizing things was a major part of Fat Eddie's organizational strength. Extra telephone lines were installed, computers and desks were grouped together, and the room became a hive of round-the-clock activity.

It didn't help efficiency much. The cops bitched about the noise and the crowding, but mostly they grumbled about Fat Eddie bringing TV crews and reporters up on the elevator and walking them to the open door, showing how he had organized things, impressing everybody with his management style, his battlefield tactics.

"There is nothing more heinous to a proud police department than the murder of a fellow officer," Fat Eddie would say, like he was saying now, standing in the doorway ten feet from Donovan's desk. An anchorwoman from one of the stations was holding a microphone in front of Fat Eddie, capturing every word, while some bearded greaseball aimed a camera into the room, panning it left past Orwin and toward Donovan. "As you can see, we have mobilized an entire task force of our leading investigative staff, dedicated to bringing the killer or killers to justice—"

The phone on Donovan's desk chirped and the camera quickened its move toward him, the cameraman zooming in on what could be a break in the case.

"Thank you, Captain Vance," the anchorwoman interrupted. "It looks like you may be getting another lead from a concerned public now." She had straight shoulder-length hair and nice eyes. Donovan smiled up at her, knowing the camera was watching him, recording everything. Fat Eddie beamed.

Donovan said his name into the telephone receiver, very casual-like.

"Hi."

He recognized her smoky voice right away. "What's up?" he asked, leaning forward and reaching for a pen.

"Probably you," Billie said. "Son of a gun, how do you stay hard so long?"

"Sorry, I can't discuss details," Donovan said, keeping a straight face. "But if you care to be more specific . . ."

"Specific?" Billie laughed. "What's with specific? Is somebody watching you right now?"

"We have total surveillance, yes." The anchorwoman was biting her lower lip, leaning way into the room with the microphone, picking up every word. The cameraman was squatting, shooting up at Donovan, capturing the tough big city cop taking another important lead in the case, the cameraman making him look like a hero warrior, thinking this'll be the lead on the evening news for sure.

"Yeah, I know about surveillance," Billie said, falling in with the joke. "I was watching you this morning, propped up there against the headboard, working away. Can you get over here tonight lickety-split, so to speak?"

"We'll follow that up," Donovan said. He was getting hard, thinking about it. "Would you repeat the address please?"

"Sure. How about eight inches south of my navel?"

"I know the location," Donovan said. "We had a man in that vicinity all night long," and Billie laughed so loud he pressed the receiver tighter against his ear in case somebody could hear.

"Listen, I called my mother a couple of minutes ago," she said. "She always asks me if I've met any new men, meaning am I ever gonna get married, okay? So I say yes and out of the blue she says, 'Is he religious?' 'cause she's tired of hearing me talk about the lowlife I meet. What she means is, is the guy respectable enough she can tell everybody about him, see?"

"Yes, that's important to know," Donovan said. The cameraman's doing a duck walk toward him, camera hoisted on his shoulder, shooting up to fill the screen with Donovan's face, bringing the talent and intensity of your police department right into the comfort of your living room, Boston. The anchorwoman is creeping behind him, whispering into the microphone to set the scene.

"So I say to her," Billie is saying, "Yeah, he's religious, Ma. He yells 'Jesus!' just before he comes," and Donovan can't help it, he snorts into the receiver and turns his head from the camera, his shoulders shaking with laughter while the cameraman and anchorwoman raise their eyebrows at each other and Fat Eddie glares from the open doorway.

"Haven't got a thing."

Ollie Schantz looked back at McGuire from his bed, his body raised to a half-sitting, half-reclining position. McGuire sat next to him, scanning the morning newspaper, catching up on his life.

"Talked to Stu Cauley yesterday," Ollie went on. "Stu calls me couple a times a week. All they know is Timmy got it with a thirty-eight. It was either one hell of a lucky shot or one damn good one, depending on your point of view."

McGuire nodded and set the newspaper aside. "Where was everybody?" he asked.

"Everybody?"

"Donovan. Peterson, the victim's ex-husband—"

"Donovan? The cop? The hell's he got to do with this?"

"You think somebody meant to shoot Timmy?"

Ollie blinked twice. "I know where you're coming from," he said. "Been thinking the same thing since I heard about it. Either they meant it for Timmy or they meant it for you."

"Different motives, different perps."

"Yeah, but Donovan? He's got porridge for brains but hell, Joseph . . ."

"Think about it, Ollie. Either somebody's waiting for me to show up or they're surprised in the act of doing something. Because nobody knew Timmy was going over to my place."

"One shot, Joe."

"Which tells us what?"

"Either it's all he needed . . ."

"Or he shoots in panic, surprise maybe, then sees who he's got and gets the hell out of there."

"You gonna do anything about it?"

"About what?"

Ollie's right hand moved in a spastic, dismissive gesture and his voice became an angry bear's bellow. "About some human shithouse killing one of your buddies on your own goddamn doorstep! You gonna leave it to Fat Eddie and those toe-suckers they got left over on Berkeley Street to screw everything up?"

"Like hell," McGuire said quietly.

"The I.A. guy, what's his name?"

"Zelinka."

"That's him. Been calling here couple times a day, wanting to know how you are. Had some surveillance teams cruising by too, nothin' serious, just checkin' up on your ass. Oh yeah, Danny Scrignoli and your ex-wife've been calling. Hell's bells, Joseph, you're gettin' as popular as a bottle of bleach at a Klan convention."

"How's Micki?" McGuire asked.

"She could use a little pat on her head from you. Like everybody else, she can't believe what happened to Timmy. Hell of a thing."

"What do I owe her, Ollie?"

Ollie Schantz knew what McGuire meant. Ollie had been there when McGuire discovered Micki's betrayals and from that day forward, Ollie and Ronnie became more protective of him, aware of something fragile within McGuire that he had managed to conceal through all of his adult life. "You spent six years with the woman," Ollie said. "I remember, every time you looked at her, you got an expression on your face like a ten-year-old kid on a new bicycle. What you owe her's got nothin' to do with it. It's what you *feel* about her that counts."

McGuire looked away, annoyed. "What did Zelinka and Scrignoli want?" he asked, still avoiding Ollie's eyes.

"Dan's lookin' out for the good of your health, far as I can tell. Zelinka, I figure, may be needin' some freelance help."

McGuire frowned back at his former partner.

"Something's going down over on Berkeley," Ollie said. "Fat Eddie's spinning his wheels so fast he's got smoke coming out his ass. Does interview sessions all day long on Timmy's murder, talking about theories and suspects and the like. Truth is, he hasn't got two ideas to rub together and everybody knows it. Zelinka's the one who'll put this all together but he has to move slowly, there're trip wires all over the place."

"I don't get it."

"Your sister-in-law. Used to be anyway. The dead one?"

"Heather."

"Yeah, her. The word is, she might have been dealing poon-tang to a cop. She said she was scared of somebody heavy, and the rumor's there."

"Sure as hell wasn't me."

"Some people think it could be. Think she gave you reason to lay some tattoos on her with a baseball bat. Hell, you gave them reason enough, Joseph. It's your voice on the tape."

"That was . . ."

"What?"

McGuire shook his head slowly. "She made me some kind of business offer. Wanted me to hold some money for her. Said her ex-husband was going to do it but she didn't trust him."

"What made her trust you?"

"She had something else." McGuire rubbed his temples with his fingertips. "It comes back in little bits, the memory . . ."

"Maybe you better try harder to remember. Anyway, Zelinka and Scrignoli, they're buying the idea it's not you she was talking about. Fat Eddie, bunch of others're working on the theory that it *was* you somehow."

"Hell of a waste of effort, two separate investigations going on."

"If both were horses coming down the stretch, which one'd have your money on it?"

"You mean you think I should help Zelinka?"

"Might as well. Hang around this place too long, Ronnie'll have you baking muffins and changing my diapers."

Within the next half hour the telephone rang three times and all three callers wanted to speak to McGuire.

"Hear you went clean," Dan Scrignoli said. "Hear you cold turkey'd it."

"I think so," McGuire said. He was sitting at the kitchen table. Ronnie Schantz placed a plate of hermit cookies in front of him and he began to nibble one cautiously.

"Jesus, you're one helluva piece of work, McGuire." Scrignoli dropped his voice. "You know what's going on down here? You hear about Timmy, what they're looking for?"

"I heard."

"Who told you?"

"Zelinka. He's been talking to Ollie. Thinks I should help out, unofficially."

A long pause. Then: "You gonna?"

"It'll keep me off the streets."

"Let's get together, pool what we know."

"I better talk to Zelinka first."

"Okay, but we have to deal with this Heather Lorenzo thing. I'll bring you up to speed on it, see where we go from here. Pick you up at Ollie's in an hour."

McGuire was working on his second hermit cookie, urging his stomach to quietude as he swallowed, when Zelinka called.

"We should talk." The Hungarian's voice was deep and gruff.

"About what?" McGuire asked.

"About trouble. Yours, mine, Captain Vance's, everybody's trouble."

"You want me to help," McGuire said. A flat statement.

"I want help from anybody at all. You're nobody special. You're just somebody who can assist me. Besides, I think I can trust you."

"I don't have to get involved."

"In what? In these two murders? You're right, McGuire. You don't have to become involved. Just as I don't have to become involved in preventing the prosecuting attorney from issuing a warrant for your arrest as a material witness in two homicides, including one of a highly regarded police detective. Who left a grieving widow and an orphaned young daughter."

"Timmy was a good guy."

"Here's your chance to be one too. And stay out of Nashua Street."

"You don't believe I had anything to do with any of that shit," McGuire said.

"No, and I don't believe my eight-year-old boy will grow old and feeble and senile some day either because I will not be here to see it. But let us deal with reality, McGuire. Reality is, like it or not, that you are involved in these matters. You may try to avoid them, of course. But you cannot avoid the fact of your involvement."

McGuire sat upright in the chair. "Why're you handling this thing on your own? You're I.A. What's this got to do with you?"

He heard a long exhalation into the telephone before the Hungarian said, in a tired voice, "That is one of the things I want to talk to you about."

McGuire arranged to meet Zelinka at an office in the old courthouse near Government Center at two o'clock. He had just left the kitchen on his way to visit Ollie's room when the telephone rang a third time. Ronnie called him back to the table, holding the receiver in her hand and averting her eyes from his.

It was Micki.

"I've called every day," she said. "Ronnie told me what you were doing, all on your own. I told her it's just like you to do that, quit a habit like that on your own. . . ."

"Where are you?" McGuire said.

"At Heather's. I'll be staying here another day or so. It's creepy but I couldn't stand the tourist home anymore. The guy who runs it kept coming up to visit me in my room. And I didn't feel like going back to Florida. Not yet, anyway." Her voice began to crack. "My God, wasn't that terrible about Tim Fox? I couldn't believe it . . . and some people are saying it was *you*, that *you* did it."

"You're really staying at Heather's? Must be tough."

"You mean do I get the shivers?" She gave a short laugh, a release. "Yeah, a bit, I guess. But she's got so many locks on the door plus the security system.

238

And the guy who owns the art gallery downstairs, I'm pretty sure he's gay but he's really nice and comes up to see me now and then."

Heather's locks, McGuire reminded himself. Lots of security and none of it damaged. "Do you want to meet some place?" he asked. "Drinks maybe? Dinner, I don't know . . ."

"That'd be great," she said. "Dinner would be terrific. Any place special?"

"You choose it," McGuire said. "I'll meet you there, at Heather's apartment. About six, something like that." Then he added, "I, uh, I don't have a lot of money . . ."

"Good," she said. "Then you'll let me pay for a change."

The day was bright and unnaturally warm for November. The sun shone through bare branches of trees flanking the Paul Revere Mall behind the Old North Church, casting filigree shadows onto the brickwork forming the plaza. Italian mothers crossed the Mall pushing baby carriages with one hand and using the other hand to cling to a toddler or gesture at an elderly woman walking with her, the older women all wearing black skirts, sweaters, heavy stockings and bandannas, widow's apparel.

McGuire watched them all, unmoving, unsmiling, feeling shudders race through his body. Take two, three pills, he was thinking. That many will get me through the day. Just taper them off, cut the dosage in half today, in half again tomorrow. . . . Why not? Why the hell not?

In the middle of the Mall, Paul Revere watched McGuire from astride his bronze horse. The animal seemed ready to rear up at some unseen danger in front of it, the sculptor's unsubtle method of suggesting the horse was as sprightly and ferocious as its rider.

On benches or from their positions near the wall of the church, knots of Italian men watched the women solemnly, nodding their heads and smiling before leaning toward each other again to resume their conversations.

Sitting next to McGuire on the stone bench facing the Revere statue, his legs crossed, Dan Scrignoli licked a lime gelato and watched the scene with approval. In his heavy dark-patterned sweater over gold woollen slacks and brown Clark's desert boots, he looked more like a Harvard liberal arts professor than a street-wise cop. Flecks of gray in his thick, curly hair were highlighted by the sun and his face creased into a smile as he studied the people in the plaza, commenting on them one by one.

"See the guy over there in the green windbreaker?" he said, leaning toward McGuire and pointing with his gelato cone. "Name's Poliziani, Mico Poliziani. How tall's he? Maybe five-one, five-two? Nice harmless old guy, likes to sip espresso, play a little dominoes with the boys. Son of a gun's a Bronze Star winner, Korean War. Back in 1950 he got left behind when the Chinese attacked and the Eighth Army panicked and retreated. Everybody took off and left the little dago lugging his Browning machine gun. Mico took a hit in the leg and when nobody went back to help him he rolled down into a gully, set up his Browning and started picking off the Chinese. One of our recon

240

planes flew over and saw him there, bodies all around him, and sent a rescue team in to pull him out. He's wounded three times, nearly out of ammunition, and they counted ten, fifteen dead men all around him, Mico still aiming with the Browning."

Scrignoli shook his head and bit into his gelato. "They gave other guys Medals of Honor for less than that and what's old Mico get? A Bronze Star. You know why?" He looked at McGuire. "You wanna know why?"

"Because he didn't have blue eyes and his name ends in a vowel," McGuire said. He leaned back against the bench, his arms stretched across the top, and felt the sun warm and cleanse him. Why not? Just a couple of pills, just for the headache. Why not?

"Damn right," Scrignoli said, still staring across the mall. "Mico looked like a rat, smelled like a garlic patch and knew maybe thirty, forty words of English. So he gets a Bronze Star from some two-bit colonel and goes back to being a tailor over there on Commercial Street and if it wasn't for people like the Italian American Club, the Christopher Columbus Society, all of them, nobody'd know about it. Nobody *still* knows about it except people here in the North End and everybody thinks we're all Mafia, Cosa Nostra types, running cribs of whores and pumping dope into the blacks." He waved the gelato cone in front of his face. "Aw, hell, I get on my soapbox too much now and then. Sorry about that." He looked at McGuire. "You okay? Can I get you something?"

McGuire turned his head slowly to face Scrignoli. "What happened to Timmy?" he asked.

Scrignoli looked away and stared down at his gelato as though he had never seen it before and had no idea how it had arrived in his hand. "Shit," he said softly, then turned from McGuire and flung the cone into a concrete trash container. He lowered his head into his hands and stared at the cracked concrete between his feet. "He was a good guy, wasn't he?"

"Yeah." McGuire waited for him to continue.

"I don't know what happened," Scrignoli said. "Nobody knows what happened."

"What do you *think* happened?"

Scrignoli turned his head to look at McGuire. "You got anything in your room somebody might need?" he asked. "Really bad?"

"Like what?"

Scrignoli shrugged. "I don't know. But maybe that's what Timmy was there for."

"Or maybe somebody thought Timmy was me. We're about the same size."

"Yeah," Scrignoli said. "Against the light like that, how could anybody tell who was coming through the door?"

McGuire nodded, lost in thought. Finally, "It's got something to do with Heather Lorenzo, hasn't it?" He rubbed his temples, where the roots of the pain were.

"What, Timmy gettin' it?" Scrignoli sat upright, looking at McGuire. His eyes were wet and he was blinking as he spoke. "You think they're connected? How the hell's that work?"

"Timmy was working on it, far as I know. He wasn't paying me any social call. He had nothing to do with the son of a bitch I worked over the night before, the one killing the girl in my room. Timmy was there to talk to me. And all he had to talk to me about was Heather's murder."

"What'd he want?" Scrignoli asked in a near-whisper.

"I don't know." McGuire leaned back again, staring up through the bare branches at the contrails of an aircraft flying far overhead, the white stream behind it like a gash across the sky, bleeding ice crystals. You don't need the pills, he assured himself. I'm free, he thought. But his stomach began to churn and the pain began to flow, jagged and moving like a chasm in spring ice along the circumference of his skull.

"See, if we could find out what he wanted, we'd be somewhere, wouldn't we?" Scrignoli was saying.

McGuire lowered his head and nodded, watching the old Italian men near the wall of the church, their eyelids creased and their mustaches drooping, speaking to each other in the language they had first learned sixty, seventy, eighty years ago. "Where was your guy when this happened?" McGuire asked.

"Guy?" Scrignoli said. "What guy?"

"The one you turned. The one Heather was blackmailing."

"The broker? You want to know where he was? How should I know where he was?"

"You checked?"

Scrignoli grinned and passed his hand in front of his face. "Listen, I can tell you something. My man had nothing to do with this thing. Nothing at all. He doesn't even know you're alive, McGuire. He doesn't even know the Flamingo exists, for Christ's sake. Look, this guy never goes south of the Common unless his chauffeur takes a shortcut to the airport."

"What's his name?"

"What?" Scrignoli watching McGuire, still grinning.

"The broker. You never mentioned his name."

"Hell, McGuire, this is a Team Green case, I told you."

"Was she seeing a cop?"

"Who? Was who seeing a cop?"

"Heather Lorenzo."

"Where'd you hear that?"

"She was afraid of somebody important, somebody who could hurt her. Could have been a cop. Maybe my voice on her answering machine started the rumor, who knows?" The pain was a living thing and its offspring were in McGuire's stomach, kicking against the walls.

Scrignoli shifted his body. "News to me, she was doin' it with a cop. News to me. But I did hear that tape with your voice on it. You were really pissed at her, weren't you? What got your balls in such a knot?"

"I'm not sure. I took a lot of pills that night and drank some wine. Stuff used to do strange things to my head. I'd be awake, I'd be talking, moving around, and the next day there'd be nothing in my memory. Damn." He felt the perspiration on his forehead, exquisitely cool and foreboding. "S'cuse me a minute." He walked to a trash barrel, leaned over it and vomited.

When he collapsed on the bench again, his hands shaking and his eyes unfocused, Scrignoli touched his arm gently. "Bad, huh?" he asked, and McGuire nodded. "You're a tough son of a gun," Scrignoli said. "You'll make it."

McGuire nodded again. "Damn right," he said weakly. Jesus, only a couple of pills. Why not? Why not? Why not?

Scrignoli leaned toward him. "You ever remember, you let me know, okay? It could be important."

"Remember what?" The shivers were passing and the slight breeze was drying his skin.

"What this Lorenzo woman said to you. To piss you off so much."

"You involved in the case? Heather's murder?"

"I'm on the fringes, me and my broker partner. With Timmy dead, they're lookin' for connections all over. So I gotta be careful, right?"

"Too careful to tell me."

"I need time to think about it, is what I mean."

"Who's DeMontford?"

Scrignoli's head snapped around. "Where'd you hear that name?"

"That's him, isn't it? Zelinka asked me if I knew him. Said I was cross-indexed with him on a Team Green file. That must've been *your* file, Danny. So what am I doing on it?"

Scrignoli exhaled slowly. "You know."

"No, I don't."

"Timmy asked Brookmyer to do a search on my guy. I don't know where Timmy got DeMontford's name but he did. Anyway, Brookmyer got access to Team Green files through I.A. codes and the stupid son of a bitch came up with your name."

"There's a link between me and DeMontford?"

"The computer thinks so."

"I don't even know the guy."

Scrignoli shrugged. "You think somebody's trying to fuck you over?"

"From the beginning." McGuire watched two gray-haired Italian men playing checkers across the square. "How'd DeMontford's name turn up at all?" he asked.

"Telephone records. They did a goddamn cross-search of Heather Lorenzo's calls and made the connection. She tried to reach him that night at an apartment he keeps downtown and got the answering machine. Didn't leave a message but the record was there."

"So your cover's blown."

Scrignoli nodded. "My cover's blown. But I'm still keeping it in the Team Green code. Limited access, I.A. and undercover only."

"Why didn't you tell me about it before now?"

"Wanted to know how much you knew. How much the guys on Berkeley have been spilling, jerkoffs like Donovan and Fat Eddie."

"You could ask them yourself."

"You know damn well I couldn't. Soon as I mention a name, they'd be off and running. Without Team Green protection, Donovan'll be crashing in on my guy and the whole outhouse hits the fan."

"So Fat Eddie, Donovan, none of them know about DeMontford?"

"Not yet. Not unless you or Zelinka tells him. Or somebody else accesses the file, goes fishing for DeMontford."

"But Timmy knew."

"Yeah. From the stuff Brookmyer gave him."

"Brookmyer tell Vance, anybody else?"

"He checked with me. Told him I'd look after it, investigate the connection."

"And?"

Scrignoli exhaled slowly. "Harley DeMontford was in Palm Beach making a speech to the American

Investors' Society at the exact moment Tim Fox got shot. Two, maybe three thousand people sat there and watched him. TV cameras covered it. The *Wall Street Journal* reported it. You can look it up."

"So Brookmyer's not chasing that one."

"Not anymore. Doesn't go anywhere."

McGuire absorbed it all for a moment, took a new tack. "Why wouldn't you use a code for DeMontford?"

Scrignoli sighed, smiled and looked away. "Don't need one for Green Files. There's supposed to be restricted access."

"And Vance, Donovan, none of them know anything about the link, about Heather and DeMontford?"

"Only Timmy." Scrignoli shrugged.

"You gonna tell them?"

"Not unless I have to."

"You're concealing information about a murder investigation."

"No, I'm not. Zelinka's the connection. I'm covering my ass that way."

McGuire nodded. Something had begun to turn in his mind. Cogs engaging, facts falling into place.

"Whattaya think of Donovan?" Scrignoli asked. He was sitting back again, staring across the square, working a thumbnail between his teeth.

"He tries too hard."

"Heard you belted him one. Heard he's ready to charge you with assault."

"Hasn't yet."

"He can be a mean and stupid bastard, can't he?"

"What're you trying to say?"

"The guy's an animal is all."

"You got more on your mind."

Scrignoli shrugged and turned away.

"What's the time?" McGuire asked.

Scrignoli checked his watch. "One thirty. You got somewhere else to go?" He stood up and scanned the Mall, nodding and waving to people he knew.

"Drop me off at the Common," McGuire said. "I need to think."

"Zelinka shouldn't've said anything about DeMontford to you," Scrignoli said.

"He's involved in Timmy's murder. He'll do whatever it takes, Danny. You know that."

"But they're not connected, Timmy and him. No way at all."

"Yes, they are," McGuire said, standing up. "One way or another they are. And I'm it."

"You think Brookmyer or Zelinka'll tell Donovan or Fat Eddie about DeMontford? Or the Lorenzo thing? After I told him there's no way he could be involved, he was with me that whole night?"

"I don't know."

"Couldn't have yet, could he? Or they'd be on my guy like flies, right?"

"Probably."

"You know what I figure?" Scrignoli leaned forward to catch McGuire's eye, his brow furrowed. "I figure Zelinka's fingered Donovan somehow. He's got me telling him DeMontford's not it and if Vance goes after DeMontford and blows it, we screw up two cases. And he's already got something on Donovan. What d'ya think?"

McGuire shrugged. "Zelinka . . ." He hesitated, thought better of it. "Zelinka's a strange guy. Anybody in I.A.'s gotta be a little strange. So who knows what he's thinking?"

"Yeah," Scrignoli nodded. "Who knows?"

McGuire smiled to himself and he stood there and stretched his arms above his head in the morning sunshine. The realization that he hadn't thought about the pills, Django's candy, for several moments elated him, like a man who had been climbing a mountain for several days and finally had a handhold on its peak.

FOURTEEN

Rudy Zelinka looked out his third-floor office window at the gray stone Romanesque court-house across the square and fingered a round, hard peppermint before sliding it into his mouth.

Zelinka and his staff of two middle-aged secretaries represented the entire Internal Affairs branch of the Boston Police Department, a staff that had once numbered ten people. But the potent combination of budget cuts and complaints from the Boston Police Officers' Benevolent Society about I.A.'s "heavy-handed activities and open intimidation" eventually diminished the department's size and power.

Before joining I.A. when it was at the height of its powers, Rudy Zelinka had been a competent if unspectacular detective on the Burglary squad, working out of

Berkeley Street. One day, while making an arrest in a Chelsea tenement, he found himself sympathizing with the suspect, a black man who hugged each of his five hysterical children and sobbing wife one by one while Zelinka and two uniformed officers stood by, one of the cops, handcuffs dangling loosely from his hand, suppressing a grin. The other cop kept his revolver drawn, and Zelinka stood shifting his weight uneasily from one foot to the other.

The black man, whose name Zelinka would always remember as Hollingsworth, was sentenced to three to five years in jail and died six months later in Deer Island prison, caught up in a riot. A week later, six police officers, led by the cop with the handcuffs and the cynical grin, were implicated in a shakedown scheme, extorting money from drug runners on Dorchester Avenue, and the next day Zelinka applied for a position in I.A.

"You're nuts," his captain said. "What you wanta work for the internal snoops for? Nobody you ever knew on the force'll have anything to do with you, you're in I.A."

"Sounds fair to me," Zelinka said.

Zelinka's sense of ethical standards, never articulated but always in his mind, was the source of his admiration for McGuire. The two men were, as unlikely as they might appear when seen together, reflections of each other.

For many years the antics of Joe McGuire and Ollie Schantz had outraged supervisors on the force, people like Jack the Bear Kavander and Fat Eddie Vance who constantly complained about their disregard for procedures and insubordination.

"But they never take a penny," Zelinka would say to anyone who questioned how McGuire and Schantz had managed to avoid serious censure when they ignored precepts that other members on the force were pressured to follow. "Not an apple from a fruit stand, not a parking ticket left unpaid, not a quick lay from a street whore. All those things other cops accept as perks, these guys ignore."

Big fucking deal, Zelinka's colleagues would grumble.

Zelinka would nod and say, "Exactly. It is a very big deal."

Now he sucked on the hard round candy and stood three stories above Courthouse Square watching one of the few incorruptible men he had ever known walk distractedly toward his office window, head down and kicking at scraps of newspapers.

You and me, Zelinka said silently to McGuire from his window. McGuire and Zelinka.

It's about time.

"I hear you succeeded in ridding yourself of the addiction."

Zelinka watched McGuire stretch his legs in front of him. He was seated in the office's only side chair, a patched leather affair whose springs threatened to break through at various locations.

McGuire was gazing out the window at people in the square below. There had been no small talk when McGuire arrived, just a perfunctory offer of coffee from Zelinka answered by a shake of McGuire's head before Zelinka ushered the other man into his cramped office with its two windows facing west toward the old courthouse.

Zelinka settled himself behind his desk in the wooden swivel chair that creaked like a rodent and waited for McGuire to respond.

"Wasn't as hard as I expected," McGuire said finally. The light through the window reflected back from his eyes in white pinpoints, and he ran a hand through his hair. "Like having a bad case of the flu."

"You still have pains?" Zelinka folded his hands across his stomach.

"Not like before." McGuire continued staring out the window. "I wasn't taking them for the pain. The pain was part of the withdrawal. I was taking them because they made me feel good."

"They made you feel nothing, you mean."

"No difference." McGuire turned to face Zelinka. "What's up?"

"Same as before. Two murders, one of a policeman."

"You don't believe I did them."

"I don't believe you did them, no."

"Internal Affairs doesn't look into homicides."

"And I'm not. Others are busy doing that. I'm looking into what I am supposed to look into. Allegations of serious misconduct by police officers. The homicides, they're perhaps the effects, not the causes, of my interest."

McGuire frowned. "What the hell're you talking about?"

Zelinka leaned forward, resting his weight on his arms. "You understand segregation, McGuire?"

"What about it?"

"Not racial segregation. That's what everybody thinks, every American, when they hear the word. I mean isolation, exclusion, separation."

McGuire watched the Hungarian warily.

Zelinka smiled, ducked his head and scratched his scalp. "I love the English language, it's wonderful in its ability to express so much. In Hungarian we have one word, it means, oh, perhaps compartmentalize, and it does it all, you see. But in English . . ." He shrugged his shoulders.

"I still don't know what you're talking about."

The amusement left Zelinka's voice and his words flew at McGuire, clipped and precise in the voice of a man who, as a teenager in a South Boston tenement, had learned to speak English from phonetic spellings in the Oxford Dictionary.

"I am talking about keeping information in one area, McGuire. I am talking about access codes and holding knowledge to one's bosom, hoarding it from others in secrecy. I am talking of people who follow regulations like . . . like rats through a maze. Turn here, turn there, do not stop to think, do not become distracted."

McGuire watched Zelinka carefully. He had never seen the Hungarian display so much emotion.

"You like computers, McGuire?" Zelinka's voice was more relaxed and he leaned back in his chair, which gave an obedient squeak. Before McGuire could respond, Zelinka said, "I despise them. Do you know why I despise them? Because they segregate information, McGuire. Because as long as facts are in computers and as long as access to those facts is limited because of secrecy, people like me cannot do our job. There is no, how do you say it, paper trail in briefcases or filing cabinets. And so when someone such as me needs to follow information, I encounter secret codes and limited access."

"You're I.A.," McGuire said. "You can go to the top and get permission—"

"The top does not create codes, McGuire. Everyone with computer access can use their own codes now. It is not like having a key or combination to files."

"Codes can be broken—"

"By specialists. By experts. But only with permission from the top, McGuire. Do you know what it takes to get permission from the commissioner's office to access a detective's private file?"

"I would think the murder of a cop, Timmy Fox's murder, would be enough."

Zelinka grinned coldly and his mustache creased in the middle. "Yes, as a matter of fact, it is, McGuire," he said. "To a point."

McGuire shook his head and looked out the window again. "I still don't know what you're getting at."

"This Lorenzo woman. There are rumors that she was being threatened by a police officer. We do not know who but it is enough, in a homicide investigation, for me to pursue some facts. The death of Detective Fox was a spur. Because I believe there is a link that extends beyond you."

"Who've you got in mind?"

"No one. Yet."

"What're you looking for?"

"Connections. Links. Splices." The Hungarian smiled and his teeth shone like snow beneath his mustache. "You see what I mean about the English language? So many words for one meaning. So many subtleties."

"You've already found a link, haven't you?" McGuire said.

"I have found a name that arises where it should not." Zelinka crunched down on a mint and chewed thoughtfully. "The name appears in a Team Green file which has nothing to do with the murder of the woman over on Newbury Street." His heavy eyebrows arched.

"Heather Lorenzo."

"And you also know the businessman's name. Because I gave it to you."

"DeMontford."

"What else do you know of him?"

"Scrignoli turned him for some stockbroker investigation. He's using DeMontford to funnel information about a bunch of scams being committed downtown."

"And his relation to this Lorenzo woman?"

"DeMontford? She was blackmailing him. Like she did a bunch of other men. It was a hobby to her. Could've written a book. How to fuck rich men for fun and profit."

"Why did Scrignoli tell you about him?"

"Because he's afraid if this guy is linked to Heather's murder and a lot of crap starts coming out, he'll refuse to play with Scrignoli. And Danny says this guy couldn't have done the murder anyway because both of them were on the Cape that night, going through files." McGuire smiled tightly. "But I'll bet you already know that, don't you?"

Zelinka was not amused. "Of course I know it," he said, standing up. "Without that alibi I could lay out a case that would toss Scrignoli's entire investigation through the window. We would sacrifice a dozen stockbroker convictions to get one murderer of a police officer, you know that." Zelinka scratched his ear distractedly. "But we have a record of a call from her apartment to DeMontford's apartment at eight p.m. Then a long distance telephone record from DeMontford's Cape Cod home to Berkeley Street at two fifteen a.m., just as Scrignoli said he made. We have DeMontford's credit card receipt at a Hyannisport restaurant where the two men had breakfast and a witness who confirms they were there."

"Wait a minute, wait a minute." McGuire leaned forward. "First you tell me I.A. doesn't investigate homicides, yet we both know the department would blow the whole headquarters building to hell if it meant finding who killed Timmy. Now you tell me you've checked DeMontford's alibi on a case that's right out of your jurisdiction. So what the hell's going on? If you've got something happening here, why don't you cut loose, nail somebody, grill their ass off?"

"Because it would be a high-risk gamble. And I cannot afford to be wrong. DeMontford has a company called Bedford Investments over on Winthrop Square. It is quite large, very successful and totally untainted by any scandal to this date." Zelinka sat down again, crossed his legs, put his hands behind his head and leaned back in the chair. "Bedford Investments is also a major contributor to the election campaigns of several leading politicians and supports a number of key charities." He smiled coldly. "These things are supposed to be irrelevant, of course."

McGuire watched in silence, waiting for him to continue.

"It's been four days since you began your, ah, retreat, McGuire," Zelinka said. "Do you have any idea how much progress has been made on Detective Fox's case since then?"

"Not a hell of a lot."

"Not a hell of a lot," Zelinka echoed. "I suppose Ollie Schantz filled you in on that fact."

"And Danny Scrignoli. He did too."

"Really?" Zelinka's eyes caught McGuire's.

"He's a good cop."

Zelinka watched McGuire in silence. His mind seemed to be a million miles distant.

"Dan Scrignoli," McGuire said, as though the other man hadn't heard. "Got a good rep, works hard."

"Yes," Zelinka said, and sat forward. His chair squeaked in protest.

"You want me to do something."

"I think you know what it is."

"You want me to turn over stones," McGuire said.

"In a manner of speaking." The Hungarian was staring past McGuire, lost in thought. "This investigation concerning DeMontford and his business associates is very important to Scrignoli. I don't have enough yet to jeopardize it." He opened a file folder on his desk, removed four sheets of paper stapled at the corners and handed them to McGuire. "Here is a copy of the murder investigation report. On the Lorenzo case. Just a summary. You may wish to read it for your own amusement or . . ." Zelinka shrugged.

McGuire folded the papers without looking at them and slid them into a trouser pocket. "You've got something in mind, someone you need me to make the connection with."

"Something like that, yes."

"DeMontford?"

Zelinka raised his eyebrows in mock surprise and pleasure. "That is a wonderful idea."

"You can't do it officially."

"Even if I could, I have no staff, no facilities. When I obtain sufficient proof, I will approach the commissioner. Until then . . ." He shrugged.

"And you're not going to tell me what you've got in mind, what you're looking for precisely."

"That is privileged police business."

"And now that I'm a civilian, I don't have access to that kind of speculative horseshit."

"Not a particle."

"So why should I do anything at all? The hell's in it for me?"

Zelinka nodded and stared back at McGuire. Then he opened his desk drawer, withdrew the plastic bag of mints, reached in again and pulled out a photograph set in a small brass picture frame. He studied the snapshot carefully as though reading a business contract before turning it to face McGuire, holding the picture by the edges of the frame and watching for McGuire's reaction.

"You're a son of a bitch, you know that?" McGuire said. He lowered his head.

"So are you," Zelinka said.

McGuire raised his eyes to the picture again. Timmy Fox was wearing a red golf shirt and casual slacks, walking toward the camera with his daughter hoisted on his shoulders. The little girl had her head thrown back and her tiny hands were gripping her father's hair. Tim's wife, in a yellow shirtwaist dress, walked beside them, looking proudly at her family and laughing freely.

Zelinka returned the picture to his desk drawer. "Please read the case summary," he said. "And tell me your opinion, if you have one." He showed McGuire his snowy teeth again. "I think we two sons of bitches would make a very good team, McGuire."

"May I tell Mr. DeMontford who is calling, please?"

The receptionist's tone was wonderfully warm to McGuire who was leaning as far as he could into the open-air telephone booth, the wind sweeping across the Common at him as though on some vengeful mission.

"My name is McGuire," he said. "I got your boss's name from Dan Scrignoli."

"And is this regarding an investment situation, Mr. McGuire?"

"No," McGuire said, forcing himself to smile, warming up his voice maybe to the warmth of the woman's. "It's regarding DeMontford's future as a free citizen."

The receptionist went off the line. McGuire thought she had simply hung up on him but he waited, determined to count slowly to sixty and she returned at twenty-eight.

"I'm sorry, Mr. McGuire." My, how the temperature of her voice had dropped. "But Mr. DeMontford has no idea what you are talking about and assumes that you have made some sort of error."

"Tell DeMontford," McGuire said in a voice supersaturated with caloric content, "that there *is* an investment involved after all and it involves the one he made with Heather Lorenzo."

The woman assured McGuire that Mr. DeMont-ford would indeed receive the message.

McGuire hung up and stood grinning to himself for a moment. Jesus, it all comes back so easily, doesn't it, he thought.

Stepping out of the booth he heard the music for the first time, the sound of an entire band of musicians, drums and horns and keyboards and bass carried on the wind to him, the instruments prodding a gravelly voice singing an old Joe Turner blues McGuire remembered from his youth.

He looked over at the band shell on the Common but it was empty except for two black kids wearing baseball caps backwards on their heads and black Raiders jackets, staring sullenly off in the distance. He looked in the other direction, across Tremont and up three doors where a large black man sat behind three portable keyboards and two speakers the size of suitcases, all of it set in the doorway of a bankrupt music store. Three battered car batteries with elaborate wiring sat beside him powering the amplifiers, and the man's fingers flew from keyboard to keyboard, eliciting a flash of trumpets here, a wail of saxophones there, all riding over an electronic drum pattern and a walking bass line played by the man's foot as it skipped across an array of pedals beneath the stack of keyboards.

He sounds like the whole damn Basie band, McGuire thought, and stood there watching and listening. A compact boom microphone set at the level of the man's mouth captured his singing and McGuire realized from the heavy dark glasses and the musician's total intensity that he was blind. A plastic pail sat atop one speaker and McGuire walked across the street to hear the man's music more clearly and to read the words printed on the container in thick black letters: Blind Charlie Decker thanks you and God blesses you. Have a nice day.

Breakfast dishes in the sink,
Come on, baby, let's have a little drink,
Sit yourself here on my knee,
Whoa there, baby, you killin' me!
Mornin' noon and night,
Mornin' noon and night,
Love ya, pretty baby,
Mornin' noon and night . . .

A small crowd was gathering, pedestrians standing and smiling, each with a foot tapping, some shyly stepping forward to deposit money in Blind Charlie's plastic container while the black man's voice soared over lyrics as old as pain and as familiar as each onlooker's name.

Down in the barnyard pickin' up chips
Comes the moo cow swingin' her hips,
I get lonesome ever' day
'Cause my baby kinda walks that way.
Mornin' noon and night,
Mornin' noon and night,
Love ya, pretty baby,
Mornin' noon and night . . .

McGuire stepped forward and dropped a handful of coins in the pail. Instead of acknowledging the donation, Blind Charlie Decker swung into a blues riff that echoed across the Common and off the walls of the Park Street Church.

But McGuire felt blessed anyway.

FIFTEEN

Django was thinking maybe he should just go upstairs, knock on Billie's door, flash her a smile. Billie always liked him, she'd probably ask him in for a drink, tell him where the Jolt is.

Standing under a light across the street from Billie's apartment, he cradled his crippled hand in the other and twisted from side to side in rhythm.

Now why's Grizz want to do away with the Jolt? Django frowned at the thought, shook his head. What'd McGuire do, piss off Grizz so bad? Nothin', that's what. Ain't Grizz that's pissed, it's somebody else, somebody Grizz owes, tells Grizz, "You do the man, hear?" and Grizz'll do it, see that it's done. That's the way Grizz works. That's the way Grizz'll act if Django says he can't, says he won't finger the Jolt. Grizz'll demolish *me* . . . .

And then there she was, coming out of the front door of the apartment building looking good, dressed like she's got somewhere to go, some place *special*, maybe out to meet the Jolt . . .

And then there's some white dude behind her and he's talking to her now, a hand pressed against her back.

Jesus, Django thought. Guy looks like a cop. Billie's going out, looking good, with a cop. Django could spot a cop hiding in a herd of elephants. How you gonna talk to Billie, finger the Jolt, all a that, with a cop on her ass? The cop hears Django ask Billie about McGuire one day, the next day the Jolt turns up, him in one end of an alley and his guts at the other end, and Django's the guy they get after, Django's the one whose ass they haul down to Berkeley Street.

Billie's walking away now, her head down and her hands in her coat pockets, the cop trailing along, keeping up easy with her, tall red-haired guy, out for the night with Billie who maybe knows where the Jolt is.

Django remained across the street, walking a little behind Billie and Donovan, following and watching, wondering if maybe this is the time when it all comes down on his head like he always knew it would eventually.

"There's a guy coming around tomorrow, giving me a price for everything. The furniture and Heather's jewelry, I mean. The rest of it, her clothes and all, I'm giving to a charity."

Micki pursed her lips together and studied her reflection in the mirror of her compact. An open makeup bag sat on the small kitchen table, its contents spilled out. "The good stuff, the antiques, I'm selling to what's-his-name downstairs, the antique guy, he's taking the good pieces. He'll probably screw me out of what it's really worth but I don't care."

"You plan to take anything of Heather's with you?" McGuire asked. He was sitting across from her, an untouched cup of black instant coffee in front of him, watching Micki in fascination as she painted and prepared her face, watching her perform her practised application of foundation cream and rouge and eye shadow and liner the way he used to watch her in the good years of their marriage. She wore an old, pale blue silk blouse stained with makeup and buttoned low so he could see the lacy fringe of her brassiere. Her hair was pulled back with a simple elastic band. A sand-colored mohair sweater lay across the back of a chair.

"Nothing." She folded the compact closed and placed it in her purse. "There's nothing here I want."

"It's a nice apartment."

"It's okay. Actually, it's pretty nice. Sometimes I almost forget about . . . about what happened to Heather here."

"Mind if I look around?"

She looked at him, then away for an instant and back again. "Will you tell me something? Honestly?"

"Sure."

"Were you ever here? With Heather?"

"No. I was never here before. With anybody."

"But you knew where she lived. How did you know that?"

"She told me."

"Why?"

"I can't remember."

Micki turned away and removed the elastic band from her hair. It cascaded onto her shoulders, catching the light and shining like crimped silk. "I think she was attracted to you in a way," she said. "I think she was even a little jealous when we were married."

"She was always jealous of you," McGuire said, standing. "That was something you never fully understood, how much she envied you. Not for me, but for who you were. You were better than her. Prettier, nicer, more popular."

Micki reached for her brush and began stroking her hair, her eyes avoiding McGuire's.

He crossed the kitchen to the bottom of the stairs and began climbing to the upper level of the apartment. The door at the summit stood ajar and he pushed it open silently. On the threshold a large square portion of broadloom, the carpet thick and crusty with Heather's dried blood, had been cut away and removed, exposing the hardwood floor beneath the spot where she had bled to death.

McGuire's eyes traced a path of freshly scrubbed carpeting from the patch of bare floor to the bathroom entrance, the trail marking Heather's journey as she crawled toward the door before losing consciousness. Other patches led across the rug from the bedroom into the upper office. McGuire followed the trail to Heather's telephone answering machine on the oak desk, its lights dead, the power cord removed.

He left the office, crossed the alcove again and entered Heather's bedroom. The sheets and blanket of Heather's bed had been pulled loosely up to the pillows by Micki. Heather's collection of vases stood on the high shelf near the ceiling where scatterings of fingerprint dust remained from Norm Cooper's forensic kit. McGuire stepped back far enough to examine the holes for the mounting screws with which Heather had fastened the motor-drive camera aimed at her bed. Tim Fox's report speculated that the camera was equipped with a timer, blinking every minute or so in near darkness illuminated by infrared light.

He sat on the edge of Heather's bed and glanced around. A compact stereo system, several fringed pillow shams, a telephone, a photo of a teenaged Heather delivering what seemed to be a high school valedictorian address, china figurines of small children with animals . . .

McGuire frowned, stood, walked out of the bedroom to the top of the stairs again.

There had been flecks of blood leading from the bedroom through the hallway and into the office.

He retraced the route into the office, visualizing the fleeing woman, already wounded by a blow or the thrust from a weapon.

There was more blood in the office, suggesting another vicious assault, and a return from there to the bathroom . . . .

McGuire lowered himself slowly onto a large leather sofa, his eyes flicking from the heavy oak desk to the doorway and back again.

She hadn't tried to flee downstairs. There was no blood on the door at the top of the stairs, no indication that she had even attempted to escape that way. Why not? Wouldn't that be the natural instinct?

He rose and returned to the alcove area in front of the bathroom, standing on the bare floor where a woman he once despised as much as he thought possible had died a week earlier.

Why not escape down the stairs? he wondered again.

Something nagged at him, standing there with the image of a mortally wounded Heather running in panic through the second floor of her apartment.

"Joe?"

McGuire turned and opened the door inward, looking down the stairs.

Micki was waiting, her makeup complete, her hair tied back with a golden ribbon. She had replaced the silk blouse with the mohair sweater worn over a tight camel's-hair skirt, and she stood looking up at him expectantly.

"I'm starving," she said. "Can we go now?"

McGuire inhaled deeply, his eyes smiling down at her, marveling at the power of a woman's beauty, however contrived, however temporary, to ransom his resolve.

Donovan ignored the little black guy at first, didn't know it was Django, thought it could be just some street tough figuring he's cool, nothing to worry about.

Donovan was about to say something, come up with a wisecrack that'd make Billie laugh, walking with her arm through his, but he turned away to look across the street and behind, and there he was again, same little guy, matching their pace, walking with that funny bounce like he's getting ready to dance, do a number with his feet for spare change from the tourists or something.

Thing is, Donovan'd rather've just gone to bed with Billie soon's he arrived. Ten hours of chasing each other's tails in the Task Force room, three days of crap, and they still didn't know much more about Fox's murder than that somebody put a thirty-eight into his chest. It wears a guy down.

All day Donovan had thought about hiding his face against Billie's chest, all that nice smooth flesh. Then he shows up half an hour ago and she's dressed like they've been invited to the governor's mansion for tea, long blue velvet dress with some kind of frilly neckline, makes her look like a stripper getting set to teach a first grade class.

"Ever been to Jingles?" she asks him, and he says, "What, that little dive behind the Hilton?" She tells him, "It's not a dive, it's a nice quiet place where you can have some drinks and dance a bit. I wanta go dancing," she says, and Donovan says, "God-damn, I'm really tired," and she pouts.

"Okay," he says finally, "drinks, coupla dances, if it makes you happy, we'll do it."

Things a guy's gotta do to get laid these days . . .

So here they are on Mass Avenue and some little black guy's tailin' 'em across the street, all the way from Billie's place.

Jingles was on the mezzanine level of a new office building, you rode up in a stainless steel elevator one floor. Inside, the place was dark and shiny, a lot of chrome and black leather, big darkened windows looking out on Boylston, and three guys playing some kind of jazz rock next to a glass dance floor lit from underneath. Some guy in a tuxedo with a little pencil-thin mustache met them at the door and showed them to a table next to the windows.

Billie turned her back to Donovan so he could remove her topcoat. Then she fluffed her hair and sat down, but as Donovan started to shrug out of his coat he paused with it half off his shoulders, looking through the window at the other side of the street. "Order me a beer," he said, slipping into his coat again.

"A what?"

"A beer. Any kind."

"Where you goin'?"

"Outside for a minute."

Billie made a face and turned her head to look out the window. Traffic was light and three young kids in baseball caps were walking past on the street below, their shoulders hunched and their hands thrust in the pockets of their jeans. At a bus stop, a heavy black woman stood patiently, her eyes moving from side to side behind heavy-rimmed glasses. Billie watched Donovan emerge from the building, trot across Dalton and disappear around the corner, heading for the Sheraton. Then he was back again, this time keeping himself close to the buildings for the first few steps before breaking into a sprint just as a small black figure burst from behind a concrete pillar of the Hynes Convention Center across the street.

Django didn't know what was in the office building, ten maybe twelve stories of it. What's this cop want with Billie in an office, this time of night? The cold was getting to him, standing there, watching people come out of the Sheraton down the way and the

Hilton across the street, flagging down cabs, heading out for a little fun, big dinner, few drinks maybe. He was thinking about the rooms in those hotels, how they must look, got your own bar fridge in there, got your cable TV with porno movies, flick the switch, got room service, send you up some steak and ribs, what you want to go outside for, night like this?

Then the cop was out the door alone now, heading for the Sheraton. Django watched him disappear from sight, wondering if Billie was alone now up in that office building, if maybe Django walked in the front door, looked around, he could figure where she might be. Or should he just stay where he's at, wait for Billie to show on her own?

He took some time thinking about that, about what he should do, and he decided maybe he'd go in the front door of the building, see what's happening. But he took one step out from behind the pillar and the man was on him, one big pink hand grabbing Django's shoulder, the other flashing a gold badge at him.

"What're you up to, asshole?"

Donovan spun Django around, taking a good look at his face, knowing him from somewhere, then shoved him face first against the locked door of the Hynes Convention Center.

"Nothin', darlin'," Django managed to say.

"Cut the crap." Donovan slipped his badge back into his coat and used the hand to yank Django's arm up his back. "You've been on our ass for six blocks. You think I didn't spot you, you two-bit amateur? What's goin' on?"

"I'm lookin' out for her's all."

"Lookin' out for who?"

"For Billie. She a friend a mine, you ask her. Ask her if she ain't a friend a Django's."

Donovan released him and stood staring at Django who turned calmly around and smoothed the sleeves of his coat. "You hang around the Flamingo," Donovan said.

"Used to." Django examined the buttons on his coat and stepped deeper into the shadowy doorway, out of sight. "Don't no more. Bird's closed for good 'cause a what happened to MaryLou and the Afro cop."

"You're a dealer."

Django looked at him blankly. "Ain't never been convicted. Ain't never even been charged."

"You supply McGuire, right?"

"I know the Jolt." Django looked up and down the street. No percentage in being seen talking to the law, even this far from home ground. "Seen him in the Bird a few times, that's all."

"Bullshit."

"I gotta go, man." Django thrust his hands into his pockets. "You tell Billie Django says hey an' I hope she's stayin' well, keepin' healthy, eatin' right."

Donovan clamped a hand on the small man's shoulder. "Tell me what else you know about McGuire."

Donovan was enjoying it, watching Django squirm there in the darkened doorway. Little black prick was a source, you could see it. Dealing on the street, feeding McGuire what he needed, he was a *source*.

"The Jolt's okay, he all right."

"He could be involved in two murders, you know that?"

"Not for me to know." Django's eyes were flying around in their sockets like a couple of ping-pong balls.

"If you're hiding anything on him, I'll nail your ass as an accessory and you'll spend ten years at Cedar Hill, you got that?"

"Ain't nothin' to know." Django shook his head and forced himself to look into Donovan's eyes.

"You ever meet Fox?"

"Good-lookin' dude, got shot in the Jolt's door? No, sir."

"You ever meet a woman named Heather Lorenzo?"

Django shook his head.

"Your buddy McGuire did her, over in her apartment. . . ."

Django's eyes shot to the left and he said something.

"What'd you say?" Donovan asked.

"Maybe—"

"Maybe what?"

"Maybe I met her once." Oh, Jesus, Django thought. Oh shit, here it goes, and he remembered Elsie.

Donovan let go of Django and Django slumped against the door. "You wanta tell me about it now?" he said, smiling. "Or you wanta tell me when your balls are between my shoe and the sidewalk?"

Could save the Jolt's life, Django thought. Maybe save mine too. They get me down on Nashua Street, Grizz think I'm talking, he'd do it, spread the word whether I'm talking or not, and Grizz'll get a guy, bury a shiv in my ribs. 'Sides, this has nothin' to do with Grizz, the woman on Newbury. Nothin' to do with him.

"She give me a message," Django said. "She finds me one day, her and her car. Leans out the window, gives me a message for the Jolt. That night she's dead. But it ain't the Jolt did it."

"'Course it ain't." Donovan leaned casually against the side of the doorway, watching Django. "So tell me the message. Tell me what she wanted you to say to McGuire."

"She want him to come see her, hold some money, somethin' like that."

"Why'd she pick you to tell him?" Donovan looked Django up and down. "You're hardly the Newbury Street type."

"Saw me once. Over by the river. On the 'Splanade. Then she see me in front of the Bird, come to find the Jolt. Gave me twenty bucks, find McGuire, tell him something."

"Tell him what?"

"Just come see her, else him and me, we'd both be in trouble."

"Him and you?"

"That's what she say." Django drew circles on the concrete with the toe of a shoe. "You tryin' to nail the Jolt for what happened, that woman?"

"Maybe."

"And the black cop, got his ass shot at the Bird, goin' in Jolt's apartment?"

"What's that to you?"

"I seen him."

"Who? McGuire? You saw McGuire?"

Django felt sick. Right there he felt his stomach

do a flip and he told himself, here we go. Here we go, fool.

Through the window of the dance club Billie had watched Donovan sprint across the street and disappear into the shadows of the buildings along Dalton. A waiter appeared and spoke to her, and by the time Billie had turned to order drinks and then looked out the window again, a bus had arrived, blocking the view. When the bus pulled away the shadows were black and lifeless again. Billie finally gave up and leaned back in her seat, watching the waiter arrive with a beer and a C.C. and water.

She was halfway through the C.C. and water when Donovan returned, walking with his hands in his topcoat and his head down, looking at the floor and frowning. When he slid across from her and sipped his beer without looking at her, she knew he reminded her of something or somebody, and when she sat back against the booth and he raised his head to give her a small smile that looked as though he wanted it to explain everything, she knew what it was. Or who. He reminded her of McGuire, the surface toughness over the quizzical expression, like a small boy puzzling over a riddle he knew he could never solve.

"Sorry about that," Donovan said. He shrugged out of his topcoat. "Police business."

"Hell of a way to treat a lady," Billie said. "Who'd you go after out there?"

"Your buddy Django."

Her face tightened with anger. "What'd you do, rough him up?"

"He was following us. Had been since we left your front door."

"So that gets you uptight? Maybe he wants to talk to me, maybe he needs something. Django wouldn't hurt me, for Christ's sake." She turned her glass in circles with both hands, staring angrily at it. "You rough him up or what?"

"Just talked to him a little bit."

"About what?"

Donovan avoided her eyes, wanting to be somewhere else. "Your friend McGuire."

"So what about him? Is he in more trouble or what?"

"I don't know," Donovan said.

SIXTEEN

"You don't like this place?" Micki asked when they were seated in the restaurant.

McGuire's reply was a grunt. He opened the menu. It was illustrated with color cartoon characters and featured omelets and salads. The ceiling was hidden by a mass of hanging plants and the waiter introduced himself as Jonathan and announced that Jennifer would soon be along to take their order.

"I think it's nice," Micki said, looking around. The dominant decorating features were plants, brass and unpainted wood. "Guess it's not masculine enough for you, huh?"

"Long as the food's good."

Micki leaned toward him. "When I made the reservations I asked if they served Kronenbourg beer and they said they did, so I said okay." She was smiling at him like a young child, eager to please.

"Thanks," McGuire nodded.

Ten minutes later, their drinks had arrived, they ordered their meals and Micki sat watching McGuire carefully over the rim of her wineglass while McGuire let his eyes roam around the room, lighting upon hers briefly, then wandering away again.

"You nervous?" Micki asked.

"A little."

"You weren't nervous with me in Florida last year."

"A lot of stuff has happened since then. Heather's dead, Timmy's dead . . ."

"Are you still upset about what happened on that boat? In the Bahamas?"

"Maybe." McGuire sipped his Kronenbourg. "How much do you know about that?"

"As much as Tim Fox told me. How you almost died. Then how you got addicted. Are you sure you're over it? I mean, if you had some now—"

"Would I take them? No. But that's because I don't have any. Drop a couple of Demerol on the table and then ask me." He wiped his eyes. He was tired of this bullshit. Somebody always seemed to be testing him. Fat Eddie, Ollie, Ronnie, Micki . . . And the toughest of them all, McGuire himself.

"Ronnie Schantz said you were as stubborn as ever but this time you put it to good use." Micki smiled at him, almost coyly. "Lot of people get hooked the way you did. I knew a woman in Florida, she was injured in a car accident and she'd have sex with her doctor just so he'd write out codeine prescriptions for her. It starts with pain and after your body's healed it still needs the drugs."

"My body had nothing to do with it."

"What do you mean?"

"I wasn't taking the drugs for the pain in my body. I got headaches, sure, but they were withdrawal symptoms. The drugs were covering other stuff."

"Like what?"

McGuire stared down into his drink for several moments before replying. "While I was in the hospital, the woman on the yacht was found floating in the harbor at Green Turtle. Her name was Patty. Her husband said they had been drinking and around midnight she decided to go for a swim before bed. He fell asleep in the cabin, woke up about three, couldn't find her anywhere. Two guys in the crew said they were asleep in bed too. The husband, name's Charlie, roused them and called the police on Treasure Cay. They found her when the sun came up. Said it was an accident or maybe suicide."

"You don't believe it was either one?"

McGuire breathed in and out slowly. "Friend of mine in New Plymouth sent me newspaper clippings about it. He underlined the names of the crew members. Same two guys Charlie brought down from Chicago to kill me. Besides," McGuire raised his eyes to meet hers, "Patty couldn't swim a stroke."

"Maybe she committed suicide."

"Or maybe she was walking on the water and tripped over an anchor chain."

"You think you were responsible for her death."

"Don't know. But one day I might be responsible for something that'll happen to her husband."

"You're not serious."

McGuire nodded. "Patient too."

"You've been planning to get revenge all this time?"

"Only while I was lying in Ollie and Ronnie's house shaking off the meperidine. As long as I was taking that crap, I didn't have to deal with it. Now that I'm off it . . ." He shrugged. "She was a nice person. Good woman in a bad marriage."

"Happens all the time."

McGuire grunted, staring into his beer, remembering Patty's thick hair, the way she'd combed it back from her face.

"What about Tim Fox?" Micki asked. "And Heather? They're both dead. What're you planning to do about them?"

McGuire shrugged. "Out of my hands. Don't give a damn."

Micki sat back and folded her arms, and when she spoke her voice had that little-girl softness which made her words all the more bristling. "Who the fuck are you trying to kid?"

Billie can't believe it. They dance a little bit, okay, he's not Fred Astaire but she can live with that, she just likes feeling a man's body rubbing against her, gets her wet, gets her ready. Then she says, "Let's go back to my place but this time I want to take a cab," and he's somewhere else, he mumbles, "Okay," like she's asked him if he wants a second cup of coffee.

Then, in the back of the cab, she grabs him right by the crotch, gets a real handful, and all he does is wince.

"What's your problem?" she says, really getting pissed now.

He says he's got a lot to think about. Big deal, she knew what he was thinking about when he came by to pick her up, couple of hours earlier. He's thinking, let's do it, let's roll across that hay, and that's *all* he was thinking. She was too, she just wanted to tease him a little, dancing and drinks and knowing it's going to happen later, that's ro*mance*, for God's sake.

But it doesn't happen later. They have a fight in the car, or anyway she gets mad, says some dumb things and gets out at her place, slams the cab door shut and yells, "See you around, asshole!" as the cab pulls away, and goes upstairs alone.

Like she's done a hundred times, a thousand times.

Micki was laughing with him, throwing her head back and bringing a hand to her throat the way McGuire remembered she did when he could make her laugh in their marriage. She asked for another glass of wine instead of coffee and McGuire considered a third bottle of Kronenbourg but decided against it. The meal had been omelets and salads and the conversation had been everywhere. Several times Micki had leaned toward him and reached to touch his hand with hers while speaking to him and when she did, his skin had jumped.

Her laughter subsided and she took a long drink from her wineglass, set it aside, placed her elbows on the table and rested her chin on her hands. "God, I miss you sometimes," she said.

Before McGuire could answer, the waitress brought the check and Micki peeled a number of bills from her wallet and looked back at him. "Let's go," she said.

Remembering his embarrassment with Billie, McGuire hesitated when she turned at the top of the stairs and kissed him, open-mouthed. He held her, feeling uncertain and foolish, her lips moving against his, until she pulled away and stared at him. "You okay?" she said.

"I don't know."

"Obviously I'm not turning you on."

McGuire smiled.

"This isn't the same guy who took me to Key Vaca, is it?"

McGuire shook his head and she turned abruptly from him. "Does anybody turn you on anymore?" she said, dropping heavily into an upholstered chair and avoiding his eyes.

He was standing on the bare patch of floor where Heather had died and he stared down at it and at his shoes, scuffed and worn. "I don't know," he said again.

Micki sat there, one leg hoisted over the arm of the chair, her fingers at her mouth. Then she stood and walked away from him, her hands at the hem of her sweater, hoisting it above her head and entering Heather's bedroom. With the bedroom door open and McGuire watching from the top of the stairs, she unbuttoned her skirt, lowered the zipper, and let it drop to the floor. She kept her back to McGuire while she reached around to unfasten her bra, and when she bent forward to let it fall from her shoulders, McGuire drew a sharp intake of breath at the sight of her breasts, the nipples round and pink, rosebuds the size of kisses.

She turned to face him, her eyes avoiding his, raised one foot to the bed, and removed her shoe.

She repeated the motion with the other foot, then tucked her thumbs under the waistband of her pantyhose and removed them as well. Standing on the other side of the bed, her legs slightly apart, she threw her head back and released her hair, letting it cascade onto her shoulders. Then she lay on the bed and only then did she catch McGuire's eyes with hers, her expression defiant, and watched until he closed his eyes briefly, smiled in the somehow sad way she remembered from a life or two ago and walked toward her.

"I want to do everything we used to do," Micki was saying, her face against his and her lips at his ear. Her hands, small hands, were at the back of his head, gripping him to her as though McGuire were a weightless thing and she were the earth, holding him against her body with her hands and periodically her tongue, grasping him within her, her legs fluttering against him like flames.

"I want to do it, do it . . ." and the last words repeated themselves over and over, fading like the sound of running footsteps in a dark and distant cave until she lay crying under him and he kissed her tears and removed one hand from beneath her to stroke her thigh, never wanting to rise from her, fearing that to rise from her now would be to leave behind too much of himself and he would hobble through the remainder of his years with less of himself than ever. So he lay within her, watching her eyes until they opened and regarded him with fear, not of him but of something else, until she closed them again and sought his mouth with her tongue.

And the motion began again in a rhythm that was unfrantic and measured and steady until he moaned and she urged him to speak her name aloud and he did and she asked him to tell her he loved her and he shook his head from side to side, his eyes closed, until she asked him again and he did.

In the dark, facing away from him, McGuire with one arm extended beneath her head, the other holding her to him, his hand cupping a breast, hearing her breathe, hearing her choke down small sobs as she had been doing since she turned away from him.

"What?" he asked.

"I'm sorry."

Not for tonight. Tonight had been wondrous, a recapturing of part of the past, and McGuire remembered someone describing lovemaking as "two bodies laughing together." No, Micki was apologizing for past sins and past rejections.

"Me too," McGuire said, and Micki began a long, slow tumble of quiet sobs, shaking in his arms like an animal craving freedom.

"You don't . . ." she began, and started again. "You don't know what I did . . . some of the things I did . . . after I left."

"You made a mistake," McGuire said. "I told you before. We all make mistakes. Dumb mistakes. All of us."

She shook her head violently. "No, no, no, more than that, more than that . . ."

"So tell me."

"I can't."

"Why? Was it so bad?" He lay there watching a pattern of lights on the ceiling. Wishing he weren't where he was. Wishing she had never started this conversation. Wishing he didn't want to know, didn't need to know.

"Yes."

McGuire exhaled. You don't need to ask, he told himself.

"Yes," she said again.

She cried again and drifted off to sleep, leaving McGuire inhaling the aroma of her perfume and her hair and the warm musk of her body. He withdrew his arm and rolled onto his back and refused to think of what Micki might have done since leaving McGuire and whom she might have done it with.

Instead, he thought of Heather.

It had begun earlier, before they left for dinner, when McGuire had traced Heather's route through the apartment. From the bedroom to the top of the stairs. From the top of the stairs to the office. From the office back to the bathroom. Tim Fox had told McGuire she had been beaten at each location, probably with a baseball bat.

He rose from the bed and tread silently, nakedly, out of the room to the top of the stairs, from the top of the stairs to the office, from the office back to the bathroom. Why didn't she escape, he wondered. Why didn't she try harder to escape?

"Joe?"

Micki's voice sounded back to him from the bedroom and before he could answer she was through the door and into the vestibule, her skin shining in the soft light drifting in through the windows from the street.

"I thought you had gone," she said, walking toward him and resting her head on his shoulder. "I don't think I want to stay here anymore. Not alone."

"Okay," McGuire said, wrapping her in his arms. "You won't. I promise." And he led her back to the bedroom where she lay down and he buried his face in her neck and nuzzled her until she cried aloud and launched her hands on an excursion of his body.

SEVENTEEN

Grizzly ran other dealers, Django'd always known it. Grizz told Django he was the favorite of the Grizz. Hell, Grizz had saved Django's black ass, blowing away that dude right there in the alley, hadn't he? Took Django in, got the Gypsy to bandage his messed-up hand, gave Django a bit of action, some walking around money. Most of all, Grizz gave him protection, staying close under Grizzly's wing, yes.

Django had met a couple of them, guys who worked other neighborhoods for Grizzly, but Grizzly made everybody keep their distance from the others, never liked getting them all together. Fact is, Grizz couldn't trust guys like them. They're liable to get together, figure out how much action Grizz is making off them, taking no risks, carrying nothing on his own self, even staying in three different places, three different addresses. Bunch of rooms in the wormy old Warrenton, paying Django's rent. And a place down on Dorchester, corner of a warehouse, just a john and a cot but Grizzly didn't need much more. And a little old house in the South End out on Albany, kitchen and all. The Gypsy liked that place best but it was too far from the action for the Grizz, he needed to be downtown, needed to see things happen.

Grizzly operated like a company sales manager, products and territories, everybody had their own. Django, he did the medicine, other side of Tremont, down among the gooks and the deadheads left over from the old Combat Zone. There was a Spanish guy, maybe a Cuban, tough little hood named Garcia but Grizzly always called him Garce, he worked the waterfront, selling mostly hash, good Moroccan shit, running it for Grizz, turning a profit.

And a skinny white-faced peckerwood, Drew something his name was, pumped crack and anything else the Boston University kids wanted, working out of Kenmore Square, never carrying, always arranging drops for kids he knew, keeping the risk down, feeding the Good Green back to Grizz.

It was Drew, last name Middleton, birthplace Knoxville, Tennessee, it was Drew Middleton who Grizz told to watch Django while Django was watching Billie, Django hoping she'd lead him to McGuire. It was Drew who timed his stroll across Dalton Street so he could pass Donovan just as the cop re-entered the dance club after nailing Django in the dark doorway of the Convention Center,

Django talking a blue streak before hustling his ass back downtown.

What's Django doin' meetin' a cop up here, so far from home turf, Drew wondered. Drew never thought much a Django. Selling little white pills, that was pussy work.

Drew spiked Donovan as a cop, told Grizzly about it the night before, gave Grizzly all night to think about what he had to do, how he had to know what Django was up to, stupid dumb fuck talking to a cop when he's supposed to be nailing the Jolt.

Early in the morning, not a good time for him but business was business, Grizzly made a couple enquiries around, subtle stuff, till he got a call from the man he wanted, the man who made things go, and then he sent the word for Django to come around, Grizz had to talk with him right now, so haul ass. Sent the word with Drew and Garce and Dewey, let Dewey know about it, Dewey back on the street with the Bird gone, Dewey looking for some action of his own now but not thinking about working for Grizz, not forever, no sir Dewey'd want to run his own show and there wasn't room for Grizz and Dewey together, but that was a problem Grizz'd deal with later.

Dewey, Garce, Drew, they'd get the message to Django, see that he got his little black ass back to Grizz, count on it.

Grizz climbed the stairs to the second floor of the Warrenton Hotel and stomped along the corridor to the four rooms at the end that he shared with the Gypsy and Django, the force of his footsteps shaking the old brass wall fixtures as he passed.

Inside the room the Gypsy was huddled naked on the floor in the corner, her legs drawn up, her chin resting on her bony knees, her eyes wild. "Get some leather on," Grizzly said, and he peeled off his heavy coat, looking to kill some time searching for new perversions, his crotch jacked already just thinking about what he might have to do when Django showed up.

McGuire left Micki sleeping, curled like a child in the oversized bed where her sister had taken countless men, driven there by the frenzy of their own libidos. She had always hated getting up, she loved to stay warm in her bed, and so he left her there. He stepped into his trousers, put on his shirt and tiptoed from the room.

He shrugged into his jacket and descended the stairs, emerging in the late morning traffic on Newbury Street to find a newspaper, put himself in touch with the world again. At a newsstand on Boylston across from the Lenox, he bought a *Globe* from the newsdealer who sucked on a hand-rolled cigarette set in the middle of his mouth, the man shifting his weight from side to side, trying to warm himself with the motion. McGuire scanned the headlines and the sky and walked back to Newbury, feeling something close to affection for the people he passed, street people and Back Bay condominium residents, B.U. students and delivery people, all of them more driven by than engaged in their lives, rarely questioning themselves, and he envied them for it.

On his way to the apartment McGuire thought of Heather, picturing her face, its quick smile and dark eyes, and her compact body: square shoulders, deep chest, hips that flared from a taut waist and dancer's legs, the thighs strong, the calves delicately sculpted.

He had never known a woman so entranced with her own place in the world, so firmly fixed upon her own status and so driven toward some goal or objective visible only to her, her progress measured according to her own secret calibrations.

McGuire and Heather had shared nothing warmer than a truce, although more than once at parties and social events, Heather passed behind him and drew the fingertips of one hand across McGuire's buttocks, murmuring "Nice ass" from the corner of her mouth before breaking into that strange laughter she had, that way of finding every incident that touched her life either secretly humorous or sinister and dangerous.

In the beginning McGuire told himself the gulf between the two of them existed because they both loved Micki and Heather, as the older sister, the protective sibling, would always be jealous of McGuire's influence over Micki, filling a role that had once been her own.

But Heather's view was different. "You know why we don't get along, gumshoe?" she once said to McGuire, a glass of wine in her hand and a laugh poised to explode from her mouth. "It's because we're too much alike." And before McGuire could reply, there was the laughter and she added, "Of course, I'm also a hell of a lot smarter than you are."

There had been a desperation about Heather, McGuire recalled, unfathomable in its source, and in combination with Heather's anger it would drive her to achieve any goal, no matter how outrageous. "What makes her so angry?" McGuire once asked Micki, and Micki said it was something that had happened to Heather when she was a child, something about an uncle who had sexually abused her, something the family never openly acknowledged or discussed.

"Heather told me once," Micki said, "that when Mom heard about it, she blamed Heather for leading Uncle Jack on and Heather realized later that Mom had been jealous. Mom hadn't been angry about her husband's brother screwing her daughter, she was jealous." Micki had smiled and shook her head and said, "Aren't some families totally messed up?"

It was Heather who detonated the explosion that destroyed McGuire's marriage by telling him of Micki's lover, revealing her long-term affair with a lawyer in Cambridge, and when McGuire awoke to the meaning of Micki's many lies and disappearances over recent weeks, it was Heather who had laughed and mocked him, who taunted him as a cuckold.

When Tim Fox and Micki told McGuire of Heather's crude blackmailing of her lovers, McGuire knew that Heather had gained more enjoyment from the dominance, from the fear her threats generated in the men she betrayed, and from the rush of power and danger than from the money it earned her.

McGuire climbed the stairs to the kitchen, made coffee and ascended the steep stairway to the fourth level. He crossed the alcove beyond the bedroom where Micki was still sleeping, and walked down the short hall to the office.

He remembered.

It had begun returning to him on the street, watching the people, envying them their concerns, their purposes. Now the memory was crystallizing, solidifying, the facts butting edge to edge like cellular growth.

Heather had sent a message to him with Django, a note on her personal lilac-colored stationery, Django handing it to him furtively across a table in the Flamingo. He remembered that.

And before that, a week after their meeting in the Esplanade, she had found McGuire in the Public Garden, waiting for Django to appear. She proposed the idea then, the first time.

"Make yourself some money," she told him. "You still have friends over on Berkeley Street, haven't you? All you have to do is tell me a few things about them, about one of them anyway. And maybe hold on to some stuff for me."

He recalled how she was dressed: a fur coat swinging open over a flowered print dress, her neck ringed in heavy gold and large diamond earrings flashing fire in the low autumn sun.

In the most eloquent manner he could summon at the time, McGuire had told her to go away.

"Hey, if you won't do this for me," she had said, "I'll find somebody who will." And that quick cold smile. "But I'd rather get you to do it for me. And I will."

And then the note delivered by Django, saying she knew how much McGuire relied on Django and what Django did, what he sold McGuire. "You do this for me, loser," she had written. "Or I'll see that the guy delivering this gets his ass in jail and yours in the harbor. Call me tonight."

Why me, McGuire had wondered, and the answer came back: Because she wants to humiliate you, because she despises you for rejecting her. And because, as an ex-cop, you know things she doesn't, you have access to something she needs.

He remembered the murder investigation summary Zelinka had given him and he withdrew it from his pocket, unfolded it and sat heavily in the chair at Heather's desk. Scanning its contents, thinking of all he had absorbed and pondered since Heather's death, he pictured Heather fleeing her attacker in the bedroom, running down the hall to this office, turning abruptly again for the door, seeking refuge in the bathroom . . .

And he knew.

He sat back in the chair and nodded his head.

He knew.

Garce found Django in a doughnut shop on Charles Street, there in a back booth, stretching a coffee, trying to stay cool, wasting the morning. "Grizz wanna talk," Garce said, standing there over the booth, hands in his pockets, a crazy black beret on his head, black nylon windbreaker done to the neck.

"What for?" Django said. "Saw Grizz last night. Don't need to see the man now."

"Hell you don't," Garce said. He had an upper tooth missing in the front, a black hole in his mouth that made him look like some kid maybe fell off his skateboard or something. "Man says you come, you come."

"He mad?"

"Grizz never get mad." Garce stepped aside for Django to get out of the booth, staying close. "Grizz jus' get along. With evr'body. You know that."

Django nodded and rose to follow Garce, feeling something inside him, something scratching and clawing, telling him not to go, just run but don't go, and he ignored it.

Grizz wouldn't hurt him. Even walking down the corridor to Grizz's room, Garce behind him now, Django kept telling himself there's nothing to worry about, just have a talk with Grizz, find out what's on the man's mind.

Standing outside Grizzly's room, Django didn't know what was going on inside from the sounds coming through the door. Grizz would put something across the Gypsy's mouth, maybe a leather strap to bite on, Django never knew. But now he could hear her moaning or screaming or whatever behind the door.

Took three knocks on the door by Garce before it opened and there's Grizz standing there, big belly hanging out over the pants he just pulled on, the Gypsy lying back on the bed, her face red and her hands flying in the air like bats or something, like she can't control them.

Grizz looked really pissed at first, then he smiled when he saw Django. "Need to talk, you 'n me," he said. "Gimme couple minutes, go wait in your room."

Garce had never been in Django's room before, Garce hardly ever came to the Warrenton, had his own place in Charlestown. But he came in now, followed Django in and leaned against the door frame like he's being cool while Django sat on his bed, saying here it comes, here it comes to himself, trying not to show the shakes.

Grizz opened the door maybe five minutes later and said, "We gotta talk, over inna alley. Let's go."

They walked down the stairs and out onto Washington Street, crossing the road among Oriental families carrying food in plastic bags and gawking tourists looking for what was left of the Combat Zone. They went up the alley to the square formed by the back of the empty buildings, Tremont Adult Novelties and Shawmut Imports and others, Grizz leading the way, Garce behind Django, Django's mouth dry and his knees weak. In the middle sat the forty-gallon drum, all rusty, two feet of ashes in the bottom.

"You not sayin' much." Grizzly slapped the side of the rusted drum as he passed, heading for the back door of Tremont Adult Novelties. "Garce, you ever see Django with his mouth not flappin'?"

"Sure ain't," Garce said.

Grizz stopped near the back of the building, turned around, looked up at a sky as cold and gray as the broken concrete Django was staring down at. "Not like the way it was flappin' at that cop last night." He looked at Django. "Like I hear."

"That cop?" Django grinned, looked around, looked at Garce and Grizz, back and forth. "He a jive turd, Grizz." Django shrugged. "Man jump me 'cause I was trackin' Lady Billie, jus' like you say, and he see me. No big deal, Grizz. I tell him I'm lookin' for cars to hot-wire, tha's all. Jus' lookin' for cars, Buick, Benz, somethin', but I was gonna lay off, yes sir, stay on my own turf . . ."

Grizzly's hand flew at Django's head, catching Django just at the corner of his eye, right where Grizz had aimed, and Django was on the ground, his legs drawn up, waiting maybe for a kick.

"Hey, Grizz," Django said. "What you wanna do that for?"

"You talk at cops," Garce said. Sometime while Django'd been talking, Garce had pulled a knife from his jacket and he held it now in one hand, lightly, like he was weighing it, judging how heavy it was. Long blade, cut out at the top, ending in a nasty point.

"I answer the man," Django said. He watched the knife, he couldn't take his eyes from the knife. "He thinks I trackin' him and Billie, tha's all. . . ."

"Wha's his name?" Grizzly said.

"Man didn't tell me his—"

This time it was Grizzly's boot. Django saw it coming and turned his head so that the boot caught him beside the ear and he lost it for a second, blackness and then flashes of light and then the pain, funny how there was that little bit of time when you wait for the pain to come.

"Donovan," Django said. He kept his eyes closed. If more was coming, he didn't want to see it.

"Talk to a cop an' know his name?" Garce said, like he's surprised and impressed, like Django just told him he'd won a million dollars in a lottery.

"Talk to the Jolt an' know his name," Django said. "Grizz know that. Jolt's a customer, Grizz give me the goods to make a sale, I find him . . ."

"You didn't find no Jolt," Grizz said. "Tell you do somethin' an' it don't get done, hell kinda way izzat to work? Huh?"

"I'm lookin', Grizz." Django lay where he was, wondering if he was going to be sick.

"Garce say you lay somethin' heavy on this cop." Grizz knelt down, got his face closer to Django's. "That right, Garce?"

"Tha's right." Garce was tossing the knife from one hand to the other now, back and forth.

"What'd you tell him?" Grizz said. "What'd you tell this cop, make him so impress with you?"

Do it, Django thought. Let it go, can't hurt you. Can't hurt you now. "I tell him what I see," Django said. "The night the black cop get his, behin' the Bird, up at the Jolt's place."

"You see somethin' then?"

Django nodded, biting his bottom lip.

Grizz, still watching Django, held a long arm up at Garce, the massive hand open, fingers splayed. Garcia took a step forward, placed the knife in Grizzly's hand, the white mother-of-pearl handle first.

"Don' move," Grizzly said. His voice was calm, gentle. "Don' move a thing," and he brought his hand back and lay the blade of the knife on Django's cheek, the feel of it cold and angry, and he slid the blade until the needle point tickled the inside corner of Django's right eye, below the bridge of his nose. "You feel that?" Grizzly asked.

Django was afraid to move his head so he whispered, "I feel it, Grizz," and Grizz said, "Good," and then Grizz asked him to tell him everything Django had told Donovan, especially what Django had seen in the alley behind the Flamingo the night Tim Fox was killed.

***

Micki came downstairs with sleep and hair in her eyes. "I smelled the coffee," she said to McGuire. "Thought you might bring me some."

McGuire was sitting at the kitchen table, the *Globe* spread open in front of him next to a cup of black coffee, but he hadn't been reading. He had been thinking of Heather's murder and Tim Fox's death. "Go back to bed," McGuire said. "I'll bring a cup up to you."

"Come with me," she said.

She led him by the hand upstairs and back to the dishevelled sheets and they lay together, Micki folded into him, her head on his shoulder while he stroked her hair.

"Who are you mixed up with?" McGuire asked.

"What do you mean?"

"Down in Florida. What are you up to?"

"Nothing special."

"Like the guy in Lauderdale, the dope dealer? You said he was nothing special either."

"He wasn't."

"You lived with him two, three years."

She shifted against him, avoiding his eyes.

"And when he got caught, he pulled you right in with him. Nice guy."

"I never said he was nice."

"You never said you loved him either."

"I didn't."

"You spent three years of your life with him. Still be with him, maybe, if he hadn't got caught in a D.E.A. raid. What'd he get? Five to ten, something like that?"

She twisted her head to look at him. "Why now?"

"Why what now?"

"Why bring all this up now? Down in Florida, when you came to see me, we never talked about this stuff. We didn't talk much about anything."

"Maybe it matters now. More than it did then."

She exhaled slowly and her eyes drifted. "He reminded me of you."

"Just what I want to hear. My ex-wife shacks up with a drug dealer because he reminds her of me."

"I meant you're both . . . dangerous in a way. That's what attracted me to you in the first place."

"Were we that much alike, him and me?"

"No. In other ways you weren't alike at all. He was cocky, arrogant. You . . . you were always a little sad, a little, I don't know . . . kind of blue."

"You miss him?"

"No." Not a moment's hesitation in answering.

He wanted to speak, considered the phrases he would use, explored how he might express the anger, the hatred, the way he despised all she had done, but almost as soon as they sprang into his mind, he discarded them and continued to stroke her hair with his hand, wondering how they had arrived at this place and this time, the both of them, together.

Grizzly had cut Django some, little nick under the eye, little slice down his cheek, just laying the edge of the knife in, let him know how sharp it was, how much it could hurt. While Django remained frozen there, his eyes closed, feeling the blood run across his cheek, Garce did what Grizzly told him to do, wrapping a length of wire around Django's wrists, binding them together behind his back.

"Get up," Grizzly said when Garce finished. He grabbed Django by an elbow and lifted.

Django stood, opened his eyes, looked at Grizzly. "Grizz, I never did nothin' 'gainst you," Django said. He twisted his body to look at Garce who was watching, eyes half-closed in that funny way of his, never know if he was stoned or sleepy or maybe just nearsighted.

"Never said you did," Grizzly said. He opened the wooden rear door of Tremont Adult Novelties that led into the storage area, a space smaller than Django's room at the Warrenton. Beyond it was a heavy steel-clad door, barred from the inside. "Move your ass," Grizzly said.

Django took a small step forward, waiting for his eyes to adjust to the darkness until Grizzly shoved him from behind, sending him sprawling to the concrete floor, and something skittered off among empty cardboard cartons stacked against the wall. He landed on one shoulder, trying to protect his hands, and his head struck the concrete, opening a gash above an eyebrow.

"Didn't piss me off," Grizzly said. He angled his head at Garce who brought the heavy door closed, shutting out the sunlight. "Pissed other people off's what you did."

Django heard something shoved through the hasp of the door, locking him inside.

The clinging warmth rising from his groin to his scalp exploded in the release, and he was crying words with meaning but without shape. Then he was lying beside her while she watched him catch his breath and swallow and blink several times before covering his eyes with his hand.

"Never in bed," Micki said, tracing circles on McGuire's chest with her forefinger. "We never had any problems in bed."

"In bed with each other, you mean." McGuire removed his hand and stared across the room at the wall, thinking of nothing.

"You always bring up the good stuff," she said sarcastically. She smiled and wove her fingers together. "If we only got along, you know, in the rest of our lives as well as we do in bed. . . ."

"We didn't do that badly." He twisted his head to look at her. "What happened this morning? Everything was fine and then . . ."

"I don't know." She folded her hands and lay her head on them, like a child preparing for sleep. "I heard you come in, I knew you had the morning paper and I thought, 'It's like those Sundays when Joe'd go for a walk in the morning and I'd hear him leave and go back to sleep and wake up and smell bacon and coffee and toast and we'd have breakfast together and talk.' But it's not like that . . ."

"Would've been for one day." A weight settled in McGuire's chest. "That's what I was going to do. . . ."

"That'd be dumb, wouldn't it?"

"What?"

"Trying . . ." She pulled a tissue from a pocket of the robe and dabbed at her nose and eyes with it as she spoke. "Trying to act like nothing's happened, having breakfast, pretending it was ten years ago when it's not."

"Even last night?"

"No, last night was terrific." She smiled at him. "Wasn't it?"

McGuire nodded.

"I meant thinking we could ever have a life together again." She bit her bottom lip and looked away. "I'm sorry. Maybe I'd better go back to Florida."

McGuire rose from the bed and began putting on his clothes. "Make it soon," he muttered. "Soon as you can."

"Why the hell not, Eddie?"

Phil Donovan stood shaking in the captain's office, watching Fat Eddie trying to stay cool, popping another thick tablet into his mouth.

"You know why," Vance said. "It's classified. You tell me what you're looking for and I'll locate it for you."

"I told you, I got an eyewitness description—"

"From a convicted felon, a street person, probably addicted to the same chemicals he peddles on the streets. You think I'm going to break the commissioner's instructions on something that weak? Now if you want to bring your witness in here where we can question him correctly and in some depth. . . ."

"The guy's not gonna risk his ass comin' down here, not unless we arrest him. And then there's nothing in it for him if he talks, we got nothing on him."

"Yes, we have." Vance smiled. "We could lay trafficking charges very easily, you know that."

"And he still won't talk unless we get him protection." Donovan walked to Vance's window and back. "Can you promise him that?"

"I can't promise anything," Vance said. "But if you want to find this witness and bring him in here, we could assess things."

"Do you know who he saw?" Donovan asked. "Do you know who he described?"

"I think so," Vance said. Something was doing somersaults in his intestines. "But I don't believe it."

Donovan stared back at Vance, then turned and left, leaving the captain alone in his office reaching for his antacid tablets.

Should he tell Zelinka, Vance wondered. Zelinka, sitting up there in his cubbyhole near Government Center, spinning off requests for files that even Vance himself would normally not have access to except with the commissioner's directive. Files from everywhere, few of them connected with anything except some convoluted bookkeeping among a few downtown businessmen, none of it decipherable to Vance, none of it directly linked to the murders of Heather Lorenzo and Tim Fox.

No, he decided. There was nothing to tell, all Donovan had was a wild tale from some half-crazed street person. He would rather find a way to rein in Donovan, let him know if he was going to explode like he just had, he'd better back it up with results. That's what McGuire and Schantz had done.

McGuire and Schantz.

There were times when he almost missed them.

* * *

Grizz my buddy, Django repeated to himself. He tell me once, he say, "You okay, some day I let you have a little taste of the Gypsy, show you what a real woman can do, she love a man 'nough."

Never say that to nobody else, Django assured himself.

He was cold, the concrete beneath his body like the floor of a freezer chest, and the wire cut into the skin of his wrists. The blood on his cheek had hardened to a crust and in spite of his fear and panic he was weary. When Grizzly came and let him go, he'd head back to the Warrenton, crawl into bed, have a good sleep, refresh himself.

Django couldn't judge time, never owned a watch, but less than an hour had passed before he heard footsteps on the bare dry earth of the square surrounding the rusting barrel. No voices. Just footsteps and a fumbling at the hasp. Django sat up painfully on his haunches, facing the door.

When the door swung open, the gray light that flooded in on Django was like life itself, and he smiled back at the silhouettes of Grizzly and Garce looking down at him. Behind them stood the Gypsy in the massive oversized gray parka, muttering to herself, one hand rising to stroke a fresh raw welt on the side of her neck then falling, rising and falling, over and over, like a mechanical device marking the time or signaling danger.

"Hey, Grizz," Django said. "Everything cool, right?"

Grizzly looked back at Django, his face cold and unyielding like the pitted concrete floor, and when

Django looked at Garce, the Cuban turned his head away and Django began to panic.

"Goddamn it, Grizz!" Django tried to rise to one knee but with his hands behind his back he had no balance, no momentum, and he fell sideways, feeling more vulnerable than ever. "I good to you, Grizz," Django said. "I good to you, I your man, Grizz!" He rose to his knees again, a man shouldn't die on his knees but he didn't want to die lying there on the floor, giving up, either.

Garce had taken a step back from the door and stood with his hands in his pockets, looking around, staying cool.

"Tol' you," Grizz said. "You good to me but other people, they better to me, you know that. Need them more'n I need you. An' they don' need you at all. Don' even want you around."

Grizzly held a hand out toward the Gypsy, keeping his eyes on Django, and the Gypsy, still muttering to herself, reached inside the parka and withdrew a blue-steel snub-nosed revolver.

At the sight of the gun, Django panicked and tried to stand and run until Grizzly's boot shot out and the blow to Django's chest sent him rolling on his side, deep within the storage shed, facing the open door, watching it all.

The Gypsy was staring down at the gun, turning it over in her hand like maybe her name was written on it somewhere.

Grizzly raised his right arm again, stretching it out toward the Gypsy, his fingers moving in an impatient give-it-to-me motion while Django watched, unable to take his eyes off her and the gun in her hand.

The Gypsy was still muttering something to herself and her other hand, the free one, rose to stroke the welt on her neck. She took a step toward Grizzly, raising the gun.

Django didn't hear what she said, never heard anything above the sound of traffic out on Washington, but Grizzly heard it. A puzzled expression crossed his face, and when the big man turned to look at her for the first time, she raised the gun to the level of his head and fired.

The bullet struck Grizzly in the face, shattering his lower jaw. He dropped to his knees, keeping his arm outstretched to her, still wanting the gun and she repeated the words and fired into his shoulder. Still Grizzly remained kneeling until a third and a fourth bullet entered his chest, the Gypsy talking to herself between each squeeze of the trigger. She stepped toward Grizzly's prone body and shot him again, repeated the words and shot him a sixth time before squeezing the trigger on an empty chamber.

Garce had ducked against the building at the first shot, crouching there, watching it all. Now the Gypsy raised the gun in his direction and pulled the trigger again, then swung her arm toward Django and tried to shoot him. Django heard the hammer click harmlessly, watching as the Gypsy slouched to the ground where she sat and stared openmouthed at Grizzly's body.

Django wriggled through the open doorway. Garce, circling Grizzly's body, his eyes on the river of blood running down the slight incline toward the alley, almost tripped over him.

"He'p me, Garce," Django said. "Get the wires. Or cops'll find me, we all be in shit." Garce knelt beside Django and untwisted the wire before bolting away, Django behind him, glancing briefly back at the Gypsy who was still watching Grizzly, the empty gun pointed at him like she was daring him to get up. Like she could do anything about it if he suddenly came alive to hurt her again.

Django and Garce ran together down the lane and along Washington in the direction of the Common until Garce noticed people watching them, a Cuban and a black, street people, running in panic, one of them with fresh blood on his face. Had to be bad news, keep an eye on those hoodlums, and Garce and Django ducked around the corner on Oak Street, through a parking lot and down a service lane. At the end Garce sat against a dumpster smelling of rotting Oriental food and rested his head in his hands, his breath sounding like a steam engine at rest.

Django paced in circles in front of him. "D'ja know he doin' that?" Django said. "He ready to blast me?"

Garce shook his head. "Said you had a lesson comin'," Garce said. "Din't know wha' kind."

"Listen," Django said. "Hear?"

They both held their breath as a police siren approached from the north, and Garce leaned forward to look down the lane toward Washington, watching two police cars scream past.

"See you 'round," Garce said, standing. He grinned almost shyly at Django. "You gotta be the luckiest black man in Boston."

Django nodded. He was thinking of his hotel room, the few belongings he had, the little bit of his money stashed away behind the loose baseboard under the bed. Two thousand dollars nearly. Enough to get him started, set him up, think about where he'd go, what he'd do.

Garce was already walking down the lane, hands in the back pockets of his tight black jeans, swivel-hipping away.

"Hey, Garce," Django called.

Garce stopped and turned to look at Django warily. "Wha'?"

"What she be sayin'?" Django asked. "The Gypsy, she mutterin' somethin', I couldn't hear. You hear what that crazy woman sayin'?"

Garce smiled and nodded. "She prayin'. But she couldn't get pas' the firs' par'."

"Prayin'?"

Garce nodded again. "She say, 'Our father, who art in heaven, hallow be thy name,' thas' what the craz' bitch sayin' over and over. Craz' bitch."

EIGHTEEN

"You have a message," Ronnie Schantz told McGuire over the telephone.

McGuire lifted a coffee cup to his lips. From upstairs he could hear the sound of the shower. "What is it?" he asked. "Somebody invited you to dinner tonight. He just called a few moments ago, said this was the number Berkeley Street gave him."

"Who?"

"Man named Harley DeMontford. Ever heard of him?"

"Yeah," McGuire said. "I've heard of him."

It swept over him again, propelled by the prospect of pain, the knowledge that Micki was already planning another departure from him, the awareness that he would be able to hold back the distress and depression for only a few hours until it crushed him again.

And he wanted a taste, a ripple of the wave that the meperidine could ride to him. He wanted to escape with it on the warm wave of vertigo he had ridden for so many weeks. . . .

Ronnie was speaking to him. He rubbed his forehead, told himself to dredge up some goddamn courage and listen to her voice.

"Sounded very nice on the telephone. Very cultured. If you go, you may have to come up and change into one of your suits. Dinner's at six o'clock. In the dining room at the Four Seasons."

McGuire released a slow whistle. "Let me talk to Ollie."

He heard a click on the line before Ollie's voice rasped through his speaker phone. "Joseph!" his former partner barked. "Where are you?"

"Newbury Street," McGuire said. "Heather Lorenzo's apartment."

"Scene of the crime. One of 'em anyway. What the hell you doin' there?"

"I'm with Micki."

Ollie waited a beat or two before speaking, more slowly, more gently now. "Ronnie tell you about your dinner date?"

"She told me."

"Who's Harley DeMontford?"

"Owns a stock brokerage. Dan Scrignoli fingered him in a Green Team operation and turned him, got him to name some names."

"And DeMontford gets off the hook."

"Scrignoli says he's one guy in a big bunch, he's a small price to pay."

"So what's he want with you?"

"Heather Lorenzo was blackmailing DeMontford. There's no evidence, no paper trail. Scrignoli told me about it."

"This guy DeMontford, he married?"

"So I hear."

"Lemme guess. Once a month his accountant adds up his net worth, pays him a visit and says, 'Harley, you really love your wife, don't you?' and old Harley looks at the balance sheet and says, 'Sure as hell do.'"

McGuire smiled. "That's what it sounds like."

"And if it spills that DeMontford was doing elbow push-ups on Heather Lorenzo, DeMontford threatens to take his chances in court instead of testifying against his country club buddies, that the way it works?"

"Without DeMontford, Scrignoli's case might not even make it to the grand jury."

"Who talked to him from Fat Eddie's group?"

"According to Scrignoli, nobody."

"They nuts over there? Timmy Fox is dead, it's got something to do with the Lorenzo thing, he's banging her for bucks and nobody's talked to him?"

"Calm down, Ollie," McGuire began.

To McGuire's surprise, Ollie did. McGuire heard three long noisy breaths drawn in and exhaled, then Ollie's voice again. "You know something, don't you?"

"Yeah, I do," McGuire said.

"What?"

"I know DeMontford's involved."

"Where was he that night the Lorenzo woman was killed?"

"On Cape Cod with Dan Scrignoli, pulling all the parts of Danny's case together."

"So what're you saying, DeMontford got some goon to do her?"

"No," McGuire said, leaning back in his chair and stretching his legs in front of him. "That's not what I'm saying at all."

Billie was out of cigarettes, which was a royal pain in the ass. She was also on her second pot of coffee, sitting there watching the goddamn television, bunch of crazy people on talk shows, where the hell do they get these freaks?

Maybe the telephone wasn't working. It had happened before, Dewey trying to reach her one afternoon and some jerk working on the roof clipped the telephone lines, didn't tell anybody about it.

Don't be stupid. The telephone's working.

So why hasn't he called?

Go out and get some cigarettes and he'll call for sure. Why didn't she get an answering machine last month when she saw them on sale, fifty bucks? Could use one now.

Maybe she'd have a drink, a little taste of Wild Turkey from the bottle in the cupboard behind the oatmeal.

She stood up, took three steps toward the kitchen and detoured past the telephone, picked up the receiver.

Damn thing's working.

* * *

"I'm going for a walk." Micki handed McGuire a brass key. "Take this in case . . . in case I'm not here when you get back, okay?"

Micki stood in the open bedroom doorway watching McGuire, who lay back with his hands clasped behind his head. He had been thinking of small white pills.

"I don't belong here anymore." Her face shattered like a fearful child's. "No, don't, please," she added as McGuire began to rise from the bed to reach for her. "I'm going back to Florida tomorrow. I'll let you know where I am, what I'm doing. Okay?"

"What happened?"

The question seemed to stun her. "What?"

"What are you afraid of?" McGuire said gently. "What's the worst that can happen? We try to make it work again and it doesn't? Is that what scares you?"

"Yes." She raised her eyes to the ceiling and bit her lower lip.

"But isn't it worth trying anyway?"

"No." She shook her head vigorously, like a terrier. "Not unless I know for sure."

"There's nothing to know for sure."

"*I never knew you!*" She held her small hands at her waist, her fists clenched like an angry schoolgirl's, and when she spoke she kept her eyes closed, maybe concentrating on her words, maybe blocking out the sight of McGuire, he didn't know. "I don't know who you are. Who are you? Do you know? Are you some tough son of a bitch like other people, the ones you work with, think you are? But you're *not*. There were times when I wanted you to

314

get angry with *me*, just to let it out, but you didn't or you couldn't, you just withdrew, over and over, until something would happen, I never knew what, and you'd put your head on my chest and cry like a baby and . . ."

"Micki—"

". . . and I never knew why, you'd never tell me. Who the hell are you anyway? I mean really, inside? Do you know yourself?"

"Maybe I never gave a damn. About knowing who I was."

"Yes, you did, yes, you did. You were just *scared* to find out. You were *scared*, and it frightened me, it scared the hell out of *me*. That's what made you dangerous, can't you see that? Other men, they can hit me or threaten me, I can deal with that because . . . because it's *there*, it's in front of me, but you . . . It was all hidden, it's *still* all hidden and . . . Can't you *see*?"

McGuire couldn't see. Looking that deeply and darkly within himself would be like asking him to see the back of his head without a mirror. "Why are you saying all of this now?" he said. "Why now?"

"Because . . . because I started feeling something for you all over again and I had to remind myself that . . . that I need somebody who knows who he is, not some big kid who acts tough and really isn't and will never know. Don't you understand how that can scare somebody close to you? Don't you?"

McGuire lay there for a very long time after she turned and descended the steps, after the door at the bottom of the stairs had closed and after his body had shook with spasms of sadness and despair.

* * *

"You will at least have an enjoyable meal."

Rudy Zelinka smiled at McGuire across his untidy desk. Outside, on the square in front of the old courthouse, a weak sun cast pale shadows across empty concrete walks and over flower beds crowded with frost-killed flowers.

"And a wonderful view of the Public Garden," Zelinka added. "I understand DeMontford has a table reserved for his exclusive use in one of the bay windows on Boylston Street."

"I didn't expect him to do something like this," McGuire said. "Inviting me to dinner. I called just to poke him a little, see if he'd panic."

Zelinka thrust out a bottom lip. "It fits the man's personality, from what I know of him. Stay aloof, in control. You come at him in a vulgar manner, he responds with formality."

"What do you figure he'll talk about?"

"He'll want to impress you with his power. Discover perhaps how much you know, in an atmosphere where he cannot incriminate himself." The cold smile returned. "Perhaps he will offer you a job. He'll certainly want to protect himself." Zelinka made a tent with his hands. "I should tell you that enquiries have been made at Berkeley Street, delicate discreet enquiries by a prominent criminal lawyer acting on Mr. DeMontford's behalf."

"Wondering what you've got on his client," McGuire said.

"Yes, but more pointed than that. The lawyer is aware of DeMontford's agreement to cooperate with Scrignoli's investigation and suggested that he could advise his client to cease such activities unless Dan Scrignoli is the only officer dealing with him. Anybody else approaches him and he'll simply refuse to cooperate."

"Scrignoli's the only one he trusts?"

Zelinka smiled and watched McGuire.

"Still doesn't make sense," McGuire said. "I'm on the fringe of things. All I know is what you and Scrignoli tell me."

"I believe you know more than anyone else, perhaps even me."

"I've got some suspicions, ideas . . . ."

"You have far more than that," Zelinka said. "I think you have worked many problems out in your head to this point, hmm?" The Hungarian pursed his lips and raised his eyebrows.

"A few." McGuire was hesitant, unsure about how much he should share with Zelinka. "Tell me again why DeMontford, who probably never heard of me before I called him, invites me to dinner."

"Never heard of you?" Zelinka spread his arms wide. "Don't be so modest. He knows of you. Mr DeMontford is very active in church diocese activities and he remembers your involvement in the serial killer of priests several years ago. To him, you are perhaps a minor celebrity."

Zelinka lowered his hands and leaned forward, fixing McGuire with his dark eyes.

"But I suspect it's because you are unthreatening to him. And you may be a source of information, a conduit even. The man is fearful, McGuire. He maintains a cool exterior but beneath it he is panic-stricken. Within a few months he could find himself bereft of his marriage, his business and his freedom." He smiled. "I love that word, bereft. It addresses the feelings the man will have while pondering his foolishness."

"How do you know so much about DeMontford?" McGuire said. "You're Internal Affairs, DeMontford's a Team Green source."

"I said I despise computers, McGuire. I did not say I refuse to use them. You may have noticed the terminal in the outer office."

"Somebody's opening files for you, sending you reports from Berkeley Street."

"I'm learning all I need to know without leaving any fingerprints."

"From who? Brookmyer?"

"It doesn't matter who." Zelinka looked away, smiled to himself, looked back at McGuire. "Brookmyer handles the transmissions and the commissioner has authorized his cooperation. Brookmyer himself is not accessing the files. You may be surprised at who is."

"So tell me."

"Captain Vance."

It was McGuire's turn to smile. "Fat Eddie? He's running things for you?"

"Don't underestimate him." Zelinka shrugged. "Due to the complexities of this case, access to information must be restricted to higher levels of authority. Whenever higher levels of authority are involved, Eddie Vance suddenly discovers new abilities neither he nor the rest of us were aware of." Zelinka withdrew a pen from the inside pocket of his worn tweed jacket. "Now if you'll tell me what you know of Tim Fox's death and any related information, I will tell you what you may want to know before having dinner with the elegant Mr. DeMontford."

At the door, Zelinka touched McGuire on the shoulder. "Have you won?" he said.

"Won what?"

"Whatever you win when you divest yourself of something that is destroying you."

"Nothing to win," McGuire said. "Nothing to lose."

Descending the stairs, McGuire realized that Zelinka had been referring to his meperidine addiction and not to Micki.

Well, she'd be damned if she'd call *him*. Phoned him twice this morning, left messages both times, how much more can a girl do?

Billie rose from her chair, fell back, rose again and reached out to steady herself against the battered walnut end table.

Out of cigarettes, out of bourbon, out of men, she thought. Then she grinned. Hell, I'm out of a job too. So what do I need first?

"Cigarettes and bourbon," she said aloud. Then look for a job. Get a job, get out and around, find another man, men're the easiest part. It's the *good* men, the decent ones, guys you can *trust*, they're the hard ones to find and hold on to.

She dressed in an old pair of slacks, heavy sweater, flat shoes. Ran a brush through her hair, smeared a little lipstick on her mouth, sprayed some L'Air du Temps on her neck, never know who you might meet on the street. Checked herself in the mirror, frowned, pulled her sweater up to her neck and removed her bra. Walked into the bedroom to find another one, a French model with wire under the cups, give her a better bust line.

She had the old bra off and the new one in her hands when she heard the knock at the door.

Well, hot damn, she thought. About time. She tossed the lace bra back in the drawer, pulled the sweater down over her breasts, her nipples getting hard already, you could see them poking against the fabric.

She walked to the door, fluffing her hair on the way. She had something to get off her chest at *him*, damn it, and swung the door open, a pained expression on her face but remembering to keep her stomach pulled in, her shoulders back, let him know what he's been missing, how close he came to losing it for *good*.

McGuire rode the Blue MBTA line to Revere Beach, arriving in the late afternoon, the sky gray and grieving. There was little wind but the sea beyond the breakwater roiled and threatened, and the sound of the waves and whitecaps were a constant background noise, like machinery humming on a distant production line.

Ronnie greeted him at the front door of the small white house, ushering him quickly into the warmth and clucking with concern at his light jacket, inadequate against the dampness and cold. "I pressed your gray trousers and sports jacket," she said. "I picked out one of Ollie's ties, a red and gray stripe, and ironed a white shirt for you. Want some coffee?"

McGuire kissed her on the forehead, a gesture he knew she disliked, and took the mug of coffee into Ollie's room.

"You see Zelinka?" Ollie demanded without greeting McGuire first.

McGuire said he had.

"You tell him what you told me, what we talked about this morning?"

"Most of it," McGuire said. He settled himself in the chair next to Ollie's bed.

"He buy it?"

McGuire nodded. "He suspected it all along."

"So what's he gonna do?"

"Wait and see what happens tonight with DeMontford."

"Doesn't have proof," Ollie said.

"And DeMontford's got some heavy lawyers." McGuire took a long swallow of coffee, set the mug aside, crossed his legs, folded his arms.

"DeMontford'll try to figure out what you know."

"Zelinka wants me to spook him a little bit."

Ollie grinned, the action creasing his face until his eyes almost disappeared. "You're good at that, Joseph. You'll spook him 'til he's like a half-fucked fox in a forest fire."

"I'm looking forward to it," McGuire smiled.

"Oh, I'd love to be there and watch you work. God, what I'd give to be there."

"I'll tell you all about it, soon as it's over." McGuire stood up. "I'd better get showered and dressed."

"The Four Seasons, huh?" Ollie watched McGuire. "Might as well hold back, get yourself a

321

good meal out of it first. And don't you forget to call me, give me all the dirt, damn it!"

At the door Ronnie caught up with him and said, "Take this." She tucked some money into McGuire's worn woollen topcoat, the dull gray garment smelling faintly of mothballs. McGuire tried to brush her hand away but she fixed him with those black Irish eyes and said, "Take it and let me and Ollie know you're all right, you hear me?"

McGuire said he heard her and kissed her on the forehead again. "You know I hate it when you do that," she said, and slapped his arm in mock anger as he turned to leave.

"I'm really proud of you," she said.

"For what?"

"For doing what you did. Giving up those pills. You're a pretty tough guy."

McGuire studied her face, grunted and leaned to kiss her gently again.

"How's Micki?" she called to his back as he walked into the night, and he shrugged his shoulders in reply.

Lily Cathcart, who lived in apartment two, never cared for Billie Chandler, never wanted anything to do with a woman who made her living parading around naked in front of a bunch of men, what kind of way was that to live? Lily Cathcart had raised three children and never slept with anyone except her dear late husband for thirty-eight years, and in all that time nobody ever saw *her* naked except Mr. Cathcart, bless his soul, and her family doctor.

Maybe Billie Chandler was at heart a good person, Mrs. Cathcart told herself, just another nice girl
caught in a bad situation. Mrs. Cathcart heard that
Billie lost her job when the terrible place she worked
in was closed down because the black detective was
killed there, gives you some idea of the kind of people Billie associated with, doesn't it? And then that
police officer knocking on her door the other day,
he looked mean enough to . . . well, as mean as anybody Lily might expect to meet on the street.

Goodness knows Billie was always pleasant
enough and kept to herself, Lily Cathcart admitted.
Usually had a smile for her and the other tenants in
the building. Never played her radio or TV too loud
either. Although sometimes Mrs. Cathcart would
hear Billie come in late at night and there'd be
somebody with her, Lily could hear a man talking
and Billie telling him to keep his voice down. And
later, if Mrs. Cathcart got out of bed and went to
the kitchen to make herself a cup of tea and the kettle wasn't boiling and Mrs. Cathcart sat on the far
side of the room closest to Billie's apartment, she
could hear their voices in Billie's bedroom on the
other side of the wall, sometimes talking low and
sometimes making groans, animal sounds.

That's what she thought she heard late that afternoon. Groans, animal sounds, doing it in broad day-
light for goodness' sake. And then the man going
downstairs, his footsteps clump-clump-clump onto
the street, just like that. No goodbyes, not a thing.

Well.

Billie taking off her clothes in some dirty club
downtown was one thing. But if she was trying to

make money as a prostitute in her own apartment, men coming up to her room like that, if Mrs. Cathcart discovered that's what she was doing to make ends meet, there would be nothing for her to do except tell the landlord and insist that Billie be evicted.

In a city justly famous for its many old and elegant hotels, the Four Seasons sits like an overly confident and audacious newcomer, occupying almost an entire city block on Boylston Street across from the Public Garden. Heavy with brass and polished walnut, the ground-floor dining room is on display through a series of smoked-glass bay windows, and it was these windows that McGuire studied, standing in the shadows of the Public Garden, hunched against the cold in his topcoat.

Four of the six window tables were occupied. McGuire scanned them from the other side of Boylston Street, squinting to identify the diners. A middle-aged couple eating dinner without speaking to or acknowledging the other, three men and a woman in business suits sampling drinks and opinions, a young couple studying a menu nervously, two elderly women sipping tea.

One of the tables held a small discreet white card and McGuire walked along the garden pathway to position himself opposite it just as a tall man in a shiny gray suit appeared in the window accompanied by two men in tuxedos, a waiter and the maitre d'. The waiter pulled the chair out for the man and whisked the white tent card away while the maitre d', his white-gloved hands holding each other at waist level, bowed and spoke to the hotel guest. The man in the shining suit nodded and smiled. Both hotel staff quickly disappeared from view, leaving him alone at his table.

The man at the table smoothed his tie and looked casually out the window, his position slightly elevated above the level of pedestrians hurrying by, shopkeepers and office workers on their way toward the subway or to dinner at less prestigious establishments where there would be no view of the Public Garden and no white-gloved waiters to pull out their chairs.

Despite the best efforts of Boston's arguably best hotel, social realities abided beyond the double-insulated glass windows, and while they could not intrude they at least remained visible and vexing to the guests.

McGuire watched one of them: a street beggar of indeterminate age shuffling along Boylston Street an arm's length from the dining-room windows. He wore a long, graying beard, and thatches of unkempt hair spilled out from beneath a knitted cap while he shook a paper cup at passing pedestrians, pleading for spare change. A filthy cloth jacket was buttoned to the neck, and as he walked his oversized shoes slapped the pavement, revealing scabrous bare feet black with dirt. On his hands were mismatched knitted gloves, and when he wasn't begging for coins, he would turn his back to the hotel windows, a street person retaining his dignity in the presence of ostentatious wealth barely a short distance, but several levels of society, away.

The beggar paused at the window where the man in the shiny suit studied him with expressions of interest and disgust. At that moment the waiter arrived with a crystal glass to set in front of him before glaring out the window at the homeless street person. His customer smiled and shook his head at something the waiter said and in an instant the waiter was out of sight again.

The homeless man, unaware of the minor distress he had caused behind him, resumed shuffling by, shaking his paper cup at pedestrians and imploring with watery eyes for handouts.

McGuire crossed the street, the collar of his worn gray wool topcoat turned up and his hands thrust deeply in his pockets. From the corner of his eye he saw the man in the window watch him approach.

At the hotel entrance the doorman avoided eye contact with McGuire who swept past and into the lobby, crossing to the dining room where the maitre d' smiled pleasantly and asked how he could help McGuire.

"DeMontford's expecting me," McGuire said, and the maitre d' closed his eyes long enough to bow his head and turn to lead the way.

DeMontford rose from his chair as McGuire approached. Various parts of the man reflected light in the dimness of the room—a glitter of diamonds in the face of the heavy watch on his wrist, a sheen from the silk fabric of his suit, a twinkle from the gleaming cuff links, a luster from the starched white shirt and a flash from the man's clear lively eyes.

"Joe McGuire," DeMontford said, reaching past the maitre d' to seize McGuire's hand. "A pleasure to meet you finally." His words were carefully modulated and, in place of the expected broad Boston accent, DeMontford enunciated with a vaguely British delivery. "I've been aware of your police career for many years."

"Your coat, Mr. McGuire?" the maitre d' asked.

"I'll hold onto it," McGuire said. He shrugged out of his topcoat as the maitre d' pulled McGuire's chair out for him. McGuire tossed his coat on one of the empty chairs, generating a wave of mothball aroma, and sat down.

"Glenfiddich, neat." DeMontford, who had returned to his chair, held the crystal tumbler up for McGuire's inspection. "Join me?" His voice was deep and raspy with a texture like tree bark.

"Got any Kronenbourg?" McGuire asked. The maitre d' lowered his eyes and nodded. "Make it a cold one," McGuire said.

"I ordered the salmon," DeMontford said to McGuire. "Poached in Chablis with bernaise sauce. Magnificent. Will you have some?"

McGuire said sure, and the waiter nodded again and half backed away, half turned to disappear into the measured gloom of the dining room.

"You certainly got my secretary's attention with your telephone message," DeMontford said. "I assume that was your objective. It worked."

McGuire sat back in his chair and drank in the man's appearance for the first time. The eyes, unwavering and fastened on McGuire's own, were pale blue and McGuire thought inexplicably of cornflowers. The skin was taut and tanned, framing a firm nose, slightly humped, set above a pewter mustache and thin lips. When the lips parted in a wide smile they revealed unnaturally white and even teeth.

"It wasn't what I planned to say to her," McGuire said. He glanced around the half-filled dining room, the tables set far enough apart to prevent eavesdropping, the diners at each table adding to the atmosphere of discretion by speaking in low tones like conspirators.

"And what would that have been?" DeMontford appeared amused, watching McGuire as though he were a stand-up comic about to deliver a monologue.

"I wanted to tell her your nuts were on an anvil and I had a hammer in my hand," McGuire said.

At first, DeMontford responded as though he hadn't heard McGuire. His smile, if anything, grew slightly wider but he gave himself away by narrowing his eyes ever so slightly before shaking his head and lifting his glass to sample the expensive single-malt scotch. "Well, well," he said, sipping from the glass and looking casually around the room. "Well, well, well."

This was all together too much.

Some other man had come bounding up the stairs, making far more noise than necessary, and began pounding on Billie Chandler's door as though he were trying to wake the dead. Then he began shouting her name over and over, saying, "I know you're in there, let me in."

Lily Cathcart opened her door, leaving the chain attached, and spoke across the second-floor landing at him. "Please," she said. "There are others living here, you know."

The man turned his head to glare at her and Mrs. Cathcart retreated slightly from the open door, recognizing his sharp features. "She in there?" he demanded.

"I have no idea," Mrs. Cathcart said, "but I do wish—"

"She's in there, isn't she?" the man said angrily. He took a step toward her and Mrs. Cathcart backed away even further, preparing to slam the door if necessary, frightened by the fury in his eyes. "You hear her go out today?"

"I have no idea who comes and goes," Mrs. Cathcart said.

"That's a load of crap," the man said. "I'll bet you know everything. You see anybody come in here today?"

"If you don't leave, I'm calling the police," Mrs. Cathcart said.

The man glared at her for a moment, then turned back to the door. "Billie!" he shouted. "Goddamn it, open up."

Mrs. Cathcart closed the door and returned to her living room. If he doesn't leave in one minute I'll do it, she promised herself. I will call the police. This is outrageous.

But the man left shortly afterward and she remained where she was, shaking with anger and remembering that she had seen the same man at Billie's door recently, perhaps just a day or so ago. And she would tell the police all about it if he should ever return.

"How much do you know about my association with the police department?" DeMontford asked. He was sitting back in his chair, watching McGuire expectantly, as though waiting for an amusing play to begin.

"You're supposedly cooperating in an undercover investigation concerning fraud," McGuire said. "In exchange for immunity from prosecution."

"Not quite." DeMontford leaned forward and rested his arms on the table. "The fact is, there is no record of my having broken any law. Or committed any transgression. None at all. So there is no risk of prosecution. By working with Dan Scrignoli, I am fulfilling my duty as a concerned and involved citizen."

"Sure, there's no record," McGuire said. "All part of the deal."

"No record." DeMontford's hand cut the air in a horizontal motion across the table. "Nothing. Remember that."

"All right," McGuire said. "So talk to me about Heather Lorenzo."

DeMontford sat back again as the waiter arrived carrying McGuire's beer and a chilled Pilsner glass on a silver tray. "Thank you, Vincent," DeMontford smiled, and he watched the waiter leave before speaking to McGuire. "Any idea how many women Jack Kennedy screwed in the White House?"

McGuire shrugged, pouring the beer into the tall glass. "The hell's that got to do with Heather Lorenzo?"

"I heard close to two hundred," DeMontford said. His voice was tinged with admiration, as though measuring an associate's wealth. "Considering he was in office less than three years, that's a new one about every five days."

McGuire watched DeMontford, waited for him to continue.

"And a lot of people still think he may be the best president we ever had. Don't you find that interesting?"

"Not really." McGuire sipped his beer.

"The point is," DeMontford said, "what a man does with his libido isn't important. Not nearly as important as what he does with his mind."

"Heather Lorenzo," McGuire said, setting the beer glass down, "was not killed by somebody's mind. She was killed by a baseball bat swung at her body and by a knife plunged into her gut. A particularly brutal death."

"Brutal?" DeMontford said. "You're shocked by brutality? A Boston homicide cop? I suspect you don't read much history, do you?" Before McGuire could respond, he waved the question away with his hand. "Of course you don't. You're probably too practical, or consider yourself to be."

DeMontford sat back and stroked his mustache with his fingertips.

"In World War Two, the toughest resistance fighters against the Nazis were the Serbian Chetniks, the meanest, most fanatic guerillas of the war, and when they weren't setting up massacres of the Germans, they were fighting among themselves or wiping out Croats and Muslims."

DeMontford shrugged. "Things haven't changed that much, have they? Anyway, the Chetniks had a favorite method of executing prisoners. Do you know what it was? I'll tell you what it was. They would choose two men of equal weight or better yet, a man and a woman, that was a favorite, and they would hang them from opposite ends of the same short length of rope tossed over a tree limb. Then they would remove the binds from their hands."

DeMontford paused to watch McGuire's reaction. When he saw none, he continued.

"The poor devils would start clawing at each other, trying to pull themselves up for another breath or two while the Chetniks stood around and laughed. Now that's brutal, McGuire."

"And I hear the Turks had a special way of punishing unfaithful women," McGuire offered. "Something about tomcats."

"Yes." DeMontford smiled again. "I'm impressed. You're more widely read than I thought. The Turks would strip the woman naked, place her in a gunnysack with two tomcats and a heavy stone, tie it all up and throw it in the sea. I've always found that fascinating. What went on inside the gunnysack, I mean. The tomcats in a frenzy, the woman hysterical . . . Every death is filled with terror, McGuire. Of one kind or another. You of all men should know that."

"How much terror did Heather Lorenzo suffer before she died?" McGuire asked.

"I have no idea."

"There was blood everywhere. In the foyer, down the hall, in her office, back up the hall. Everywhere."

"You know quite a lot about her death. How much did you know about her life?"

"I was related to her," McGuire said. "By marriage."

"I know that. I meant the little scheme she had. The music piped into her room. The camera aimed at the bed. The special lighting she used, invisible to the human eye but very good at creating images on infrared film. The cute little way she had of threatening to destroy a man's life, his reputation. The woman had no feelings at all, McGuire. Except anger. No compassion. She wanted only to sell her dirty pictures like they were some sort of . . . some kind of commodity, for God's sake."

"Just another business deal," McGuire said.

"It was blackmail, McGuire." DeMontford's face had grown red with anger but he still managed to smile. "What made it so good, what made her so effective, was that she could be romantic about it. I mean, she wasn't interested in one night stands. She went after a kind of commitment, relationship. The kind a married man cannot easily explain away. The kind that leads to confrontations and lawsuits. The kind he'll pay thousands to avoid."

"The kind that would drive him to kill her," McGuire said.

DeMontford nodded. "Agreed. And there were dozens of men who might have. You know that. She told me when she showed me the pictures. Our pictures. She said there were dozens of other men, all wealthy, all successful and all weak enough to be seduced by her. All carefully selected and used. Trying to make it easier for me to capitulate, sign the check, chalk it up to experience."

He shook his head in admiration.

"You know, when Heather first came to me with those pictures and sprang everything on me, she was so cool and specific about the terms I considered hiring her on the spot. The idea actually crossed my mind. I thought, 'This woman could outperform every securities salesman on my staff.'"

"You didn't offer her a job."

DeMontford drained his glass.

"You killed her," McGuire said.

DeMontford lowered the glass and looked out the window at the pedestrians scurrying past on Boylston Street, their collars turned up against the chill. "Don't be ridiculous," he said. His amused expression had faded. "I was at my home on the Cape with Dan Scrignoli all night. Preparing material for the investigation."

"Bullshit." McGuire sat back in his chair.

DeMontford looked back at McGuire, visibly annoyed. "You're a damn fool," he said angrily. "What makes you think you can intimidate me? You have no legal standing, you have no respect, you have nothing."

McGuire shrugged.

"You used to be a hero," DeMontford said. "I remember reading about you in the newspapers. How you went up against that priest killer a few years ago. Now you're just a bum. They wouldn't have let you through the front door of this place if I hadn't told them to."

DeMontford's words seemed to amuse him and the anger faded, replaced with a dry smile.

"I thought I would do you a favor. Dan Scrignoli told me what a good man you once were. He said you'd had a string of bad luck and now you were trying to turn things around. I'm a good Catholic, I remember how you solved those priest killings. And I'm concerned about maintaining my reputation as a civic leader. So I thought perhaps we could talk. I might even be able to offer you something, a helping hand perhaps. But you don't deserve it. You deserve nothing but my contempt. You're just another street bum."

McGuire watched DeMontford carefully and in silence, which appeared to annoy the other man. His words tumbled out in longer sentences.

"Remember when I said the things a man does with his libido aren't nearly as important as what he does with his mind?" The elegant tone had vanished from DeMontford's voice, replaced by an edge, a low growl that was both measured and relentless. "Well, I built the best privately owned securities operation in the northeast. The very best. I count the governor, three United States senators and a former president among my friends. All these connections were made by me, my hard work, my energy, all of it with my mind. I have status, McGuire, something you're not even within shouting distance of. Status and standing and responsibilities, and I am married to a woman from a family that represents the finest of American society. And I would not risk any of it, not a shadow of it, for another woman, especially one like Heather Lorenzo."

"But you did," McGuire said. "You slept with her."

DeMontford dismissed the thought with a shake of his head. "I've slept with many women without risking my position. She was just one more."

DeMontford leaned toward McGuire and dropped his voice even lower. "You may have been related to her, McGuire, but unless you were intimate with her, you wouldn't know. You'd *never* know what that woman could do for a man. Heather Lorenzo had more qualities that attract a man than you could ever imagine. I don't mean just physical qualities. I mean a kind of total package, a vibrancy, a . . . an insatiability, if that's the word—"

"She was a hot fuck," McGuire said.

DeMontford smiled tightly. "I suppose that's the kind of phrase you prefer."

"And I'll bet your wife's about as much fun in bed as a bag of lobsters."

DeMontford sat back in his chair and inhaled with fast, shallow breaths. "I was mistaken," he said. "You're not a bum, McGuire. You are a pig."

The two men continued staring at each other, DeMontford with indignation, McGuire with a cool detachment, wondering how much more it would take to trigger an explosion in the other man. Before either could speak, the maitre d' arrived at the table and presented a cordless telephone receiver to McGuire.

"A call for you, sir," he said, then turned to DeMontford. "The salmon is on its way."

DeMontford nodded, still glaring at McGuire, who brought the receiver to his ear and spoke into it.

The voice at the other end was Zelinka's. "Have I interrupted the main course?" the Hungarian asked, but his voice said he didn't care if he had.

"I hear it's on the way," McGuire said, watching the waiter approach, pushing a teak and silver serving cart toward the table.

"Perhaps you should ask for a doggy bag then," Zelinka said. "I am in my car, turning onto Arlington Street. I will be there in three or four minutes."

The waiter arrived and with a flourish removed the ornate sterling silver cover from the serving dish revealing two large salmon fillets, pink islands in a sea of thick lemon-colored sauce. DeMontford kept his eyes on McGuire and gave the waiter a flick of the hand that could have been a gesture of either approval or dismissal.

"You want us to set a place for you?" McGuire asked.

"No," Zelinka said. "Meet me outside. At the curb." Zelinka's cellular telephone crackled. "There has been a murder reported. I am heading there now."

"Who?" McGuire said.

He heard a moment or two of traffic noise, another crackle in his ear, and the line died.

McGuire reached for his topcoat, stood up and shrugged into it. Then he stood over DeMontford. "You killed her," he said, staring into the other man's eyes.

The waiter continued to prepare DeMontford's plate as though he were totally deaf to the words being passed back and forth between the two men.

"I know why," McGuire said. "And I know how. And I know that when Zelinka and I pull everything together, a herd of lawyers won't be able to save your rich status-seeking well-connected ass, DeMontford."

If anything, McGuire's words seemed to calm the other man. "I don't believe we have any reason to talk further." The waiter set a plate of salmon in front of him. "I have said everything I wanted to say and you have said everything you need to say."

McGuire glanced to his left, through the bay window that looked out onto Boylston Street. The beggar was returning, shaking his battered paper cup and thrusting it toward passersby. "No, I haven't," he said, and spun on his heel toward the door.

Outside, the air had the sharpness of a knife's edge and McGuire buttoned his coat to his neck before trotting along the sidewalk to catch up with the beggar. He spoke a few words to him, thankful that the brisk wind carried the man's body aroma away from him. The beggar glanced back at the bay window where DeMontford sat watching McGuire. Then he exposed a mouth of brown teeth with his smile and extended a hand to McGuire who placed a ten-dollar bill in it.

At the sound of a horn, McGuire glanced around to see a gray Plymouth waiting at the curb, Zelinka behind the wheel. He jogged toward it, opened the door and slid into the car's musty warm interior, but before Zelinka could pull away, McGuire touched his shoulder and said, "Wait a second."

Zelinka followed McGuire's eyes back to the bay window of the hotel where Harley DeMontford had just placed the first morsel of Chablis-poached salmon into his mouth. All three men watched the beggar, his eyes gleaming and his mouth working in silent laughter as he approached the window, his hands at his hips. Then, in a gesture as explicit as it was timeless, the beggar pulled his trousers down to his knees and backed up to press his buttocks against the window inches from DeMontford who ceased his chewing and turned his head away, an expression of disgust visible on his face just before he covered it with his starched white dinner napkin.

NINETEEN

"You know a woman named Billie Chandler."
Zelinka shifted the car into gear and pulled into
the evening traffic.

"Billie?" McGuire turned away from the scene at
the hotel window. "What about her?"

"She is dead."

McGuire stared at Zelinka, waiting for him to
continue.

Zelinka swung the car to the right, down Charles
Street. "She was found strangled in her bed. It happened some time this afternoon."

"Who found her?"

"Your friend Donovan and two uniformed officers he flagged down in the street. They broke in,
on Donovan's suspicions."

"We're going there now?"

Zelinka grunted.

"Why do you want me along?" Billie. Jesus, poor Billie.

"Because things are beginning to come together very quickly and I'm certain this woman's death is part of it," Zelinka said.

"I don't see how," McGuire said.

"Patience." Zelinka swung right again, turning west. "I think Donovan is prepared to explain many things."

McGuire sat in silence for another moment or two. Then, "You said you were looking into a lot of different stuff to do with Heather Lorenzo's murder."

"I was."

"Did that include Scrignoli's investigation into fraud charges, the Green Team stuff that started with DeMontford and spread to a bunch of other heavyweights in town?"

Zelinka smiled and nodded.

"So what'd you find?"

"Minor indiscretions by DeMontford's company."

"And the rest?"

Zelinka shook his head. "Smoke. Suspicions. That's all."

It was McGuire's turn to nod. "I thought so," he said more to himself than to the other man. "I thought so."

Zelinka flashed his ID and the two men swept past the uniformed officers at the door to Billie's apartment building and through a knot of tenants gathered in the lower foyer. At the top of the stairs Mel Doitch stood unwrapping a stick of gum which he wadded into his mouth before greeting Zelinka with

340

a nod and McGuire with a sudden arching of his eyebrows.

"Got a time?" Zelinka asked.

"Between noon and two." Doitch was watching McGuire. "What's he doing here?" he asked Zelinka.

"I'm researching a book," McGuire said, stepping around the medical examiner.

He walked down the corridor past Billie's kitchen to her large bedroom with the double bay windows and the oversized brass bed with its ivory lace duvet and matching pillow shams.

Billie lay on her back, fully dressed in sweater and slacks. One leg was pulled up as though she were making herself comfortable. Both arms were bent at the elbows, her hands alongside her head in a position that said I give up, I surrender. Her eyes were partially open, staring somewhere beyond the ceiling. A pair of pantyhose had been pulled so furiously around her neck that deep blue furrows had been carved into the flesh.

Two forensic men, newcomers unknown to McGuire, were lifting fingerprints from the surface of the bed, the night table and the telephone, speaking in low tones to each other as they worked.

Leaning against the wall, staring out the window, was Phil Donovan. He looked at McGuire without expression and turned his head away.

"You know her?" McGuire asked Donovan.

Donovan turned slowly around to look first at McGuire, then at Zelinka. "Get him out of here," he said to the I.A. man.

Zelinka said nothing. He walked to the foot of the bed, his hands in the pockets of his topcoat, and stared down at Billie with great sadness.

"Hey."

It was Donovan glaring at Zelinka, who looked at Donovan as though seeing him for the first time.

"McGuire is here because he is involved," Zelinka said. "You know that."

"He's here because he used to fuck her," Donovan said.

The two ID men paused to glance at Donovan, then at each other, before resuming their work.

McGuire felt weary, beaten. In some other world, a better one, Billie would have married an insurance man a few years ago and be living in Needham, raising kids and crabgrass, and the biggest danger she'd face would be a leaky microwave oven.

And some other woman would be here now, a voice reminded him. You don't eliminate this stuff, you just change names and faces.

"You were as well, I understand," Zelinka replied to Donovan. He raised a hand to stroke his mustache. "Is that why you were here today?"

"She got pissed at me last night." Donovan was staring out the window again. "I needed to check some stuff I picked up." He jerked his head in McGuire's direction. "From his drug pusher, his street connection."

"Django?" McGuire said. "You talking about Django?"

"Little black bastard was followin' us last night and I nailed him outside the Convention Center. Prick acts tough but he's a cream puff. Put the squeeze on him and he'll squeal on his own grandmother."

"What did he tell you?" Zelinka asked.

The ID men had finished and were putting their instruments in oversized black briefcases. Donovan watched them snap the cases closed and leave the room before pushing himself away from the window and walking to the bed where he stared down at Billie as he spoke.

"Django, whatever his name is, he was at the Flamingo the night Fox got it." He breathed deeply and McGuire realized the detective was on the edge of tears. "He was going up to your room," he said to McGuire without looking up, "and saw Fox open your door, goin' in. He turned to leave, heard the shot and ducked into the shadows near the fence. The perp came out, ran down the stairs and vaulted the fence maybe ten feet from your friend. Never knew his black ass was there."

"But he saw the man?" Zelinka asked. "He was able to describe him?"

Donovan nodded.

"Danny Scrignoli," McGuire said.

Donovan turned to him. "You knew?"

"Figured it out. Zelinka and I, we figured it out."

"So why didn't you *do* somethin'?" Donovan's voice was a howl of anger and pain.

"We needed more," Zelinka said. "More time, more proof. More assurance that there was no one else with him. We couldn't risk making a false accusation."

"He killed her," Donovan said, extending a hand toward Billie's body. "He came up here at noon and killed her, probably to learn what Django'd told me. The little bastard's missin' and the guy who was runnin' him, Grizzly, he's dead, down near the JFK, his loony girlfriend's bouncin' off walls at Mass

General and Django's probably chopped into cat food by now. Or haulin' his ass to California."

McGuire looked over at Zelinka. It's not all coming together, McGuire said silently. It's all falling apart.

"Where were you today?" Zelinka asked Donovan. "Before you found her?"

Donovan released a deep breath. "Chatham. On the Cape. Checkin' out how long it took to drive from Newbury Street to there. Talked to a waitress, works the early morning shift at Denny's. Asked if she remembered seeing Scrignoli and DeMontford there."

"And she did."

"Sure she did. Said they were both like a couple a monkeys in heat. Couldn't sit still. Ordered breakfast, hardly touched a thing. But here's the kicker. I found an Exxon attendant, station near Hyannis, who remembered seein' DeMontford about midnight, sittin' in a Buick, fits the description of Scrignoli's car. The guy used to work at a station near DeMontford's place so he sees him in the passenger seat, Scrignoli's drivin', positive identification, both of them. Scrignoli fills up, comes in the booth and pays cash. The guy watches DeMontford through the window but doesn't say anythin' because he knows DeMontford's got the big bucks, except he doesn't look it."

"Doesn't look it?" McGuire asked.

"Dressed like a laborer, that's what the gas attendant says. I told you, the attendant used to work at a station near DeMontford's place on the Cape, years before. He sees him from inside the booth this night and thinks the poor bastard's lost it all, maybe he's doin' construction work, somethin' like that. So he's a decent guy, he's not gonna embarrass

DeMontford who sure as hell didn't know this guy anyway. DeMontford's hardly the type to buddy up with a gas station attendant."

"Why does DeMontford look like a laborer?" Zelinka asked.

"Both of them did." Donovan turned away and stared at the floor. His voice was lower, as though telling the tale had drained him of energy. "Scrignoli and DeMontford. They were wearin' coveralls and old sweatshirts. And that's why the attendant remembered. Never saw DeMontford in anythin' but Brooks Brothers."

"And six hours later they're back ordering breakfast at Denny's," McGuire said.

Donovan nodded.

"But they weren't wearing coveralls."

"Golf sweaters and sports jackets," Donovan said. "And smellin' of smoke. That's what the waitress remembered. They had this odor of smoke comin' off them."

"One provided an alibi for the other," Zelinka said.

"They both killed her, that's what I figure." Donovan walked back to look out the window, down at the evening traffic.

"That's why she ran, all through the apartment," McGuire said. "That's why Heather didn't try for the door. She wasn't killed by one man. She was killed by two men. They stalked her, taking turns beating her with baseball bats probably. Then they stabbed her and left."

"Burned the clothes somewhere between here and Chatham," Donovan said. "They'd be covered in blood, the clothes."

"And the baseball bats," Zelinka added. "They would have burned them too."

"There's a record of a telephone call from DeMontford's place to Berkeley Street at two fifteen in the morning," Donovan said. "But that's a chickenshit alibi these days. Any two-bit computer with a modem could make the call, right? Programmed to access Scrignoli's electronic mail, Berkeley Street computer picks it up at the other end, telephone company registers it as a call. Danny figured he could use it, prove they called for messages, another nail in the story."

"Why Scrignoli?" McGuire asked. "What got him involved?"

The question seemed to amuse Donovan. "You kiddin' me? Guy beats up on a broad like that, it's gotta be for one of two things, am I right? Love or money. Am I right? And with that bitch it was always both."

"Have you placed a call to Berkeley for Scrignoli?" Zelinka asked.

"Goddamn right," Donovan said. He was staring at Billie's body again. "Goddamn right. I'm not sittin' on my ass like you guys did. Look what happened." He gestured toward the bed, but there was neither malice nor anger in his voice. "Look what it did for Billie."

"Good work," McGuire said as he left the room. "You did good work, out on the Cape."

"Fuck off, McGuire," Donovan said. "You think I need you tellin' me what a good cop I am? Huh? Well, fuck you, asshole, because I don't."

Zelinka told Donovan to calm down, relax a little bit, and the red-haired detective swore and turned away, leaning against a wall and lowering his head.

* * *

There was no response at Scrignoli's apartment and a squad car was assigned to watch it through the night. McGuire rode with Zelinka through the streets, monitoring reports that Scrignoli had been sighted at various locations in Boston and Cambridge, all of them proving empty and futile.

At midnight McGuire accompanied Zelinka to Berkeley Street where the Task Force facility set up to find the killer of Tim Fox was now the nerve center of the hunt for Boston Police Sergeant Daniel Scrignoli.

"Where is Captain Vance?" Zelinka asked one of the detectives.

"With the commissioner." The detective popped the remaining half of a jelly doughnut in his mouth.

"Plotting strategy?" Zelinka said.

The detective shifted the doughnut to one side of his mouth. "Drafting news releases," he said around the wad of pastry.

"Stay here," Zelinka said to McGuire and left the room, striding down the corridor toward the commissioner's office.

McGuire walked to the coffee machine, nodding in response to muted greetings from the officers who recognized him. He was pouring a second cup when Zelinka returned and collapsed on a chair at a nearby table. He waved McGuire over.

"General agreement is, Scrignoli killed Fox." Zelinka looked toward the front of the room where three officers were bent over a city map. "As you suggested." He shook his head sadly. "Figured there was something in your room that might point to him and DeMontford. Fox surprised him, Dan panicked and shot."

"How did he get involved in the first place?" McGuire asked. "With Heather?"

"Danny was squeezing DeMontford, that's what we figure. Uncovered some dirt on DeMontford, maybe threatened to widen the investigation, or maybe DeMontford made the first move by offering a bribe. Anyway, Danny took it. Dan's been looking the other way on a bunch of stuff for a while now. That's why I got involved in the first place. We were collecting evidence, getting ready to call him in, show what we had and give him the opportunity for a graceful exit. Then the Lorenzo woman was murdered. When DeMontford's name turned up in both Danny's green file and the Lorenzo woman's telephone records, the connection seemed more than coincidental. What if Heather had learned about Danny's deals with DeMontford and some others? Maybe the news got back to Heather Lorenzo from other sources, or maybe DeMontford himself couldn't resist bragging that he had a cop in his hip pocket. That he was buying whatever he needed from Danny. Time, information, whatever."

Zelinka angled his head, reacting to a thought, and when he spoke it was more slowly and distinctly, as though he were describing a new and complex machine. "I'm willing to bet that Heather Lorenzo tried putting the squeeze on Danny herself. Anyway, it's almost certain that they had a relationship, if that's the term. All three of them. Heather and DeMontford. Heather and Scrignoli. Scrignoli and DeMontford. Variations on the same old triangle. Except that two sides joined forces against the third when Heather sought something from both."

"Jesus," McGuire said. He thought of Heather, remembered her intensity, her drive to seize every advantage, gain every benefit offered to her. Then he smiled in dark admiration. "That'd be her style. Blackmail DeMontford for the pictures. Then blackmail Danny for taking a payoff from DeMontford."

"Remember, we have no proof that she slept with him," Zelinka said. "Danny, I mean. But that's not important."

"She puts the squeeze on both, DeMontford and Scrignoli get together, each tells the other what she's doing to him and they work out the idea."

"One provides an alibi for the other," Zelinka said.

McGuire drained his coffee, set the cup aside and rubbed his eyes as he spoke. "One of them gets into Heather's apartment, maybe promising another payoff, then he lets the second one in and they take turns chasing her through her apartment, beating her with baseball bats. Probably toying with her, letting her think she's getting away, making a break for the office or for the door, but there's always one of them there, herding her like a couple of collie dogs."

He sat in silence for a minute. "You really had him early like you said, didn't you? You had Scrignoli down."

"A little. Just a little perhaps."

"That's why you got in this. As an I.A. man."

"I had some help."

"From who?"

"Captain Vance."

"Fat Eddie? Fat Eddie knew about this?"

"He did more than gain access to the computer. It

was the cap:ain's idea to float the rumor. About Heather's inv)lvement with a police officer. To see what might happer.. Although I must tell you, he said starting the rumor wa; the kind of thing you would do. He felt it was underhanded but effective. Said you and Ollie Schantz would start unfounded rumors like runaway trains and watch to see who jumped from the path."

"Fat Eddie?" McGuire said again. He shook his head and smiled, then looked up at the clock. It was almost one o'clock. "What do you figure Danny's doing now?"

"Running." Zelinka sat in a chair too small for the bulk of his large body, like a parent in his child's kindergarten class. "Sleeping. Maybe dead." He swiveled his head toward the door behind McGuire. "Something come up, Captain?"

McGuire turned to see Fat Eddie Vance watching him with sleepy curiosity. Vance's eyelids were half closed, his face was puffy and his shoulders sagged. He reminded McGuire of an overweight dog just awakened for dinner and pondering whether it would be worth the effort to move.

"Joe," Vance said, nodding at McGuire. He lowered himself into the chair next to Zelinka, passed a hand over his eyes and said, "We just received a call from a lawyer representing DeMontford. He told us he'll be accompanying his client here in the morning, nine o'clock, to discuss DeMontford's possible involvement in Heather Lorenzo's murder."

"He'll try to cop a plea," Zelinka said.

Vance yawned and nodded.

"And throw Danny to the dogs," McGuire said. "Turn on him to save his ass."

"One more off the slate," Vance said. "Nothing on Scrignoli?"

"Nothing we've heard," Zelinka said.

Vance nodded again and stood up.

"Hey, Eddie," McGuire said.

The captain turned to look at McGuire.

"You lost some weight?"

"A little." Vance frowned, watching McGuire carefully.

"Looks good," McGuire said. "You're really looking good these days."

"Thanks." The captain glanced at Zelinka and smiled, almost shyly, before shuffling away to his office.

Zelinka drove McGuire to Heather's apartment, promising to call the moment he heard anything about Scrignoli.

As soon as McGuire entered the third-floor foyer, even before he saw the note on the small kitchen table, he knew she was gone.

He walked to the cabinet in the office area, poured three fingers of J&B into a glass tumbler, walked back to the kitchen, sat at the table, ran his hand through his hair and drank half the scotch. Then he picked up the note.

> Joe:
> I wrote you like this once before, didn't I? Maybe I'm getting good at it. That was a joke by the way. Not very funny, is it? Anyway, I guess this doesn't make a lot of sense but I got so scared and I don't know why because I was having so much fun and it felt so good to be with

you again. So why should it scare me? But it did anyway. I tried to tell you why last night and this morning, but I don't think I made much sense.

Maybe I can take you just in small doses. I hope you understand and if you do maybe you can explain it someday. I've got a seven o'clock flight to West Palm in the morning. It was all I could get, so I'm staying at a motel near the airport. Please don't call me. Some men are coming for the furniture tomorrow. I sold them everything, I don't want a bit of it. I promise to let you know when I'm settled. I'll call or write Ollie and Ronnie. They love you, Joe. Just in case you hadn't noticed.

Micki
P.S. So do I.

"Hell of a way to show it," McGuire said aloud. He drank the rest of the scotch, walked to the outer office and lay on a floral-patterned settee, recalling all the motels he knew near the airport, wondering which one she had chosen and why.

It seemed only a moment after he closed his eyes. He opened them at the sound of what? A telephone? Gray light seeped through the windows off Newbury Street, another cold goddamn November dawn.

The telephone rang again. McGuire sat upright and lowered his head while the room settled around him, then he stumbled to the kitchen.

"I am starting to feel like some kind of immoral chauffeur," Zelinka said in his ear. "Picking you up from your evil assignations."

"What's going on?" McGuire asked. He saw Micki's note on the table where he had left it a few hours ago and he snatched it up and stuffed it in his pocket.

"They located Scrignoli's car on Hull Street. No sign of him. Do you care to join me and the rest of the tired posse?"

McGuire nodded. Speak, you dumb bastard, he told himself. "Yeah," he said. "When'll you be here?"

"When?" Zelinka said. "I am downstairs now. Let's go."

"We know a little more," Zelinka said after pulling away from the curb. "About Dan Scrignoli."

"How much more?" McGuire looked at the clock on the car's dashboard. It wasn't yet seven. His mouth tasted like the bottom of a garbage pail.

"He cultivated some contacts among narcotics dealers." Zelinka glanced across at McGuire who was leaning his head against the window glass. "Among them was the man everyone seems to know as Grizzly."

McGuire stared straight ahead. "Danny was working with Grizzly?"

"Passively."

"What, he'd pass the word along when the pressure was on, when a roundup was coming?"

"It appears that way. Danny, of course, never handled narcotics himself."

McGuire nodded. "And you can bet it wasn't a one-way street."

Zelinka glanced briefly at McGuire.

"Grizzly would tell Danny what he needed to know," McGuire said. "What was happening on the street, who he was dealing with maybe." McGuire remembered the meperidine pills on his food tray in the jail. "He would've told Danny what Django told Donovan. The same thing Donovan probably told Billie. About Django seeing Danny leaving my place the night Tim Fox was shot."

Zelinka grunted and wheeled the car onto Commercial Street.

And about me, McGuire realized. He would have told Heather about me and Django and the pills he sold me. That's how she knew.

"What about Django?" McGuire asked. "Anybody seen him?" Ahead two cruisers blocked Hull Street, the gumball lights on their roof flashing red and blue. A police officer, his hand raised, began walking toward the car before recognizing Zelinka and waving him through.

"I have heard nothing." Zelinka pulled to the curb. "There may be nothing here except his car," he said to McGuire, nodding at Scrignoli's Buick. "But the engine was still warm when it was located half an hour ago."

"You been to sleep yet?" McGuire said, opening the door.

Zelinka smiled and shrugged. "Soon, maybe."

Three more police vehicles and two detective cars were parked at angles on the narrow street which abutted Copps Hill Burying Ground, the pre-revolutionary cemetery whose ancient gravestones still bear the scars of bullets fired by British soldiers using the markers for target practice.

Phil Donovan stood in the middle of the street writing in a wire-bound notebook. Knots of police officers were knocking on doors of the old brick houses facing the burial ground, rousing the residents from sleep or breakfast to ask questions. Some neighbors stood watching the activity from their windows, dressing gowns and bathrobes gathered about them, absorbing the street drama.

McGuire walked through the scene. Donovan nodded curtly at him before barking commands to a newly arrived group of police officers. Zelinka was conferring with Brookmyer and another ID specialist seated in a blue sedan next to Dan Scrignoli's Buick.

He's not here, McGuire realized. Not in any of these houses, not on any of these streets.

He turned on his heel, brushed between two cops and walked south through the dull morning air down the hill toward the Old North Church. He skirted the building and entered Unity Street where the Paul Revere Mall stretched behind the church down to Hanover Street.

A white-haired man was crossing the tiled plaza, walking a golden retriever on a long leash. They were about to pass a younger man who sat on a concrete bench set against the east wall holding his head in his hands. The dog paused to sniff the man's shoes and wag its tail in greeting as he passed but when the man on the bench failed to respond, the dog found other things to interest him, encouraged by a tug on the leash from his white-haired owner who looked back at the man on the bench with a sad expression before nodding to McGuire as he and the dog continued their early morning walk.

McGuire approached the bench, halting a few feet away to scan the plaza, empty except for the seated man and a knot of pigeons scratching for food beneath the concrete benches. A police car sped down Hanover Street at the opposite end of the Mall. When it disappeared from view, McGuire said, "How you doing, Danny?"

Dan Scrignoli raised his face to meet McGuire's. His eyes were red-rimmed and a facial muscle twitched with an irregular rhythm, pulling one corner of his mouth aside like a stuttering half-smile. He was wearing a black leather bomber jacket over worn corduroy trousers and scuffed tennis shoes.

"Hey, Joe." He smiled, turned his head away. His voice was weak, reedy. "I been better, you know?"

"They found your car on Hull Street." McGuire raised a foot and rested it on the bench. "Donovan's got twenty, maybe thirty guys up there, rousing the neighbors. Figures you're inside with a buddy, maybe went in through a window or something."

Scrignoli bit down hard on his lower lip and nodded, staring across the plaza at the pigeons. "They're gonna be pissed," he said. "The neighbors. Bunch of cops peeking in their closets and stuff. Early in the morning."

"DeMontford's showing up at Berkeley Street with his lawyer in a couple of hours," McGuire said.

"He . . ." Scrignoli cleared his throat and began again. "He told me. Called me last night. After he heard about . . ." He closed his eyes and shook his head.

"Billie?"

Scrignoli nodded. "That was too much. Too much for him."

356

"Heather I can understand," McGuire said. "You, me, a dozen other guys, maybe we all could've done what you and DeMontford did to her. And Timmy was an accident, right?"

Scrignoli nodded again, avoiding McGuire's eyes.

"But why Billie? Goddamn it, Danny, why Billie?"

Scrignoli's shoulders heaved and he lowered his head. "I lost it, Joe." He breathed deeply and raised his head again, tears glistening on his face. "After . . . after DeMontford, what . . . what we did to Heather that night, we were . . . we were standing around a barbecue pit at some abandoned farm near Rockland . . ."

"Burning the overalls and baseball bats."

"Yeah. And the pictures and stuff we took out of her files. Threw the camera and other stuff into the pond there." Scrignoli cleared his throat. "And it hit us, you know? I mean it felt *good* bashing her at the time, it was so fucking *easy* because God, she was such a bitch, Joe, she was ready to ruin everybody and everything, me, DeMontford, our careers . . . . I showed up first and she laughed at me, she told us she'd love to see us on our asses. And then I let DeMontford in and in a couple minutes it was over and I remember thinking Jesus, we *did* it, we actually *killed* her, and I got the shakes. I couldn't believe we *did* it. And then Timmy, Christ, I almost died when I saw it was Timmy . . . ."

"You thought it was me."

"I didn't think at all. That's the point. I had the gun in my hand, a stupid thing to do, but I figured if anybody found me going through your stuff, I'd either bluff my way out or maybe just fire one in the air, scare their asses down the steps, I don't know. . . ."

McGuire waited for him to continue. On Hanover Street a police car cruised past. McGuire watched as its brake lights flashed red and the driver suddenly shifted into reverse, providing him with a clear view of the Mall.

Scrignoli smiled coldly. "DeMontford, he was happy when he heard about Timmy. Timmy'd called his office, Timmy'd found something on him. I kill Timmy and DeMontford's in Florida somewhere when it happens, smelling like a rose."

"What were you doing in my place anyway?" McGuire said.

"I had somebody feeding me, on the street . . . ."

"Grizzly."

"Yeah."

"And Django."

He shook his head. "I just dealt with Grizzly. And the guy who ran the Flamingo, Dewey. They . . . they told me Django had given you something from Heather, when they heard she was dead. They thought *you* did it, like everybody did. I figured maybe it was something that might connect me with her. DeMontford, him and I, we talked it over, he called me from Florida when he got the message that Tim wanted to talk to him, and he thought it'd be a good idea to check your place out. I wanted Grizzly or Dewey, one of *them*, to score your place but they wouldn't touch it, and then that night, after you beat up on the guy who was killing that hooker, I heard . . . well, I heard you were back on the pills, outta circulation for a while. . . ."

He cleared his throat, swallowed hard and wiped his eyes dry. "I'm in there, I'm lookin' in your bathroom and there's somebody on the steps. I figure if it's you I bluff, if it's not I show the gun. I talked to enough witnesses, you show 'em a gun and that's all they remember, they never remember your face. Then this guy looks like he's chargin' through the door at me and it's Timmy and he's only stumbling, kinda fallin' forward but I don't *know* it's Timmy, not yet, and it's a reflex, Joe, it's a goddamn reflex and I . . . I shoot him. Jesus, Joe . . ."

McGuire saw the cop step out of his car, standing on Hanover Street, watching them over the roof of the cruiser, speaking into his radio.

"What happened to Billie?" McGuire asked.

"Django. It all had to do with Django."

"He saw you leave. When you shot Timmy."

Scrignoli nodded. "Grizzly told me Django'd confessed to him that he told Donovan he saw me, recognized me. Grizzly passed the word along . . ."

"Where's Django?"

A shrug. "Grizzly said he'd look after everything for me." Scrignoli smiled, embarrassed. "He said not to worry about you, what you'd do. He'd take care of you, pay back what he owed me. I'm, uh, I'm glad he didn't get to you. If that means anything . . ."

"Grizzly's dead."

Scrignoli looked at McGuire as though he had been told it would rain later that day, started to speak, then shrugged again as though it didn't matter. "I'm sorry about Billie," Scrignoli said. "I lost it, Joe." Scrignoli was shaking his head. "I lost it with her. I wanted to know what Donovan knew, how much he told her. She wouldn't tell me anything and I started to choke her and . . . I just lost it."

McGuire heard the squeal of brakes on the street behind the Old North Church, then the slamming of several car doors and a series of quick, cautious steps approaching.

"You know . . ." Scrignoli hadn't seen the cop on Hanover Street, didn't respond now to the sounds from behind the church. He smiled, staring across the plaza at the pigeons. "You . . . you were the guy I always wanted to be. I got out of the academy and I watched you working, even before you and Ollie were a team, I decided you were the best kind of cop. When I came to see you on Nashua Street, I just wanted to find out if you'd be fallin' with the charge, you know? Because that's what I'd heard, you'd be takin' it and that was too bad for you but real, real good for us, right? And then, Jesus, Joe, you looked so bad, I felt so goddamn sorry for you, I got some Demerol slipped on your tray and I . . ."

"You carrying?" McGuire snapped.

"What?" Scrignoli seemed to be waking from a dream.

"Are you armed, for Christ's sake?" McGuire hissed.

"Oh, Jesus." Scrignoli looked down toward Hanover Street for the first time. A second cruiser had joined the first and was angled across the road, three uniformed officers poised behind it, their guns aimed down the Mall at McGuire and Scrignoli.

"Put your weapon on the ground and your hands over—" McGuire began.

"Yeah, yeah." Scrignoli spoke like a man in a trance, dropping his head again and reaching inside his jacket.

"*Hold it, asshole!*" Donovan's voice cut the air from behind McGuire.

Without turning, McGuire waved a hand in Donovan's direction, a gesture of dismissal, more concerned about the police officers at the other end of the Mall on Hanover Street.

"Listen, Joe . . ." Scrignoli began, his hand half out of his jacket, gripping the pistol, when his words were cut off by a sudden exhalation of air, like a man punched in the stomach, and the crack of three quick shots from Donovan's gun.

McGuire reached out to catch Scrignoli as he fell forward off the bench, his face contorted in shock and surprise.

"*Get away from him!*" Donovan screamed. McGuire knelt to catch Scrignoli and, holding him by the shoulders, lowered him gently to the ground. Another shot cut the air like a whip-crack and the ground beyond the bench exploded with the impact of the bullet.

McGuire was still gripping Scrignoli, trying to avoid the volcano of blood erupting from his abdomen, staring into the other man's eyes, watching them grow dull and distant. Footsteps clattered behind him, a knot of men running toward him. He heard more footsteps from the direction of Hanover Street and then Donovan's voice near his ear, screaming at him again.

"*Move!*" Donovan shouted like a man on the edge of control. "*Now, goddamn it!*"

McGuire lowered Scrignoli to the pavement, rose slowly and turned to face Donovan who was standing ten feet away, red-faced in his firing stance, feet set wide apart, his Police Special thirty-eight in a two-handed grip, arms extended. "He was giving me his gun, Phil," McGuire said.

"He was preparing to use his weapon." Donovan angled his head toward Scrignoli, who was rolling from side to side in agony. Two police officers broke from the group, knelt next to the wounded man and began loosening his jacket.

"You gonna call an ambulance?" McGuire asked. Behind Donovan he saw Zelinka approaching, speaking rapidly into a hand-held radio.

"You're under arrest." Donovan kept his gun aimed at McGuire.

"Are you gonna call an ambulance?" McGuire said again.

"I said you're under arrest."

"And you're a pathetic prick." McGuire turned his back and began walking away.

"*McGuire!*" Donovan screamed.

Zelinka approached Donovan from behind, positioned himself directly in front of the detective and raised one large hand to gently push Donovan's gun aside. He stared into the younger man's eyes with a solemn, weary expression until Donovan lowered the gun and glanced down at Scrignoli. "Get him an ambulance," Donovan snapped, and Zelinka said, "There is already one on the way."

Zelinka exhaled, a long, noisy sigh. He shook his head in sorrow and resignation, and watched McGuire round the corner alone onto Hanover Street, his shoulders hunched, his head down. Above the Mall the flock of pigeons that had exploded into flight at the sound of the shots whirled in panic, around and around.

362